D0483054

CHILDREN
of the
FOG

Cheryl Kaye Tardif

Praise for Cheryl Kaye Tardif

CHILDREN OF THE FOG

"A chilling and tense journey into every parent's deepest fear." —Scott Nicholson, *The Red Church*

"A nightmarish thriller with a ghostly twist, CHILDREN OF THE FOG will keep you awake...and turning pages!" —Amanda Stevens, author of *The Restorer*

"Reminiscent of *The Lovely Bones*, Cheryl Kaye Tardif weaves a tale of terror that will have you rushing to check on your children as they sleep. With exquisite prose, *Children of the Fog* captures you the moment you begin and doesn't let go until the very end." —bestselling author Danielle Q. Lee, author of *Inhuman*

"Ripe with engaging twists and turns reminiscent of the work of James Patterson, Tardif once again tugs at the most inflexible of heartstrings...*Children of the Fog* possesses you from the touching beginning through to the riveting climax." —Kelly Komm, author of *Sacrifice*, an award-winning fantasy

SKELETONS IN THE CLOSET & OTHER CREEPY STORIES

"Tonight I read Cheryl's SKELETONS IN THE CLOSET. My hands turned to ice, my blood ran cold, and my body shook with the shivers. Cheryl writes scary stories." —Eileen Schuh, author of *Schrodinger's Cat*

"Cheryl Kaye Tardif had me gasping with fright...many times over. These stories are shocking! Frightening! Original!" —Betty Dravis, author of *Dream Reachers*

"A thoroughly entertaining and unabashedly Canadian collection of horror shorts - a straightforward, in-your-face, goosebump raising, skin crawling creep fest with brilliantly conceived endings..." —Paul Weiss, Top 1000 Amazon Reviewer

"If you like Stephen King's quirky short stories or are a fan of the Twilight Zone, you will enjoy 'Skeletons in the Closet.'" —John Zur

WHALE SONG

"Tardif's story has that perennially crowd-pleasing combination of sweet and sad that so often propels popular commercial fiction...Tardif, already a big hit in Canada...a name to reckon with south of the border." —*Booklist*

"*Whale Song* is deep and true, a compelling story of love and family and the mysteries of the human heart...a beautiful, haunting novel." —NY Times bestselling novelist Luanne Rice, author of Beach Girls

"A wonderfully well-written novel. Wonderful characters [that] shine. The settings are exquisitely described. The writing is lyrical. *Whale Song* would make a wonderful movie." —*Writer's Digest*

THE RIVER

"Cheryl Kaye Tardif has once again captivated readers in her third novel and latest suspense thriller, *The River*. Set in the wilds of Canada's north, *The River* combines intrigue, science, love and adventure and is sure to keep readers clamoring for more." —*Edmonton Sun*

"Exciting and vivid...A thrilling adventure where science sniffs harder, desperate to find the fountain-of-youth." —*Midwest Book Review*

DIVINE INTERVENTION

"An exciting book from start to finish. The futuristic elements are believable...plenty of surprising twists and turns. Good writing, good book! Sci-fi and mystery fans will love this book." —*Writer's Digest*

"[An] excellent suspenseful thriller...promises to keep readers engrossed...Watch for more from this gem in the literary world..." —*Real Estate Weekly*

"Believable characters, and scorching plot twists. Anyone who is a fan of J.D. Robb [aka Nora Roberts] will thoroughly enjoy this one...*Divine Intervention* will undeniably leave you smoldering, and dying for more." —Kelly Komm, author of *Sacrifice*, an award-winning fantasy

REMOTE CONTROL

"DON'T TOUCH THAT REMOTE! If you like some of Stephen King's quirky short stories or Twilight Zone episodes, you will really enjoy this short story from Cheryl Kaye Tardif. It will definitely put a smile on your face." —John Zur, reviewer on Amazon.com

DIVINE JUSTICE

"Divine Justice is a powerfully-written chill ride that will give you nightmares. Best to keep the lights on with this one." —Rick Mofina, bestselling author of *In Desperation*

"This fast-paced thriller should be a runaway best-seller. Divine Justice reminds me of CSI or Medium. If you like J.D. Robb's In Death series, you'll love Cheryl Kaye Tardif's Divine series." —*Midwest Book Review*, Betty Dravis, co-author of *Dream Reachers* series

"One of those 'sitting on the edge of your seats' read as the team unravels the mystery and tries to solve the case. It is a unique blend of action, mystery...This book is highly recommended." —Margaret Orford, *Allbooks Review*

Praise for Cherish D'Angelo (aka Cheryl Kaye Tardif)

LANCELOT'S LADY

"Romance, mystery, danger, black-mail, and twists and surprises, this tale contains them all... Despicable intentions threaten every character in this finely crafted tale of sweet tension...Lancelot's Lady is a non-stop adventure combined with the agonizing struggle to not give in to the magnetism between them. Enticing. Fun." —*Midwest Book Review*

"From the cold rocky shores of Maine to the extravagant mansions of Miami to a lush tropical island in the Bahamas, Cherish D'Angelo takes her heroine through a series of breathtaking romantic adventures that mirror the settings, often in surprisingly ironic ways. A page turner in the best possible sense." —Gail Bowen, author of the award-winning Joanne Kilbourn series

"Cherish D'Angelo has got that mythical "voice" down to a fine art." —Jennifer L. Hart, author of *River Rats*

"*Lancelot's Lady* is riveting. It holds on and won't let you go! Cherish D'Angelo's descriptive powers are amazing. She summons up scenes like genies from bottles!" —Susan J. McLeod, author of *Soul and Shadow*

CHILDREN OF THE FOG

Copyright © 2011 by Cheryl Kaye Tardif. All Rights Reserved.

No part of this publication may be reproduced, stored in a retrieval system, or transmitted, in any form or by any means, electronic, mechanical, photocopying, recording, or otherwise, without prior written permission from the author.

This is a work of fiction. Names, characters, places and incidents either are the product of the author's imagination or are used fictitiously. And any resemblance to actual persons, living, dead (or in any other form), business establishments, events, or locales is entirely coincidental.

http://www.cherylktardif.com

FIRST EDITION

Imajin Books

ISBN: 978-0-9866310-6-1 (2011 trade paperback edition)

eBook editions also available at various ebook retailers

Cover designed by Sapphire Designs - http://www.designs.sapphiredreams.org

Novels by Cheryl Kaye Tardif

Whale Song
The River
Children of the Fog
Submerged

Series by Cheryl Kaye Tardif

The Divine Series:
Divine Intervention
Divine Justice

Short Stories by Cheryl Kaye Tardif

Remote Control
Skeletons in the Closet & Other Creepy Stories

Novels by Cherish D'Angelo (aka Cheryl Kaye Tardif)

Lancelot's Lady

This novel is dedicated to

Sebastien, Jason & Ben

and all 'missing' children...

To those who have been taken too early,
Who left on their own accord,
Who were given away in love,
Or those stolen from caring parents.

To the ones who have disappeared in spirit,
Lost souls on our city streets,
And those whose minds have betrayed them,
We will always remember the real 'you.'

To those who have been left behind,
Searching endlessly and tirelessly
For mother, father, sister, brother, daughter or son.
May you find Strength and Hope.

For the abandoned, forgotten and missing,
May you find an eternity of love,
And for those who are still, always and forever missed,
May you all find your way...Home.

~CKT

Acknowledgements

Thank you to my early editors and readers: Francine, Marc, Kelly, David and Eileen, who offered wise advice and smart editing suggestions.

A special thanks to Lynn Hoffman, wine expert and author of *bang-Bang*, who suggested the perfect wine for this story. Cheers!

Thank you to ALL my fans—readers, book clubs, schools, libraries, bookstores, reviewers, etc—for trusting me to provide you with an entertaining and hopefully emotional story.

And my eternal thanks to my husband Marc and daughter Jessica for always believing in me and my work.

prologue

May 14th, 2007

She was ready to die.

She sat at the kitchen table, a half empty bottle of Philip's precious red wine in one hand, a loaded gun in the other. Staring at the foreign chunk of metal, she willed it to vanish. But it didn't.

Sadie checked the gun and noted the single bullet.

"One's all you need."

If she did it right.

She placed the gun on the table and glanced at a pewter-framed photograph that hung off-kilter above the mantle of the fireplace. It was illuminated by a vanilla-scented candle, one of many that threw flickering shadows over the rough wood walls of the log cabin.

Sam's sweet face stared back at her, smiling.

Alive.

From where she sat, she could see the small chip in his right front tooth, the result of an impatient father raising the training wheels too early. But there was no point in blaming Philip—not when they'd both lost so much.

Not when it's all my fault.

Her gaze swept over the mantle. There were three objects on it besides the candle. Two envelopes, one addressed to Leah and one to Philip, and the portfolio case that contained the illustrations and manuscript on disc for Sam's book.

She had finished it, just like she had promised.

"And promises can't be broken. Right, Sam?"

A single tear burned a path down her cheek.

Sam was gone.

What reason do I have for living now?

She gulped back the last pungent mouthful of Cabernet and dropped the empty bottle. It rolled under the chair, unbroken, rocking on the hardwood floor. Then all was silent, except the antique grandfather clock in the far corner. Its ticking reminded her of the clown's shoe. The one with the tack in it.

Tick, tick, tick...

The clock belched out an ominous gong.

It was almost midnight.

Almost time.

She drew an infinity symbol in the dust on the table.

∞

"Sadie and Sam. For all eternity."

Gong...

She swallowed hard as tears flooded her eyes. "I'm sorry I couldn't save you, baby. I tried to. God, I tried. Forgive me, Sam." Her words ended in a gut-wrenching moan.

Something scraped the window beside her.

She pressed her face to the frosted glass, then jerked back with a gasp. "Go away!"

They stood motionless—six children that drifted from the swirling miasma of night air, haunting her nights and every waking moment. Surrounded by the moonlit fog, they began to chant. *"One fine day, in the middle of the night..."*

"You're not real," she whispered.

"Two dead boys got up to fight."

A small, pale hand splayed against the exterior of the window. Below it, droplets of condensation slid like tears down the glass.

She reached out, matching her hand to the child's. Shivering, she pulled away. "You don't exist."

The clock continued its morbid countdown.

As the alcohol and drug potpourri kicked in, the room began to spin and her stomach heaved. She inhaled deeply. She couldn't afford to get sick. Sam was waiting for her.

Tears spilled down her cheeks. "I'm ready."

Gong...

Without hesitation, she raised the gun to her temple.

"Don't!" the children shrieked.

She pressed the gun against her flesh. The tip of the barrel was cold. Like her hands, her feet...her heart.

A sob erupted from the back of her throat.

The clock let out a final gong. Then it was deathly silent.

It was midnight.

Her eyes found Sam's face again.

"Happy Mother's Day, Sadie."

She took a steadying breath, pushed the gun hard against her skin and clamped her eyes shut.

"Mommy's coming, Sam."
She squeezed the trigger.

1

Sadie O'Connell let out a snicker as she stared at the price tag on the toy in her hand. "What did they stuff this with, laundered money?" She tossed the bunny back into the bin and turned to the tall, leggy woman beside her. "What are you getting Sam for his birthday?"

Her best friend gave her a cocky grin. "What *should* I get him? Your kid's got everything already."

"Don't even go there, my friend."

But Leah was right. Sadie and Philip spoiled Sam silly. Why shouldn't they? They had waited a long time for a baby. Or at least, *she* had. After two miscarriages, Sam's birth had been nothing short of a miracle. A miracle that deserved to be spoiled.

Leah groaned loudly. "Christ, it's a goddamn zoo in here."

Toyz & Twirlz in West Edmonton Mall was crawling with overzealous customers. The first major sale of the spring season always brought people out in droves. Frazzled parents swarmed the toy store, swatting their wayward brood occasionally—the way you'd swat a pesky yellowjacket at a barbecue. One distressed father hunted the aisles for his son, who had apparently taken off on him as soon as his back was turned. In every aisle, parents shouted at their kids, threatening, cajoling, pleading and then predictably giving in.

"So who let the animals out?" Sadie said, surveying the store.

The screeching wheels of shopping carts and the constant whining of overtired toddlers were giving her a headache. She wished to God she'd stayed home.

"Excuse me."

A plump woman with frizzy, over-bleached hair gave Sadie an apologetic look. She navigated past them, pushing a stroller occupied by a miniature screaming alien. A few feet away, she stopped, bent down and wiped something that looked like curdled rice pudding from the corner of the child's mouth.

Sadie turned to Leah. "Thank God Sam's past that stage."

At five years old—soon to be six—her son was the apple of her eye. In fact, he was the whole darned tree. A lanky imp of a boy with tousled black hair, sapphire-blue eyes and perfect bow lips, Sam was the spitting image of his mother and the exact opposite of his father in temperament. While Sam was sweet natured, gentle and loving, Philip was impatient and distant. So distant that he rarely said *I love you* anymore.

She stared at her wedding ring. *What happened to us?*

But she knew what had happened. Philip's status as a trial lawyer had grown, more money had poured in and fame had gone to his head. He had changed. The man she had fallen in love with, the dreamer, had gone. In his place was someone she barely knew, a stranger who had decided too late that he didn't want kids.

Or a wife.

"How about this?" Leah said, nudging her.

Sadie stared at the yellow dump truck. "Fill it with a stuffed bat and Sam will think it's awesome."

Her son's fascination with bats was almost comical. The television was always tuned in to the Discovery Channel while her son searched endlessly for any show on the furry animals.

"What did Phil the Pill get him?" Leah asked dryly.

"A new Leap Frog module."

"I still can't believe the things that kid can do."

Sadie grinned. "Me neither."

Sam's mind was a sponge. He absorbed information so fast that he only had to be shown once. His powers of observation were so keen that he had learned how to unlock the door just by watching Sadie do it, so Philip had to add an extra deadbolt at the top. By the time Sam was three, he had figured out the remote control and the DVD player. Sadie still had problems turning on the TV.

Sam...my sweet, wonderful, little genius.

"Maybe I'll get him a movie," Leah said. "How about *Batman Begins*?"

"He's turning six, not sixteen."

"Well, what do I know? I don't have kids."

At thirty-four, Leah Winters was an attractive, willowy brunette with wild multi-colored streaks, thick-lashed hazel eyes, a flirty smile and a penchant for younger men. While Sadie's pale face had a scattering of tiny freckles across the bridge of her nose and cheekbones, Leah's complexion was tanned and clear.

She'd been Sadie's best friend for eight years—*soul sistahs*. Ever since the day she had emailed Sadie out of the blue to ask questions about writing and publishing. They'd met at Book Ends, a popular Edmonton bookstore, for what Leah had expected would be a quick coffee. Their connection was so strong and so immediate that they talked for almost five hours. They still joked about it, about how Leah had thought Sadie was some hotshot writer who wouldn't give her the time of day. Yet Sadie had given her more. She'd given Leah a piece of her heart.

A rugged, handsome Colin Farrell look-alike passed them in the aisle, and Leah stared after him, eyes glittering.

"I'll take one of those," she said with a soft growl. "To go."

"You won't find Mr. Right in a toy store," Sadie said dryly. "They're usually all taken. And somehow I don't think you're gonna find him at Karma either."

Klub Karma was a popular nightclub on Whyte Avenue. It boasted the best ladies' night in Edmonton, complete with steroid-muscled male strippers. Leah was a regular.

"And why not?"

Sadie rolled her eyes. "Because Karma is packed with sweaty, young puppies who are only interested in one thing."

Leah gave her a blank look.

"Getting laid," Sadie added. "Honestly, I don't know what you see in that place."

"What, are you daft?" Leah arched her brow and grinned devilishly. "I'm chalking it up to my civil duty. Someone's gotta show these young guys how it's done."

"Someone should show Philip," Sadie muttered.

"Why—can't he get it up?"

"Jesus, Leah!"

"Well? Fess up."

"Later maybe. When we stop for coffee."

Leah glanced at her watch. "We going to our usual place?"

"Of course. Do you think Victor would forgive us if we went to any other coffee shop?"

Leah chuckled. "No. He'd start skimping on the whipped cream if we turned traitor. So what are you getting Sam?"

"I'll know it when I see it. I'm waiting for a sign."

"You're always such a sucker for this *fate* thing."

Sadie shrugged. "Sometimes you have to have faith that things will work out."

They continued down the aisle, both searching for something for the sweetest boy they knew. When Sadie spotted the one thing she was sure Sam would love, she let out a hoot and gave Leah an I-told-you-so look.

"This bike is perfect. Since his birthday is actually on Monday, I'll give it to him then. He'll get enough things from his friends at his party on Sunday anyway."

Little did she know that Sam wouldn't see his bike.

He wouldn't be around to get it.

∞ ∞ ∞

"Haven't seen you two all week," Victor Guan said. "Another day and I would've called nine-one-one."

"It's been a busy week," Sadie replied, plopping her purse on the counter. "How's business, Victor?"

"Picking up again with this cold snap."

The young Chinese man owned the Cuppa Cappuccino a few blocks from Sadie's house. The coffee shop had a gas fireplace, a relaxed ambiance and often featured local musicians like Jessy Green and Alexia Melnychuk. Not only did Victor serve the best homemade soups and feta Caesar salad, the mocha lattés were absolutely sinful.

Leah made a beeline for the washroom. "You know what I want."

Sadie ordered a Chai and a mocha.

"You see that fog this morning?" Victor asked.

"Yeah, I drove Sam to school in it. I could barely see the car in front of me."

She shivered and Victor gave her a concerned look.

"Cat walk over your grave or something?" he asked.

"No, I'm just tired of winter."

She grabbed a newspaper from the rack and headed for the upper level. The sofa by the fireplace was unoccupied, so she sat down and tossed the newspaper on the table.

The headline on the front page made her gasp.

THE FOG STRIKES AGAIN!

Her breath felt constricted. "Oh God. Not another one."

A photograph of a blond-haired, blue-eyed girl sitting on concrete steps dominated the front page. Eight-year-old Cortnie Bornyk, from the north side of Edmonton, was missing. According to the newspaper, the girl had disappeared in the middle of the night. No sign of forced entry and no evidence as to who had taken her, but investigators were sure it was the same man who had taken the others.

Sadie opened the newspaper to page three, where the story continued. She empathized with the girl's father, a single dad who had left Ontario to find construction work in Edmonton. Matthew Bornyk had moved here to make a better life. Not a bad decision, considering that the housing market was booming. But now he was pleading for the safe return of his daughter.

"Here you go," Victor said, setting two mugs on the table.

"Thanks," she said, without looking up.

Her eyes were glued to the smaller photo of Bornyk and his daughter. The man had a smile plastered across his face, while his daughter was frozen in a silly pose, tongue hanging out the side of her mouth.

Daddy's little girl, Sadie thought sadly.

Leah flopped into an armchair beside her. "Who's the hunk?"

"His daughter was abducted last night."

"How horrible."

"Yeah," Sadie said, taking a tentative sip from her mug.

"Did anyone see anything?"

"Nothing." She locked eyes on Leah. "Except the fog."

"Do they think it's *him*?"

Sadie skimmed the article. "There are no ransom demands yet. Sounds like him."

"Shit. That makes, what—six kids?"

"Seven. Three boys, four girls."

"One more boy to go." Leah's voice dripped with dread.

The Fog, as the kidnapper was known, crept in during the dead of night or early morning, under the cloak of a dense fog. He wrapped himself around his prey and like a fog, he disappeared without a trace, capturing the souls of children and stealing the hopes and dreams of parents. One boy, one girl. Every spring. For the last four years.

Sadie flipped the newspaper over. "Let's change the subject."

Her eyes drifted across the room, taking in the diversity of Victor's customers. In one corner of the upper level, three teenaged boys played poker, while a fourth watched and hooted every time one of his friends won. Across from Sadie, a redheaded woman wearing a mauve sweatshirt plunked away on a laptop, stopping every now and then to cast the noisy boys a frustrated look. On the lower level, one of the regulars—Old Ralph—was reading every newspaper from front to back. He sipped his black coffee when he finished each page.

"So..." Leah drawled as she crossed her long legs. "What's going on with Phil the Pill?"

Sadie scowled. "That's what I'd like to know. He says he's working long nights at the firm."

"And you're thinking, what? That he's screwing around?"

Leah never was one to beat around the bush—about anything.

"Maybe he's just working hard," her friend suggested.

Sadie shook her head. "He got home at two this morning, reeking of perfume and booze."

"Isn't his firm working on that oil spill case? I bet all the partners are pulling late nights on that one."

Sadie snorted. "Including Brigitte Moreau."

Brigitte was her husband's *right-hand-woman*, as he'd made a point of telling her often. Apparently, the new addition to Fleming Warner Law Offices was indispensable. The slender, blond lawyer, with a pair of breasts she'd obviously paid for, never left Philip's side.

Sadie wondered what Brigitte did when she had to pee.

Probably drags Philip in with her.

"It could be perfectly innocent," Leah suggested.

"Yeah, right. I was at the conference after-party. I saw them together, and there was nothing innocent about them. Brigitte was holding onto Philip's arm as if she owned him. And he was laughing, whispering in her ear." She pursed her lips. "His co-workers were looking at me with sympathetic eyes, pitying me. I could see it in their faces. Even *they* knew."

Leah winced. "Did you call him on it?"

"I asked him if he was messing around again."

Just before Sam was born, Philip had admitted to two other affairs. Both office flings, according to him. "Both meant nothing," he said, before blaming his infidelities on her swollen belly and her lack of sexual interest.

"What'd he say?" Leah prodded, with the determination of a pit-bull slobbering over a t-bone steak.

"Nothing. He just stormed out of the house. He called me from work just before you came over. Said I was being ridiculous, that my accusations were hurtful and unfair." She lowered her voice. "He asked me if I was drinking again."

"Bastard. And you wonder why I'm still single."

Sadie said nothing. Instead, she thought about her marriage.

They'd been happy—once. Before her downward spiral into alcoholism. In the early years of their marriage, Philip had been attentive and caring, supporting her decision to focus on her writing. It wasn't until she started talking about having a family that things had changed.

She flicked a look at Leah, grateful for her loyal companionship and understanding. Fate had definitely intervened when it led her to Leah. Her friend had gone above and beyond the duty of friendship, dropping everything in a blink if she called. Leah was her life support, especially on the days and nights when the bottle called her. She'd even attended a few AA meetings with Sadie.

And where was Philip? Probably with Brigitte.

"Come on, my friend," Leah said, grinning. "I know you really want to swear. Let it out."

"You know I don't use language like that."

"You're such a prude. Philip's an ass, a bastard. Let me hear you say it. *Bas...tard."*

"I'll let you be the foul-mouthed one," Sadie said sweetly.

"Fuckin' right. Swearing is liberating." Leah took a careful sip of tea. "So how's the book coming?"

Sadie smiled. "I finished the text yesterday. Tomorrow I'll start on the illustrations. I'm so excited about it."

"Got a title yet?"

"Going Batty."

Leah's pencil-thin brow arched. "Hmm...how appropriate."

Sadie gave her a playful slap on the arm. "It's about a little bat who can't find his way home because his radar gets screwed up. At first, he thinks he's picking up radio signals, but then he realizes he's picking up other creatures' thoughts."

"That's perfect. Sam'll love it."

"I know. I can't believe I waited so long to write something special for him."

A few months ago, Sadie decided to take a break from writing another Lexa Caine mystery, especially since her agent had secured her a deal for two children's picture books.

"It's been a welcome break," she admitted. "Lexa needed a year off. A holiday."

"Some break," Leah said. "I've hardly seen you. You've been working day and night on Sam's book."

"It's been worth it."

"Is it harder than writing mysteries?"

"Other than the artwork, I think it's easier," Sadie said, somewhat surprised by her own answer. "But then, Sam inspires me. He's my muse. Kids see things so differently."

"Wish I had one."

Sadie's jaw dropped. "A kid?"

"A muse, idiot."

Sadie grinned. "How's the steamy romance novel going?"

"I'm stumped. I've got Clara trapped below deck on the pirate ship, locked in the cargo hold with no way out."

Since the success of her debut novel, *Sweet Destiny*, Leah had found her niche and was working on her second historical romance.

"What's in the room?"

Leah gave her a wry grin. "Cases of Bermuda rum."

"Well, she's not going to drink it, so what else can she do?"

"I don't know. She can't get the crew drunk, if that's what you're thinking. "

"What if the ship caught on fire?"

Excitement percolated in Leah's eyes. "Yeah. A fire could really heat things up. Pun intended."

They were silent for a moment, lost in their own thoughts.

"Hey," Sadie said finally. "I've been tempted to cut my hair. What do you think?"

Leah stared at her. "You want to get rid of all that beautiful hair? Jesus, Sadie, it's past your bra strap." In a thick Irish accent, she said, "Have ye lost your Irish mind just a wee bit, lassie?"

"It's too much work," Sadie said with a pout.

"What does Philip think?"

"He'd be happy if I kept it long," she replied, scowling. "Maybe that's one reason why I want to cut it."

Leah laughed. "Then you go, girl."

Half an hour later, they parted ways—with Leah eager to get back to the innocent Clara and her handsome, sword-wielding pirate, and Sadie not so thrilled to be going back to an empty house. As she climbed into her sporty Mazda3, she smiled, relieved as always that she had chosen practical over the flashy and pretentious Mercedes that Philip drove.

She glanced at the clock and heaved a sigh of relief. It was almost time to pick Sam up from school.

Her heart skipped a beat.

Maybe there's been some progress today.

2

The instant Sam saw her standing in the classroom doorway, he let out a wild yell and charged at her, almost knocking her off her feet.

"Whoa there, little man," she said breathlessly. "Who are you supposed to be? Tarzan?"

"We just finished watching Pocahontas," a woman's voice called out.

"Hi, Jean," Sadie said. "How are things today?"

Jean Ellis taught a class of children with hearing impairments.

"Same as usual," the kindergarten teacher replied. "No change, I'm afraid."

Sadie tried to hide her disappointment. "Maybe tomorrow."

She studied Sam, who could hear everything just fine.

Why won't he speak?

"Did you have a good day, honey?"

Ignoring her, Sam pulled on a winter jacket and stuffed his feet into a pair of insulated boots.

"It was a great day," Jean said, signing as she spoke. "Sam made a friend. A real one this time."

Sadie was astounded. Sam's first real friend. Well, unless she counted his invisible friend, Joey.

"Hey, little man," she said, crouching down to gather him in her arms. "Mommy missed you today. But I'm glad you have a new friend. What's his name?"

When Sam didn't answer, Sadie glanced at Jean.

"Victoria," the woman said with a wink.

Grinning, Sadie ruffled Sam's hair. "Okay, charmer. Let's go."

With a quick wave to Jean, she reached for Sam's hand. She was always amazed by how perfectly it fit into hers, how warm and soft his skin was.

Outside in the parking lot, she unlocked the car and Sam scampered into the booster seat in the back. She leaned forward, fastened his seatbelt, then kissed his cheek. "Snug as a bug?"

He gave her the thumbs up.

Pulling away from the school, she flicked a look in her rearview mirror. Sam stared straight ahead, uninterested in the laughing children who waited for their parents to arrive. Her son was a shy boy, a loner who unintentionally scared kids away because of his inability to speak.

His lack of desire to speak, she corrected.

∞ ∞ ∞

Sam hadn't always been mute.

Sadie had taught him the alphabet at two. By the age of three, he was reading short sentences. Then one day, for no apparent reason, Sam stopped talking.

Sadie was devastated.

And Philip? There were no words to describe his erratic behavior. At first, he seemed mortified, concerned. Then he shouted accusations at her, insinuating so many horrible things that after a while, even she began to wonder. During one nasty exchange, he had grabbed her, his fingers digging into her arms.

"Did you drink while you were pregnant?" he demanded.

"No!" she wailed. "I haven't had a drop."

His eyes narrowed in disbelief. "Really?"

"I swear, Philip."

He stared at her for a long time before shaking his head and walking away.

"We have to get him help," she said, running after him.

Philip swiveled on one heel. "What exactly do you suggest?"

"There's a specialist downtown. Dr. Wheaton recommended him."

"Dr. Wheaton is an idiot. Sam will speak when he's good and ready to. Unless you've screwed him up for good."

His insensitive words cut her deeply, and after he'd gone back to work, she picked up the phone and booked Sam's first appointment. She didn't feel good about going behind Philip's back, but he'd left her no choice.

By the time Sam was three and a half, he had undergone numerous hearing and intelligence tests, x-rays, ultrasounds and psychiatric counseling, yet no one could explain why he wouldn't say a word. His vocal chords were perfectly healthy, according to one specialist. And he was right. Sam could scream, cry or shout. They had heard enough of *that* when he was younger.

Sadie finally managed to drag Philip to an appointment, but the psychologist—a small, timid man wearing a garish red-striped tie that screamed *overcompensation*—didn't have good news for them. He sat behind a sterile metal desk, all the while watching Philip and twitching as if he had Tourettes.

"Your son is suffering from some kind of trauma," the man said, pointing out what seemed obvious to Sadie.

"But what could've caused it?" she asked in dismay.

The doctor fidgeted with his tie. "Symptoms such as these often result from some form of…of abuse."

Philip jumped to his feet. "What the hell are you saying?"

The man's entire body jerked. "I-I'm saying that perhaps someone or something scared your son. Like a fight between parents, or witnessing drug or alcohol abuse."

Sadie cringed at his last words. The look Philip gave her was one of pure anger. And censure.

The doctor took a deep breath. "And of course, there is the possibility of physical or sexual—"

Without a word, Philip stormed out of the doctor's office.

Sadie ran after him.

He had blamed her, of course. According to him, it was her drinking that had caused her miscarriages. *And* Sam's delayed verbal development.

That night, after Sam had gone to bed, Philip rummaged through every dresser drawer. Then he searched the closet.

She watched apprehensively. "What are you doing?"

"Looking for the bottles!" he barked.

She hissed in a breath. "I told you. I am *not* drinking."

"Once a drunk…"

She cowered when he approached her, his face flushed with anger.

"It's *your* fault!" he yelled.

Guilt did terrible things to people. It was such a destructive, invisible force that not even Sadie could fight it.

∞ ∞ ∞

She looked in the rearview mirror and took in Sam's heart-shaped face and serious expression. She wondered for the millionth time why he wouldn't speak. She'd give anything to hear his voice, to hear one word. *Any* word. She'd been praying that the school environment would break through the language barrier.

No such luck.

Suddenly, she was desperate to hear his voice.

"Sam? Can you say Mommy?"

He signed *Mom*.

"Come on, honey," she begged. "*Muhh-mmy*."

In the mirror, he smiled and pointed at her.

Tears welled in her eyes, but she blinked them away. One day he *would* speak. He'd call her Mommy and tell her he loved her.

"One day," she whispered.

For now, she'd just have to settle for the undeniably strong bond she felt. The connection between mother and child had been forged at conception and she always knew how Sam felt, even without words between them.

She turned down the road that led to the quiet subdivision on the southeast side of Edmonton. She pulled into the driveway and pushed the garage door remote, immediately noticing the sleek silver Mercedes parked in the spacious two-car garage.

Her breath caught in the back of her throat.

Philip was home.

"Okay, little man," she murmured. "Daddy's home."

She scooped Sam out of the back seat and headed for the door. He wriggled until she put him down. Then he raced into the house, straight upstairs. She flinched when she heard his bedroom door slam.

"I guess neither of us is too excited to see Daddy," she said.

Tossing her keys into a crystal dish on the table by the door, she dropped her purse under the desk, kicked off her shoes, puffed her chest and headed into the war zone.

But the door to Philip's office was closed.

She turned toward the kitchen instead.

The war can wait. It always does.

Passing by his office door an hour later, she heard Philip bellowing at someone on the phone. Whoever it was, they were getting quite an earful. A minute later, something hit the door.

She backed away. "Don't stir the pot, Sadie."

Philip remained locked away in his office and refused to come out for supper, so she made a quick meal of hotdogs for Sam and a salad for herself. She left a plate of the past night's leftovers—ham, potatoes and vegetables—on the counter for Philip.

Later, she gave Sam a bath and dressed him for bed.

"Auntie Leah came over today," she said, buttoning his pajama top. "She told me to say hi to her favorite boy."

There wasn't much else to say, other than she had finished writing the bat story. She wasn't about to tell him that she had ordered his birthday cake and bought him a bicycle, which she had wrestled into the house by herself and hidden in the basement.

"Want me to read you a story?" she asked.

Sam grinned.

She sat on the edge of the bed and nudged her head in the direction of the bookshelf. "You pick."

He wandered over to the rows of books, staring at them thoughtfully. Then he zeroed in on a book with a white spine. It was the same story he chose every night.

"My Imaginary Friend again?" she asked, amused.

He nodded and jumped into bed, settling under the blankets.

Sadie snuggled in beside him. As she read about Cathy, a young girl with an imaginary friend who always got her into trouble, she couldn't help but think of Sam. For the past year, he'd been adamant about the existence of Joey, a boy his age who he swore lived in his room. She'd often catch Sam smiling and nodding, as if in conversation. No words, no signing, just the odd facial expression. Some days he seemed lost in his own world.

"Lisa says you should close your eyes," she read.

Sam's eyes fluttered shut.

"Now turn this page and use your imagination."

He turned the page, then opened his eyes. They lit up when he saw the colorful drawing of Cathy's imaginary friend, Lisa.

"Can you see me now?" she read, smiling.

Sam pointed to the girl in the mirror.

"Good night, Cathy. And good night, friend. The end."

She closed the book and set it next to the bat signal clock on the nightstand. Then she scooted off the bed, leaned down and kissed her son's warm skin.

"Good night, Sam-I-Am."

His small hand reached up. With one finger, he drew a sideways 'S' in the air. Their nightly ritual.

"S…for Sam," she said softly.

And like every night, she drew the reflection.

"S…for Sadie."

Together, they created an infinity symbol.

She smiled. "Always and forever."

She flicked off the bedside lamp and eased out of the room. As she looked over her shoulder, she saw Sam's angelic face illuminated by the light from the hall. She shut the door, pressed her cheek against it and closed her eyes.

Sam was the only one who truly loved her, trusted her. From the first day he had rested his huge black-lashed eyes on hers, she had fallen completely and undeniably in love. A mother's love could be no purer.

"My beautiful boy."

Turning away, she slammed into a tall, solid mass. Her smile disappeared when she identified it.

Philip.

And he wasn't happy. Not one bit.

He glared down at her, one hand braced against the wall to bar her escape. His lips—the same ones that had smiled at her so charismatically the night they had met—were curled in disdain.

"You could've told me Sam was going to bed."

She sidestepped around him. "You were busy. As usual."

"What the hell's that supposed to mean?"

She cringed at his abrasive tone, but said nothing.

"You're not going all paranoid on me again, are you?" He grabbed her arm. "I already told you. Brigitte is a co-worker. Nothing more. Jesus, Sadie! You're not a child. You're almost forty years old. What the hell's gotten into you lately?"

"Not a thing, Philip. And I'll be thirty-eight this year. Not forty." She yanked her arm away, then brushed past him, heading for the bedroom.

Their marriage was a sham.

"Doomed from the beginning," her mother had told her one night when Sadie, a sobbing wreck, had called her after Philip had admitted to his first affair.

But she'd proven her mother wrong. Hadn't she? Things seemed better the year after Sam was born. Then she and Philip started fighting again. Lately, it had escalated into a nightly event. At least on the nights he came home before she went to sleep.

Philip entered the bedroom and slammed the door.

"You know," he said. "You've been a bitch for months."

"No, I haven't."

"A *frigid* bitch. And we both know it's not from PMS, seeing as you don't get that anymore."

Flinching, she caught her sad reflection in the dresser mirror. She should be used to his careless name-calling by now. But she wasn't. Each time, it was like a knife piercing deeper into her heart. One of these days, she wouldn't be able to pull it out. Then where would they be? Just another statistic?

Philip waited behind her, flustered, combing a hand through his graying brown hair.

For a moment, she felt ashamed of her thoughts.

"Are you even listening to me?" he sputtered in outrage.

And the moment was gone.

She sighed, drained. "What do you want me to say, Philip? You're never home. And when you are, you're busy working in your office. We don't do anything together or go any—"

"Christ, Sadie! We were just out with Morris and his wife."

"I'm not talking about functions for the firm," she argued. "We don't see our old friends anymore. We never go to movies, never just sit and talk, never make...love."

Philip crossed his arms and scowled. "And whose fault is that? It's certainly not mine. You're the one who pulls away every time I try to get close to you. You know, a guy can only handle so much rejection before—"

"What?" She whipped around to confront him. "Before you go looking for it elsewhere?"

He stared at her for a long moment and the air grew rank with tension, coiling around them with the slyness of a venomous snake, fangs exposed, ready to strike.

When he finally spoke, his voice was quiet, defeated. "Maybe if you gave some of the love you pour on Sam to *me* once in a while, I wouldn't be tempted to look elsewhere."

He strode out of the room, his footsteps thundering down the stairs. A minute later, a door slammed.

She released a trembling breath. "Coward."

She wasn't sure if she meant Philip...or herself.

Brushing the drapes aside, she peered through the window to the dimly lit street below. It was devoid of any moving traffic, just a few parked vehicles lining the sidewalks. The faint rumble of the garage door made her clench the drapes. She heard the defiant revving of an engine, and then watched as the Mercedes backed down the driveway, a stream of frosty exhaust trailing behind it. The surface of the street shimmered from a fresh glazing of ice, and the car sped away, tires spinning on the pavement.

Philip always seemed to get in the last word.

She watched the fiery glow of the taillights as they faded into the night. Then the flickering of the streetlamp across the road caught her eye. She frowned when the light went out. One of the neighbors' dogs started barking, set off by either the abrupt darkness or Philip's noisy departure. She wasn't sure which.

And then something emerged from the bushes.

A lumbering shadow shuffled down the sidewalk, a few yards to the right of the lamp. It was a man, of that she was sure. She could make out a heavy jacket and some kind of hat, but she couldn't distinguish anything else.

The man paused across the street from her house.

Sadie was sure that he was staring up at her.

She shivered and stepped out of view, the drapes flowing back into place. When her breathing calmed, she edged toward the window again and took a surreptitious peek.

Gail, a neighbor from across the street, was walking Kali, a Shih Tzu poodle. But other than the woman and her dog, the sidewalk was empty.

Sadie locked all the doors and windows, and set the security alarm.

3

After Sadie dropped Sam off at school the next morning, she drove to Sobeys for milk and laundry detergent. Walking past the bakery section, she was flagged down by Liz Crenshaw, a vivacious food demonstrator who talked a mile a minute.

"Sadie! I was just thinking about you. How are you?"

Though the petite woman was in her early fifties, she looked closer to thirty-five. Liz had three grown children and four grandchildren who all lived back East. Without her family around to spoil, she was a sucker for Sam. And Sam adored her.

"How's your little boy doing?" Liz asked, smoothing a stray auburn curl behind one ear. "It's Sam's birthday soon, isn't it?"

Sadie tucked the milk under her arm and reached for a custard pie sample. "Monday. But his party's on Sunday. He's excited about all the birthday gifts he'll be getting."

Liz passed her a plastic spoon. "What did you get him?"

"A new bike," Sadie said between mouthfuls. "I'm not giving it to him until Monday though."

"I'd like to get him something. From Auntie Liz. What does he want, hon? Games? Books?"

Sadie grinned. "A pet bat."

The woman shuddered. "Ugh. That boy's got strange taste."

Sadie frowned at the empty sample dish in her hand, then greedily eyed the others on the stand. "Yeah, I'm trying to talk my husband into getting him a puppy as a compromise."

"Aw, I bet Sam'll love that."

"Yeah, but Philip hasn't said yes yet."

And he probably won't.

After two more samples, Sadie headed home. As she drove, she thought about Philip's relationship with Sam. He barely saw his son. Whenever he did, there was always an uncomfortable strain in the air. He never said anything to Sam, unless he wanted him to pick up something off the floor, and then Philip's voice was always so intolerant. And he never played with Sam. He was always too busy, or he didn't want to wrinkle his shirt or get his pants dirty.

She let out a sigh. She'd give anything to see Philip on the floor beside his son, both of them playing with dinosaurs or action figures—anything.

Entering the house, she headed straight for the kitchen and put the milk jug in the fridge. In the laundry room, she started a load of darks and threw the whites into the dryer. The morning passed quickly as she lost herself in her regular routine of housework.

After a bite to eat, she sat down at the small desk in the corner of the living room. She pulled out some watercolor paper and began drafting the cover for Going Batty. By two o'clock, she had created outlines of the cover and the first four pages.

"Looking good," she murmured.

She packed away the drawings and began straightening the pillows on the two sofas. Flicking a look around the room, she scowled at its stark white simplicity. She had wanted to decorate the spacious room with fresh flowers and colorful prints. But Philip wouldn't have it. He liked things the way they were. Everything in its place, no frivolous touches. The only room she'd been allowed free reign was Sam's.

The phone rang. It was her agent in Calgary.

"Hey, Jackson," she said. "I thought you'd forgotten me."

There was a feigned gasp on the other end. "I could never do that. You're a Starr, remember?"

Starr Literary Agency, run by Toronto native Jackson Starr, was giving the bigwigs in New York a run for their money.

"Any word on the conference tour?" she asked.

"That's why I'm calling. I have you booked in five cities in September, including the Crime Writers Conference in Toronto and Criminal Minds at Work in New York."

She grinned into the phone. "How rich did you make me?"

"Five thousand, plus hotel and travel expenses."

"Well, that made my day. Thanks."

"Any time. I'll deposit the check into your account this afternoon." There was a ruffle of paper. "So when you coming to visit us?"

Sadie's gaze was drawn to Philip's office door. He was at work, but she still felt his presence, his disapproval. He didn't like Jackson, was jealous of him.

"Sorry, Jackson. I won't be able to get away for a bit. Maybe when I finish Sam's book."

"How's it coming?"

She filled him in on her progress, then hung up.

The thought of the extra money in her private account elated her. Philip maintained control over most of their money, which he had tied up in investments. He gave her a weekly household allowance with the agreement that any money she made would be used for Sam's basic expenses and her own. Thank God, she made a decent income. Maybe this summer they could finally go to Disneyland.

Thoughts of a family vacation, sunshine, castles and rides filled her mind and she practically danced into the laundry room. When the third load was dry, she folded Sam's clothes and placed them in a basket, along with a pair of Philip's socks that she'd discovered behind the laundry hamper. Gripping the basket under one arm, she trudged upstairs.

In the master bedroom, she opened the top drawer of the tallboy dresser and tried to ignore the five airplane bottles of alcohol that clinked together. Philip had made a halfhearted attempt to hide them under his long johns.

Five bottles, five drinks.

She tossed the socks in and slammed the drawer shut. Then she moved into the hallway, hesitating outside the door to Sam's bedroom. She wasn't sure why, but when her hand touched the brass doorknob, the hair on the back of her neck stood up. With a nervous laugh, she turned the knob and stepped inside.

A quick survey of Sam's room told her that nothing was out of the ordinary, so she set the laundry basket on the bed, next to a Batman t-shirt that had been tossed on the pillow.

She sniffed the shirt. "Clean."

Folding it, she placed it on top of the clothes in the basket. Then she gathered up the toy T-rex, raptors and pterodactyls that were scattered on the floor and put them in the treasure chest. A few minutes later, Sam's clothes had been put away in the dresser, with the exception of an Oilers jacket.

She moved toward the closet, the jacket in hand.

Ssss...

The sound brought her to a halt.

"Get a grip. What would Philip say if he saw you?" She laughed derisively. "He'd say you're being a stupid fool."

She hauled the door open.

The closet was a jumble of toys and clothes. On the floor, jammed between two stuffed animals, a red balloon left over from the Valentine's Day parade hissed at her mockingly.

As it deflated, she echoed the sound. "Idiot."

She hung up the jacket, tossed the balloon in the garbage and went downstairs. An hour later, she headed out to pick up Sam, the balloon long forgotten.

∞ ∞ ∞

"It's Friday," she said as they left the school. "Park day."

Sam let out a whoop, his mouth lined with orange Kool-Aid.

She frowned. "We have to wash that face before Daddy sees."

They crossed the parking lot and followed the sidewalk to the playground. A light blanket of snow still covered the grass, but that didn't deter the dozen or so children that played in the park.

She settled Sam on a swing and closed her fingers over his.

"Hold on tight, honey. Don't let go."

She gave the swing a gentle push. Then another.

Sunlight danced in Sam's black hair and he closed his eyes and leaned backward. He rose higher and higher, pumping his legs in delight. One of his boots slipped off and landed a few yards away. Sam didn't even notice.

"You're flying," Sadie said, grinning. "Like a bat, Sam."

Watching him, she had a sudden urge to freeze the moment, savor it forever. Times such as these made her wish she had brought a camera.

She heard his soft giggle. It built slowly, then exploded into a bout of contagious laughter.

Even the young mother next to her couldn't help but smile.

"He's having a good time," the woman said.

Sadie nodded. "Oh, to be young and carefree."

"You got that right—Andrew!"

Distracted by the antics of a lanky, freckle-faced boy climbing on top of the covered slide, the woman rushed off, leaving her daughter—still a toddler—in the baby swing next to Sam.

Sadie stared after her in disbelief. What on earth was the woman thinking? How could she leave her daughter with a complete stranger after a girl had been kidnapped?

Her gaze drifted over the school park.

A cluster of mothers chatted at a picnic table, while an olive-skinned boy of about four wandered precariously close to the busy parking lot. A few feet away, an older boy—maybe thirteen—pushed a chubby girl off the steps to the slide, and a toddler of indiscriminate gender played in the sandbox, feasting on gourmet dirt laced with God knows what else. And all of that, ignored by the women at the table.

The child in the baby swing let out a soft cry.

Shaking her head in frustration, Sadie slowed Sam's swing. As she helped him down, she was torn between wanting to take him home and not wanting to leave the little girl alone.

Huge brown eyes captured hers. "Mama?"

Sadie sensed her fear. "Your mommy will be back soon."

The girl whimpered, her eyes pooling with tears.

A few minutes later, the mother rushed over. "Jeez, you'd think he'd been killed, the way he was carrying on." She nudged her head in the direction of the freckled boy.

Sadie's lips thinned. "Your daughter was getting worried."

The young woman's eyes widened as she let out a coarse snicker. "Daughter? She's not my kid. Neither of 'em are. I'm their nanny."

Sadie was shocked. "Their nanny?"

"Hey, people mistake me for their mom all the time," the woman said, as though motherhood were nothing more than a badge one could buy at the local Dollar Store.

While the woman helped the toddler from the swing, Sadie gave her a disparaging look and bit back a reply. Without another word, she took Sam's hand and led him back to the car.

"Snug as a bug," she said, clicking his seatbelt into place.

She climbed into the driver's seat. As she reached for the door, something made her look across the street.

A lone man wearing reflective sunglasses and a cowboy hat pulled low over his face waited in a gray sedan with the window rolled halfway down. She couldn't make out his features, but she did see the proud smile on his face as he watched his son or daughter playing in the park.

I wish Philip would take the time to bring Sam here.

She backed out and eased toward the parking lot exit.

That's when she noticed the man in the car again. He wasn't looking toward the playground anymore. His shadowed gaze was directed at her. Passing the man, she was relieved when he looked away.

4

"Give me a call and let me know if you'll be home for supper," Sadie said in response to Philip's voice mail greeting.

Despondent, she hung up the phone.

It was almost six and she needed to talk to him—before things got further out of hand.

Maybe therapy would help.

She let out a huff.

The day Philip went for any kind of counseling would be the day that pigs, sheep *and* cows flew.

A dull *thump* came from Sam's room.

"Honey, you okay?"

She listened at the bottom of the stairs, but he wasn't crying, so she strolled back into the living room.

The phone rang. "Hello?"

All she heard was breathing—heavy breathing.

She hung up. She'd been getting a lot of crank calls lately.

The phone rang a second time.

She picked it up. "Hello?"

More breathing.

"Is anyone there?" She sighed, irritated by the silence. "Is that the best you can do?" When there was still no response, she said, "I hope this is as good for you as it is for me."

A hooting laugh erupted on the other end.

"Leah," she muttered.

"Hey, Sadie," her friend said with a snort. "What've you got planned for tonight?"

"I'm not sure. I was hoping Philip would be home early for a change. What about you?"

"I need to get out. My neighbor has a party every Friday night and I swear they're going to come through the ceiling any minute. Of course, it wouldn't be so bad if they invited me."

Sadie heard the frustration in Leah's voice.

"Why don't you come here for supper then?" she said.

"You don't mind?"

"Of course not, you twit." *But Philip might.*

Although she'd never say *that* to Leah—even though her friend already knew that Philip wasn't her number one fan. He had issues with Leah. He didn't agree with her lifestyle, her fashion, or her influence on Sadie. He'd been trying for years to get Sadie to hook up with some of the wives from the firm. It would look good for him.

"Well..." Leah drawled, pretending to ponder the offer of free food. "Okay, I'll come over. I'll be there in twenty minutes. But as soon as Phil the Pill shows up, I'm outta there. Got it?"

"Got it."

"What's for dinner anyway?"

Sadie smiled. "Sam's favorite."

"KD?" Leah whined.

"No," Sadie said, chuckling. "His other favorite. KFC."

"Awesome! I'll be there in ten."

Leah showed up at the door wearing a pair of tight black pants that flared at the ankles and a flamboyant gypsy-style blouse in colorful bronzes and silver trim.

"Hey, it's Friday night," she said when she saw Sadie's raised brow. "I'm going out later. Now, where's the man of the house?"

"Sam! Auntie Leah's here!"

A ball of energy flew down the stairs and landed in her friend's outstretched arms.

Leah groaned. "You're getting big, buddy."

Sam looked up at Leah and a devilish grin developed.

"Tomorrow you'll be six," she said, kissing his cheek.

"Well, officially he's six on Monday," Sadie reminded her.

Leah lifted a slim shoulder. "Semantics." She set Sam down. "Are you excited for your birthday?"

He nodded, then giggled and raced back upstairs.

"Supper'll be here soon," Sadie said, heading for the kitchen.

Leah followed her. "I take it the esteemed legal eagle isn't back yet?"

"No."

"You still thinking he's—"

Sadie's prickly gaze halted her.

"Ah..." Leah murmured. "You know, until you have proof, I wouldn't get too hung up on this idea. For all you know it could be perfectly innocent."

Sadie made a sour face.

"Or you could be right," Leah added quickly.

"I don't know what to do."

"You gotta talk to the man. But be prepared. You might not like what you hear." Leah's voice softened. "God, you don't deserve—"

The doorbell rang.

"Chow's here," Sadie said, grateful for the interruption.

She headed for the living room, grabbed a couple of twenties from her purse and opened the front door. An attractive older man wearing a damp hooded raincoat stood on the porch. He held a paper bag in one hand and the bill in the other.

"Thanks," she said, handing him the money. "Hey, where's Trevor?"

The man smiled. "You must get a lot of chicken if you know us guys by name."

"My son is hooked on KFC."

The man nodded and passed her the bag. "Trevor's in the hospital getting his appendix out."

"Ouch. Hope he gets better soon."

"Yeah, well, you have a good night," he said.

As she closed the door, Leah snickered behind her.

"He was *so* checking you out, Sadie."

Sadie blushed. "I think he was checking *you* out, my friend."

"Nope. He was disappointed to see me here. Gee, should we arm wrestle for him?"

"I'm married."

Leah gave her a hard stare. "Married, maybe. But you ain't dead, sistah friend."

"You know I won't do *that*. I made a vow to Philip and I intend on keeping it. Even if he doesn't."

"I admire you for that, Sadie. So should your husband."

After supper, Leah tucked Sam into bed, leaving Sadie to tidy up. When she was finished, she stared at the phone. Philip still hadn't called.

"I think he just pulled in," Leah said behind her.

A few minutes later, Philip walked into the house. Ignoring Sadie, he tossed his briefcase on the dining room table and sent an irritated look in Leah's direction.

"What's for supper?" he asked, eyes flashing.

"KFC," Sadie replied. "It's in the fridge."

His mouth thinned as he eyed Leah, his disapproving gaze moving from her head to her feet and back up again. "What, another sleazy party tonight?"

"Nope," Leah said dryly. "Not unless *you* know where a good one is."

"Aw, bite me."

"I would, Phil, but I don't eat pork."

Philip's eyes narrowed and he strode out of the kitchen.

"Time for me to go, Sadie," Leah said, chagrined. "I feel a storm a brewin'. Sorry, hon."

"*I'm* sorry. I don't know why he has to be so rude to you."

"He's jealous of our friendship. But no worries. We're friends for life. Right?"

Sadie hugged her. "For life."

∞ ∞ ∞

As she changed into an oversized t-shirt for bed, Sadie threw a hesitant glance in Philip's direction. He'd hardly said a word to her since Leah had left. No, "How was your day, Sadie?" Or, "What did you do today?"

"Any new developments in your case?" she asked hesitantly.

Philip grunted as he peeled off his pants. "You know I can't discuss it."

Then talk to me about something else.

She tried again. "Sam had a great day at school today."

Philip paused in the doorway to the bathroom. "Did he say something?"

She bit her bottom lip and shook her head.

"Then he didn't have a great day," he said with a scowl.

When the bathroom door closed behind him, she slumped on the edge of the bed. She didn't understand what was going on with him. Why was he so distant, so cruel?

Sliding between the cool sheets, she stared at the spackled ceiling, wondering how much more indifference she could take. Philip had always been driven by his passion for success. He handled multinational corporate trials with ease, winning his fair share of high-profile cases. He kept long hours and often slept on the sofa bed in his office.

Or so he said.

The bathroom door creaked.

She rolled away, just before Philip turned off the lamp and climbed into bed beside her. A whiff of floral perfume emanated from his body. The perfume wasn't hers. It had traces of honeysuckle. Sadie hated honeysuckle.

Feigning sleep, she waited for his breathing to slow. Or for the snoring to begin. For a long moment, she wondered whether she should say something. Then she felt heavy breathing in her ear, and a hand fumbled beneath the t-shirt and stroked her thigh.

"I need you to help me with a little problem, Sadie."

You haven't needed me for a long time, she itched to say. *Now you want sex? What about my needs?*

"I need to talk," she said when Philip reached higher.

His hand froze. "What about?"

"You know what. I think we need help."

He snatched his hand away as if her words had burned him.

"If you want to see a shrink, go see one."

"Both of us," she insisted.

The mattress shifted.

She sat up, turned on the lamp.

Philip stood beside the bed, wearing nothing but a rapidly dwindling erection. He sent her a piercing stare, glaring at her as though she had lost her mind.

Had she?

"I don't need a goddamn shrink, Sadie. I'm not the one with the problem."

"Our marriage is in trouble," she said, scrambling from the bed. "We need counseling. If you won't do it for me, then at least do it for Sam's sake. Please!"

"Sam's sake? Jesus Christ, Sadie! Everything lately has been for Sam's sake. We moved out of the apartment into this house for him. Now I have to drive almost an hour instead of fifteen minutes to get to the off—"

"That apartment wasn't suitable for raising a child."

Philip stabbed a finger in the air. "*You* once thought it was the perfect place for us. Until your meddling friend got her nose out of joint."

"What's that supposed to mean? Leah had nothing to do with why I wanted to leave that apartment."

"She's changed you, Sadie. So has Sam. If you can't see that..." He shrugged.

She stared at him, baffled. "Of course having a child changed me. What did you expect? There's someone else to consider now, not just the two of us."

Philip's jaw flinched, but he remained silent.

"My God," she whispered. "You're jealous of him? Of Sam?"

Philip let out an angry huff, grabbed a pillow and stalked toward the door. "I am *not* jealous of my son. I just don't like the changes I see in you." Cursing, he stormed out of the room.

"And I don't like the changes I see in you," she mumbled, slumping on the bed. *Why am I still with him?*

That was a stupid question, of course. She stayed because of Sam. Because a small part of her still believed that Philip could change. *Would* change.

She recalled the night her life began to crumble.

"I don't want kids," he'd told her. "I'm happy with the way things are. I don't understand why you'd want to jeopardize everything."

"What would be jeopardized?" she'd asked, stunned. "You'd still have your career and I'd have mine. But I want children too."

"Well, I don't."

That was the end of that discussion.

Believing he'd change his mind and feeling she had no other choice, she secretly went off the pill. Bad move. When Philip discovered the unopened prescription box, he refused to speak to her for the rest of the day. A week later, she found out she was pregnant. She was ecstatic. Philip was pissed. He screamed at her, calling her a conniving bitch.

She miscarried the next day.

Yeah, they'd been the happy couple, the envy of all their friends, especially the ones who thought Sadie and Philip had everything. They didn't realize that she was putting on a façade. In public, she'd smile and tell everyone that things were wonderful. However, in private...

There was no denying it. She was a miserable mess.

It started with the occasional drink before bed. To calm her nerves since Philip was always late. But one drink became two. Then three. Before she knew it, she started drinking during the day, hiding bottles where Philip would never find them.

A second miscarriage sent her into a bout of severe depression and she was sure she was being punished, that she'd never have a baby. She spent most nights with her other 'best friend'—a bottle of rum.

Then Philip started staying out later and later.

Her life changed forever the night he was promoted to partner. At a special banquet, a new partner and his wife were celebrating the arrival of a baby boy. The attention they received and the accolades from the senior law partners made Philip reconsider the idea of children. Suddenly, having a child seemed the perfect way to elevate his social and professional status.

A year later, Sam was born.

Sadie had quit drinking the moment she found out she was pregnant. It had been rough at first, but with Leah's help and Sam as the reward, she'd fought all her demons and won.

She'd been sober ever since.

∞ ∞ ∞

As she slipped into bed, she clamped her eyes shut, blocking off tears that threatened to escape. She was not going to cry. Not over Philip.

Outside, a dog barked.

"I guess a puppy for Sam is out of the question then."

It seemed as though she had just closed her eyes, when the sound of breaking glass woke her. A piercing scream sent her heart racing and she flew out of bed.

When she left her bedroom, the first thing she noticed was the chill that swept down the hall. The second thing she saw was Sam's half-open door.

She pushed it. *"Jesus!"*

Her son's bedroom blasted her with frigid air. When she glanced toward the far wall, she spotted the culprit. The blinds were wide open and the window was shattered. On the floor, a foot from Sam's bed, was a brick.

"What's going on?" Philip demanded, flicking on the light.

Speechless, she reached a hand to her throat as her eyes swept over the room, then screeched to a stop on Sam's bed.

His *empty* bed.

Panic seared through her, hot and fearful. "Sam?"

Behind her, the closet door creaked. She moved closer, but Philip beat her to it. When he whipped it open, she was overwhelmed by relief. Her sweet boy was curled up in the corner, tears flooding his face.

She swept Sam into her arms. "Only my bat boy would hide in the closet," she murmured, stoking his hair. "Philip, who would do such a thing?"

"Shit, I don't know. Probably just kids out carousing. Tuck Sam back into bed and we'll clean this up."

"I'll put him in our bed," she said dryly. "He's not sleeping in here tonight."

"Fine. I guess I'll clean up the glass then."

Sadie hefted Sam to her hip and made for the door. She could feel his heart beating rapidly, and it didn't slow until she reached her bedroom and tucked him into the king-sized bed. When he reached up, she kissed his forehead. "No worries. You're safe, honey. I promise."

Lugging the vacuum behind him, Philip paused in the doorway. His gaze wouldn't meet hers.

"I'll report it first thing in the morning," he said before disappearing.

A minute later, the vacuum roared to life.

These were the moments—although rare—that reminded her of why she had married Philip. He always took care of business.

5

Leah arrived just after one-thirty on Sunday afternoon.

Sadie took one look at her friend's downcast face and knew instinctively that something was wrong.

"What?" she demanded.

"They didn't have your cake order, Sadie."

"But I called it in last week. How could they—" She caught sight of Leah's sly grin and twinkling eyes. "What's going on?"

"April Fools!"

Leah darted down the sidewalk, then returned a minute later bearing a sweet gift. Sam's Batman birthday cake.

"April Fools' Day ends at noon, you know," Sadie muttered.

"Not in Canada, silly. Besides, I couldn't resist."

Sadie gave her a saccharine smile. "No problem. I'll get you back next year."

Juggling the cake box, Leah kicked off her shoes and made a beeline for the kitchen. "There's no room in the fridge."

"Leave it on the counter then," Sadie said, emptying a bag of steaming microwave popcorn into a bowl. "Are you ready for this?"

"It's a kids' party. How bad can it get?"

Sadie opened her mouth, but then clamped it shut. Leah didn't have kids.

And after today, she'll be very thankful of that fact.

When they entered the living room, it was already in a state of chaos. Toys and kids were scattered on every piece of furniture. In one corner, twin boys jumped on the sofa, fighting over a plastic sword. Victoria, Sam's new school friend, stood nearby with her hands on her hips.

"Stop it!" the little girl demanded. "Put that down and stop fighting!" Her blond pigtails bounced with every word.

In the middle of the room, a copper-haired boy sat on the floor, eyes glued to a movie. Beside him, Sam was busy pretending to be a T-rex, his voice competing with the screams of his friends and the deafening volume of the TV. So far, he was in the lead.

The look of sheer horror on Leah's face was almost comical.

"Oh…my…God," she said. "How on earth are you gonna survive all these monsters?"

Sadie grinned and passed her the popcorn bowl. "That's what I have you for."

Leah's face paled. "Hey, you only asked me to pick up the cake. You never said anything about me staying."

"Then you don't get any cake."

"But that's…blackmail!" Leah sputtered. "Fine then, but I'm leaving after the ice cream."

The doorbell rang.

Sadie wiped her fingers on a dishcloth and hurried to the front door. When she opened it, she was relieved to see that the entertainment Philip hired had arrived.

Clancy the Clown stood on the porch, his curly orange hair flapping in the wind. His face was caked with white paint and a bulbous red nose covered his own. An exaggerated crimson smile took up the lower half of his face. To Sadie, it seemed more grotesque than happy.

"Hey, Mrs. O'Connell," the man said in a nasally tone. "Sorry I'm late. My car broke down and—"

She waved him inside. "Don't worry about it. I'm just thankful you made it. You look very…uh…colorful."

The clown sported a blue and orange striped jacket, a white shirt and bright yellow baggy pants held up by lime green and gold suspenders. A tiny top hat was perched on his head and a huge daisy was pinned to the left lapel.

Sadie suspected that one sniff would get her drenched.

"Do you want cash or a check?" she asked.

"Cash, if you have it."

She pulled a wad of twenties from her pocket. She counted out three hundred dollars, paused, then added an extra forty.

You'd better be worth it, Clancy.

Handing him the money, she said, "Three hours, right?"

The clown nodded, placing the bills inside a canvas bag. "I'll let myself out at…" He checked his watch. "Five-fifteen. Then you're on your own."

"Gee, thanks."

Clancy smiled. "Did you call the agency?"

"I've had my hands full with these kids."

The crimson smile stretched further. "The boss doesn't know I'm late then. Thanks."

A snort sounded from behind Sadie.

"If you want to thank her," Leah said wryly, "then round up the little hooligans and do your thing."

The clown's brown eyes shifted to Sadie. "No problemo. Su casa es mi casa."

With a bob of his head, Clancy and his neon red, size fourteen shoes clomped into the living room. He was welcomed by a boisterous Sam who shrieked with delight.

"Oh, Jesus," Sadie moaned.

"Just think how loud things'll be when Sam starts talking," Leah said. "Once he starts, you won't be able to shut him up."

"That will be the best day of my life."

Leah's expression grew sad. "I know."

Sadie watched Sam and his friends play with Clancy. The kids were fascinated by the clown, pulling on his suspenders and stepping on his huge shoes, and shrieking when he sprayed them with the daisy.

"Hey," Leah said, jabbing her. "Let's grab a glass of chocolate milk. I need something to wash down this popcorn. "

As Sadie followed her into the kitchen, she peered over her shoulder. Sam's beaming face brought a smile to her own.

"You're a lucky mama," Leah said softly.

"I know. Sam is the best thing in my life."

∞ ∞ ∞

When the door closed behind the last child, Sadie and Leah released a collective sigh, looked at each other and laughed.

"Birthdays were way easier when he was a baby," Sadie said.

Leah pushed back her limp hair. "I just have one thing to say to you, my friend. I'm going to have a root canal this time next year. It'll be a slice of heaven compared to this."

"If you can get a two for one special I'll come with you."

"Yeah, but that would mean Phil would have to actually show up," her friend said sourly.

The smile on Sadie's face faded.

"Hey," Leah said. "I'm sure he's got a good reason for not making his own kid's birthday party."

Sadie raised a brow. "You think?"

"Well, he must have. He may be a jerk to me and treat you like crap most of the time...but he loves Sam."

"I know, but sometimes I think he loves himself more."

"Well, cheer up," Leah said, eying the mess in the room. "Sam's party was a complete success."

Sadie slumped into a chair. "Yeah. Thank God for Clancy. He did a great job keeping the kids entertained. I was so busy in the kitchen trying to get those darned sparklers to light that I didn't even see him leave."

"And lucky you, you get to do it all over again tomorrow."

"Yeah, the family birthday party. You'll be here, right?"

"Wouldn't miss it. Sam'll be so happy when he sees that bike you got him."

"I'm going to take him to the park to practice on it next weekend. Do you want to come?"

"Sure."

Leah disappeared into the kitchen and Sadie heard her rummage through the fridge.

"Ah-ha!" her friend called out. "The perfect year."

When she reappeared, she had two glasses of peach iced tea. She handed one to Sadie. "Drink up. Then I'll help you clean up this mess before Philip sees it."

Sadie's woeful gaze drifted around the living room. Paper plates were piled everywhere. They had somehow gone astray and hadn't made it into the garbage can that she had so thoughtfully provided next to the dining room table. Plastic cups, some half full of pop, were on every table and counter space. There were more cups than there had been kids.

"Ugh," Leah said behind her.

Sadie followed her friend's gaze.

A chocolate cake smear—so dark it almost looked like dried blood—stretched across the kitchen wall, three feet from the ground, a small handprint at the end.

"Your house is a disaster," Leah said unnecessarily.

Sadie sighed. "Well, at least it's quiet."

Sam had gone upstairs to his room, tired from all the excitement and junk food. The last time she had seen him, he was lying on his bed.

"He's probably asleep," Leah said, reading her thoughts.

Sadie gulped down her iced tea, then set to work on the kitchen, while Leah looked after the living room. After an hour had passed, all that was left to do was run the vacuum over the carpets and turn on the dishwasher.

"All done," Leah said, wiping a bead of sweat from her brow.

"Thanks. I can handle what's left."

As Sadie watched Leah climb into her car, a part of her wanted to holler, "*Come back!*"

"You're being silly," she muttered.

Sadie closed the door and slid the deadbolt into place. Then she locked up the rest of the house, set the alarm for the night and went upstairs to check on Sam.

When she opened the door to his room, she smiled. Sam was stretched out across his bed. On top of the blankets. A soft snore issued from his half-opened mouth. He had passed out from exhaustion, his face covered with chocolate cake, white, black and blue icing, and an orange pop mustache.

"Happy birthday, little man," she whispered, tucking an extra blanket around him.

She closed the door and headed downstairs to wait for Philip.

∞ ∞ ∞

Sadie was abruptly roused from a deep sleep. She jerked to a sitting position, inhaling deeply, and looked at the space beside her. It was unoccupied, the blanket still tucked under the pillow. She had waited for Philip downstairs for hours. Eventually, she had given up and gone to bed.

She peered at the bedroom clock. It was half past midnight. She'd only been asleep for about forty-five minutes. In the murky shadows of the room, she felt a foreign presence, a movement of air that was so subtle it could have been her own breath.

A draft?

She squinted at the window. It was closed.

Somewhere in the house a floorboard creaked.

Philip must be home.

Tossing the blankets aside, she slid from the bed and walked to the door. Remembering the brick thrown through Sam's window, she froze. Her stomach fluttered as she imagined a gang of teen hoodlums breaking into the house.

But the alarm would go off, silly.

Still, she pressed an ear to the door and strained to listen.

At first, there was silence. Then another creak.

"Philip," she mumbled.

She was about to open the door when she heard an unfamiliar ticking sound. Had Philip bought a clock for the hall?

She listened again.

Tick... tick, tick.

Whatever it was, it was coming closer.

Her heart began to pound a maniacal rhythm and her breath quickened. When a shadow passed underneath the door, she held her breath. Her heart thumped almost painfully in her chest.

Then the shadow was gone.

Cautiously, she opened the door. Just a crack.

The hall was empty.

And no ticking.

Maybe I dreamt it.

With a tremulous laugh, she flung open the door, a show of false bravado. Maybe Philip was working in his office. Maybe he'd gone to check on Sam.

"Philip?"

She walked down the hall and stopped in front of Sam's room. Her toes tingled as a draft teased her feet. She shivered, then opened the door.

The window that Philip had replaced gaped open—black and hungry—like a mouth waiting to be fed. The curtains flapped in the night wind, two tongues lashing out.

She frowned. Philip hadn't left the window open. He'd gone to work early, without a word to either of them. And Sam couldn't have opened it. He wasn't tall enough.

Did I leave it open?

She crossed the room, barely looking at the mound in the bed. She reached for the window and tugged it shut. The lock clicked into place, the sharp sound shattering the stillness.

Then she glanced at the bed.

Sam hadn't even stirred. But then again, he never did. He was almost comatose when he slept and nothing could wake him early, short of a sonic boom.

She tiptoed to the bed and touched his hair. Then, closing her eyes, she leaned down, kissed his warm forehead and breathed in his sweet child scent. He smelled of chocolate and sunshine.

"Snug as a bug," she whispered.

She stepped back, her foot connecting with something soft and furry. Reaching down, she fumbled in the dark until she found the stuffed toy dog that Philip had given Sam the night before. She moved quietly toward the closet, inched the door open and tossed the toy inside. Then she stepped out into the hall, shutting the bedroom door behind her.

Her gaze flitted to the far end of the hallway, where shadows danced between silk trees that stood in the alcove. Beside the trees—two-thirds up the wall—was a small oval window, and through it, a new moon was visible. It hung in the cloudless sky, a pearlescent pendant on invisible string.

It was a beautiful night, one that was meant to be shared.

Loneliness filled her, but she shrugged it off and plodded down to the kitchen to get a glass of juice. Five minutes later, she went back upstairs, with every intention of crawling into bed and ignoring the fact that Philip hadn't even bothered to call on the night of their son's birthday party.

As she passed Sam's door, a flicker of light beneath it caught her eye. Then she heard a soft thud. Sam must have fallen out of bed again. He had done that on two other occasions. Usually he woke up screaming.

She opened the door and sucked in a breath as her gaze was captured by something that made no sense at all.

The window was open again.

She blinked. "What the—?"

Moonlight streamed through the window, illuminating the bed. It was empty.

"Sam?"

She reached for the light switch.

"I wouldn't do that if I were you."

At the sound of a stranger's hoarse whisper in her son's bedroom, she did the most natural thing.

She flicked on the light.

6

A black-hooded monster held her son in his arms.

Sam wasn't moving.

The oxygen was instantly sucked from the room, making it impossible for Sadie to breathe. The glass slipped through her fingers, orange juice pooling at her feet. Speechless, she took a trembling step forward. "Please—"

"Don't move!" the stranger growled from the depths of the sweatshirt hood. "You have ten seconds to make a decision. Let me walk out of here with the kid, or your son dies." He shifted Sam's limp body in his arms and a glint of metal flashed.

A gun. It was aimed at Sam's head.

She trembled uncontrollably. *Oh Jesus...*

"Let him go," she said in a shaky voice.

He snorted, as if he found her comment amusing. When he twisted his head to glance over his shoulder at the open window, she saw a ghostly face with a hooked nose that looked like it had been broken a few times. A red smear gleamed in the crease that ran from the side of his nose to his wide, thick lips. His cheek was pale alabaster and flecked with spidery imperfections.

Pockmarks, she guessed.

The man turned, examining her just as closely. "Are you that fucking stupid? Turn off the goddamn light!"

Although her hand trembled noticeably, she obeyed.

Dressed in black, the man blended into the shadowed corner.

She hissed in a breath. "What did you do to my son?"

"Just gave him something to make him sleep." The man sighed, frustrated. "Why'd you have to go and mess things up? If you'd stayed asleep I'd be outta here already."

"I want my son," she said with a whimper. "Just let him go. Leave. I won't tell anyone. Please. Just give him to me and walk out the door."

"That ain't gonna happen."

The man did something unexpected. He moved into the moonlight, sat down on the bed and propped her son in his lap, like a ventriloquist's doll.

"Is it, Sam?" He gripped Sam's chin and turned his head from side to side. "No, Mommy," he said in an eerie, childlike voice. "I'm going with this man."

Sadie staggered against the wall. "No, he's not."

The man tossed Sam on the bed. "Shit, shit, *shit!*"

She shivered at the pure madness in his voice.

"I'll tell *you* how this is gonna play out," he muttered. "First, you're gonna promise not to leave this room for twenty minutes."

"Wait!" she cried, tears flowing down her face. "Take me instead. You don't need him. I'll come with you, do whatever you want."

"I don't need you." He stroked the gun against Sam's hair. "I have what I came for. Five seconds."

She hitched in a breath, her heart aching, burning…dying.

"You sick…*per*vert," she said between gritted teeth.

"I'm no perv."

"Then what do you want with my son?"

"For fuck's sake, shut up! You've already screwed things up enough. No one's ever seen me. No one!"

That's when it hit her.

The Fog.

She shrank back against the wall. "I won't let you take my son."

The Fog laughed mockingly. "You won't *let* me?"

She stood slowly, quivering from head to toe. "No. I won't."

In a flash, she lunged for the gun. The man backhanded her across the face. Pain exploded in her left temple. Enraged, she roared and hurled herself at him again. This time she managed to dislodge the gun from his hand.

She dove for it.

He kicked her in the ribs. "Stupid bitch."

Forcing her away from the gun, he kicked her again. And again. Then he reached down, hauled her up by her hair and flung her across the room. A sharp twinge pierced her side as she landed with a sickening thud against the dresser. She let out a pained gasp. When she looked up, Sam was lying helpless in the man's arms.

"I'm walking out of here," The Fog said. "With the kid. And you're not gonna stop me. You know why?"

She shook her head, unable to move or speak.

"Because if you try to stop me…" He pressed the gun to Sam's head and pretended to pull the trigger. *"Bam!"*

"I can give you money," she cried out. "I've got twenty-five thousand in my checking account."

He sneered. "Is that all he's worth to you?"

"I'm begging you…a *hundred* thousand! Whatever you want, I'll get it. Please! Just tell me how much you want."

The Fog tossed Sam over his shoulder with the ease of someone hefting a sack of potatoes. Then he strode toward her and leaned down, his shadowed face bare inches from hers.

"What I *want* is to see nothing in the papers," he said, his breath a simmering stew of cigarettes, onions and beer. "No description, no nothing. I want you to go back to bed and pretend you never seen me."

"I can't do that."

"Yes, you can. And you will."

"But the police—"

"Fuck the police! You want your kid to live?"

Sadie shuddered. "Yes, I want Sam to live."

"Don't leave this room for twenty minutes."

She stretched out a trembling hand. "Don't take my baby."

The Fog straightened. Then he yanked the door open and the light from the hall illuminated him for a brief moment.

"Please," she wept.

"Please," he mimicked scornfully. "You're pathetic."

She closed her eyes in agreement. Then, in a last ditch effort, she clawed her way across the floor, writhing in agony as a hot wave threatened to pull her under.

The Fog watched her, his thin lips twisting into a sinister smile. "I see one description—you even say you saw me—and I'll send the kid back to you all right. In little *bloody* pieces. You got that?"

She couldn't answer.

"Two seconds!" he snapped, raising the gun to Sam's head.

"Okay! Take him! Just please…don't hurt him."

Then Sadie did the only thing she could do. She let a madman take her son.

Alone, she cried in the dark, scared to move, scared not to.

"God help me," she sobbed. "Help Sam!"

But God wasn't listening.

∞ ∞ ∞

Philip stumbled into the house at one fifteen. And *stumbled* was an understatement. Upstairs in Sam's room, Sadie heard the sound of glass hitting the floor. It was followed by a belligerent curse.

She stared at the bat signal clock on Sam's wall.

The twenty minutes were up. Five minutes ago. They had passed slowly, like a never-ending funeral dirge for the Pope. She had mentally shut down and collapsed on Sam's bed in a haze of overwhelming pain, grief and guilt.

She pulled herself to her feet, ignoring the throbbing spasms in her ribs. Her legs shook, her heart raced and her head pounded.

What do I do? What do I tell Philip?

She moaned. "Oh, God. Sam…"

She stepped out into the hall, one hand on the doorframe for support. Her throat burned as heavy footsteps lumbered up the stairs.

Philip turned the corner and lurched to a stop when he saw her. "Sadie?" he slurred. "Whatcha doing? Waiting up for me?"

"Philip, I n-need—"

"I need you to blow me." He grinned lecherously and tried to grab her.

She batted his arm away. "Philip, stop it!"

"So I'm a little drunk," he said, pouting. "We can still—"

"Sam's gone," she whispered. "He took Sam."

"What?"

"The Fog…took…him, Philip." Her voice caught in the back of her throat as deep, wracking sobs hiccupped to the surface.

Philip stared at her. "What the hell are you talking about?" He pushed her aside and staggered into Sam's room. "Sam's sleeping in his—"

He stopped, confused. Then he strode to the closet and flung the door open. "Where is he, Sadie?" He whipped around, almost colliding into her. "What've you done with my son?"

She was stunned. "I haven't done anything, Philip. I told you, Sam's been kidnapped."

"Kidnapped?" His glazed eyes went immediately sober and his face blanched. "Oh shit." He looked as though someone had sucker punched him in the gut.

She moved slowly toward their bedroom.

"What are you doing?" he demanded, following her.

"Calling the police."

"You haven't called them yet?"

She reached for the cordless phone. "I just…found him gone."

Philip sank down on the bed and watched her dial.

When the 911 operator answered, Sadie's composure crumbled. "My son's been kidnapped," she wept into the phone.

The man took her information, then instructed her not to hang up. "The police will be there soon."

Phone in hand, she stood by the window and stared at the street below. There were no signs of life. No cars, no lights.

No Sam.

Then she heard the siren wailing in the distance.

"Did you see anyone?" Philip rasped.

She hesitated and swallowed hard, remembering The Fog's parting words. *'If you even say you saw me, I'll send the kid back to you all right. In little bloody pieces.'*

She believed him. If she said anything, Sam was as good as dead. And how would she live with *that* on her conscience? But she realized something else. Once she started lying, there was no turning back.

She choked back a muffled sob. "I heard something. I thought he fell out of bed. But when I went to check on him..." She stared at the phone. "Sam was gone."

The lies had begun.

7

Two police detectives showed up on her doorstep. The younger of the two, a tall man with closely cropped sandy hair, looked as if he were fresh out of college, while the other was balding and probably nearing retirement. They were followed by three crime scene unit investigators carrying metal cases.

Philip greeted them with a slurred, "C'mon in, officers."

"Mr. and Mrs. O'Connell, we're terribly sorry," the older detective said, offering Sadie his hand.

"Actually, my last name is Tymchuk," Philip cut in. "My wife kept her maiden name. For her writing."

The detective's wrinkled eyes arched. "Ms. O'Connell, then. Detective Lucas, and this is my partner, Detective Patterson." He reached into his shirt pocket and handed Sadie a plain white business card.

Detective Jason Lucas, Robbery Unit.

"Robbery?" she asked, confused.

"We handle abductions too."

She led them upstairs and paused in front of Sam's door.

"Is this your son's room?" Patterson asked.

When she nodded, the young detective disappeared into the room with the crime scene investigators. She leaned against the wall, afraid to breathe or move, afraid that she was in the way, yet afraid that if she went downstairs they would miss something.

"I need a drink," Philip muttered, veering unsteadily toward the stairs. "Want one?"

She scowled. "I think you've had enough."

"I meant coffee." He headed downstairs, shoulders slumped.

Detective Lucas cleared his throat. "Ms. O'Connell, I have to ask you some questions. Can we go downstairs?"

She shook her head. "I need to stay up here. Close to Sam's room."

The man gave her a sympathetic look. "Is there someplace we can sit?"

She nodded and led him to the bedroom. "Sorry for the mess," she said, wincing as she picked a nightgown and a mauve robe—a Christmas gift from Leah—off the floor.

"Don't worry about it." He looked at her closely. "Ms. O'Connell, you have blood above your left eye."

She touched her forehead. Her fingers came back sticky.

"It's just a scrape," she said quickly. "I tripped down the stairs. After I found Sam missing."

"Do you need to go to the hospital?"

"I'll go later." She perched on the edge of the bed, her hands twisting the sheets beside her. "You *will* find him, Detective—" She broke off and looked up. "I'm sorry. What did you say your name was?"

"Call me Jay."

Jay, a man in his early fifties, dragged a chair across the floor and positioned it in front of her. He was average height, about thirty pounds overweight, with thinning gray hair. His brown eyes looked tired and the shadows beneath them were etched with deep wrinkles, suggesting he had witnessed too many terrible things. Nevertheless, they were kind eyes.

"The first seventy-two hours are critical, Ms. O'Connell. The more you can tell me, the more we have to go on."

She hissed in a slow breath. "I'm ready."

He pulled out a notebook and pen. "You were in the house alone?"

She nodded. "Philip was…working late."

"What time did you go to bed?"

"Eleven forty-five."

"You said a noise woke you. What time was that?"

"Twelve-thirty."

Jay scribbled a few notes in the notebook, then looked up. "What did you do?"

"I went to open my bedroom door, but I heard something."

"What?"

"A clock ticking." She paused. "Or at least I thought it was. But we don't have a clock in the hall. Philip hates clocks. Ticking ones."

She knew she was rambling, but she didn't care.

"Maybe if I had turned on the light the first time…" Her gaze wandered around the room and landed on Sam's photo beside the bed.

"The first time?" There was surprise in the man's voice.

Her eyes latched onto his. *Careful. Don't screw this up.*

"I went to check on Sam when I first woke up. He was sleeping, but the window was open. So I closed it. Then I went downstairs for a drink. When I came back upstairs, I heard a thump. I thought Sam had fallen out of bed. When I opened the door..." She caught her breath. *Steady.* "He was gone."

"The time doesn't add up."

"What?" She gave him a blank stare.

"You called 911 at one eighteen." He studied his notes. "How long were you downstairs getting your...drink?"

"I don't know." *Timeline, you idiot!* "Maybe half an hour. I-I tidied up the kitchen too."

Jay leaned forward. "What exactly were you drinking?"

It took her a moment to realize what he was suggesting.

"Orange juice," she said evenly. "I don't drink alcohol. I'm an alcoholic." When the detective raised a brow, her lips thinned. "I've been sober almost seven years."

"Is there anyone you know of who would want to hurt you or your family?" he asked, writing something in the notebook.

"No, but some kids threw a rock at Sam's window the other night."

"Did you report it?"

"Philip did," she said, massaging her forehead. "Look, Sam's kidnapping isn't...personal. It was The Fog."

Jay looked up. "You saw him?"

She drew in a deep breath, mentally kicking herself. "Who else kidnaps children in the middle of the night?"

Patterson stepped into the room. "We need Ms. O'Connell to identify something. Do you recognize this? We found it under your son's bed." He held up a plastic bag marked *EVIDENCE.*

"Oh my God," Sadie moaned, reaching for it.

The bag contained one object. Clancy the Clown's red shoe.

When she flipped it over, a sparkle caught her eye. A silver thumbtack was stuck in the heel.

Tick, tick, tick.

"We hired a clown for Sam's birthday," she said in a hoarse voice. "Clancy. But of course that's not his real name."

"We'll get him, Ma'am," Patterson said.

"I'll need the name of the company you hired him from," Jay said. "And the phone number."

She stared at the shoe in the bag. "Philip has all that. Hiring the clown was the one thing I asked him to do." She squeezed her eyes shut, fighting a wave of nausea.

It was her fault. She had let The Fog into her house. She had talked to him, paid him three hundred and forty dollars to entertain a room full of innocent children. She had watched him play with her son, and obviously he had never left since the alarm hadn't gone off.

"Clancy must have hidden somewhere," she said.

"Where?"

The answer came to her in a flash. "Sam's closet. Oh, God. I let The Fog into my house."

"I don't think it was him," Jay said, taking the bag from her.

"W-what do you mean? Of course it was—"

He shook his head. "No. The M.O.'s different. The Fog never leaves behind evidence. He's too smart for that. It could be a copycat."

That didn't make sense to Sadie. Not one bit. She had been inches from the man. She'd seen him flinch when she mentioned *The Fog*. But she couldn't tell Jay that.

"Couldn't he have changed his M.O.?"

"Trust me, Ms. O'Connell. We'll be looking into every possibility." He jerked his head toward the doorway. "What about your husband?"

"What about him?"

"He's a lawyer, right?"

She nodded. "Corporate law."

"Perhaps someone is trying to get at him."

"No," she argued. "It was *him*. The Fog."

Jay's eyes narrowed. "How do you know?"

"I just do."

Philip chose that moment to be a gentleman. He entered the room, a steaming mug in his hand. "Here, Sadie. I thought you could use some coffee."

She gaped at the mug, turning it in front of her eyes. It was the one Sam had given her last Mother's Day, the one Leah had helped him pick out. On it was a cartoon alien boy with his mother in a spaceship. *To the best Mom in the Universe.*

She stifled a sob as tears streamed down her cheeks.

"Oh shit," Philip muttered. "I'm sorry, Sadie. I—"

"Mr. Tymchuk," Jay interjected. "I need to know where you were tonight. Between midnight and one-twenty this morning."

"Yeah, Philip," Sadie scoffed. "Please, tell us where you were. And who you were with. We'd *all* like to know."

Philip's face reddened. "I was at the office, working late."

"And where is that exactly?" Jay asked.

"Fleming Warner Law Offices, downtown on Jasper."

"Were you alone?"

Philip's eyes shifted toward Sadie. "No. I was with Brigitte Moreau." He paused. "She works there too."

Jay cleared his throat. "And what exactly is the nature of your relationship with Ms. Moreau?"

Sadie crossed her arms. "What the officer is so politely asking you,

Philip, is whether you're discussing oil spills with her or screwing her." To the detective, she said, "I've been asking him that same question for months."

"What's my relationship with Brigitte got to do with my son being kidnapped?" Philip demanded.

"Just answer the question, please," Jay said.

"Brigitte and I are associates." Philip slumped down on the bed beside Sadie. "And…lovers."

There. It had finally been said. The answer to a question that had been eating her up inside for months. An answer that would have ripped her apart yesterday, maybe even hours ago. Strangely enough, she didn't care now.

A snicker escaped.

"What's so funny?" Philip asked, eyeing her.

She stared at her husband, the man who had belittled her for years, who had neglected her. The man who had screwed around on her.

"I don't care, Philip."

"That I slept with Brigitte?" he asked, confused.

She smiled at him as if he were a stupid child. "No. I don't care about you, period. I don't care what you do, or who you do. As long as it isn't me. The only one I care about is Sam. *He* is important." She jabbed a finger against his chest. "Not you. You're nothing but a—"

"Ms. O'Connell," Jay cut in. "How did you find Clancy?"

Sadie glanced at Philip. "My husband hired him. From some party company downtown."

Philip scowled. "What, are you saying this is my fault? You're the one who wanted the damned clown in the first place."

"Well, you should have checked him out more carefully."

Philip jumped to his feet. "Don't you dare blame me, Sadie!"

"Mr. Tymchuk," Jay said calmly. "This isn't about blame right now. It's about finding your son. Every second we waste means it will be that much harder to find him. Do you understand what I'm saying?"

Philip sagged back onto the bed. "I understand. I'm sorry."

"Okay. Tell me about the clown."

"A few weeks ago, when I got to my office, there was a flier for the clown company on my desk. So I booked him."

"Do you still have it?"

"I think so."

Philip disappeared. A moment later, he returned with the flier and handed it to Jay. The detective scanned it, then dialed a number on his cell phone. He spoke to someone in a low voice. A few seconds later, he hung up.

"It's a cell phone. And it's not in service."

"Can't you trace the GPS?" Philip demanded.

Jay nodded. "We will, but he's more than likely tossed it already. He's well organized."

"So he set us up?" Sadie asked in disbelief.

The detective nodded. "He's had this planned for a while. He knew where you worked, your routines, and he knew that Sam had a birthday coming up."

He opened a plastic bag and indicated to Philip. "Slide the flier in here. I'll get it tested for fingerprints. You're the only one who's touched it, right?"

Philip nodded. "Me and whoever put it on my desk."

"Here's the number for Victim Services." Jay thrust a card toward Sadie. "You can contact them any time if you need to talk or…anything."

"We don't need to talk to strangers," Philip said.

"That's your choice. But the service is there if you need it."

"He doesn't like talking about our problems," Sadie scoffed. "Do you, Philip? You'd much rather have everyone believe that we're the perfect family and you're the perfect husband. Well, you're son's missing, Philip. Sam is gone!"

Philip stood up and moved toward the door, but not before she saw the tears in his eyes.

"I'll be downstairs," he said without looking back.

When he was gone, she stared after him, feeling bereft and slightly ashamed of the spiteful words that were spewing from her mouth. Regardless of anything he had done in the past, he was still her husband…and they had a child together. A child who needed them.

"I think it's best if we question you separately at the station," Jay said quietly. "I-I'm sorry I had to ask him about Brigitte."

"Don't be. Before, I only suspected my husband was messing around. Now I know." She took a deep breath. "What are the chances of finding Sam?"

The detective shifted uncomfortably. "The truth?"

She nodded.

"Every hour that passes narrows his chances. But you have to stay positive, believe he's coming home and hold onto hope."

"Hope is all I've got."

"In the meantime, we'll check into Ms. Moreau."

"She didn't have anything to do with Sam's disappearance."

"Jealous lovers have been known to do almost anything," the detective said as he moved toward the door. "But don't worry, Ms. O'Connell. The truth always comes out in the end."

His words made her tremble. There was no way the police or Philip could ever find out that she had seen The Fog.

Sam would die.

And she would die too.

8

After the detectives and crime scene investigators had left, the house was quiet. Philip had locked himself in his office, refusing to talk to her. So she did the one thing she could. She took a sleeping pill and crawled into bed. Dark discolorations had appeared under her breasts. Her ribs were bruised, maybe broken. But that wasn't important. What mattered was Sam. Was he hurt? Was he cold, hungry, afraid?

Of course he's afraid, you imbecile!

She lay awake, fighting her increasing remorse. She watched the shadows in the room, half-expecting The Fog to reappear.

What's he doing to Sam?

Two hours later, she was still awake. How could she possibly sleep with Sam gone and a single thought hammering at her?

It was Monday. *Sam's birthday.*

She pushed up on her elbows, groaned at the slow burn in her ribs and flicked on the lamp. It was 4:35 and still dark outside. She dropped back, head pounding, and thought about something Jay Lucas had said.

"The truth always comes out in the end."

A cemetery of restless ghosts walked over her grave and she shuddered. If the truth came out, Sam would be dead.

"You have to keep quiet," she whispered. "Don't say a word. Not yet."

Her gaze settled on the nightstand. The portfolio case, a black leather-bound binder with all the preliminary drawings for Sam's book, peeked from the half-closed drawer.

Sam...

There was no more sleep for her. She swallowed back the tears and sat up. Then she reached for the binder. Easing back the zipper, she studied the colorful drawing of a comical brown bat with lopsided eyes.

He was hiking up baggy shorts that kept sliding down.

She smiled, wiping away a tear. "Sam's going to love you, Batty." There was a hitch in her voice, but she caught it.

Now's not the time to lose it. Sam needs me.

She flipped through the drawings, allowing them to take her back to happier times. Mere hours ago. She recalled Sam's laughter, his grinning face as he opened his birthday presents.

She moaned. "He didn't get his bike."

Maybe she'd never see him ride it. Maybe she'd never see him—

"Stop it!" she hissed. She shook her head hard. "Sam *will* come back. They'll find him."

They have to find The Fog first, her conscience reminded her. *And only one person knows what he looks like. Sort of.*

Her eyes fell on a blank piece of paper.

The Fog's warning echoed in her mind. *"If I see one description—if you even say you saw me…"*

Did she dare?

She strained to hear footsteps or voices.

The house seemed vacant.

She reached for a pencil. Then, with a ragged breath, she started drawing the face of The Fog. A drawing that no one could ever see. She shaded, erased and chewed the end of the pencil as she concentrated on creating his face—his hooked nose, deep-set hooded eyes and pockmarked left cheek. She surrounded his face with a hood, and when the picture was finished, she glowered at it. It was a bit vague, but it was him. The Fog.

"Don't hurt my son," she whispered tearfully.

She was tempted to tear the paper into shreds. Driven by a need to confess, she made notes of everything the man had said and done, and what he had worn. Then she tucked the drawing between two fresh sheets and slid everything back into the binder. She wouldn't have to worry about Philip coming across it. He wasn't interested in her work.

Or in me, for that matter.

As she opened the drawer to fit the binder inside, her eyes fell on Sam's school photo. It had somehow toppled into the drawer. Thankfully, the glass hadn't broken.

She picked it up, recalling the day she had found out she was pregnant, the day Sam was born, the morning they had taken him home, his first steps, first laugh—what a joyous sound that had been—and his first day at school. So many firsts. So many more yet to come.

She clutched the photo to her chest and overwhelming sorrow engulfed her, burying her in a violent storm of hot tears and anguished sobs that tore at her very soul.

"Sam…my baby. Oh, God…*Sam!*"

∞ ∞ ∞

By six-thirty, she gave up trying to go back to sleep. Her sides ached rebelliously as she sat up, reached for the phone and called Leah.

"Hey," her friend croaked, half asleep. "How come you're calling so early? Is Philip being an ass—?"

"I need you, Leah." That was all she said.

Leah's voice came back, strong and reassuring. "I'll be there in fifteen minutes. Whatever it is, we'll get through this."

The line went dead.

Sadie headed for the shower. It was while she was washing her hair that she realized she had forgotten to remove her panties. Afterward, she dressed so quickly that she pulled on the same socks she'd worn the day before.

She stepped into the sunlit hallway and as she passed by Sam's door, she lurched to a halt. The door was wide open. Sam always left it that way in the morning. She peered inside, half-expecting to see Sam sitting on his bed.

But the room was empty.

"Sam."

Leaving the door ajar, she continued downstairs. She paused on the bottom step when she heard the rattle of dishes. "Leah?"

"Oh good, you're done your shower," her friend said as Sadie entered the kitchen. "I've made us some coffee and toast. So, what's going on? Is it Philip?"

Sadie looked at her friend and felt the sting of fresh tears. She blinked them back. "It's…Sam."

"Is he okay?"

Sadie shook her head. "He's gone, Leah."

"Gone where?"

A sob caught in the back of her throat. "The Fog took him."

Leah's eyes widened in horror. "No! Not Sam."

Sadie nodded, not trusting her voice.

"No, Sadie," Leah wailed.

As soon as she spotted the tears in her friend's eyes, Sadie's shoulders quivered and she lost it. Sobs wracked her body. Leah gathered her close, rocking her like a baby, stroking her hair and crying with her.

"He's gone, Leah. Sam's gone. What do I do?"

Leah had no answer.

Whenever Sadie grew quiet, another thought would hit her. Wave after wave of memories and anguish assaulted her until she was lost, floundering…breathless.

"I…can't do…this," she sobbed. "He has Sam. Oh, God. Why did he take my baby?"

"I don't know, honey," Leah wept. "But we'll get him back."

After a long silence, Sadie lifted her head and gazed into her friend's eyes. "What did Philip and I do to deserve this? Are we being punished? Am *I*?"

"Sadie, you didn't do anything wrong," Leah said, her voice trembling with emotion. "It's not your fault. Neither of you are being punished."

Sadie didn't believe her.

Leah drove her to a walk-in clinic where a doctor assured Sadie that her ribs were bruised, but thankfully not broken. He gave her a prescription for Tylenol 3s, scheduled an x-ray—*just to be safe,* he said—at the Gray Nun's Hospital for the next day, and told her to be more careful when going down the stairs.

Afterward, she made Leah go home. "There's nothing more you can do right now," she told her. "And I have to take care of a few things."

"If you need anything, Sadie—anything at all—call me."

"All I need is Sam."

∞ ∞ ∞

The afternoon was spent downtown at the police station. Philip met her there, half an hour late. When he apologized to Jay, the detective flicked him a steely look that made Sadie feel better. Then they were led to a crowded, windowless office with stacks of folders piled on one side of a beat up desk.

Sadie eyed the folders. *Somewhere in there is one on Sam.*

"We need to know if either of you noticed anything strange the past few days," Jay said, pulling out his notebook. "So we'd like to question you together first. Is that okay?"

"Whatever it takes," Sadie said. "I just want my son back."

A muscle jumped in Philip's jaw. "Same here."

Jay turned to Sadie. "Have you noticed any strangers hanging around your house? Or had any visitors?"

She shook her head slowly. "No one except Leah. And the clown. Oh, and a KFC delivery guy."

"And what about at Sam's school? See anyone there?"

"No. Just his teacher."

"Where else did you and Sam go this week?" Jay prodded.

She wracked her brain, trying to remember all the little things she and Sam had done together. Mostly, she had played with him in the house, since it was so cold outside. Except the day she took him to the park.

She told Jay.

"Did you see anyone there who didn't seem to fit?" he asked.

She shook her head. "It was mostly parents, mothers. Oh, and there was one fath—" She looked up and gasped. "There was a man in a car. I thought he was one of the fathers."

"Can you describe him?"

She winced. "I don't know. He was sitting in his car and he had a hat and sunglasses on. I didn't get a clear look at him. I think he was in his mid-thirties, early forties." She wasn't exactly lying.

"Did you get a look at the car?"

"I'm sorry. I wasn't paying attention. It was dark—gray or black. Four doors. That's all I remember." Before Jay could ask, she said, "And I never saw the license plate."

"Do you know the make or model?"

"Sadie can't tell a sedan from a sports car," Philip said dryly.

She sent him a look that made his mouth snap shut.

Jay jotted down a few notes. "What about the birthday party?"

"Just friends of Sam's, no strangers," she said.

"Let's get some background info," Jay said, turning to a fresh page in his notebook.

Within minutes, he had a blow-by-blow of their whole life—routines, friends and every person who had stepped into their house. He admitted that the clown was the strongest lead, since they had found the shoe in Sam's room. They were also checking into the delivery guy.

Sadie and Philip were separated for about half an hour and questioned individually. Then they were free to go.

She grabbed Jay's arm as they walked out of his office. "How long do you think before we get Sam back?"

The detective flicked an uneasy glance at her husband. Philip was standing a few yards away, glancing at his watch as if he had somewhere better to be.

"That depends on who took him, Ms. O'Connell," Jay said.

"You told me the first three days were critical. What happens after that?"

"We keep looking. You've given us lots of leads to check out."

"What if it *was* The Fog?" she persisted.

Jay's mouth thinned. "We haven't found any of the kids he's taken. But that could be a good thing. It's very possible they're all still alive. Including Sam." He looked at Philip again. "But that's *if* The Fog has taken him. Without witnesses or a description, we don't have much to go on, but we're looking into all possibilities."

Without witnesses or a description...

The detective's words made her flinch, and she hurried around the hall corner, anxious to escape the police station. As she neared the waiting area, she skidded to a stop.

Thick-lashed blue eyes met hers.

Sam!

He was sitting in a chair, crying. When he saw her, he smiled and motioned her to come closer.

Ecstatic and relieved, she turned to Jay. "You found him!"

"What?"

"Sam!" She spun around, pointing toward the chair. "He's—"

The chair was vacant.

Her mind went numb. She had seen him. He had smiled at her, waved at her.

Philip grabbed her arm, leading her out of the station. "That wasn't funny, Sadie."

"It wasn't meant to be," she snapped. "I thought...oh, never mind."

Not a word was said on the drive home. Or as Philip pulled the Mercedes into the garage. When she entered the house, she kicked off her shoes, dropped her purse on the floor and plodded upstairs. Two painkillers and a sleeping pill later, she climbed into bed.

It wasn't quite six o'clock.

9

Sadie awoke slowly, rubbing her weary eyes. They felt dry, as if someone had coated them with flour and rubbed it in for good measure. Most likely a side effect of the pills she had taken the night before.

She blinked.

It was day two and a piece of her was missing.

Sam.

She sat up and swung her legs over the side of the bed. A low moan boiled in the pit of her stomach, slithering upward, a coiled snake ready to strike. It burned between her ribs, up to her throat and then erupted from her mouth in a keening wail.

"Sam!"

Wherever he was, he was scared. She knew that without a doubt and she wanted to comfort him, take away his fear. He should have been getting ready to go to school, just as he did every Tuesday morning. Instead, he was with…

The devil.

"Oh, God. Why'd you let him take my baby?" She pounded the mattress. "Why?"

Swatting back tears, she reached for the phone.

"It's Sadie O'Connell," she said when Jay Lucas picked up.

"I was going to call you. Can you come to the downtown station?"

"Why? Have you found Sam?"

There was a brief pause. "No, but we do need to talk to you again."

"Should Philip come too?"

"No, just you."

She hung up and dressed quickly, distracted by her thoughts.

Why did Jay want to talk to her alone? Had he somehow guessed she'd been lying? Did he suspect she had seen the man who had taken her son?

∞ ∞ ∞

After signing in at the front desk, she was escorted to a small office where she sat down uneasily. Jay entered the room, carrying a gray folder. He shook her hand, then sat down behind the desk.

"Ms. O'Connell," he began. "What I'm about to tell you is highly sensitive and cannot leave this room. I shouldn't even be discussing this, but it could be pertinent to Sam's case. A word of caution though. If you mention any of this to your husband or anyone else before it becomes public, we'll be forced to charge you with interfering in our case. Do you understand?"

"I-I…yes, I understand."

"Are you aware that your husband is being investigated for fraud and embezzlement?"

"What?" she sputtered. "What are you talking about?"

"Fraud division's been investigating him for the past year. I didn't see the connection at first because I had you both listed under the name of O'Connell, since you called it in. But when I amended your husband's last name, it was flagged."

"B-but that's impossible. Philip would never—"

"Your husband's associate Morris Saunders is under investigation too. We suspect they've been siphoning their clients' funds into offshore accounts. About eight million dollars in total."

Eight million dollars?

She couldn't believe what she was hearing. Her husband—Mr. Defender of Justice—was an embezzler, a thief.

"Aren't people supposed to be presumed innocent?" she asked in alarm.

The aging detective gave her a rueful look. "Fraud had someone undercover. Someone who knows your husband quite well."

"Who?"

"I can't tell you right now. But you'll know soon enough."

Sadie was silent for a long moment.

"Ms. O'Connell?"

"I…I thought you wanted to talk to me about Sam. I thought maybe you had found—" Her voice broke and she slumped forward, her hands covering her face.

"I'm sorry, Ms. O'Connell."

"Please," she said into her hands. "Just call me Sadie."

"Look…Sadie. I know you don't need any more on your plate, but—"

Her head snapped up. "But what? Eight million dollars is more important than my son? Is that what you're trying to say?"

Jay reached a hand across the desk. "Please, hear me out for a minute. Most kidnappers are related to the victim. Often it's a spouse. Philip could have staged the kidnapping—"

"You think he took Sam? For what, ransom money?"

"He may have thought the bank would loan him money, or that he could get it from family or the law firm. If he thought he could get the money to pay them back and save himself, he could have taken Sam somewhere."

Sadie was outraged. "No! Philip would never do that!"

"Desperate people do desperate things, Ms. O'Con—Sadic."

Shoving her chair back, she jumped to her feet. "My husband may be a coward and a thief, but he would never put Sam's life in danger for money. Never!"

Jay shifted in his chair. "It's also possible that one of Philip's clients took Sam. Your husband took money from some very dangerous people. People who would do anything to get it back. Do you understand what I'm saying?"

She gaped at him. "You think they took Sam to get back at Philip?"

"It's possible."

"No! It was The Fog."

Sharp eyes pierced hers. "How do you know that?"

She opened her mouth, readying to tell him everything. But then the Fog's hoarse voice filled her ears. *"Little bloody pieces."*

Her stomach twisted in knots.

Should she say something? Tell him what she knew?

"Mrs. O'Connell, if you know something—"

"No," she said, turning away. "I don't know anything that would help you find Sam."

"Then why are you so sure it was The Fog?" Jay repeated.

Careful, Sadie.

"I just know. Call it instinct." She paused in the doorway and gave the detective a hard look. "When you find The Fog, you'll find my son."

∞ ∞ ∞

Afterward, Sadie drove to Gray Nuns Hospital. She'd been feeling a bit better as the day progressed, but she wanted to ensure that nothing was broken. Her ribs weren't so tender—until the technician asked her to flounder around like a fish out of water on the x-ray table. Turn on her right. Then on her left. Then on her back. She was in more pain when she left the hospital. She drove home and took a couple of Tylenol.

With nothing else to do, she waited.

And waited some more.

When Philip returned home that evening, he retreated to his office. Sadie stared after him as fury boiled in the pit of her stomach. She was infuriated that the police weren't looking for The Fog and stunned by the revelations of her husband's criminal activities.

She knocked, then opened the door. "Philip, I need to talk—"

The words caught in the back of her throat.

The office was in absolute chaos. It looked and smelled like a bachelor pad. The sofa along one wall was covered with twisted sheets and blankets, while a pile of Philip's clothes had been kicked into the corner. It was impossible to tell if they were clean or dirty. Empty pizza boxes and other take-out containers covered a table by the window, and two Fleming Warner coffee mugs, half-filled with congealed week-old coffee, sat on the oak desk. One of them had left a coffee ring on the wood surface.

But what shocked her even more was Philip.

He had a gun.

"What are you doing?" she asked slowly.

Philip calmly wiped the weapon with a cloth and placed it in a cedar box. "Don't worry, Sadie. It's just for show."

"Show for who?" she sputtered. "Are you crazy? We can't have a gun in the house. Not with Sam—" She broke off and glanced at the floor.

"It's not loaded," he said, like that made any difference.

"It's *illegal*. How'd you get it in the first place?"

She watched as he pushed away from the desk, strode toward the closet and nudged the box onto the top shelf.

"Someone got it for me," he said. "He owed me a favor."

"And you think you need it—a gun."

She looked at him closely, wondering why he was so nervous, why a man who had followed every law—except fidelity—had a weapon that was meant for one purpose. To kill.

Her mouth thinned. "You're afraid of whoever you took the money from, aren't you?"

Philip looked shocked. "They contacted you?"

"No, the police did. They told me everything."

"That's impossible," he said with false bravado. "They don't know everything." He sat down at his desk.

"They know enough to drag me into the station and threaten to charge me if I told you they talked to me."

"Then why are you telling me?"

She sank into the chair across from him. "The police think that

Sam's disappearance is related."

"It isn't," he said, shaking his head firmly. "My associates wouldn't take him. They would've taken me for a ride instead, maybe slashed my tires as a warning. There's no way they took Sam." He sounded as if he were trying to convince himself of this.

"I believe you, Philip. But we don't need the police wasting time on your associates when they should be out looking for The Fog. That's who took Sam. I'm certain of it." She frowned. "Wait! How did *you* know about the investigation? The police said it was an undercover operation."

Philip massaged his temple. "I got a call from one of the investors. He has some connections in the police department and found out that Morris and I were being investigated. He threatened to kill me if I said anything about his business transactions. And believe me, he'd do it that way before he snatched a kid."

"Who *are* these people you stole from?"

He shrugged. "Drug dealers mostly."

She gritted her teeth, resisting the temptation to reach across the desk and slap him. "Jesus, Philip! Did you honestly think they'd let you steal their money?"

"I was desperate. We've got a heavy mortgage, bills that just keep adding up and you always need money for—"

"Don't make excuses," she snapped, jumping to her feet. "And don't you dare lay this on me. *You* stole the money. *You* messed with the wrong people."

A million questions filled the prolonged silence.

Then Philip said, "What do you want from me? Blood?"

"I don't want anything from you," she said tightly before stalking out of the room.

Finally, she had the last word.

∞ ∞ ∞

The next day there was still no sign of Sam.

Frustrated by the police department's lack of progress, she made up posters with Sam's face on them. She was careful not to mention The Fog. She taped the posters on postal boxes, bank windows, grocery store bulletin boards and any other place she could think of. Then she delivered them to every house in a five-block radius, hoping that someone had seen something. A license plate, a car…Sam. Anything.

Twice, she picked up the phone to call Matthew Bornyk, the father of the latest missing girl. But what could she possibly say to him?

Hi, you don't know me, but we have something in common. Both of our kids were taken by an insane maniac, and I saw him and spoke to him, but didn't tell the police.

"Jesus, Sadie," she muttered under her breath. "He'll think you're just as insane."

A part of her yearned to talk to someone who knew exactly how she felt, someone who was just as scared, just as empty. Every time she saw Cortnie's father on television or heard him on the radio, she could tell by his eyes and voice that he felt his daughter's loss just as deeply as she felt Sam's.

She secretly clipped every newspaper article about The Fog. She even went to the *Sun* and *Journal* and bought old papers. She kept everything in a plastic container in her closet, taking them out every few hours to sort through them and make notes. However, she refused to look at the other children in the photos.

Except Sam. She cried each time she saw his face.

Her brother and sister-in-law called from Halifax. Brad, a Master Seaman in the Canadian Armed Forces, was preparing to be deployed to Afghanistan. They apologized for not being able to drop everything, find a sitter for their two young kids and fly to Edmonton. Sadie told them not to worry, that by the time they got here, the police would have found Sam and brought him home.

She wanted so desperately to believe this.

Then her parents called. They wanted to fly up from Arizona where they'd been enjoying the snowbird life, but Sadie persuaded them not to. Their questions were already driving her half-crazy.

"There's nothing you can do anyway," she told them.

"But we want to be there for you," her mother said tearfully.

"I know."

And she did. Her mother always meant well, but Sadie just couldn't deal with listening to her mother's sobs each night.

"Call us if you hear anything," her mother pleaded.

"I will. Thanks, Mom."

"And honey, if you need anything—"

"I'll call. Love you."

When Philip returned home that night, he reeked of Jack Daniels and culpability. He sprawled on the sofa beside her.

"I think the investors *did* take Sam," he slurred. "If I'd only known what they'd do, I'd never have taken their money. Not if I knew they'd take my boy." He slumped to the floor in front of her and clung to her legs like a baby. "I screwed up, Sadie."

"Yeah, you did," she said stiffly.

"I don't know what I'll do if I'm locked away," he moaned. "I'm not made for prison."

She was disgusted. "*That's* what you're worried about?"

In that instant, her husband went from Godlike legal legend to a sniveling coward. She pushed him away, then stormed across the room. Pausing in the doorway, she was tempted to leave him drowning in his guilt.

"The Fog took Sam," she said bitterly. "You had nothing to do with it. Neither did any of your clients."

Philip's head rose, a half-crazed expression in his eyes. "You think so?" He wiped his nose and staggered to his feet. "Yeah. You're right, Sadie. It's not my fault. It can't be."

She left him in the living room, talking to himself, and when she reached their bedroom, she closed the door and locked it.

Philip would get the message. *If* he made it up the stairs.

10

After Philip left for work the next morning, she turned on the television, hoping to catch news about Sam. But Philip's face was plastered on the screen instead. Underneath, two words in bold print flashed in alarm. *FRAUD INVESTIGATION!*

A reporter brushed something off her tailored suit jacket, then gave a brief announcement stating that two employees at Fleming Warner Law Offices were being questioned about allegations of fraud. The woman named Philip and Morris Saunders as co-conspirators.

The next segment was on hockey, so Sadie turned off the TV. With nothing else to do, she drew up the courage to call Matthew Bornyk. He picked up on the first ring.

"Hello?" His voice was husky, whether naturally or from lack of sleep, she didn't know.

She sucked in a breath. "Mr. Bornyk, this is Sadie O'Connell. You don't know me but—"

"I know who you are." His voice sounded wide awake all of a sudden. "Is there any news about your son?"

"No, nothing." She paused, embarrassed. "I-I'm not sure why I called."

"I'm glad you did. I was going to call you."

"Really? It seems a bit…odd. Talking to someone I've never met, I mean."

"I have an idea. Why don't you meet me for coffee? You and your husband."

The offer surprised her. She wasn't sure what she had thought the call would accomplish, but she hadn't expected to meet the man face-to-face.

"Name the place and the time," she said.

"Borealis Café, downtown on Jasper Ave," he said. "I can be there in an hour. Do you need directions?"

"No. I know exactly where it is." She hung up.

Borealis Cafe was right across from Fleming Warner Law Offices. In addition, it showed up often on their VISA bill. Philip took Brigitte there quite often. For business lunches, he said.

Yeah, right!

∞ ∞ ∞

Matthew Bornyk had aged ten years since the photo she had seen in the newspaper. Although there wasn't a trace of gray in his sandy-blond hair, the lines under his gray-blue eyes and the pallor of his face spoke of sleepless nights and unbearable pain.

"Have a seat," he said, indicating the chair across from him. "Do you want some coffee? They make a wicked house blend. Or if you're hungry, the caramel apple pie here is excell—" He looked away, frowning. "Sorry, I'm rambling."

After a young waiter filled their mugs with the Borealis house blend, Matthew leaned forward. "Your husband couldn't make it?"

"He's tied up with…business meetings."

There was an awkward silence before the man said, "I heard."

"Hard not to. It's all over the news."

Matthew took a sip of coffee. "I'm sorry."

"Philip always wanted to live like a king." The words were out of her mouth before she realized what she was saying.

"What about you?" Matthew asked.

"I'm no queen. I only need one thing. My son."

Her hand trembled as she lifted the mug, and Matthew did something unexpected. He reached across the table and grasped her hand. His warm touch drew a soft gasp from her. Not knowing what else to do, she stared at the hand that covered hers. It was strong and tanned, except for the pale circle of skin on his left ring finger.

"We'll find them," he said. "Both of them. As soon as we get a break, a witness—"

She snatched her hand back.

How could she look this man in the eye? He wanted a witness and had no idea he was having coffee with one. The humiliation and uncertainty was eating her alive.

What if I told him?

The answer hit her immediately.

Then Sam will die.

Matthew cocked his head, watching her. "I hope we hear something soon."

"Me too," she said tiredly. "Did you see anything? When Cortnie was taken?"

"I was asleep. Didn't even know she was gone until the next morning." He stared into his coffee mug. "She always had coffee with me before school." He smiled. "Hot chocolate for her."

For the next half hour, they swapped stories. She told him about Sam's obsession with bats. How he'd quit little league because he believed the wooden bats were related to his furry 'friends.'

"The next day, he drew faces on a bat that Philip bought on eBay." At Matthew's puzzled look, she grinned. "A baseball bat. It was autographed by the Toronto Blue Jays."

"Yikes. That probably didn't go over well."

"No. Not at all."

Needing a moment to clear her head, she waved to the server and pushed her mug toward him. Matthew did the same. The kid filled both mugs, then left them a handful of creamers.

"Cortnie's obsession is books," Mathew said, stirring his coffee. "She's read every Harry Potter. Sometimes I'd find her reading under her blankets. With a flashlight. She also reads those Cup of Soup books."

Sadie snickered.

"What?" he asked.

"Chicken Soup books."

He gave her a rueful look. "Figures you'd know about those books. You're a woman."

She shook her head. "I'm a writer."

"What do you write?"

"Fiction. Mainly mysteries. Right now, though, I'm working on an illustrated children's book for Sam…" Her smile faded.

"He'll read it," Matthew said softly.

Sadie's gaze flickered to the window.

A woman in a teal jacket stood on the street corner. Her white-blond hair shone in the sunlight as she waited for the crosswalk light to flash. A young boy held her hand. He had his back to Sadie, but his hair reminded her of Sam's.

She frowned. *Even his build is like—*

The boy turned abruptly, his familiar eyes latching onto hers. His mouth opened and he mouthed one word.

Mommy.

Her heart splintered into a million miniscule pieces.

"Sam?"

She lurched to her feet, oblivious to the spilled coffee pooling on the table and the strange look from Matthew.

"Sadie, what's wrong?" he asked, standing quickly.

Brushing past him, she flew out the door and veered around the corner. Across the street, the woman in the teal jacket meandered down the sidewalk, staring into shop windows every now and then. Alone.

Zigzagging between cars, Sadie ignored the blaring horns as she ran toward the woman, grabbed her arm and spun her around.

"Hey!" the blond yelled. "What the hell are you doing?"

"Where is he?" Sadie demanded.

"Who?"

"Sam! The boy you were with."

The woman eyed her as if Sadie were a street beggar. "Are you nuts? I wasn't with any boy."

Sadie gaped at her, speechless. Something was wrong—off. The woman's hair didn't seem quite as pale up close, and she seemed younger than the woman Sadie had spotted from inside Borealis Café.

But she's wearing a teal jacket.

She twisted around, searching the sidewalk. But there was no other blond-haired woman in teal.

"Sadie, what's going on?" Matthew said, rushing toward her.

Bitter tears trailed down her cheeks. "I saw him. Sam! He was walking with *her*." She whipped her head around, but the woman was gone. "Where did she go?"

"Look, Sadie, why don't I drive you home?"

"I'm not crazy, Matthew! I saw Sam. I swear it."

He gently took her arm. "I believe you."

"He looked at me and said…*Mommy*."

"I imagine seeing Cortnie sometimes," he murmured, steering her across the street. "At the park. At her school. But it's never really her."

"I didn't imagine it," she argued. "It was Sam."

Matthew sighed. "Sadie, do you want to talk—?"

"No. I just want to go home."

"Do you want me to drive you?"

"No, I'm fine." She rolled her eyes. "Well, as fine as I can be under these circumstances."

He took her car keys from her fumbling fingers, unlocked the car door and waited while she climbed in. Then he passed her the keys and a business card.

"My home, office and cell numbers."

She thanked him, then sped away. As she watched him in the rearview mirror, Matthew Bornyk stood motionless, a miserable expression on his handsome face.

No father should ever look that way.

Unable to help herself, she drove around the block three times, looking for the blond-haired woman in the teal jacket. But there was no sign of her. Or Sam.

When Sadie arrived home, she sat on the cold cement steps of the front porch, mindlessly sipping a cup of coffee while scanning the cars that passed by. After an hour, she could have sworn she had seen Sam three times. But in her heart she knew it wasn't him. Her baby was gone, taken by a madman, and with each passing moment she was more and more convinced that she needed to tell the police what she knew.

Maybe tomorrow.

The rest of the day dragged on. She paced around the house, the cordless phone attached to her belt.

"In case there's any news of Sam," she said to Leah, who had dropped by.

"You can't just wait by the phone every day, Sadie. You should get out, get some fresh air."

Sadie stared at her. "What do you expect me to do? Go tanning? Or out for coffee?"

"No, I didn't mean it like that," Leah said, throwing her hands up defensively. "I just don't want to see you holed up in your house for days on end. It's not…healthy."

"I can't act as if nothing's wrong, Leah. Not when somewhere out there my son is waiting to be found."

"They'll find him."

Leah hugged her, but Sadie felt smothered and pulled away.

Her friend didn't understand. No one did.

That evening, she vacuumed Sam's room.

"For when he comes home," she told Philip firmly.

11

The following day, there was still no sign of Sam.

Jay called to say that the clown shoe was a dead end.

"And we got nothing off the sheet of paper," he added.

There were no prints, no DNA, nothing to lead them to the kidnapper.

"We're trying to trace the manufacturer of the shoe," he said. "Maybe we'll find the store he bought it from."

Sadie's heart sank. "But that won't do any good if he paid with cash."

"Yeah, but we might get lucky. The store may have a security camera. We just need a break, Sadie. One solid lead and we'll find Sam."

All day long she wracked her brain trying to think of ways to help the police locate Sam without having to describe the man she had seen, but nothing came to her, so she ventured outside and plastered more posters of Sam all over the neighborhood until his eyes followed her everywhere. She knocked on doors, asked questions about a strange vehicle in the neighborhood and showed Sam's photograph. But no one had seen a thing.

She even tried to rely on fate. It had become a habitual joke all these years, something to play with, like *we'll buy the house if the previous deal falls through.* Or *I'll know the time is right to write something different when I'm given a sign.* Fate had been her best friend back then, but now that she really needed divine intervention, it had abandoned her.

The next day, she waited by the phone. By suppertime, it hadn't rung, so she called Jay's number.

"Sadie, we don't have any news yet. Sorry."

"You told me the first three days were crucial," she said, trying to keep the panic from her voice. "Why is it taking so long?"

"We're doing everything we can," he assured her. "We're hoping someone in your neighborhood will call in. Someone had to have seen something."

Yeah, I did.

Although the words were on the tip of her tongue, she just couldn't spit them out. She feared for Sam. She had no doubt that The Fog would kill him, just like he promised. And there was no way she could live with Sam's death on her hands.

∞ ∞ ∞

A week went by. A week of pure hell.

Sadie wanted nothing more than to slip away into a cloud of drugged oblivion. But the stubborn part of her kept her heading out each morning to replace the ripped, blurred, rain-splattered posters of Sam.

On the tenth morning, she remained in bed, refusing to get up or eat anything. She'd even ignored the incessant ringing of the phone, although Leah had called twice and left frantic messages on the answering machine.

Sadie didn't want to talk to anyone.

Except Sam.

She missed him fiercely, and not a moment passed when she didn't think of him. Was he alive? Was he being abused?

The angry Xs scratched across the days on the calendar beside her bed glared back at her.

"Ten days…"

Sam's picture was pressed up against her. She peeled it away, noticing the red imprint the frame had left on her arm. Placing the picture back on the nightstand, she reached into the drawer beside her bed and removed the binder—the one with the drawing of The Fog.

She eased it open.

A sharp gasp escaped when her eyes latched onto the face of the man who had taken Sam. She slipped the paper from the binder and rested it on top of the duvet.

"When they find you, I'll make sure you rot in prison for the rest of your life."

It was a promise she intended on pursuing, no matter what it took. This stranger had entered her home, assaulted her and stolen her son. What horrific crime had she committed to warrant such terror in her life?

Her eyes flitted across the room toward Philip's sock drawer. She experienced the familiar pang of need and the relentless voice she had long ago silenced began its litany of reasons why a drink would be indisputably justified.

Just one small drink.

She shook her head and looked down at the picture of The Fog, but her eyes were drawn against her will back to the drawer that promised instant relief.

To calm my nerves. No one would blame me.

She shivered as a draft wafted over her.

"You're awake."

Philip stood in the doorway.

She stuffed the drawing under the covers and was about to read him the riot act for sneaking up on her when she noticed something peculiar. Her husband was fully clothed, ready for work. And wearing the same suit as yesterday.

"You stayed out all night?" she asked, stunned.

His shoulders lifted in a nervous twitch. "Sadie—"

"Don't! Don't make up any more excuses. We both know where you were and who you were with. I would think the least you could do is be honest for once in your pathetic, miserable life." She wondered if the expression on her face matched the sour, rotten taste in her mouth.

Without a word, Philip turned on one heel and disappeared.

As soon as he was gone, she flung back the duvet and smoothed the drawing before placing it at the back of the binder, which she slid into the drawer of the nightstand. Curling up in a fetal position with Sam's photo clasped close to her heart, she drifted into a restless sleep and stayed there all day.

∞ ∞ ∞

The next morning, Philip officially moved into his office.

At first, she was relieved. Then anger consumed her. While she went to bed each night—alone and lonely—he stayed out until the wee hours of the morning. Part of her resented him, and part of her was thankful that he was so busy. They sometimes passed in the hallway and gave each other chilly nods. But they said very little. What was there to say?

Later that afternoon, she called Jay and was transferred to his voicemail.

"I just want to know if you've heard anything," she said. "Do you have any new leads? It's been almost two weeks. Please call me back." She hung up, shoulders slumped in despair.

Sam's disappearance had left her barren. Childless. Loveless. And full of agonizing remorse. Every minute, she battled with her secret. Should she talk or stay quiet? What if the police could find Sam before he got hurt? Sometimes she was a breath away from confessing that she had seen The Fog, albeit vaguely. And that she had drawn him.

When Jay called her back, his voice was weary. "We have nothing new. Sorry, Sadie. None of your neighbors heard or saw anything."

"What about the Amber Alert?"

"We've had nothing but false leads so far."

"Like what?"

Jay sighed. "One man reported strange lights over Edmonton the night Sam was taken. He swears Sam was abducted by iridescent, tentacled extraterrestrials. And a woman in Calgary, who swears she's psychic, said he was taken by a one-legged woman in a flowered dress."

He told her that Sam had been sighted at Vancouver's Stanley Park, at Niagara Falls, in Texas—even as far as Mexico. In the end, all reports were discredited.

"Thanks anyway," she said before hanging up.

Sinking into a chair, she fought back tears of frustration. Sam had vanished from the face of the earth.

Except I keep seeing him.

She saw him everywhere. The backyard, Sobeys, the bank, even in the back seat of the car. Sometimes she could swear she heard his voice, which was ridiculous since Sam didn't speak.

Philip was no help at all. He kept telling her that Sam was more than likely dead.

"The bastard probably buried him somewhere," he'd said just the other morning.

She knew Sam was alive. She could feel him, sense him.

Philip's heavy footsteps thumped overhead, reminding her that there was some unfinished business to attend to. There was one thing she wanted from her husband. Something she'd kept putting off.

"Just ask him," she muttered.

The bedroom was silent when she entered. Philip was sitting on the bed, his back turned to her, unmoving.

"Philip," she said, hovering in the doorway. "I want a divorce." When he didn't move, she added, "I think you want it too. Our marriage is…over." *Dead.*

Philip's head swiveled, his hardened glare catching her off guard. "You *bitch*!"

"Phil—"

"You saw him?" He held up a piece of paper.

The Fog's face stared back at her, the face that she had so carefully drawn. Her pulse raced and she grabbed onto the doorframe for support. "I-I can explain."

"Can you? I was looking for a piece of paper. Instead I found *this*." He waved the paper at her. "And a complete account of what happened that night on the back."

She took an unsteady step forward. "Philip, I—"

"You what? You forgot to tell me? You forgot to tell the police that you saw the bastard that took our son? What the hell's wrong with you?"

"You don't understand," she stammered. "He was going to kill me."

"You? What about Sam? I can't believe you were more concerned about your—"

"He had a gun, Philip! And he hurt me. That's why my ribs were bruised. I couldn't move." Her voice grew hoarse. "And then he said he'd kill Sam if I told anyone I'd seen him. Or if I described him. I didn't know what to do!"

"You should have told the truth."

She stared at him in disbelief. "Don't you dare lecture me on truth, you...you ass."

"You lied, Sadie. You said you didn't see anyone." He shook the drawing at her. "This is the man who took our son. The police have been running around, chasing their tails for almost two weeks, and all along you had this. His face, for Christ's sake!"

"He said he'd send Sam home in pieces!" she screamed.

Philip stared at her as if *she* were the monster. Then he shook his head and without a word, disappeared into the hall, the drawing in his hand.

A door slammed downstairs and she flinched.

"What have I done?" she cried out in anguish.

12

The following morning, Sadie's whole world came crashing down around her. Her deception made headline news. Every channel broadcasted reports of how the mother of the latest abducted child had known all along what The Fog looked like. Every newspaper across the country carried her drawing. Reporters were scathing in their contempt of a mother who would conceal such a vital lead. Even the police looked at her differently.

Except Jay.

"You're a victim in all this too," he told her.

Terrified, she had holed up inside the house, refusing to answer the door. Every time the phone rang, she winced, especially when she saw Matthew Bornyk's number. She couldn't face him now.

When Philip packed his bags and moved into a hotel, she knew that nothing would ever be the same. Her life was a train wreck and there were no survivors.

Later that morning, Leah showed up in the kitchen. She had let herself in through the garage when no one answered the door.

Sadie took one look at her friend's watery eyes and broke down. "He's going to kill my baby, Leah. Sam is so scared, I can *feel* him. And there's nothing I can do to comfort him."

Leah hugged her tightly. "Jesus, Sadie. I'm so sorry."

"It's my fault."

"No, it isn't. You did what you thought was right."

Sadie shook her head. "Maybe if I had told the police what The Fog looked like someone would've recognized him."

"And maybe he would've done what he said he'd do," Leah argued. "Listen. No one can blame you. You were given an ultimatum, right?"

Sadie met her gaze. "Would you have kept quiet?"

"I honestly don't know what I would've done if I was in your position. Maybe I would've told the police and hoped they'd keep it out of the papers. I mean, no one else saw him. You saw his face. That's a pretty important piece of information."

Sadie backed away. "You don't think I thought of that?"

"I know—"

"You don't know anything. You don't know what it's like to love a child, to be a mother, to hold life in your hands and watch it grow into something beautiful. You don't know what it's like to watch a monster rip away your son, knowing you might never see your baby again. Not a single day goes by that I don't blame myself, wonder if I should have said something, done something."

Leah held out her hands. "Sadie, you—"

"No! You can't judge me. No one can. You weren't there. I want my son alive. Don't any of you get that? I'd rather Sam be alive and living with that—that *monster*, than dead."

The doorbell rang.

"I'll get it," her friend said quietly.

Sadie welcomed the uneasy truce. She hadn't had much peace lately. Everyone demanded something from her. Detective Lucas, Philip...even Leah. Like bloodthirsty piranha, they tore at her, stripping away her confidence, her last remnants of hope.

"Your neighbor across the street dropped this off," Leah said, handing her a small package wrapped in brown paper.

"My neighbor?"

"Yeah. Gail. The one with the yappy dog. She said someone left this on her porch by mistake."

Sadie's gaze dropped to her hands. "No..."

The package mocked her. Her name and address were written on it in black marker, but that was it. No return address, no stamp, nothing to indicate that Canada Post had ever processed it.

She let out a yelp and flung the package on the kitchen table.

Leah grabbed her. "What's wrong?"

"He said he'd send Sam to me. In little bloody pieces."

Leah stared uneasily at the box. "You don't really think..."

"No, I don't think. I know."

Sadie's breathing grew shallow and strained, and her tongue stuck to the roof of her mouth as if coated with sand. She moved toward the table, half expecting the package to burst into flames when she touched it. When it didn't, she swallowed hard and her churning stomach threatened to rebel.

"Maybe we should call the police," Leah suggested.

Sadie shook her head. She wasn't about to wait for the police. She had to know what was in the package *now.*

"I'm calling that detective," Leah said firmly, reaching for the phone.

Sadie ignored her and peeled the paper from the package.

It was a hair color box. *Sun-kissed Blond.*

She opened it carefully and peered inside. There was no card, just a crumpled wad of black tissue. When she unfolded it, something rolled onto the table.

A small, bloody finger.

An ear-piercing scream shattered the air.

It took Sadie a few moments before she realized it was hers.

∞ ∞ ∞

After the police left, Leah tucked her into bed.

"We don't know if it's Sam's," she said.

"I do."

Sadie stared at a smudge on the wall. She'd missed a spot in her cleaning. She'd have to remember to wash the walls in the morning. After all, she didn't want a dirty house. Sam would be coming home soon and everything had to be ready for him.

Leah hovered over her, a worried look in her eyes. She gently smoothed Sadie's bangs. "The pills should kick in any time."

Sadie grabbed her hand. "What would I do without you, Leah? You're the only one who's stuck by me in all this."

"You need to rest. I'll be downstairs if you need anything."

Sadie frowned, recalling her harsh words earlier. Had she really said those things to Leah? That was so unlike her. She was mortified by her behavior.

And ashamed of that spot on the wall.

She made a mental note. *Clean the walls.*

"I love you, my friend," Leah said, choking back a sob.

The door closed behind her.

Sadie looked at her hands. They were shaking. For a moment, she stared at them, at her fingers. She was fascinated by her pinky.

So tiny...and covered with blood. Where had the blood come from?

She shook her head, remembering.

From Sam's bloody finger. In the package.

The police said they'd keep it on ice. It would take a day to match the DNA, but she knew it was Sam's baby finger. She had kissed his little hands plenty of times. She also knew something else. This was just the beginning. She knew she could expect a piece of Sam on her doorstep. Maybe a finger every day.

No! Don't think of that!

Desperate to drown out those horrible thoughts, she threw back the blanket and stumbled to Philip's sock drawer. She rummaged around furiously, then upended the drawer on the floor. Three mini bottles of rye rolled past her feet.

"You'll do just fine."

Twisting the first lid open, she raised the bottle in a silent salute to years of sobriety. Then she downed the rye. The bitter alcohol burned at first, then grew warm, soothing. *Familiar.* A fond memory of a long-lost friend. She emptied the last two bottles, then staggered back to bed with one thought on her mind.

Without you, Sam, I have nothing to live for.

She wept until there was just an empty pit where her heart had been. Then sleep stole her away.

∞ ∞ ∞

When she awoke a few hours later, she discovered that Philip had moved back in.

"Temporarily," he stated. "Until you're feeling better."

He made her some soup for lunch.

"You have to eat," he said, placing the tray on her lap.

She gave him a blank look. "Why?"

"You need to stay strong."

"But I'm not strong," she said miserably. "I'm weak and—"

"You're the strongest person I know. That's the God's honest truth. I'm the weak one. Not you." He leaned down and kissed her forehead. "Stay strong, Sadie. For Sam."

After Philip had left, she picked at the food on the tray. Her stomach heaved in rebellion and she just made it to the bathroom before she was overcome by nausea.

What is The Fog doing to Sam now?

Two more pills gave her the dreamless sleep she craved.

∞ ∞ ∞

At six that evening, Jay showed up on the doorstep.

The minute she saw him, she braced herself against the wall and held her breath. Then she hollered for Philip, who was working from home.

"We found the car, the sedan," Jay told them. "It was a rental. No fingerprints, no traces of the perp, just some strands of Sam's hair in the back seat."

"Where'd you find it?" Philip asked.

"The airport. We checked all flights. They didn't get on a plane. It would have been impossible anyway, since Sadie said Sam was unconscious."

"So he must have had another vehicle," she surmised.

Jay nodded.

"What about the...finger," she asked timidly.

Jay's mouth thinned. "The finger was numbed before amputation. We found traces of a local anesthetic, which leads us to believe he has a medical background. He may be a paramedic or a doctor. Something like that."

"And?"

"And...the finger is Sam's."

Sadie lost it. She howled with anguish and sank to the floor, working herself into such a frenzy that Philip couldn't calm her.

"Whoever did this, they knew what they were doing," Jay said, trying to comfort her. "That means he would have made sure there was no infection. I think Sam is still alive."

There was no comfort in the detective's words.

When he was gone, she doubled over, weeping. "The bastard hurt Sam, and it's all my fault."

No it isn't, Mommy.

"Yes it is," she argued with her son's ghost.

Without a word, Philip isolated himself in his office. In that one move, he had virtually washed his hands of her. And they both knew it.

She stumbled upstairs to the bedroom, reached into the drawer of the nightstand and pulled out a manila envelope. Inside were the documents that Philip had signed the night before.

"I know I was a rotten husband," he'd told her. "But I don't want you to hate me, Sadie."

She stared at the divorce papers, pen poised, ready to lay down her signature—until uncertainty overwhelmed her. She wasn't sure why. Their marriage had been over years ago.

So why *was* she hesitating?

Maybe because she was afraid that if she signed them, signed away her marriage, that Sam would never return. Perhaps by holding onto her marriage it would make him come back. Maybe there was still hope for her and Philip.

She pursed her lips. "Who are you trying to kid?"

She scribbled her signature on the papers.

For a long moment, she stared at the pen stroke that wiped out her status as a wife. It had been so easy, so quick. Her marriage was over—dead.

Like Sam, taunted her subconscious.

"No," she murmured with a shake of her head.

She hurried downstairs. Philip hadn't left yet.

"Here." She dropped the envelope on the desk in front of him. "Signed, sealed and delivered. I'll be out of the house by the end of the month."

At least he had the decency to look uncomfortable.

"Where will you go?" he asked.

"I don't know exactly. I might stay with Leah for a few weeks until I find myself a new place."

"I meant what I said before. You can keep the house."

Her head jerked. "I don't want it, Philip. Someone stole our son from this house. It's poisoned now, tainted. But I do need something from you."

"What?"

"Make sure this is taken care of." She pointed to the envelope.

"I'll have it filed immediately."

"You do that."

He watched her, a wild look in his eyes. "I tried to be a good husband, but I'm just not cut out for it. I-I did love you, Sadie. The best way I knew how. But then Sam came along and everything…changed. *You* changed."

"We both did, Philip."

13

Easter used to be Sadie's favorite holiday. Not this year though. No one called her with a cheery, "Happy Easter," as in years past. No flowers from Philip, even though they'd always been bought in haste at Sobeys. And no Sam. Instead, Easter Sunday arrived with a drizzle of rain and stormy skies, perfect weather for Sadie's mournful mood.

She was cleaning the kitchen when the phone rang.

"Hello?"

Heavy breathing greeted her.

"Leah, I'm really not in the moo—"

"Sam's left you an Easter gift," a voice rasped.

Her blood ran cold. It had been two weeks since she had heard that voice.

"It's on the porch."

Her breath quickened. "Wait! Please! Don't hurt—"

Click.

Dropping the phone on the table, she tottered toward the front door and whipped it open, half hoping—half praying—to see Sam. All she saw was a small ring box.

She phoned Jay.

"I'm right around the corner," he said. "We're already searching the neighborhood."

He pulled up a few minutes later in an unmarked police car. Patterson was with him.

"We've got your phone tapped," Jay explained when he noticed her questioning look.

"Did you trace the call?"

"He wasn't on long enough."

The younger detective quickly scoped the yard, checking the

perimeter of the house, while Jay followed her to the porch.

"Did you move it?" he asked.

She shook her head. "Not an inch."

"Good."

He slipped on a pair of latex gloves, crouched down near the box and cautiously lifted the lid. Releasing a hissed breath, he gave her a fleeting look. Then he eased the box into a clear plastic bag and sealed it.

"Take this to the lab," he said to Patterson when the man returned. "I'll stay with Ms. O'Connell until her husband arrives."

Patterson drove away, tires squealing.

"What was in the box?" she asked, her stomach quivering.

"Sadie, I think we should wait—"

"Just tell me, Jay. It's better than letting my imagination run wild. What was it?"

"A child's toe."

Sadie's knees buckled and she collapsed against the house.

Jay rushed to her side. "Jesus, I'm so sorry," he said, helping her inside. "I'll call Victim Services for you."

"No!" She grabbed his arm. "I need to be alone."

As soon as the words were out of her mouth, she realized what she had said. "I don't mean you have to go. I just don't want to be surrounded by strangers. I need to think. I need to call Philip. I need…oh, God!"

She sagged into a chair at the kitchen table and rocked back and forth, trying not to think of the box. Or Sam's toe. Or the monster who took him. She hugged her arms across her chest.

Sammmm!

"Where do you keep your tea cups?" Jay asked firmly.

A flurry of thoughts bombarded her mind. *What will he cut off next? Another toe? Another finger? Something else?*

"Sadie?" Jay touched her arm.

She choked back a sob. "Sorry. What did you say?"

"Tea cups?"

"In the china cabinet," she said, watching him.

Jay found the kettle, filled it and plugged it in. When the water boiled, he looked at her and she pointed to a cupboard where she kept the teapot and tea. A few minutes later, he poured two cups of the strong brew, laced them with lots of cream and sugar, and hefted his bulk into a chair.

"I'm not very good at knowing what to do in situations like this," he apologized.

"The tea is good," she said. "Thanks for the distraction."

"My mother always used to say that the world's troubles could be solved by a pot of tea," he mumbled. "It's the only thing I can think of doing when things go bad."

She studied his tired, wrinkled face. "And things are really bad, aren't they?"

"We don't know if it's Sam's toe," he said quietly. "I'll have it analyzed right away."

She blinked rapidly, holding back the tears. "He said he'd send Sam back in pieces. First his finger, now his toe." She moaned and cradled her head in her hands.

"I wish I could do something, Sadie."

She heard the helplessness in his voice. She felt the same way.

"Thank you, Jay."

"I'm sorry that you're being taunted like this," he said. "And I'm so sorry he's hurt your son."

She nodded mutely.

"I want you to know we're doing everything..." His voice drifted away. "Hell, I know there's nothing I can say that'll make you feel any better." Frustrated, he ran a hand through his thin gray hair. "I'd give anything for a break on this case."

She felt a surge of pity for Jay. His face was lined with worry and years of hopeless cases. "Thank you."

"I've spent too many years on the job," he confessed. "It doesn't get any easier."

"There must be something you get out of it, something rewarding."

He smiled grimly. "Catching the bastards."

Good, she thought. That's what she wanted too.

"You must travel a lot," she said offhandedly.

"Not much. I have a little...problem."

Her brow lifted. "What kind of problem?"

"I, uh..." His mouth curled wryly. "I don't like flying."

"Long waits and crowded airports," she guessed. "Or nine-eleven."

"None of the above. I'm afraid of flying." He stood slowly and wandered toward the doorway to the living room. "I'm going to call your husband."

For a few moments—only a few though—he had taken her mind off the horrible reality that her son had been brutally dismembered. She sensed that Jay Lucas was not used to showing his own vulnerability. Then she thought of hers—Sam. He was her number one weakness.

However, she had one more. And it was calling her name.

"Jay," she said, standing on shaky legs. "I need to lie down for a bit."

"I'll clean up," he offered. "Oh, and Philip is on his way."

She excused herself and headed down the hall.

Her conscience argued, "Don't do it!" But she was beyond listening. All she could think of was the box with Sam's toe. She needed something to numb her pain, make her forget. And there was one thing that was guaranteed to do just that.

In Philip's office, she grabbed a set of keys from the top desk drawer. Then she unlocked the bottom drawer of the filing cabinet—the one Philip had always told her was for business.

Business? Yeah, right!

She'd discovered the bottles a month ago when she was searching for an empty file folder. Philip had left the drawer unlocked. When she confronted him, he told her that the six bottles of ridiculously expensive Screaming Eagle Cabernet had been given to him by one of his wealthy clients after a successful corporate merger.

She had never touched the bottles—until today.

The wine called to her. *Sadie...drink me...I'll help you forget.*

Seduced by its persuasive promise, she climbed the stairs, a corkscrew in one hand and a bottle in the other. As soon as she reached her bedroom, she uncorked the red wine and sniffed it. The aroma was intense and sulfurous—like a mix of earth, concentrated fruit and something murky that simmered beneath the surface.

She scrunched her face, wondering if there was any other alcohol in the house. But short of drinking the vanilla extract that her parents had bought in Mexico, this was the best she had.

"Suck it up, Princess."

She didn't even bother with a glass. Sipping directly from the bottle, she hardly tasted it at first. The wine slid down her throat, leaving a fiery trail behind. When her taste buds finally registered, she was shocked by the almost undrinkable quality of the wine.

"Must be an acquired taste," she mumbled.

She tossed back the wine, forcing her throat to swallow. As she welcomed the warm infusion of alcohol into her body, a few drops spilled from the corner of her mouth and onto the cream-colored carpet. They resembled spatters of blood.

"What are you doing, Sadie?" she whispered.

The wine found its way to her mouth again.

Forgetting.

Half a bottle later, she was more than a little drunk. Hiding the Cabernet behind her nightstand, she staggered into the bathroom where a bottle of sleeping pills waited. She shook some into her palm. It was tempting to take them all, slip into a deep and permanent sleep, but she took one and put the rest back.

Then she flopped face-first onto the bed and passed out.

∞ ∞ ∞

The days passed uneventfully.

While Jay worked overtime on Sam's case, the fraud investigation into Philip and Morris resulted in both men being hauled down to the police station for questioning. When Sadie went to meet Philip, he was in a state of panic.

"Thank God you're here," he said, gripping her hand.

She yanked it away. "I'm not sure why you want me here."

"Well, you *are* still my wife."

"Not for long. Once the divorce papers are finalized—" She broke off. "You filed them, didn't you?"

He looked away. "We can't rush that now. We have more important things to think of. It's just a matter of time before they charge me."

"You should have thought about that before."

"Damn it! I need you, Sadie! Why can't you get that?"

"You need me," she said slowly, testing each word. Her eyes flashed dangerously. "You don't want me testifying against you. You want me to defend you, support you."

"You *should* support me. We're married, for Christ's sake! I've given you everything."

She glared at him. "Everything? You've given me a life of infidelity and lies. Our marriage was a sham, Philip. Right from the beginning. My mother was right."

After that, she refused to talk to him. She sat in the interrogation room while he was drilled by investigators about his financial dealings. An oily-looking lawyer with slicked-back hair and a suit that probably cost a month's salary interrupted with the occasional whisper in Philip's ear. At one point, a police officer asked her a direct question, but she shook her head. She wasn't compelled to answer anything. And she wasn't going to.

When they left the station, she hurried ahead of Philip, refusing to say a word. She strode across the parking lot, the scornful kiss of bitter wind blasting her skin. She hated the cold. Summer was what she loved. Summer meant taking Sam to the parks, swimming in Millcreek's outdoor pool and going to the Valley Zoo.

She shook her head. *Stop!*

"So what happens now?" she asked, unlocking the car door.

Philip climbed into the passenger seat. "My lawyer told me to play dumb and let Morris take the fall."

"How can you even think of doing that?"

"If I don't, we could lose everything."

She felt sick. "We've already lost everything."

The drive home was awkward, but thankfully silent. As she pulled into the garage, she spotted a media swarm waiting on the doorstep. Ever since the fraud investigation had gone public, a toxic cloud of doom followed Philip everywhere, usually in the form of persistent reporters who waited like ravenous tigers for the right moment to pounce and rip into him.

Today, she was ready to give them a glass of wine on the side.

"Mr. Tymchuk!" a man yelled, tripping over his feet to beat the other carnivores.

Sadie scowled, pushed past the throng and slammed the door behind her, not at all feeling sorry for Philip, who was trapped outside.

"You made this mess, Philip. Deal with it."

The answering machine light flashed impatiently, demanding her attention. Setting her purse on the table by the door, she pushed the button.

"Thank you for supporting us in the past," claimed a charity that she knew damned well she had never sent money to. She skipped to the next message, a droning telemarketer selling lawn care services.

"There's still snow on the ground," she muttered. *Delete.*

The next message made her pause.

"Ms. O'Connell, this is Detective Garner. I'm working your husband's case. Please call me right away." He left a number.

With a heavy sigh, she picked up the phone.

"We'd like you to come back to the station," Garner said when she got through to him.

"I don't think I—"

"I'm sorry. I don't mean to cut you off, but are you aware that there was an undercover detective at your husband's law firm?"

Answering one question wouldn't hurt Philip's case.

"Yes."

"The detective wants to talk to you—*off* the record."

Sadie was flustered. "Why would he want to do that?"

Garner must have placed his hand over the receiver because there was a muffled sound on the other end. And another voice, an indistinct one.

"I can't get into this over the phone," Garner said finally. "Can you come down tomorrow morning around ten?"

"Fine. I'll be there."

She hung up just as Philip stormed into the house.

"Goddamn bunch of pariahs!" he ranted, heading for his office. "I don't want to be disturbed, Sadie. Got that?"

"I have no intention of disturbing you," she said dryly.

What she wanted was a drink, but she'd already finished off the bottle of Cabernet. She experienced a pang of shame. Her sobriety was over. But it wasn't the same as before. She had one glass before bed. To help her sleep. The good thing was that this time, she was in control. At least, that's what she told herself.

Her eyes wandered across the living room walls, pausing on a family portrait. She remembered that day clearly. Sam had just turned two. She had held him on her lap and tickled him until he laughed with glee. In that perfect moment, the photographer had captured Sam's spirit.

And perhaps his soul.

She thought of his troubled birth. The nurses had doubted that the tiny boy would survive, but he had fought, struggling for breath with each labored beat of his heart, and he had lived. For six years. Six *short* years.

She had loved Sam more than she loved her parents or Philip or any other—more than life itself. He was her miracle, her salvation. It was the love for her son that had made her want to get up each morning and made her life worthwhile. He had defined her entire existence.

He still did.

14

The room in the police station where she waited was small, but it wasn't as bleak as she had expected. On one wall, there was a painting of a Japanese geisha strolling in a garden of cherry blossoms. A dust-spotted silk tree in the far corner sat lopsided in a plastic pot, and in the middle of the room, padded chairs and a small, round table showed little character but frequent use.

She sat down and furtively eyed the dark glass in the middle of the wall. She knew what a tinted window meant. She watched Law & Order.

She waved, smiling through gritted teeth. "Bring it on, boys."

Five minutes passed without interruption.

She tapped her fingers. "Let's get this over with."

The door opened and a woman stepped inside.

Sadie recognized her instantly. "What are *you* doing here?"

"I'm sorry, Sadie. About Philip. About everything." A badge dropped on the table.

"You? You're the undercover detective?"

Brigitte Moreau sat down in the chair across from her.

Sadie was stunned. The last thing she expected was to find out that the undercover cop sent to spy on her husband was none other than the woman who'd been sleeping with him. The woman she had despised for the last year.

Brigitte folded her hands. "I have to admit, this is a bit awkward. My real name is Bridget Moore. I, uh...was brought in by Philip's firm once they discovered the funds were missing. My assignment was to get close to Philip, to see if he was in on it and find out where the money was going."

"Getting close to him doesn't mean sleeping with him."

Bridget unclasped her hands. "I had to take advantage of his weakness for women. Get him to trust me."

"I guess it worked."

"Look, Sadie, we both know that Philip wasn't the perfect husband. He pursued *me*—or Brigitte Moreau." Her lips curled into a wry smile. "And trust me, the sex wasn't all that great."

Sadie stared at her, wondering why Bridget's derisive comment didn't make her want to lunge across the table and grab handfuls of that perfectly coiffed blond hair. Ironically, she just wanted to laugh. Maybe have a Philip-bashing party and a bottle of *whine*. She certainly had enough to complain about.

"The sex was *never* that great," she admitted.

Bridget grinned. "You know, if I can be blunt, you're far better off without him. I wasn't the first, you know."

Sadie feigned surprise. "Really?"

"Philip told me he started sleeping around just after you were married. The last time—before me, that is—was with someone close to him, he said. Another associate, I think. But he said it was a one time thing, a mistake."

Sadie thought of Latoya Jefferson, the young receptionist who had worked at the firm a few years ago. Philip had shown an unusual interest in her. When Sadie had questioned him, he'd shrugged it off, saying she was the daughter of a friend. Latoya left in a flurry of rumors of an affair with one of the partners.

She scowled.

Bridget noticed her expression. "In my defense, Philip can be quite charming when he wants to be. Plus, it was the only way to track down the money."

"And did you?"

The woman nodded. "He left me in his office one day while he went to see Morris. I found some documents behind a picture of Sam. We're in the process of tracing the funds. If we're lucky, we'll be able to reroute them to a secure account. We're talking millions."

"So why am I here?"

"Because I needed to apologize, Sadie. And because you're going to hear some nasty things during the trial."

"If it goes to trial."

Bridget's eyes brightened. "Do you think he'll accept a plea bargain?"

"I don't know. Philip's basically a…"

"Coward?"

"I see you know him very well."

Bridget blushed. "We're planning to pick him up next week. Oh, and don't bother trying to post bail. He's too much of a flight risk. He won't be going anywhere."

"And you don't want me going anywhere either. Is that it?"

"We're hoping to keep you out of it," Bridget said. "By Philip's admission, you had no knowledge of what he was doing. He kept you in the dark. We won't need you to testify, but…"

"There's always a *but*."

Bridget sucked in a deep breath. "The press will be nasty on this one. They'll call my involvement entrapment and turn your marriage into a farce."

Sadie stood slowly. "Let them say what they will. I don't plan on being around for long."

"It's probably a good idea to start over," Bridget said. "Start a new life."

Sadie paused in the doorway. "They'll be right, you know."

"What?"

"My marriage *was* a farce. But one good thing came from it."

Bridget's eyes were full of sympathy. "I hope they find Sam."

"Me too."

In the parking lot, Sadie sat in her car for almost fifteen minutes, letting the engine idle while she replayed the latest development. If anyone had told her that she'd have a rational, almost friendly, conversation with the woman her husband had been sleeping with, she would've laughed.

Irony *was* a strange bedfellow.

∞ ∞ ∞

"We're checking out some new leads," Jay told her a few days later. "We've had to sort through calls from people claiming they've seen the man from your drawing. In the meantime, we need you to do an interview—a plea for Sam's release."

After lunch, she met him at the television station.

Philip was already there.

"Are you sure this is a good idea?" he asked Jay.

The detective gave him a tight smile. "We haven't got anything to lose at this point." When he saw Sadie cringe, he added, "If you make a personal plea to him, it could make him care more about Sam's well-being."

"If Sam's still alive," Philip muttered.

"He's missing a finger and a toe," Sadie cried. "That doesn't mean he's dead."

"Doesn't mean he's alive either."

Philip's words enraged her.

"Shut up, Philip!" she shouted. "He's alive! I know it!"

For a moment, no one spoke.

Jay sent Philip a hard stare, then turned to Sadie. "When you speak to The Fog, make sure you mention Sam's name a lot. Make it personal, Sadie. Most abductors see their victims as impersonal objects, not human beings. Show him the sweet, playful side of Sam."

"Do you think he might let Sam go?"

Jay's mouth thinned and she saw his eyes cloud over.

"That's not why you want me to make it personal, is it?" she said.

"Look, Sadie," he said. "We just don't want him to continue hurting Sam. We want him to think that his warnings have worked, that we'll back off. Meanwhile, we'll keep looking for him."

In a blur of motion, someone clipped a tiny microphone to her collar and a receiver to the waistband of her slacks.

"We've drafted up a speech to help you," Jay said, handing her a piece of paper.

She scanned the words, staring at them as if they were written in a foreign language. One word stood out clearly. *Sam.*

"We're on in five," the cameraman said, counting down.

There was a sour taste in her mouth.

Reporter Lance MacDonald introduced her.

Then time stood still.

She faced the camera, her mouth sandpaper dry, her tongue limp. *What do I say to a kidnapper, a man I let take my son?*

She read the notes that Jay had so carefully prepared.

"I want to ask you for the safe return of our son, Samuel James Tymchuk. Samuel—Sam—is our...my..." Lost in grief, she couldn't get the words out.

Behind her, Philip hissed, "Jesus! Keep going!"

"S-Sam is only six and he's..."

Her eyes welled with tears and the words before her blurred.

She tried again. "Sam is six and..."

Why was she reading someone else's words?

Crumpling the paper, she stared into the camera.

"Sam is my son. He's six years old and very smart, even though he doesn't talk. He loves to read and draw. He's a sweet, sweet boy—my baby—and I love him more than anything. I beg you...please return him to me." She hitched in a breath. "I apologize that my drawing of you got out. I'm sorry I ever drew it. But I was not responsible for releasing it to the police. Neither was Sam. He's innocent in all this and I know you don't want to hurt him. I'll give you money, time to disappear, whatever you need."

She caught sight of Jay's grim expression. He shook his head, but she continued. "If you give me back my son, give me Sam, I'll make sure you walk away. You know how to reach me. Call me. This can be between you and me. Just don't hurt Sam." She choked back a sob. "Please—"

Philip shoved her aside. "Listen, you sick freak! Give us back our son! Only a fucking coward would—"

Sadie watched in horror as Jay grabbed Philip and hurled him against the wall. Even the reporter flinched. The cameraman had the decency to turn the camera away and the crew stepped back.

"You stupid ass!" Jay hissed between gritted teeth. "What are you trying to do, get your son killed?"

"Of course not!"

Sadie clenched Philip's arm. "If you've done anything to hurt Sam—"

"Me? What about you?" He shook a finger at her. "You're the one who let him take Sam, for Christ's sake."

"You weren't there!" she screamed, unleashing her fury. "He was going to shoot Sam right in front of me. I had no choice!"

"You should've tried!" he yelled back. "You should've done more!"

She gave him a frosty look. "I will always wonder if I could have done more, Philip. I live with that every day."

∞ ∞ ∞

That night, she saw her face plastered on all the local news stations. She called Jay just before ten.

"Anything?"

"Sorry, Sadie. We haven't heard from him."

She hung up, disappointed.

In the ensuite bathroom, she downed a sleeping pill. Then she brushed her teeth and splashed cool water over her face. Groping blindly for a towel, she found one. Then she raised her head and hissed in a huge lungful of air.

A boy stood behind her.

"Sam!"

She whipped around, but there was only empty space.

"Sam? Where are you, baby?"

She wandered in her bedroom, listless and dead tired. Then she crumpled into bed and slipped into unconsciousness, her sleep haunted by disturbing visions.

Sam was standing just out of reach, surrounded by pitch-black shadows. At first, he appeared at a great distance. Then he moved forward. Behind him, the black void expanded, a tunnel racing to claim him. He peered over his shoulder, and when he turned back, the fear that radiated from his eyes almost made her heart stop beating.

"Hurry, Sam!" she screamed.

The blackness slithered over him and she ran toward him, but her legs were weighted down by some invisible, malevolent force. She was an arm's length away when her knees buckled and she sank to the ground, crying out in anguish.

"Come back to me, Sam! I miss you."

Sam leaned over her, his face a blur, and a flash freeze brushed her cheek. That's when she bolted awake, her pulse beating furiously. She could have sworn that Sam had kissed her. When she touched her cheek, it felt damp.

By morning, she was sure she had dreamt it all.

Either that or I've completely lost it.

A computerized version of Barney's "I Love You" song—Sam's choice—interrupted her thoughts.

"Is this line tapped?"

Her hand shook. "I-I don't think so."

"I saw you on TV," The Fog said. "You and your husband."

"He shouldn't have said those things," she said quickly. "He didn't mean it. Please, don't hurt Sam because of it. I'm really, really sorry."

There was a muffled moan, then the slam of a car door.

"So am I," The Fog replied. "You know the Rafferty Tree Nursery, west of Beaumont?"

She held her breath. "Yes."

"Sam's waiting for you. Be here in half an hour. Alone."

"Alone?" she repeated.

There was an impatient huff. "If I wanted to kill you, Sadie, I woulda done it that night. Oh, and in case I need to tell ya, no police."

"Wait! I—"

The line went dead.

Relief flooded her. She was going to get Sam back.

She left a message on the answering machine for Philip. "I'll be back soon. With Sam."

She stared at the flashing message light for a moment.

Well, I'm not telling the police, but if he thinks I'm going to leave and not tell someone where I'm going, he's definitely crazy.

∞ ∞ ∞

The Rafferty Tree Nursery was a twenty-minute drive to the outer edge of south Edmonton. The family-owned business grew an assortment of trees and shrubs, with acres of wooded land stretching as far as the eye could see.

As she drove, she glimpsed her reflection in the rearview mirror. She was a mess. Her long black hair was dry and dull, and she couldn't remember if she'd even brushed it that morning. The Mars-like craters under her eyes bespoke of little sleep and too much crying. Even the blue of her irises seemed washed out.

"You look like crap, Sadie O'Connell."

But she knew it didn't matter what she looked like, as long as she got Sam back. She could feel his life essence pulling her closer, urging her to step on the gas.

Hurry!

She turned down a side road, ignoring the *Private Property* sign and the warning that the place didn't open for the season for three more weeks. The eroded dirt road took her past the scraggly branches of deciduous trees—silver birch, trembling aspens and balsam poplars. The farther she drove, the more mature and thick the greenery became, until she was surrounded by a grove of lush, long-needled evergreens.

"Where are you?"

The road came to a dead end, so she parked the car and climbed out. Two footpaths led to either side of her. On the right, a red balloon hovered in the air, its string tied to the branch of a blue spruce. "This way," it seemed to beckon.

As she passed, she saw a slip of paper clipped to the string.

Snatching it up, she unfolded it.

YOU HAVE 5 MINUTES TO SAVE HIM!

A mix of adrenaline and terror kicked her into high gear.

She ran.

When a glint of metal caught her eye, she left the path and weaved between the trees, paying no attention to the brittle branches that plucked at her clothes and hair. Her legs pumped harder, faster, until they burned.

Up ahead a horn beeped.

She rounded a lodgepole pine and skidded to a halt ten yards from the back end of a rusted yellow Chevy. It was parked between two trees with its rear wheels raised on cement blocks. The heavy snow on the trunk and bumper indicated that the car had been there for a while, which was not surprising since she was farther into the nursery than customers were allowed.

She widely circled the car. Its side windows were grimy, the interior shadowed.

Then she saw him.

"Oh God."

Sam was slumped over the steering wheel, still dressed in his pajamas, a Blue Jays baseball cap pulled low over his head. His mouth was bound with electrical tape.

"Sam!" she shouted.

He didn't move.

Horrified, she raced toward the car.

A fateful mistake.

Her right foot hooked a thin metal wire before she could even comprehend what it was. From that second on, everything dissolved into a hellish nightmare and her entire world was blown off its axis. A deafening roar rocked the earth, throwing her to the ground while bits of searing metal ripped through the air.

"Nooooo!" she screamed.

A smoking, black wad landed near her outstretched hand.

Sam's baseball cap.

The Fog had fulfilled his promise.

Sam.

"Oh, Jesus, no!"

She scrambled to her feet, but a second explosion sent her flying backward through the air. Her head smacked against a rock. Sharp pain surged through her, over her, and when she touched the back of her head, her fingers came away covered in blood.

Consciousness faded in and out.

"Sam…"

Something floated above her.

The red balloon.

It hovered, then lifted into the smoke-filled sky, its thin string dangling beneath it.

She raised a quivering hand. "Come back."

A devilish face blocked the light. In a blurred shadow, it leaned down and laughed at her, its breath rancid.

"Why?" she moaned.

"I always keep my promises," it whispered.

Then Sadie slipped into oblivion.

15

"Can I come in?"

Dressed in uniform, Jay Lucas lingered in the doorway of the hospital room—a bouquet of drooping flowers in one hand, a drenched raincoat in the other.

Sadie guessed it wasn't just a courtesy call. "Of course."

"How are you feeling?" he asked, slipping the flowers into a water jug on the side table.

"Short of some scratches and a mild concussion, I'm...fine."

And she was. Physically. Mentally was another story.

It had been two days since Philip had led the police to the nursery after hearing her message on the answering machine. They had discovered the smoldering wreckage of the car, and her unconscious body nearby.

She took a deep breath. "Did you find Sam?"

Jay shook his head.

"He could've been thrown clear," she said. "Did you check the bush—?"

"Sadie, we found blood from two victims."

"Two?" She sat up, wincing from the pain. "That doesn't make sense."

"Unless there were two kids in the car."

"But I only saw Sam."

"The other could've been in the back seat or..."

"Or the trunk," she finished for him.

The detective nodded grimly.

"The blood—are you sure it's Sam's?" she asked, fearful.

"It matched the DNA from the toothbrush you gave us."

A tear leaked from one eye. "And what about other evidence?"

"We found detonator fragments. Military issue."

"That's good, right?" she wept. "Makes it easier to find him?"

"Unfortunately, nowadays, people could find one on the Internet, if they looked hard enough.

She hitched in a breath. "I have to make arrangements. To bury Sam."

"Sadie, I, uh…"

"What?"

His face drooped. "There's nothing to bury."

She eyed him blankly.

"There's nothing left of him," he said softly. "There were two bombs. They disintegrated almost everything. It's going to take weeks for forensics to sift through the remains. And even then, they're so tiny…"

She shuddered. "Little bloody pieces."

"Huh?"

"Something The Fog said to me." She turned away, drained. "What about the balloon?"

"We found it in a tree, a few yards from the scene. It's been sent to trace. If we're lucky, we'll pull a print or DNA from saliva."

Sadie studied the ceiling for a moment and found herself reliving the explosion, the fiery inferno of the car, the smell of burning flesh…the screams. *Her* screams.

She wiped her eyes. "If only I hadn't moved."

"You didn't know about the tripwire."

"But I should have called you, waited—"

Jay reached for her hand. "We'll get him, Sadie."

She looked into his eyes, comforted by the steely promise of justice. She didn't doubt the man. He would hunt down The Fog…or die trying. She hoped to God it wasn't the latter. She'd grown fond of the old man.

"Thanks, Jay," she whispered.

His face crinkled with concern. "I heard Philip is…uh…"

"In an eight by twelve foot cell," she said wryly.

Bridget had been true to her word, although apologetic about the rotten timing. Philip had been formally arrested that morning.

"He pled guilty," Sadie told Jay. "But his lawyer thinks he'll get a reduced sentence."

Jay nodded. "Because they found the money."

"Every penny of it. Philip was depending on it for his retirement plan." She shook her head. "I don't think he planned on retiring in prison though."

"You're lucky, Sadie."

Her mouth dropped. "Lucky? How can you say that?"

Jay shifted uncomfortably. "What I mean is, they could've taken your house, your vehicles, frozen your bank accounts."

"Those things mean nothing," she said in a dead tone. "They could have it all if it meant I'd have Sam back."

There was an awkward moment of silence.

"They letting you out soon?" Jay asked eventually.

"Just before supper."

"You need someone to come get you?"

She shook her head. "My friend will be here."

Jay moved to the door. "If you need anything, let me know."

She listened to the detective's footsteps echo down the hall. Then she eased herself from the bed and stumbled into the bathroom. Waves of nausea wracked her aching body and she collapsed in front of the toilet. Resting her burning forehead on her arms, she pictured Sam bound and gagged in the car.

"There's nothing left of him," Jay had said.

Then why does it feel like Sam's still with me?

She threw up. Moaning softly, she yearned to crawl into the toilet, to be flushed out with the soiled water. A nurse found her with her forehead resting on the toilet seat and helped her back to bed.

Later that afternoon, Sadie checked out of the hospital. Leah was waiting in the lobby to take her back to the house. The drive home was as endless as the pouring rain and dull gray sky, which matched her dismal mood. She said very little to Leah. There was too much on her mind.

"Thanks for the ride," she said, unlocking the front door.

Leah's eyes filled with concern. "Want me to stay with you tonight?"

"No." She stepped inside the house and began to close the door, but Leah's arm shot out.

"Sadie, don't push me away. I want to help—"

"There's nothing you can do. I just want to be alone."

"Are you sure?"

"Yeah, I'm sure. Thanks though." She closed the door and leaned against it. "There's nothing anyone can do to help me."

She drifted from one room to another, calmed by the anti-depressants the hospital had given her and by the pitter-patter of raindrops against the windows. Every time she passed in front of the door to Sam's room, she'd pause and rest a hand against it. But she could never quite bring herself to open it. Eventually, she'd have to pack away his toys, his clothes…his life.

Not yet. Later. When I'm ready.

∞ ∞ ∞

They decided to have a service, complete with burial.

"For closure," Philip had said when she visited him in jail.

At first Sadie had been hesitant. A funeral would make Sam's death more real. And she didn't want it to be real. Then there was the matter of a coffin. Philip had argued that they could just bury a plywood box, something symbolic.

"A box." She gaped at him as if he had lost his mind. "Sam deserves more than a cheap wooden box."

She ventured out alone and bought a child-sized coffin.

The morning of Sam's funeral was appropriately dreary and filled with a flurry of well-meaning but unwanted visitors who dropped off indistinguishable casseroles and obligatory fruit baskets. By lunchtime, Sadie had run out of counter space and there was no room in the fridge.

Then there was the family to deal with. Philip's brother, sister and father had bused in from Seattle, while her parents, looking tanned and healthy, had flown up from Yuma. Her brother had shipped out to Afghanistan the week before, leaving her sister-in-law Theresa with the kids.

"Damn, Sadie," Theresa said on the phone. "I'd give anything to be there. I know Brad would too. I-I'm so sorry. I'm going to miss Sammy so much. His sweet little face, his laugh, his—"

Sadie hung up on her.

She felt a flicker of remorse. She hadn't meant to be rude, but hearing Theresa talk about missing Sam made her clench her hands into fists. This is *my* loss, she wanted to shout. *Not yours!*

Philip called at lunchtime. "How are you holding up?"

"How do you think?" she said, trying to keep the resentment from her voice.

"A wreath is being delivered to the cemetery at two-thirty."

"You should be here for this, Philip."

"I tried, but they won't let me out. It's not fair."

"Sam is dead," she snapped. "How fair is *that*?"

There was an empty pause. Then she heard him clear his throat. "Say goodbye to my boy for me, Sadie."

"I can't even say goodbye to him for me," she said bleakly.

Two hours later, she allowed her father to tuck her into the backseat of the Mazda and they headed for the cemetery, her mother beside her, sniffling into a tissue. Chuck, her father-in-law, drove Philip's brother and sister in the Mercedes.

The service was painful, yet brief. Other than family, Leah, Liz, Jean, Bridget and Jay attended. Matthew Bornyk sent his condolences, even though Sadie hadn't thought to invite him. And why should she? His daughter might still be alive.

After a short prayer from a pastor her father had found, she waited while everyone placed a single white rosebud on the coffin lid. Since there were no human remains, they were burying a single object—the blackened baseball cap. Slowly, the small white coffin with its white satin lining that only Sadie had seen was lowered into a muddy pit in the Cherished Children section of Hope Haven Cemetery. She watched it disappear into the gaping hole and her heart sank with it.

Tears streamed down her face, and she shuffled closer. As she hovered at the edge, she yearned for someone to push her in. She wouldn't even fight them if they did.

She closed her eyes, inhaling the soft scent of a white rose.

Then she tossed it into the pit.

"Sleep, little man," she said in a trembling voice. "Snug as—"

She broke down, sobbing hysterically.

"Come on, honey," her mother said, gently taking her arm.

"I'm so sorry," Sadie wailed. "Forgive me, Sam!"

"Let him go, Sadie."

"How do I do that, Mom? How do I say goodbye to my baby?"

"I don't know, honey," her mother said, batting away a tear. "No mother should ever have to bury her child."

They shuffled toward the car, each engulfed in misery.

That evening, Sadie couldn't take it anymore. The constant bodies and mundane conversations in every room irritated her. She wanted nothing more than to be left alone, and she told her mother so. Finally, Philip's family went back to their hotel, and her friends went back to their own homes, their own lives.

She curled up on the sofa and rested her head in her mother's lap. "I've lost everything, Mom. Everything."

Her mother stroked her hair. "I know it feels that way, Sadie, but it *will* get better. I promise. It'll hurt less, with time."

"Time. That's all I've got left."

"Time is a gift, honey. Use it wisely. Do something for Sam, something to remember him."

But Sadie wasn't listening. Another voice spoke to her, and it was far more compelling.

"Mommy, where are you? I can't find you."

As soon as her parents went to bed, she armed herself with another bottle of Philip's Cabernet and barricaded herself in the bedroom. Within an hour, she had polished off the entire bottle and had staggered downstairs to dispose of the evidence.

Back in her room, she passed out in the chair.

The next morning, she walked unsteadily into the kitchen. Disheveled, reeking of stale wine and suffering from the most god-awful hangover she'd ever had, she almost didn't see her parents seated at the kitchen table. They were waiting for her, and the look of disapproval on her mother's face told her that something was up.

"What's wrong?" she asked.

Her mother frowned. "You look terrible."

"Gee, thanks, Mom."

An empty wine bottle was dangled in front of her nose.

"I found this," her father said. "In the garbage can out back."

"What on earth are you doing, Sadie?" her mother asked.

Sadie massaged her pounding head, then moved to the window and crossed her arms. "I'm forgetting."

What else could she say? They didn't understand.

"You need help," her mother said firmly. "Counseling, AA, whatever you need, do it. We'll stay with you for a while. Until you're better."

"I don't need a babysitter, Mom."

"No, but you do need help." Her mother moved toward her, hands outstretched, pleading. "Let us help you. You've been down this path before, Sadie. It doesn't lead anywhere good. You know that."

"Don't tell me what I know! I know my son is dead! I know it's my fault. I know that drinking makes me numb. And I *like* that."

"You're saying that because you're grieving," her mother cried. "We're all grieving. You lost your son. We lost our grandson. We don't want to lose you too."

"Just go home, Mom. I'll be—"

"We're not leaving," her father interrupted. "Not until you agree to see a psychologist and go to AA."

Sadie clenched her teeth. "You're giving me an ultimatum, Dad? I'm not a child. I'm an adult and I can make my own decisions. Right or wrong, I have to do this *my* way. If that means I drink to forget, then I drink. Right now I just want to be left alone."

She flinched at the hurt she saw in her mother's eyes.

"Give me some space, Mom. I'll call you if I need you."

"You promise?" Her mother was weeping.

"Go back to the States. There's nothing more you can do."

Her parents left the next morning, depressed and defeated.

Sadie spent the day wading through paperwork. Then she called the realtor that Philip found.

"Any news on the house?"

"We've got a buyer," the man said. "The deal's been finalized and the money'll be in the bank by tomorrow. How much time do you need?"

"I'll be out of here in a few days."

Jay called later that day.

"That bastard has us by the balls," he vented. "The balloon, the note, the bombs—they're all dead ends. But we're still hoping something will come up."

Sensing his frustration, Sadie thanked him and hung up. She'd watched enough Missing and Without a Trace to know that with each passing day there was less possibility that The Fog would ever be caught.

The following day, she stood in front of Sam's door. Holding her breath, she opened it and a rush of emotion bombarded her. This was the last place she had seen Sam alive, where she had watched a murderer take him away. She should have fought harder. Done something more. Remorse ate at her, broiling in her stomach and threatening to spew forth.

She shifted in a slow circle, taking in Sam's fuzzy slippers, the autographed baseball bat, his clothes...the empty bed. She sat down on it. Then she lay back and stared up at the same ceiling her son had looked at for six years. With her finger, she drew an invisible infinity symbol in the air. Again and again.

"I miss you, Sam."

She turned on her side, gripped his favorite blanket and cried until she was drained of everything, until an idea that had been brewing since the day Sam died became the only thing she could focus on. She couldn't—*wouldn't*—live without Sam, and there was only one way to be with him.

With a heavy heart, she began the daunting task of packing away his room. Every object seemed to be haunted by another memory, each one cutting her heart even deeper than the last. It took hours of battling emotions, memories and tears before she was done.

Then she wandered through the house. The house they had brought Sam home to when things had been happy. Memories of him were everywhere. Like ghostly dust bunnies, they haunted every nook and cranny. She wanted to ignore them, but she couldn't. His first steps, his first tumble down the stairs, his first birthday party.

His last.

"Everything's different now," she whispered.

Sam was gone. Philip was gone. Her life as she knew it was gone. Everything had dissolved around her.

Anger bubbled rebelliously to the surface, like a tablet of antacid in water. *Plop, plop. Fizz, fizz...*

But there was no relief in sight. Except in one thing.

Don't do it, Sadie!

But she couldn't resist fate.

16

She grabbed another bottle of Screaming Eagle Cabernet from Philip's secret stash. That left three in the drawer. She considered taking them too, but then changed her mind.

"I'll save you for something special."

Upstairs in the bedroom, she miserably flopped in the chair by the window and cranked up the antique radio on the windowsill. She needed something heavy, something to give her momentum, so she turned the dial until she heard the pounding bass of a rap song pumping out a rhythmic beat. A deep voice boomed scarcely recognizable lyrics about a woman walking out on her man.

"I axed you why..." the rapper sang.

Sadie held the bottle in the air. "To a life well axed."

She'd grown accustomed to drinking straight from the bottle and she tipped it back, taking a long swig. The wine's initial bitter flavor didn't shock her anymore and she savored its warmth as it trailed down her throat. Each mouthful enveloped her in mind-numbing calmness.

"What now?" she murmured.

In a burst of sudden clarity, she made two decisions.

First, she took a pair of scissors into the bathroom and stood in front of the mirror. Between gulps of wine, she chopped off her long black locks to just below her ears. She felt no regret as she watched the strands waft to the floor. When she was done, there was more hair on the floor than on her head.

She stared at her hollow, shadowed eyes. "I'm nothing. Just an empty shell."

After sweeping up the hair and depositing it into the garbage can, she wandered back to the bedroom to prepare for her second decision. Setting the bottle on the nightstand, she pulled two suitcases out of the closet and tossed them on the bed.

"There's one thing left to do," she slurred. "But you can't do it here." She paused, her hand hovering near the zipper of a suitcase. "Well, you could, but it might not go over well with the new homeowners." She giggled drunkenly.

There was an unexpected knock on the door.

Sadie slipped the half-empty wine bottle in the recycle bin just seconds before Leah poked her head inside.

"Can I come—? Sadie! What did you do to your hair?"

"I cut it."

"Yeah, I can see that," Leah replied, moving into the room.

Sadie's patience was wearing thin. "I didn't hear the doorbell."

"I rang it a few times, but when you didn't answer, I got worried. I let myself in through the garage." Leah spied the suitcases on the bed. "What the hell are you doing?"

"What's it look like? I'm leaving."

"But you can't just leave."

"Watch me."

"What about Philip? And the trial?"

Sadie tossed three pair of jeans into one of the cases. "There's nothing for me here anymore. I need to get away."

An uncomfortable silence permeated the room.

Leah sat down on the bed. When she finally spoke, her voice emitted quiet acceptance. "So where will you go?"

"Anywhere but here."

She placed Sam's photograph and a heavy photo album on top of her clothes. Then she zipped the suitcase shut. In the second suitcase, she packed away the plastic container that held all the newspaper clippings. Lastly, she tucked in the portfolio case.

"Are you going to finish Sam's book?" Leah asked.

"It'll be the last thing I do for him."

"Maybe it *is* a good idea. Take some time, get away for a bit."

Sadie nodded. "You've been a great friend, Leah. A better one than me."

"No, that's what friends are for. I'm here for you. I'll watch your house while you're gone, until you get back."

Sadie shook her head. "It's been sold."

Leah's brow arched in shock. "What? I didn't know you were selling." There was an accusatory edge to her voice.

"Look, I can't explain this. Things are different now. Now that Sam's…gone."

"Yeah, but running away won't solve anything. Jesus, Sadie! What's happening to you?"

In her anger, Leah backed into the recycle bin. When she looked down and spotted the wine bottle, she shook her head in disappointment. "Sadie, this isn't what you want—"

"Don't lecture me! I'm tired of everyone telling me how to act, what to do, how to feel. My son was taken from me, blown up right in front of my eyes. And it's my fault. So if I need to get away, that's what I'll do. If I need to drink, I'll drink. You don't understand, Leah. You never will."

Leah blinked tearfully. "You're right. I don't understand. Because you won't talk to me. You've closed me off, shut me out. And now you're drinking again? Sam wouldn't want this, my friend."

Sadie clenched her jaw. "Don't tell me what my son would want." Then she added, "Make sure you lock the front door on your way out."

Leah left without a word.

After she was gone, Sadie experienced a flash of regret.

Leah doesn't deserve this.

Part of her wanted to apologize, beg forgiveness. But that would just make things worse in the end. Leah was never going to forgive her for what she was about to do.

She strode across the room to the closet, grabbed a couple of sweaters and added them to the suitcase. She had no idea where she was going, but she wanted to be prepared. In the ensuite bathroom, she rifled through the bottles in the medicine cabinet. She hit pay dirt. Three bottles of prescription muscle relaxants and sleep aids. At least a hundred pills.

She went downstairs, making a beeline for Philip's office. The door was closed and she hesitated in front of it. There were two more things she needed. Both were on the other side of the door.

She stepped inside. Shutting the door behind her, she disregarded the mess and headed for the filing cabinet where she grabbed the last three bottles of Cabernet. She wrapped them in one of Philip's t-shirts and stuffed them into a small duffel bag that Philip used when he went golfing.

She hurried to the closet.

The cedar box was still there.

"Ok, Sadie. Now what?"

She reached for the box. It was heavier than she expected, and her hands shook as she lifted the lid. They shook even more when she touched the frigid metal of the gun. She picked up the magazine and studied it. It held a single bullet.

"I hope to God you know what you're doing."

She stuffed the gun back into the box, placed it in the bag, then searched the closet shelf for more bullets. She came up empty. She looked in Philip's desk, in the filing cabinet, in an old briefcase. Still nothing.

"Well, it's not as if you need target practice," she muttered. "How hard can it be? Point and shoot."

She grabbed the duffel bag and made for the door.

The knob turned before she touched it.

Damn!

The door opened.

"Sadie!" Leah exclaimed. "I, uh…"

"What are you doing here? I thought you went home."

Leah's eyes flitted across the room. "I was going to, but…then I remembered I left a book here."

Sadie frowned. "In Philip's office?"

"Well, I thought maybe someone moved it in here. It's not in the kitchen. Or the living room."

"What's it called? I'll help you look for it."

"Uh, don't worry about it. Actually, I think I left it in my car."

Sadie watched her friend, puzzled by her odd behavior.

Why was Leah here, in Philip's office?

The answer washed over her with tsunami force, subsiding silently, then lashing back with a vengeance.

Damn them both!

Philip must have told Leah about his hidden stash of Cabernet. And since she'd already seen a bottle in Sadie's bedroom, she'd come back to dispose of the others.

Leah said something in a low voice.

"Pardon?"

"I don't know what to say anymore," Leah said. "Or do."

"No worries."

"But I don't want things to be like this between us. Just tell me what I can do to help and I'll do it."

"There's nothing you *can* do." Sadie turned to leave, but Leah's arm shot out.

"Sadie, I…"

"What?"

The air dripped with tension.

"Nothing," Leah said finally. "Forget it."

As Sadie edged past her, the duffel bag bumped Leah's legs.

"What's in the bag?" her friend asked.

"Legal documents. Sorry, but I'm not in the mood to chat. I'm going to lie down for a bit. I'll see you to the door first."

"Fine," Leah said with an audible sigh. "Let me know if you need anything."

Sadie eyed the bag. "I've got everything I need."

∞ ∞ ∞

Just after six that evening, Philip called from prison.

"The house is sold," she told him. "I said we'd be out by the end of the month."

"No problem. I'll call a moving company. Everything's going into storage, including the furniture, right?"

Not everything.

She flicked a nervous look at the duffel bag. It sat on the table near the door. Ready, waiting.

"Yeah, put everything in storage," she agreed.

"What about your things, Sadie?"

"I, uh, haven't thought about where—"

"Just put it with my stuff. I don't mind. That way you'll have access to everything, in case either of us needs something."

"Are you sure?"

"Hey, it's not as if I'll be needing it any time soon."

Philip was right about that. He'd cut a deal and rolled over on his partner Morris, who had masterminded the embezzlement scam. With Philip's cooperation and a plea of guilty, there was no need for a trial. His sentence had been reduced from twenty to ten years.

"So you're going to stay with Leah for a few days?" he asked.

She lied. "Maybe a week or two."

There was a long pause and when he finally spoke, his voice drooped. "Sadie?"

"Yeah?"

"Will you come visit me tomorrow?"

For a second, she considered his request. "No. I need some time…away. From you, from this house, from everything."

"Fine." He sighed. "I'm sorry, Sadie. For everything."

"Me too."

"It's just that I got caught up with the wrong people. I know it changed me—changed *us*. Maybe with time we can be friends."

"Look, Philip. I'm exhausted. I need to go to bed."

"Where will you go after Leah's?"

Nowhere, Philip. I'm going nowhere.

When she didn't answer, he sighed. "Take care, okay?"

She eyed the duffle bag. "Yeah."

∞ ∞ ∞

Two days later, everything was set in place. She had managed to pack up their personal items on her own. Leah had offered, but Sadie declined. She didn't want any witnesses to her crumbling life.

That morning, a moving truck pulled into the driveway. On both sides were the words, *Two Small Men with Big Hearts*. She had seen the trucks around town, and the name had always made her smile.

But not this time.

She showed the movers into the house, thankful that they'd pack up everything else. Exhausted, she flopped on the sofa.

"Let me know when you want me to move," she said, stifling a yawn. "Mind if I turn the radio on?"

The younger of the two men grinned. "Not at all."

She reached for the remote on the coffee table, turned on the stereo and searched for her favorite station, one she never got to listen to when Philip was around.

"Ah, 91.7 The Bounce," the older man said.

"Unless you want me to change it to country."

"No!" both men said in horror.

A smile flashed on her lips. Until she realized what she was doing. Berating herself for taking any pleasure in life, she watched as they packed away her entire existence.

And Sam's.

The two men wrapped, boxed and covered all the symbolic items of her life—the dishes she'd received as a wedding gift, the new microwave Philip had bought her for Christmas, the crystal rose vase her mother had given her when Sadie had completed her first year of sobriety.

"It's all going in storage?" the older man asked curiously.

She nodded.

Within a few hours, the movers were gone, along with a truckload of furniture and boxes. On the floor near the door, the suitcases and the duffle bag with the wine and gun box claimed their last stand in a vacant house that was once filled with joy, but now echoed tragedy.

It took her two trips to drag everything out to the garage. She started automatically toward the Mazda—until a silver gleam caught her eye.

Philip's Mercedes.

"This is *my* car, Sadie," he had insisted the day he'd bought it. "I'm the only one who drives it. Understand?"

She moved closer to the car.

Did she dare?

"Well, Philip's not going to use it," she muttered.

She popped the trunk of the Mercedes and pushed aside a plastic bin filled with files and letters. She wedged the two suitcases beside the bin and dropped the duffel bag on the passenger seat. Then she climbed into the car and flicked a look at the bag beside her. The shape of the gun box was visible. Giving in to a sudden urge, she unzipped the bag, just to be sure that the gun was still inside the box.

It was.

"Okay, let's get this show on the road."

She turned the key in the ignition. The car sputtered, then purred to life. She glanced at the gas gauge and smiled.

"And a full tank to boot. Thanks, Philip."

Shifting the car into reverse, she backed down the driveway and pulled out onto the street. For a moment, she idled in front of the house, the place she had called home for over six years. Against her will, her gaze was drawn upward, to the empty window on the second floor and she saw Sam's pleading face pressed against the glass.

"I know you're not real. Goodbye, Sam."

She sped away without a backward glance.

∞ ∞ ∞

"Here," she said, handing Leah three keys. "Car, house and storage. After you get my car, just leave the house key under the front doormat for the realtor."

Leah peeked over her shoulder and caught sight of the Mercedes. "I thought I was storing Philip's car."

"I decided to take it instead."

Leah blinked. "Won't he be pissed?"

Sadie ignored the question and pulled some bills from her wallet. When Leah gave her a questioning look, she said, "My car probably needs gas."

"Oh, sure." Leah gave her a wounded look. "No problem."

"Thanks."

Sadie felt the awkwardness of their conversation, but it was a necessary evil. She had to cut herself off from everyone. That was part of her plan.

"Sadie—"

"I'm sorry, Leah. I really am. But this is what I have to do. I hope one day you'll understand. I have to go now. Make sure Philip's lawyer gets the storage key, okay?"

Leah gave a resigned nod. "Sure."

Sadie climbed into the Mercedes and drove away. It was only when she was leaving Edmonton's city limits that she allowed herself to consider the plan. She plotted the steps she would need to take, making a mental list of everything.

"Soon, Sam."

She flicked a look at the back seat, half expecting to see him staring back at her. The seat was empty. She reached for the radio, then changed her mind. She'd leave it up to fate.

"I'll drive in silence. When it's interrupted, I'll stop."

Traffic was gearing up for the afternoon rush hour as she navigated Edmonton's congested streets. Half an hour later, the traffic thinned and the bustling city was replaced by farmland. Muddy fields of dead hay lined with melting snow whizzed past, merging into a blur of endless flatlands interrupted by the occasional cattle farm. The silence and peace was mesmerizing.

Two hours passed uneventfully.

Before long, the sign for Edson appeared. She drove through the small town with barely a second thought. But then further down the highway, the traffic stalled.

The silence had ended.

17

Flashing lights and sirens greeted her.

Sadie eyed the bag on the passenger seat. "Crap!"

Obeying an orange-vested traffic cop, she slowed the Mercedes to a crawl behind a wood-paneled station wagon filled with tattooed rockers who, between the four of them, had every facial feature pierced with shards of metal. One young man in the back seat turned his head, grinned at her and made lewd motions with his spiked tongue. Ignoring him, she focused on the road.

"Come on. Move!"

A minute later, she saw the problem. Up ahead, a silver-bellied oil tanker had flipped across the meridian. Traffic was being re-routed.

She let out a frustrated sigh. "Where am I going anyway? I need a sign. Come on, Sam, show me where to…"

A crow silently watched her from the top of a wooden post. Suspended below the bird was a sign. Some of the words had faded, but she could still make it out.

Cabins for rent! Bat cave! Follow signs to Cadomin, Alberta.

And there it was. Her sign. Once again, fate had intervened.

She turned off Highway 16 and followed the road south to Robb. She was grateful for the lack of traffic, having seen one vehicle—an old Airstream trailer—by the time she reached the point where the paved road disappeared and was replaced by gravel.

"Could you possibly be any further from civilization?"

In response, the winter tires of the Mercedes kicked up rocks and chunks of melting ice. At the sound of scraped metal, she flinched. "Philip is not gonna like this."

She guided the Mercedes down the road until she passed the small town of Cadomin. Following the signs for the cabin rentals, she navigated the craters in the road and slowed for a sharp curve.

A horn blasted.

"Jesus Christ!"

A black pickup with tinted windows came out of nowhere. It careened toward her, forcing the Mercedes precariously close to the ditch.

She slammed on the brakes.

As the truck sped past, she saw the silhouette of a man in a cowboy hat. He waved an angry fist at her.

"Moron!" she yelled, even though he couldn't hear her.

In the rearview mirror, she watched the truck disappear in a trail of dust. She tried to calm her pounding heart, all the while wondering why she even cared if he had hit her. It would have been a blessing.

But you're not finished Sam's book, her conscience urged.

Easing back onto the road, she drove another fifteen minutes before the scenery changed from flat, treed land to a silver ridge of rolling hills in the distance. Far beyond them, the Rockies rose majestically, so pale that they seemed to float in the sky.

She slowed as she reached another intersection.

A sign read, *Cadomin Cave, left. Harmony Cabins, right.*

She steered right and headed down a narrow lane that wound through the trees. A few minutes later, she saw a small, hand-hewn log cabin. A sign staked into the ground near the front door designated the building as *Harmony Cabins Office.*

She let out a sigh of relief, parked the car and climbed out, stretching her aching legs.

"Travel a long way?" a voice rasped.

Sadie jumped.

A pencil-thin elderly woman with dove-gray hair sheered short like a man's stood near the side of the cabin. Her faded jeans, thin winter jacket and tanned, freckled face was evidence of someone who spent a lot of time in the great outdoors.

"Cat got your tongue?" the woman asked, swinging an axe back and forth in one hand as she walked.

Sadie stepped backward with a gasp. "I, uh…"

"You're from the city." Near black eyes squinted.

"Edmonton."

The woman reached into her jacket pocket and pulled out a slim pack of cigars. She shook one out. With the flick of a lighter, she lit up, the smoke streaming from the corner of her mouth.

"And you need a cabin," she said.

Sadie nodded. "For the rest of this month and next."

The woman took a thoughtful drag and broke into a fit of coughing.

The rattle that erupted from her chest sounded like an old freight train on a rickety track.

"There's four days left this month," she said. "I'll just charge you for May. I got one cabin left, so you're lucky. Hasn't been cleaned though."

"That's okay," Sadie said quickly. "I'll take it."

The woman turned and swung the axe hard. It sliced into a stump beside the cabin door with a resounding *thwack*. To Sadie, it was as if the guillotine of fate had just come down upon her head, slicing it clean off.

"I'm Irma," the woman said, holding out a bony hand.

Sadie shook it carefully. "Sadie O'Connell."

"Nice to meet you." The woman flicked a look at the Mercedes. "You head into town, be sure to drive careful. This road ain't the safest, 'specially with Sarge hogging it."

"He doesn't by any chance drive a black pickup, does he?"

Irma scowled. "That old heap belongs in the junkyard."

Sadie bit back a reply as her eyes latched onto a prehistoric cattle trailer parked behind the office cabin. The trailer looked like a candidate for the junkyard too. But she didn't say so.

"C'mon, Sadie. I'll show you your five-star accommodations."

Irma chuckled at her own joke, then motioned her down a well-trodden path. After a few yards, the woman paused to discard the cigar.

"You're in the last cabin," she said, using the toe of her boot to grind the cigar into the ground. She immediately lit up another one. "Want one?"

"No, thanks. I don't smoke."

"Yeah, me either." Irma grinned, displaying a mouthful of neglect and decay. "Every day I swear I'm gonna quit. Then I pick up another one. It's a bitch when you make the devil your best friend."

Sadie swallowed. "Sometimes he's your only friend. You know what they say, the devil you know..." Irma's dark eyes burned into her, so she changed the subject. "Is it this one?"

Ahead, a cabin with daisy curtains sat amidst bare poplars.

Irma shook her head. "Yours is down by the river."

"There's a river back here?"

"Well, it's more of a creek in some parts."

As they passed the cabin, Sadie noticed a sign over the back door. It had one word on it. *Peace*.

She smiled. "Nice name."

"My daughter's idea. She named all of 'em. Said it would make 'em more appealing." Irma looked over her shoulder. "Does it?"

"Well, it works for me," Sadie said, amused.

"Mine's the office—Harmony," Irma said. "Then there's two in back of mine. Hope is close to the road and Inspiration is deeper in the woods. Down here, there's Peace and Infinity."

Sadie stumbled. Had she heard right?

"Infinity?"

Irma smiled. "It's got the best view. You can see forever."

"And that one's mine?"

"Yup, only one I got left."

Sadie drew in a deep breath. The coincidence was disturbing.

"No such thing as coincidence," her mother always said.

"Does your daughter live with you, Irma?"

"Naw, she used to run this place. Before she and that husband of hers ran off to the *big city*. Country life just wasn't good enough for her once she met up with him. 'Specially after them kids were born."

"How many grandchildren do you have?"

"Five. Brenda just couldn't stop once she got going. Popped 'em out every year for five years." Irma snorted. "Now she's home-schooling 'em. In Edmonton, for Pete's sake, where there are schools galore. Lord almighty, that girl's missing a few brain cells." She shook her head slowly. "Takes after her dad, God rest his wretched soul."

Sadie gave her a sympathetic look.

"Clifford's dead," Irma stated. "Used to ride the bulls at the Calgary Stampede. He was trampled eighteen years ago by old Diablo. Blind as a bat, that one."

"The bull?"

Irma grunted. "No. Clifford. Man couldn't see his own feet."

They continued walking, both lost in thought.

"So you're out here alone?" Sadie asked finally.

"Yeah, just me and them oil workers. They're in the other cabins. Lucky for you, they're gone most days. They come back to sleep, unless they get a room in town. But they shouldn't bother you none. Probably won't see anyone, 'cept me."

Sadie paused near an uprooted tree stump. A steady stream of ants paraded along the top of an exposed root, while a bulbous-bellied arachnid crept closer to the buffet line. She shuddered when the spider snatched up a lagging ant and consumed it.

Survival of the fittest, she thought.

Irma beckoned Sadie onward. "We're almost there."

The path descended toward the thinning trees, then opened upon a winding river that trickled over rocks, around tree stumps, weaving and undulating through the woods and past the last of the defiant snow banks. In some places, it was so narrow that the water was shallow. In other areas, the river was dark and deep.

To Sadie, the view was breathtaking.

"This here's Kimree River," Irma announced.

An April breeze skipped over the water, caressing Sadie's face in a cool mist. The air was scented with a soft marshy odor—not really unpleasant, just damp and earthy. It made Sadie think of the Screaming Eagle Cabernet.

"You can keep following this path through the woods or take them stairs." Irma pointed to rough planked steps set into the icy earth. "It's easier to walk by the water if you're carrying stuff. But watch yourself. Those steps are slippery."

On the river's shore, they walked side-by-side in mutual silence. There were no other buildings to be seen, no people. Once Irma returned to her own cabin, Sadie would be on her own.

Just the way I want it.

"There it be," Irma said proudly.

Approaching from the side, Sadie got the first view of her new home. The log cabin was perched on a dry grassy knoll, its light gray roof glittering in the sunlight. Two windows on the side were framed by heavy white shutters and a small veranda with its front end on supports hung out over the river. A blue and white Coleman cooler, two worn wooden chairs and a table made from a bulging tree stump were the veranda's only adornment, except for a dwarf cedar in a terracotta pot near the sliding door.

Sadie surveyed her new home. It wasn't much to look at from the outside and most likely not much better inside. But the soothing trickle of the river would make it bearable.

"You weren't kidding when you said the cabin was down by the river," she said, chuckling.

"Just better hope we don't get a flood," Irma warned.

"A flood?"

"Yeah. A few years back, we had us a flash flood and lightning that lit up the sky for miles. Now *that* was a storm. If we get another one like that, you'll wanna close them shutters. Out here, we get some awful winds and the thunder gets pretty loud."

They climbed the steps that were set into the earth and walked around the side of the cabin. Stacks of firewood, covered with a faded forest-green tarp, were piled up against one wall. A fishing rod and an oil lamp lay abandoned in the grass.

Dismayed, she turned to Irma. "There's no electricity?"

"Not out here, dear. That gonna be a problem?"

"I need to charge the battery for my laptop and my cell."

"Well, I was gonna get me one of them fancy-schmancy generators like Sarge got, but I just can't afford it. Sorry."

"That's okay. I'll charge my things in town then."

Irma grunted. "Not in Cadomin, you won't. There's only one store, and that Louisa's a real control freak. She wouldn't even let you piss in the washroom 'cause you're an outta-towner." She wiped a grimy hand across her forehead. "You'll have to go to Hinton, to Ed's Pub. Just tell him I sent ya. He's my brother."

As they approached the back of the cabin, Sadie spotted the sign above the door. *Infinity*. It made her think of Sam, of their nightly ritual.

"Sam," she whispered.

"Who's Sam?" Irma asked. "He your man?"

"No, uh—"

"It's okay, dear. He won't find you here."

Sadie's head jerked. "What? No, you've misunderstood me."

Irma shook her head. "Naw, I don't think so. Why else would you be out here in the middle of nowhere? It's in your eyes, dear."

"What is?"

Irma ambled to the door and slid a key into the lock. "When I first saw you, I said to myself, 'Irma, that girl's running from someone. Or something terrible.' I can see it in your eyes. And eyes don't lie." She peered over her shoulder. "But it's none of my nosey ol' business."

The old woman pushed on the door. It groaned in rebellion, then swung open, releasing a cloud of black flies.

And the scent of death.

"Sweet Mary, Mother of Jesus!" Irma said in horror.

Sadie gagged. "What's that smell?"

18

Their footsteps disturbed the mud-covered floor, and a waft of fine particles—dust, cobwebs and God knows what else—ascended into the stale air, along with the overpowering stench of decomposed chicken skin, rotten fish and sour milk. It reminded Sadie of the time the garburator had clogged and backed up into the kitchen sink.

Irma rushed to open the windows. "I'm so sorry, dear. Got caught up in Brenda's problems and kept putting off cleaning this place. I guess I shoulda come sooner."

Yeah, I'd say so, Sadie wanted to say. But she didn't.

Holding her breath, she crossed the room, flung back the heavy curtains and opened the sliding door onto the veranda. Light illuminated every grimy corner, and for a moment, she was tempted to turn around and leave.

And go where?

Her mouth curled in disgust as her gaze swept across the clutter of unwashed dishes piled in the sink and on the chipped laminate counter. In one corner, a garbage can contained two fat, fly-infested fish heads and a slimy, black clump of salad greens—lettuce or spinach, maybe. A two-burner Coleman stove sat on the counter near the sink, a cast iron pot abandoned on top of it. She peered inside, then wished she hadn't. Something brown and furry covered the bottom of the pot, a feast for the black flies, fly larvae and wriggling white maggots that squirmed over it.

She fought hard not to gag. "When did the last tenant leave?"

"About two weeks ago. He was in a hurry, that one."

"I'd be in a hurry too, if I lived in a place that smelled this bad. The guy was a slob."

She stared at the jumble of sheets on the sofa bed and the dirty socks and stained t-shirts scattered across the floor.

"Why didn't he take his stuff?"

Irma shrugged. "Said he had a family emergency."

"Was he an oil worker too?"

"Naw, some kind of doctor, he said. But I tell ya, I wouldn't want him sticking no needles into me. He had the shakes real bad." Irma eyed the room. "I think he needed a woman in his life."

"Or a maid," Sadie muttered.

"Let me show you around, dear. Over here's the bedroom."

When Irma opened the door. Sadie was shocked by the state of the room. It was pristine, clean, not a thing out of place. Only a fine layer of dust on the double bed, dresser and nightstand. There was a small closet with no doors at the foot of the bed and a rectangular window facing the woods lined the exterior wall.

"Guess he didn't use this room much," Irma said needlessly.

"I wonder why."

"Dunno. Bed here's more comfortable than that sofa. Don't make much sense to me." She puttered over to the closet. "There's a bin with fresh linens on the shelf. Just drop off all the other laundry to me and I'll get it done at Ed's."

Back in the main part of the cabin, Sadie noticed something in the corner of the living room that she wasn't expecting. An old grandfather clock. A sinewy cobweb swayed above it, and although the glass in front was missing and there were a few chips in the wood, the clock seemed to be working.

"My mother-in-law's," Irma said with a scowl. "Can't stand the noise myself—even though the damned thing doesn't go off every hour like it's supposed to. It won't bother you, will it?"

"I don't think so."

"Good, cause I ain't moving it."

Irma showed her the bathroom, just off the kitchen. It boasted an antique clawed tub and a sparkling new toilet that betrayed the rustic simplicity of the rest of the cabin.

"You have to heat the bath water," Irma said ruefully. "No hot water tank."

"That's fine. I'm just thankful there's a toilet."

Irma lifted her chin. "I still say, there ain't nothing better than communing with Mother Nature in a good ol' outhouse."

You can keep your outhouse, Sadie thought. *And the nature.*

"I can't believe your last tenant left you with this mess."

Irma chuckled deep in her throat. "*Your* mess, dear." She handed Sadie the key to the cabin. "There should be a lantern in every room and oil under the sink. You gonna be all right bringing in your things? I know it's a long haul."

"I can handle it."

"Yes, you've had more to cope with." A frail hand rested on her shoulder. "Like I said, it's in your eyes, dear."

Sadie frowned. She'd have to be very careful around Irma.

"There's a fireplace for cooking and heat," the old woman continued. "You know how to get a fire going?"

Sadie nodded.

When it came to campfires, she was the queen of sparks. Three years at Girl Guides and a montage of rugged camping trips with her father and brother had taught her well. The few times she and Philip had taken Sam camping, she was the one who always got the campfire going—much to Philip's chagrin.

Irma paused in the doorway and lit up another cigar. The sweet smoke mixed with the potpourri of offensive odors, masking the stink...slightly.

"Before I leave, Sadie, you got any questions?"

"Just one. How do I store perishable food?"

"There's an old freezer outside my cabin. You're welcome to use it. It's not plugged in, but I pack it with ice every other day. Actually Ed does. And it's still cold enough at night to keep things mostly frozen. Label your food though, or them men'll eat it on you. Oh, and there's a root cellar under *that*." She pointed to a worn square rug near a wing chair. "Good for storing vegetables."

Sadie apprehensively eyed the rug. There was no way on earth that she was going to crawl around in a musty cellar. God only knew what was growing down there.

"Course, you can always use the cooler outside for the small stuff," Irma added. "I'll bring you a few things. And if you need anything else, you come see me."

"I'll be fine, Irma."

"I'm sure you will. But these woods can get pretty lonely and quiet. 'Specially for city folk. None of them all night fast food restaurants here. But we don't got that god-awful traffic either."

"Speaking of traffic, is my car okay by your cabin?"

"Yeah, just lock it up at night. We don't get fancy-schmancy vehicles like that here. And you don't wanna tempt me." Irma stepped outside and flashed her yellow teeth. "Always wanted to drive a sports car."

When the woman was gone, Sadie felt strangely bereft. One look at the interior of the cabin made her realize she'd soon be far too busy to feel lonely. With hands on hips, she surveyed the room in dread, her mouth turned down in a scowl.

"Bet you miss your central vac and Swiffer now."

She found a box of garbage bags under the kitchen sink. The sheets, towels and men's clothes went into one. The garbage and three occupied mousetraps went into another. When she opened the door half an hour later to toss the bags outside, she discovered a box with cleaning products, a bulky blue flashlight with a sticker that read *Infinity Cabin*, fuel for the stove, a map and a note from Irma.

Sady,

Here's some stuff to cleen with. If you need more just holler. The flashlight has new battries. The maps new, shows the root to Hinton and Edson. Hinton's closer. Best place for grocries is the Sobeys store. Ed's Pub has got the best liver and onions, fried chicken and fish and chips in town.

P.S. On account of the mess and you cleening it, just pay half of May.

Irma

Almost two hours later, Sadie fell into the armchair, exhausted, but satisfied. The interior of the cabin glistened, the reek of decay replaced by a fresh orange scent.

"You can't stop now, though," she said with a sigh.

It took two trips to the Mercedes to get the suitcases and duffle bag. She debated on leaving the gun behind in the car, but had visions of Irma hotwiring the Mercedes and taking it for a joyride, police in tow.

The gun box found a home under the double bed.

For a fleeting moment, she allowed herself to think of its purpose. She examined the floor, envisioning it splattered with—

Her head snapped up. "Don't go there."

She was famished. The only thing she'd eaten all day was a stale donut and coffee from a gas station. She opened a cupboard, inspecting the three cans—two tuna and one kidney bean. Her stomach rumbled and she glanced at the wall above the sink. The floral clock read *6:10*. Lots of time to get to town and back.

Securing the cabin door, she trekked through the woods, climbed into the Mercedes and headed for Hinton. Following Irma's map, she gripped the steering wheel, eyes dead ahead on the narrow gravel road. Thankfully, nobody tried to run her off this time.

She geared down to take a blind corner. The road unexpectedly dipped low, running parallel to the river. As she crossed a rickety wood bridge, she slowed the car to a crawl to admire the view. The river trickled a few feet below, cutting a path through the still-frozen ground, around a bend and out of sight. To her right, a gray roof protruded between the trees.

She squinted. It was her cabin. She was sure of it.

A sudden movement on the opposite bank caught her eye.

A man in a black cowboy hat and knee-length black jacket stepped from the woods. He made his way toward the river, crouched down—to wash his hands, maybe—then stood and stretched leisurely.

She was sure he was the owner of the black truck.

Sarge, Irma had called him.

The man's head jerked toward the bridge. Toward *her.* He was too far away to make out his face, but she got the impression he wasn't smiling. Then he darted off into the bushes.

"Great!" she muttered as she sped away. "He'll think I'm a nosy neighbor. Oh, wait, Sadie, you are."

She left the bridge behind, thankful that the man lived on the other side of the river. The last thing she needed was visitors.

∞ ∞ ∞

Ed's Pub was quiet, except for the flamboyant '50s style jukebox that belted out Johnny Cash's *Walk the Line* and the handful of customers—some just out of high school—who played pool on the three billiard tables at the far end. At a table near the door, two primitive-looking men dressed in soil-stained coveralls were drinking beer, their shaggy gray beards brushing the wet surface of the table. They looked like gold diggers from the Klondike era.

When they noticed Sadie in the doorway, their mouths dropped and the whispering began. She ignored them and headed for the bar, where a man stood with his back to her, rearranging bottles against a mirrored wall. When he turned, she knew without a doubt that he was Irma's brother.

"What can I get you, young lady?" he asked.

"Iced tea, please."

The man's mouth curled into a wrinkled smile. "What's a pretty gal like you doing in a place like this?"

She laughed. "I see originality isn't one of your strong suits."

"Hard to be original when you're a twin."

The man was a carbon copy of his sister, right down to the thin build, short gray hair and dark eyes. But where Irma's eyes were serious and knowing, his did a dangerous two-step with flirtation as he leaned down, grabbed a glass from under the counter and filled it with iced tea.

He slid it down the bar toward her. "So what are you doing here, 'sides making my heart race?"

"I'm finishing a project. I needed a peaceful place to do it, so I'm staying in one of your sister's cabins." As an afterthought she added, "And if I'm making your heart race, perhaps you forgot to take your medication this morning."

"Tsk, tsk," he said, chuckling. "You're a sharp one."

"That's what my husband says."

Ed's face fell and she nearly burst out laughing.

"Dang. You're married?"

She wasn't about to tell him about the pending divorce, so she held out a hand. "Sadie O'Connell."

"Ed Panych." He smiled. "Well, Sadie O'Connell, you just dashed away all my hopes."

She grinned and patted his liver-spotted hand, the one with the plain gold band on his ring finger. "I'm sure your wife will be relieved."

A hoot erupted from behind her. The men at the table were brazenly listening to every word.

"Yeah, Martha's gonna be very happy, Ed," one of them shouted. "Don't think shc'll wanna share ya. 'Specially since you just celebrated your fiftieth."

Ed waved his hand in the air. "Ah, shut it, Bugsy. I was just teasing the lady."

Bugsy muttered something to his companion. The other man let out a thunderous laugh that echoed in the small pub.

"Sorry," Ed told her quietly.

"Nothing to be sorry about." She grinned, raised her voice. "If you weren't married, Ed…"

"Ah, I'm way too old for a pretty gal like you," he mumbled, embarrassed. He hobbled into the back room.

Sadie sat at the bar, lost in her thoughts as a nostalgic sadness swept over her. Shc'd always thought shc and Philip would grow old together, celebrate their fiftieth *and* sixtieth anniversaries, and sit in matching rockers on the back porch.

She took a long swig of her tea, draining the glass.

None of that was going to happen now.

Ed reappeared. "Another?"

"No thanks." She rifled through her purse and dropped some coins on the bar. "Irma said you wouldn't mind if I plugged in my laptop once in a while. To charge the batteries. Is that okay?"

"You can charge my battery anytime!" Bugsy shouted.

"Hey!" Ed bellowed. "None of that, you mangy mutt. Or I'll cut you off."

Bugsy clamped his mustached mouth shut.

"You need electricity, you come see me," Ed told her. "Tell Irma I'll drop off more ice in the morning."

She nodded, then stepped outside. Above her, the sun shone brightly, glaring off the pavement and anything metal, but the air still held a chill.

There wasn't much activity in Hinton. Traffic was light, only a few cars. The Sobeys grocery store was right across the street, down a block, so she decided to leave the Mercedes in the pub parking lot. The walk would do her good.

She strolled across the street in no hurry, enjoying the quiet, when a childish laugh made her look over her shoulder. A group of teens walked toward her, the girls giggling, while the boys tried to look cool. One young man—a punked-out kid with black and violet streaked hair—walked with a swagger that would've put John Travolta to shame. His arm was thrown over the shoulders of an anorexic blond waif who looked destined for a stint at a rehab center.

"You gotta problem, lady?" the boy asked as they passed by.

"No," she mumbled, wondering if Sam would've talked like that.

She hurried into Sobeys.

Half an hour later, she headed back to the car with four bags of groceries and a bag from the nearby liquor store. Setting them on the ground, she unlocked the passenger door and maneuvered the bags onto the seat and floor.

As she left the parking lot, a black pickup sped around the corner in front of her. It barreled past, kicking up rocks into her windshield, and screeched to a dusty halt near the pub doors. She watched in the rearview mirror as a man in a cowboy hat and long jacket jumped out of the truck. Even with his back to her, she knew it was Sarge, the idiot who had almost run her off the road earlier.

And my neighbor from across the river.

She was tempted to charge in after him, give him a piece of her mind, but she chickened out. Confrontations weren't her thing. She had proven *that* more than once.

19

"There. That should do me for a while."

Sadie placed the last package of meat into the decrepit freezer outside Irma's cabin. The rusty hinges of the lid screeched when she lowered it. She winced and looked at Irma. The old woman was leaning against the cabin, puffing on a cigar as usual.

"Ed said he'll drop off more ice tomorrow," Sadie said.

Irma grunted. "So...did he make a pass at ya?"

"Just a little one."

"No such thing as a little pass, dear. Ed's a lecherous old fool. Don't know how Martha puts up with him." Irma lifted a bony shoulder. "He's harmless enough, though. All mouth."

"I can take care of myself, Irma."

"Don't doubt that for a minute. Just watch out for the townies. 'Specially Sarge."

"You mean the idiot in the black Ford?"

Irma broke into a fit of coughing. "Yeah, him."

"Does he live nearby?"

The old woman's eyes shifted to Sadie's left hand. "No ring?"

"Divorced. Well..." She gave a quick shrug. "Almost."

"No such thing—"

"As almost divorced," Sadie finished for her.

"Coulda used you for a daughter," Irma mumbled. "You're quicker than most." She pursed her lips thoughtfully. "Sarge lives across the river and down aways. He's not married, if you were gonna ask."

Sadie blushed. "I wasn't."

"Sure you weren't. Stay clear of him, dear. He's a loner and not much of a people person. 'Specially since his wife and kids died."

"That's too bad."

"A terrible tragedy, it was."

"There's a lot of that going around. Did you know them very well?"

Irma took a drag on her cigar. "His wife Carrie was friends with my Brenda. 'Cept Sarge didn't want her talking to anyone, even when he was in Iraq. Kind of possessive, that man. And them kids…poor little lambs."

"What happened?"

"House caught on fire four years ago, night of the big storm. Only Sarge made it out alive. He lost everything. Carrie. The kids. Had no insurance either. The man was so sick with grief after that, he wouldn't even level the house."

"What'd he do?"

"Left it standing—what's left of it. Ed said he won't let no one near it, or on his property. That Sarge…he's just not the same. Can't imagine what it must feel like, not being able to save the ones you love."

Sadie shuddered. "I can."

"Oh, dear. I'm so terribly sorry. Your husband?"

"My son." Sadie turned away, heading back to the car. "I can't talk about it. Sorry."

"People tell me I'm a good listener, dear."

"Thanks, Irma. But I'm here to forget."

Praying she hadn't offended the woman, she grabbed the remaining bags from the car and lugged them down the path until she reached the steps. She navigated them carefully, then enjoyed the short walk along the riverside. At the cabin, she juggled the bags and unlocked the door. After she put away the canned goods and stored the fruit and veggies in the cooler, she made a quick tuna salad sandwich, bundled herself in a wool blanket and settled into one of the wooden chairs on the veranda. She nibbled on the sandwich and stared out over the river, watching the sleepy sun begin its leisurely descent.

She thought of Sam, of how much he loved the outdoors.

"You would've loved it here, Sam."

She didn't know how long she sat there watching the peaceful ripples on the water and thinking of Sam. He was never far from her thoughts. Sometimes she felt almost smothered by malignant, cancerous guilt.

She shook off the shadows. "I miss you, Sam."

A few water birds scrabbled on the shore, occasionally calling out to each other. The chill air caressed her face, making her feel alive and free as she inhaled the fresh aroma of pine and spruce, and listened to the resonance of Mother Nature. All around her was pure peace. *Heaven.*

She shut her eyes…just for a moment.

∞ ∞ ∞

"Cawwww!"

Sadie's eyes flew open. She gasped.

A crow perched on the wood rail of the veranda, its beady eyes no more than three feet from hers. It stared at her, unmoving.

"Go away!"

It cocked its head to one side, giving her an inquisitive look.

"Stupid bird, shoo!"

She waved her hand, but the bird just hopped up and down. Bizarre behavior for a crow, she thought.

The crow emitted another raspy shriek.

"Just so you know, I hate birds," she said. "Except when they're Shake 'n Baked." She grinned stupidly.

"Squacckkk!"

She stood up, expecting her movements to dislodge the annoying pest. It didn't. She was tempted to approach the bird, but then common sense took over. Why would she want to?

Maybe it's diseased. Maybe it has the bird flu.

Ignoring the crow, she stretched. Then she frowned. The fading light made her take a second look out over the water.

It was late. She must have been asleep for a while.

"Must be the country air."

She strolled toward the sliding door, mindful of the crow. It watched her every move, and that was unnerving, so she released a pent-up breath and stepped inside. She lit an oil lamp and checked the clock on the wall. *8:55.*

With a sigh, she glanced around the room, then set to work building a fire. There was no TV to watch and nothing much to do except sleep. But she was wide awake now and somber thoughts were creeping into her mind.

What she needed was a drink.

She reached into a cupboard, her hand hovering over the three bottles of red wine. "No. I'm saving you."

She moved toward the cooler and pulled out the bottle of Jamaican rum that she'd bought in town. She opened it and poured a healthy shot into a beefy silver travel mug, topping it up with a can of cola. Then she curled up on the sofa in front of the fireplace.

The rum went down fast. Maybe too fast. Its smooth undertone made her warm, tingly. She enjoyed its mind-numbing effect, a welcome reprieve from the constant torment and grief that followed her everywhere.

She got up, poured another drink. "I'm in control this time."

Philip's condemning voice came to mind. *"Don't delude yourself,*

Sadie. You're an alcoholic. One drink is never enough."

"I can stop whenever I want, Philip. I just don't want to." She chuckled. "Is talking to yourself a sign of insanity?"

Only if you answer back.

That's what her mother always said.

Sadie finished her second mug of rum and poured another.

The glow from the lamp and the simmering fireplace radiated over the wood walls, enveloping them in a golden sheen. Yet the room lacked something tangible, something she couldn't quite put her finger on.

"What's missing here?"

The answer came to her, clear as glacier water.

She awkwardly made her way to the bedroom. When she returned to the living room a few minutes later, she had three framed photographs in hand. A small one of Sam found a place on the coffee table, and one of Leah decorated the oval table by the armchair.

Sadie gave her friend a sad smile. "I'm sorry, sistah friend."

Leah would hate her when this was all over.

Gripping the portrait of Sam in her hands, she swallowed hard. "You need a special place, little man." Her gaze was drawn to the empty space above the crackling fire. "Perfect."

She slid a chair over to the fireplace, then hung the portrait above the mantle. Sam's sweet smiling face stared down at her, full of life. She kissed the tips of two fingers, pressing them against Sam's lips.

"I love you," she said softly.

A floorboard creaked behind her.

She flicked a look over her shoulder and almost toppled from the chair. Crossing the room, she listened. Nothing. She looked at the bedroom door. It was closed. Had she left it that way?

She let out a huff. "Talk about paranoid, Sadie."

She pushed the door open, stepped inside and set the lamp on the dresser. Dropping to her knees on the hardwood floor, she lifted the bedspread and peeked underneath.

The cedar box was still there.

As she stood, her head swam and she hit her hip on the corner of the dresser, almost knocking over the lamp.

She giggled. "Just a bit tipsy, are you?"

A faint childish laugh echoed nearby.

Sadie jumped. "Hello?"

Another soft laugh.

She flew out of the bedroom, holding the lamp high above her head. She spun on one heel in the middle of the cabin. "Sam?"

No one was there.

Half a dozen uneven steps brought her to the picture window in the kitchen. All she saw outside was a pea soup fog hugging sturdy tree trunks and a sliver of moon winking between menacing clouds.

Thud!

She turned. A distorted shadow moved on the other side of the draped sliding door. Darting across the room, she yanked back the drapes. "Who's out there?"

It was so black outside that she could only make out the shape of the table and two chairs. Other than that, the veranda was unoccupied.

She slid the door open and stepped outside.

Right into a fresh mound of dirt.

She immediately spotted the culprit. The dwarf cedar lay on its side, clumps of loose soil spilling from the terracotta pot.

A shiver snaked up her spine.

Someone or something had knocked it over.

Uneasy, she peered into the shadows, but nothing moved except the river. The air was nippy, but still. No wind. Near the woods, a semi-sheer curtain of fog hung suspended a foot off the ground.

A streak of white flitted through the trees.

She squinted. "What the heck?"

Something *was* moving out there.

Her jacket hung on a peg just inside the door. She grabbed it and shoved on a pair of boots. Then she fumbled for the flashlight on the shelf above her head.

"Okay," she whispered. "Where are you hiding?"

There!

She moved cautiously across the veranda, the light from the flashlight arcing toward the woods. Whatever the white thing was, it flickered, then reappeared behind a tree a few yards away.

"Hello?" she called. "Who's there?"

A small figure shrouded in a ghostly white cloak emerged from the swirling fog. A child. Sadie couldn't make out if it was male or female. She saw no distinct features, not even an arm or leg.

Another giggle wafted in the air.

She started for the steps that led down to the grass and headed for the figure in white, praying it was human.

What if it isn't?

Emboldened by the alcohol coursing through her veins, she swept the light over the woods.

"Irma! If that's you, this isn't funny."

The figure was gone.

"Maybe you imagined it. Maybe you're just drunk." She let out a derisive snort and tottered back up the steps. "What were you thinking, Sadie? That you could just go gallivanting off into the woods after a gho—?"

Something lay in front of the sliding door.

Sadie drew the lamp closer. "A chocolate bar?"

Perplexed, she picked up the chocolate bar and examined it. It was her favorite. A Hershey bar.

But who would leave her such a treat?

20

When she awoke the next morning, there were two things on her mind. Finding the bottle of Tylenol and getting rid of the god-awful taste that caked her tongue.

"Potty mouth," she mumbled, scrabbling from bed.

She shivered and pulled her robe over the ratty oversized t-shirt that she'd slept in. Then she stepped into the small bathroom. She jolted to a stop when she caught sight of her haggard reflection in the mirror above the sink.

"You...look...*horrible*."

She gingerly touched her matted hair. The short curls were foreign to her and she couldn't decide if it made her look older or younger. Regardless, she looked terrible.

"Thank God Philip can't see you now."

She leaned closer, pushed up her bangs and traced the angry scar that gleamed high on her pale forehead—compliments of The Fog. Her eyes—the same blue as Sam's—stared back at her, faded and tired, with bags underneath that were so puffy they resembled Barbie pillows.

"Looks like you're in for more than a bad hair day."

Since she hadn't unpacked her suitcases yet, she grabbed the tube of toothpaste left by the last tenant and squeezed some on her finger. Then she spread it over her teeth and tongue, spitting out the excess. Reaching for a towel, she cursed under her breath when her hand met air. She'd forgotten to put out the fresh linens.

She wiped her mouth on her sleeve. "Time to make this place a home, even if only temporarily. You could use a few things."

The Sadie in the mirror scowled. "Like a plastic surgeon."

After a quick sponge bath with warm water from the kettle, she pulled on the jeans from the day before, a fresh t-shirt and a sweater that her mother had knitted. In the main room, she added some kindling and wood to the smoldering embers in the fireplace. Then she made a pot of coffee and began the daunting task of unpacking, all the while trying to ignore the chocolate bar that sat on the counter.

Had Irma left it for her?

In the bedroom, she lugged one suitcase onto the bed. She filled three drawers of the dresser. The other suitcase was dragged into the kitchen. She opened it and removed the art supplies and the manuscript for Going Batty. The plastic container with the clippings found a spot on the coffee table.

Battling a raging headache, she flopped in the armchair and picked up Leah's photo. Her best friend—her *soul sistah*—grinned back at her, hazel green eyes sparkling wickedly. Above her head was a colorful birthday banner.

The photo had been taken three years ago, the night Sadie had thrown her a surprise party. Leah had suspected nothing when Sadie had asked her over for dinner, claiming she couldn't get a babysitter for Sam. Some of Leah's friends and family hid in the kitchen before she arrived, but once Leah was seated on the sofa, they ambushed her. Leah looked as if someone had told her she'd won the lottery. The only sour grape was Philip's unexpected arrival after a business meeting was cancelled, but thankfully he retreated to his office. Meanwhile, Leah got so plastered she had to rest upstairs while Sadie entertained the guests. Then she left early, saying she wasn't feeling well. Sadie had to convince Philip to drive her home.

A bittersweet sigh escaped. "Home."

She had no home. Not anymore. Life in Edmonton seemed so far away, so long ago.

She returned Leah's photo to the table, then leaned back and closed her eyes. "Now what are you going to do?"

The answer arrived with a knock on the back door.

Irma stood on the porch, a navy toque pulled over her head and ears. "Thought you might wanna go for a walk with an old widow."

"If you want to walk with a divorced writer," Sadie said wryly as she grabbed her jacket.

A cigar found its way to Irma's mouth and a puff of smoke was released into the crisp air. "What do you write, Sadie? Slutty romances?"

"No, that's my friend's area. I write mysteries mostly."

"Ah," Irma said, nodding. "Nothin' better than a good mystery."

An image of the Hershey bar crossed Sadie's mind.

"I found a chocolate bar on the veranda," she blurted.

Irma snickered. "Must be from one of the men. You got yourself an admirer."

They walked through the woods in silence. Sadie felt surprisingly at peace and her headache rapidly disappeared. Rejuvenated from the country air, she got up the nerve to ask Irma something.

"You said you have grandchildren. Are they visiting now?"

The cigar dangled from the corner of Irma's mouth. "They're in Edmonton. Won't be coming back until summer holidays. Why you ask?"

Sadie stared at the icy rocks beneath her feet.

Should she tell Irma what she had seen the night before?

"What about the oil workers?" she asked. "Any of them have kids visiting?"

Irma flicked the stub of her cigar into the river. "Nope. The nearest kid is in town." She eyed her suspiciously. "Why all this interest in kids?"

"I thought I saw someone. In the—oh, never mind." Sadie groaned. "I think I drank too much last night." But she couldn't help thinking about the Hershey bar she had tossed into the cooler.

"Liquor'll kill you," Irma stated, lighting up another cigar.

They strolled along the riverside, chatting about the weather and inconsequential things. As they neared a curve in the river, Sadie noticed a pattern of half-submerged, flat-topped slabs of rock in the water, maybe two feet apart. They looked too perfectly aligned to be natural.

"Stepping stones?" she asked.

Irma eyed the rock bridge. "Yeah. Sarge put 'em in. So his kids could visit Brenda and me. It's faster than taking the road around."

Sadie stopped at the river's edge and framed her eyes with a hand to block the piercing sun.

"The water looks pretty high," she noted.

"The spring runoff. See that boulder?" Irma pointed across the river. "If the water ever gets to that orange line, it's time to pack it in and head for Cadomin. Before the bridge to town gets washed out."

Sadie eyed the river. "How often does it flood?"

"About once every three or four years."

As they headed back, Irma's words echoed in Sadie's mind. She'd have to be vigilant. A flood would ruin her plans.

"Thanks for the walk," she said when they returned to Infinity Cabin.

Irma squinted at her. "You're too young to be cooped up inside, dear. Life is meant for living. Don't forget that." With a wave, she puttered off down the path.

For the rest of the afternoon, Sadie worked on editing the manuscript for Going Batty. Until her laptop died. Frowning, she pushed it aside and made a mental note to go into town the next day to charge the battery.

Supper was a generous chef salad with shredded Canadian cheddar and bacon bits. Seated on the sofa in front of the fireplace, she thought of Philip. He would have been appalled if she had made a salad for supper. He was a meat and potatoes man. Take-out was bad enough. And God forbid if they didn't eat at the dining room table like *normal* people.

A mischievous grin crossed her face. "To hell with normal."

Once the dishes were washed, she stretched out on the sofa and stared into the flames. It was hard to resist the impulse to dive right in. In one hand, she held her cell phone. In the other, a glass of rum and cola.

"You can do this. Just one drink tonight."

First, she called her parents. They were concerned about her, naturally, but she assured them that she was taking a little holiday and getting lots of rest.

"Well, you sound okay," her father said.

Strangely enough, she felt okay. In fact, her mind had never been clearer.

"I love you, Dad. Mom too."

After a few words with her mother, she hung up and stared at the drink in her hand, swirling it leisurely.

"One more call," she said, gulping back the last mouthful.

But she just couldn't dial the number.

Half an hour later, she finished off her third glass, then made the call. After explaining to the man on the other end that her call was urgent—a family matter—she was put on hold while a guard located Philip and escorted him to the phone.

"Sadie? I was wondering when you'd—"

"I just wanted to tell you that you won't be able to contact me for a while, Philip. I don't have electricity."

"What do you mean? Where are you?"

She took a long, thoughtful sip of her drink.

Where was she? *Nowhere.*

"Sadie, are you all right?"

She stared at Sam's photo. "Yeah, I'm fine."

"I heard you took my car." His voice was tight, measured.

"How the heck—? You talked to Leah. Why?"

"It doesn't matter why. Listen, Sadie. I left some important documents in the trunk. Do you think you can pack them up in a box and mail them to me right away?"

"Sure," she said, miffed. "Next time I drive into town."

"Damn, I almost forgot. There's a problem with the starter."

"The starter?"

"On the car. If it goes you'll have to take it in to a shop."

There was a long pause.

"Sadie, do you need—?"

"No. I don't need anything. I have to go now."

"Wait! Tell me where you—"

"My cell's dying," she lied. "Bye, Philip."

She hung up on him, wondering why she had called him in the first place. Maybe so he wouldn't file a missing person's report or send someone after her. She was tempted to call Leah, give her a piece of her mind. But courage wasn't her middle name.

In the end, she found comfort in another glass of rum.

No mix.

∞ ∞ ∞

A bird screeched beyond the bedroom window without a care for the occupant inside. As the raucous chatter found its way into Sadie's restless dreams, she rolled onto her stomach and dragged the blanket over her head.

"Cawww!"

"Shut up!"

As soon as the words were out of her mouth, she moaned and scrunched her face. Her head throbbed, as if crushed in a vice. She threw back the blanket and when she opened her aching eyes, she was relieved to find that the bedroom was pitch black, except for a faint glow from the battery-operated clock on the nightstand. The double-backed curtains in the window were a godsend. But they didn't muffle the bird's incessant squawking.

She sat up on her elbows and glared at the clock.

"Two in the morning? You've got to be kidding."

Another shriek brought her stumbling to her feet.

"Okay, enough already!"

She lit the lamp, then strode toward the window, intending to shoo the irksome pest away. Hooking a finger between the drapes, she inched them back and was startled by the darkness that loomed beyond. What freaked her out most were the two black eyes on the other side of the glass.

The crow—the *same* one from last night—stared at her.

"Get lost!" She knuckled the window, but the bird didn't move. "Jesus! What's with you?"

Another shriek from the crow. Then its beak struck the glass.

Tap! Tap!

She resisted the urge to strangle the damned thing. Barely.

"Don't tempt me, you black-feathered minion."

She was about to step away from the window when something

shifted in the bushes near the back stairs.

"There *is* someone out there."

Instantly, she was dead sober. She strode into the living room where she slipped into her jacket and boots. Then she tiptoed to the sliding door.

"Spy on me, will ya. I don't think so."

The door slid open unhindered and she stepped out onto the veranda, accompanied by a flashlight and an iron fire poker. She waited. Then she took a tentative step forward and the beam of light swept across an object near her foot.

A card-sized white envelope.

She picked it up and examined it. It was blank. No address, no stamp, nothing. Cautiously, she opened it, but it was empty.

She thought of the chocolate bar in the cooler.

"What the heck's going on?"

Someone giggled nearby.

Sadie flicked off the flashlight. There was enough light from a slice of moon and its reflection off the river that she could see her way down the steps to the grass below. She crept around to the back door, sticking close to the side of the cabin. Her boots made quiet crunching sounds, and she held her breath, hoping that whoever was out there wouldn't hear. Even in the crisp night air, her palms grew sweaty and it became difficult to hold the poker handle. She almost dropped it twice.

She paused, listening.

There was a faint rustle of foliage not far from where she stood. Then a quicksilver flash of white whipped through the trees.

The ghost child from last night?

She moved onward with reckless persistence, one boot planted in front of the other. When the ground dipped, she lurched forward, her foot hovering for a second in midair. Thrown off balance, she hooked an arm around a tree trunk, spinning around it in a half-circle, like a square dancer at a barn dance.

Catching her breath, she squinted into the dark.

Where are you, damn it?

Then she saw the child—if that's what it was—half-hidden by a tree. Crouching low, Sadie waited until the white shape moved away before dashing toward the woods. She made it without mishap and leaned against a tree.

"This is crazy," she scolded herself. "What are you doing?"

She covered her mouth, partly to muffle the sound, but also to hide the mist her breath was making. Her heart thumped in her chest so loudly she was sure it could be heard.

The white shape was just ahead.

Guided by the moonlight, Sadie continued through the trees.

Six yards to go.

She peered over her shoulder to ensure that she could still see the light from the cabin. It seemed a great distance away. Still, she moved forward, the sound of the river trickling over the rocks concealing her progress. With the poker raised above her head, she took another step closer and a twig cracked beneath her boots.

Up ahead, someone muttered something unintelligible.

Sadie turned on the flashlight.

An ethereal face with wide doe eyes stared back at her.

"What are you doing out here?" Sadie asked, baffled.

21

Before her stood a young girl—eight or nine years old maybe—wearing a white bath towel over her head and body. Underneath, she had on a white cotton nightgown with a yellow peace sign on the front.

Liquid pools of blue blinked once, twice, from beneath thick, dark lashes. "I'm sorry," the girl said in a trembling voice.

"For wha—?"

A solid weight slammed into Sadie's back. The poker and flashlight flew into the air, and as she hurtled toward the ground, she flung her arms out and braced for the fall. She hit the frozen ground, knees first, and slid onto her stomach, her palms skidding, burning. She let out a pained gasp, then closed her eyes, her heart beating frantically against her chest.

It would be so easy to lie here...die here.

Footsteps tramped through the woods—away from her. She lifted her head, but saw only fleeting shadows. Her fingertips grazed cold metal. She retrieved the poker, then struggled to her feet and searched for the flashlight.

But it was nowhere to be found.

"Wait! Who are you?" She tipped her head, listening, but the woods were silent. "I won't hurt you. I just want to..."

What *did* she want?

She turned in the direction of what she hoped to God was the cabin. In the encompassing darkness, she couldn't tell. As she carefully maneuvered between bushes and trees, she paused every now and then to listen for the river. When she broke from the woods, she found herself on the beach, the cabin a few yards away. She strode toward it, throwing anxious looks over her shoulder.

Someone had attacked her. But who?

She had felt a strong body behind her, but had seen nothing, heard no one. Except the girl.

"No children around here," she muttered. "Yeah, right, Irma."

Someone living nearby obviously had a daughter.

Infinity Cabin welcomed her, undisturbed in its solitary existence. Cursing herself for losing the flashlight, she fumbled in the dark and lit the oil lamp. With determination, she strode toward the back door and slid the deadbolt into place. Staring at it, she didn't feel safe. Not one bit. So she pushed the armchair in front of the door.

"Let's see you get through *that*!"

As a final measure she jammed a broom handle against the sliding door frame. No one would be able to open it without removing the broom first. She grabbed another rum and cola and dragged the comforter from the bedroom. Then she curled up on the sofa, the poker propped up within reach.

Just in case.

∞ ∞ ∞

Morning crept into the cabin, and an ominous sound boomed through the air, then dwindled into a low drone.

Foggy-headed, Sadie sat up. She flung back the blanket and sucked in a deep breath as pain shot through her knees and hands. She stared at her palms, noting the fresh scrapes and dried blood. Her gaze went from her clothes—the same ones she had worn yesterday—to the grandfather clock, and then to the simmering fireplace.

She frowned. "Okay...why am I out here?"

The clock gonged again. It died midway, as if someone had gripped its innards in a chokehold.

Sadie looked at her watch. "It's ten o'clock and all you could manage were two gongs?" She caught sight of the chair by the door. "What the heck was I doing last night?"

She rubbed her forehead, trying to remember.

A girl! She had seen a girl in the woods.

"Or did you?"

Doubt plagued her, especially when she noticed the open bottle of rum on the counter. She staggered into the bathroom, took one look at her unkempt reflection and made a face. She picked up the hairbrush, intent on getting the tangles out of her hair, then frowned and dropped the brush on the counter.

Why bother? No one would see her anyway.

Except maybe the girl...

"You're seeing things. That's what it is. You haven't had booze for so long, you're hallucinating." She snorted. "And talking to yourself."

Confident that she had solved the previous night's events, she decided to have a luxurious bath. She had to boil water on the Coleman stove and in the fireplace—three pots at a time. It took fifteen pots of hot water and a few cold ones to fill the tub halfway. Hell, it wasn't like she had anything better to do.

Sadie soaked for a long while, allowing the past week's anxiety to melt away. She shampooed her hair, then rinsed it in the bath water. Closing her eyes, she slid underwater until she was completely submerged. She held her breath as long as she could, and when she came up sputtering for air, she was disappointed. Drowning herself was definitely out of the question.

After she towel-dried her hair, she shrugged on her jacket and reached for the sliding door. The broom handle in the track made her pause. She tugged at it, her brow furrowed in puzzlement. What was she trying to keep out?

Sweeping her thoughts under an imaginary rug, she grabbed her laptop and purse, then headed down the path. Once she reached Irma's cabin, she could hear the elderly woman singing inside. It wasn't a harmonious sound.

Sadie hesitated. *Should I invite her into town with me?*

As soon as the thought blossomed, she squashed it. Getting too involved in a friendship right now wasn't fair. Not to Irma.

The Mercedes was right where she had left it. She climbed in and the engine purred the moment she started it. The sound was comforting, and she backed the car out of the clearing and ambled onto the road. When she looked into the rearview mirror, Irma was standing near the freezer, watching her.

∞ ∞ ∞

"Back so soon, Sadie O'Connell?" Ed gave her a sly wink and set down the glass he was drying. "Just couldn't keep away from me, could ya?"

She peered over her shoulder. The table in the corner was empty. No hecklers today.

"Yeah. Plus my laptop is dead and I need to charge my cell."

"Your cell?"

She held up her phone.

"Ah," Ed said with a nod. "Never did get me one of them things. Gives you brain cancer, I hear. You be careful, young lady." He nudged his head toward the end of the counter. "Plug is over there on the post."

She thanked him, slid the laptop from its carrying case and set it on the counter. Once the laptop and phone were plugged in and charging, she settled into a stool, elbows propped up on the polished wood of the bar.

Ed slid a steaming mug toward her. "You look like you need this. Didn't get much sleep last night, did you?" His eyes strayed to her damp, messy hair and gaunt face.

"You could say that." She took a sip of coffee and let out a contented sigh. "This is heaven, Ed. Thanks. I still haven't figured out how to make coffee back at the cabin. Percolators are a bit before my time."

Ed swung a dishcloth over his shoulder. "The trick is to use a half a scoop less and a dash of cinnamon. And don't boil it too long."

"How about you just deliver me a carafe of coffee every morning," she suggested jokingly.

The grin that spread across the old man's face could have lit an entire town. "That's the best offer I've had in...well, decades." His face reddened, as if he just realized he'd spoken out loud.

Over the mug, she said, "How's the wife this morning?"

"You just had to go and spoil it," he grumbled. "Martha's doing fine. She works at the library."

He pronounced it "*lie-berry.*"

That gave Sadie an idea. She needed something to do for an hour while she waited for her things to charge.

"How do I get there?"

"Drive down to the main lights, turn south and it's two blocks past the Esso on your right-hand side."

"Is it okay if I leave these here to charge?" she asked, indicating the laptop and cell phone.

"Sure, I'm here 'til midnight. No one'll touch 'em."

A waft of cool air made her shiver. Behind her, someone had entered the pub. When she looked over her shoulder, she saw a bald man veering down the hall to the washrooms.

She turned back to Ed. "Thanks. I'll be back in an hour."

"Take as long as you like."

As she headed outside, the lyrics of *Pretty Woman* trailed after her from the jukebox. Ed's gravelly voice sang along. He sounded just like his sister. And just as bad.

Sadie drove to the 'li-berry'. In the almost empty parking lot, she slid into a spot by the door, next to a dented maroon-colored Cadillac with a vanity plate that read BUKS4U, which could have meant *bucks for you* or *books for you.*

She rolled her eyes. "Ten *bucks* says that's Martha's car."

Hinton Public Library held a modest collection of books and the walls displayed a montage of colorful posters, painted by the town's children, no doubt. The far right corner held a cozy children's nook with fluffy pastel pillows and low bookshelves. Overhead, a lifelike toy bat hung from the ceiling. A breeze—maybe from an open window—sent it fluttering the moment Sadie stepped inside. She stared at it and her mouth quivered.

"Can I help you?"

Sadie turned. A smartly dressed woman in her sixties rushed toward her, a stack of children's picture books in her arms. The woman was pleasantly rounded in a grandmotherly way, with curly gray-black hair that framed a plump face, hazel eyes and a cheerful smile. Attached to a silver chain around her neck, a pair of glasses rested against her chest. A nametag on the lapel of her jacket read, *'Martha V.'*

"I'm in town for the day," Sadie explained. "And thought I'd check out your library, Martha."

"Well, let me know if you need anything, Miss…uh…"

"Sadie O'Connell. I'm—"

The woman just about dropped the books. "Not Sadie O'Connell, the author!"

Sadie winced. "Actually…yeah, the author."

Martha's chin dropped. "Good grief! I didn't even recognize you. You look—" The woman caught herself, beamed a bright smile, then motioned Sadie to a table in the corner. "Can I get you a coffee or anything?"

"Thanks, but I think I'm all coffee'd out. I was just at your husband's pub."

Martha set the books down and settled into a chair. "Please, have a seat, Miss O'Connell. Are you feeling all right? You look a little under the weather."

Under the weather was an understatement, and Sadie knew damned well that the woman was being polite.

"I haven't been sleeping well."

"That's dreadful." Martha folded her pudgy hands primly in her lap. "So what brings you here?"

An appointment with death, Sadie wanted to say.

"I'm staying in Cadomin for a while."

A swift smile lit up the woman's face. "You know, we don't get too many authors of your status around here. Would you consider doing a reading?"

A reading was the last thing Sadie wanted to do. That meant socializing with people, lots of smiling and no time to finish Sam's book.

"I'm sorry, but I'm just passing through. I have a…deadline to meet."

Martha's smile drooped. "Maybe later then. In the summer, perhaps. Wait! How long are you staying?"

"Not long. Another month maybe."

"Well, if you change your mind..."

I won't. "I'll let you know."

"So what can the Hinton Public Library do for you?"

Sadie shrugged. "I'm trying to kill some time while I wait for my laptop and phone to charge. They're over at Ed's."

Martha rose gracefully. "Well, how about I give you a little tour, then? We have some historical memorabilia here that might interest you." She slid her glasses over her nose as they reached a wall of photographs. "This is our history wall. Hinton became a real settlement when the Grande Trunk Pacific Railroad passed through over a hundred years ago. Then in 1931, the Hinton mine opened. Ten years later, Hinton was a ghost town. Until 1955, when the first pulp mill went in." She paused, breathless. "Am I boring you?"

"Not at all."

And that was the truth. History had always fascinated Sadie, and it often found its way into her novels.

Martha tapped her mouth with one finger. "You're staying in Cadomin, you said?"

"At Harmony Cabins."

"How wonderful. Ed's always fretting about his sister being out there by herself. Well, if you don't count those men in the other cabins. It'll be nice for Irma to have another female around."

Sadie's attention drifted to a photo of a cave. "Is this nearby?"

"Cadomin Cave, one of the major sights in these here parts. It's not too far. Just follow the signs on your way back to the cabins. It's well marked."

Sadie sighed. "My son would've loved it."

"Unfortunately, it's closed. Can't go in until May, or you'll disturb the bats and kill them."

"Kill them?"

"If they wake up too early in the spring, they'll starve to death," the woman explained.

Sadie moved on to the next set of photos. Many were restored black and whites with curled edges, illustrating the progression of the town's development. In some of them, hardworking farmers plowed fields of barley and hay.

"Agriculture always was very important in this area," Martha continued. "It still is. Many Hinton families have been farmers for generations."

Farther down, a row of women's portraits graced the wall.

Sadie nudged her head in their direction. "Who are they?"

"All of our librarians."

"How come you aren't up there?"

"I'm just a volunteer," Martha said, looking disappointed.

Sadie patted her arm. "I'm sure you're much more than that."

She studied the portraits, admiring the artists' techniques. It was interesting to see the progression of fashion styles and facial expressions. In the earlier paintings, the women stared straight ahead, unsmiling. Halfway down, that changed.

But it was the portrait on the end that made her pause.

The woman in it looked vaguely familiar. She sat in a green plaid wingback chair, her pale blond hair swept up into a loose bun. She had a half-smile on her face, but it didn't reach her vacant blue eyes.

Martha cleared her throat. "Did you know Carissa?"

"She looks…familiar. I think I've seen her recently."

"That's not possible." Martha's response was quick, almost breathless.

"No, I'm sure I've met her. Somewhere."

"She's passed on."

"Passed on?" Sadie caught sight of the mournful expression in Martha's eyes. *Dead, you idiot. Like Sam.*

"Yes. Four years ago."

"Hey, you wouldn't happen to have any of my books here, would you?" Sadie asked, adroitly changing the subject.

"Of course we do," Martha replied proudly. "We have all of them. It was Carissa who discovered you, when she went to the city the year before she died." She waddled over to a bookcase and pulled a hardcover from the shelf. "Here we go. *Deadly Diamonds*. It's one of my favorites."

Sadie dug in her purse for a pen. "Can I sign some of them?"

"Really? Oh my! That would be wonderful."

On the title page of *Deadly Diamonds*, Sadie wrote a dedication to the library and signed her name. Then she signed three more books and handed them to Martha.

"The rest have been checked out," the woman said. "Of course, we'll have to keep an eye on these, make sure no one checks them out *permanently*." She let out a girlish giggle and her double chin shook. "Maybe I can get you to sign one of mine sometime."

"I'll be back in two days. My laptop doesn't last much longer than that. I'll try to stop by."

"I'm here every day 'til two."

Sadie peeked at her watch. Her laptop had been charging for almost an hour. It was now past one, past lunch. She was getting hungry. Time to go home and dig into the bologna and cheese she had in the cooler.

"Well, I'd better get back to the pub." On the way out, she remembered something. "Martha, what kind of car do you drive?"

"A red Caddy," the woman replied. "Why?"

"Just curious."

Sadie smiled. Ten bucks! She'd get takeout.

At Ed's Pub, she picked up her laptop, phone and an order of fish and chips. She bought a small yellow flashlight—the only one in stock—and extra batteries at the hardware store and drove back to the cabin. Passing the sign for Cadomin Cave, she felt an impulsive urge to turn down the road, but remembered Martha's warning—the cave was closed until May.

She thought of the blond-haired librarian in the photo.

It wasn't until she was eating her lunch on the veranda that she remembered where she had seen her before. The woman had been wearing a teal jacket.

And holding Sam's hand.

22

In a daze of confusion, she struggled with the impossible idea that she had seen a dead woman.

And Sam.

"So, what—you're seeing ghosts now? I see and hear dead people. Great. Now what would Philip say to that?" At the sound of her husband's name, she recalled something. "Damn!" She'd forgotten to mail his documents.

Intent on packing everything into a box and bringing it to town the following day, she hurried down the path and unlocked the Mercedes. She grabbed the plastic bin, hefted it to her hip and slammed the trunk. Then she started back, walking cautiously, since she couldn't see her feet.

By the time she reached the cabin, she was covered in a thin layer of sweat and every muscle in her arms ached. She pushed aside the back door with her hip, realizing too late that she'd nudged it a bit too hard. The door hit the inside wall. Then it rebounded back at her and threw her off balance. The bin flew out of her hands and upended on the ground, scattering papers, binders and file folders everywhere.

"Shit!"

Startled by her unusual outburst, she covered her mouth and giggled. Leah was right. Swearing *was* liberating.

"Shit, shit, shit!"

Grinning, she swept the mess of papers and files into a pile, and as she dumped everything back into the bin, a plain white envelope caught her eye. It was addressed in block letters to Philip. At his office. Besides the fact that it had no return address, there was something peculiar about the envelope, but she couldn't put her finger on it.

She opened it.

The letter had one paragraph of typed print and was dated over two years ago.

Philip, it began. *Leave me alone! I told you that night was a mistake. It can never happen again. Ever! I will never forgive myself if Sadie finds out.*

It was signed *L.*

"LaToya," she said, scowling. "I knew it. Just another notch in Philip's belt."

Since there was no time to surrender to jealousy and regrets, she tucked the letter back inside the envelope and tossed it into the bin, which she dropped on a kitchen chair and hastily put out of her mind.

She spent the afternoon outside on the veranda, painting and soaking up the warm sun. The drawings had evolved to watercolors, and time flew by as she lost herself in her work.

"Soon you'll be done, Batty."

More and more, she caught herself talking to the comical little rodent on the paper. Around four o'clock, she finished shading the entrance of a forbidding cave and she would have continued painting, but a strong breeze made her look up. The sapphire sky was being gobbled up by ravenous charcoal clouds.

"Damn. Time to pack it in."

She brought everything inside, and the moment she shut the door, the wind kicked up, howling in rebellion like a toddler in a full-blown temper tantrum. Immediately, the skies unleashed a torrential downpour that pounded the roof. Between the rain, wind, crackling fire and occasional sickened gong from the grandfather clock, Sadie felt as though she were sitting front row at a symphony that was seconds from an earsplitting crescendo.

Since there wasn't much else she could do, she curled up on the sofa with a mug of hot chocolate and a photo album. It was the perfect time to do something she had been putting off for weeks—a melancholy but necessary trip down memory lane.

Taking a deep breath, she flipped open the album.

Her mouth lifted. "You were so tiny, Sam. So perfect."

The photo had been taken in the hospital the day Sam had been born. His eyes were open and his skin emanated a healthy blush. She remembered how her heart had ached for nine months, wondering if he'd be born healthy or if she'd miscarry like the others. After Sam was born, she kept asking the nurses, "Are you positive he's okay?" They assured her that he was.

"He'll be bringing home girlfriends soon enough," the doctor had said with a chuckle.

Sadie had believed him.

The next page showed Sam on his chubby little knees, a line of drool hanging from his smiling, toothless mouth. He was crawling to Mommy. Another photo showed Philip sleeping with a colicky Sam next to him. None of them had slept much that night.

Sadie turned the page and giggled. She had taken the picture a few months before Sam had turned three. He was sitting on the bathroom floor, an open box of tampons scattered in front of him. By the time she had discovered him, he had devilishly unwrapped every tampon and was throwing them like darts at the door.

The next page held one of her favorite photos. They had taken Sam to Galaxyland Amusement Park at West Edmonton Mall. All three of them were happy in the photo, especially Philip, who was grinning from ear-to-ear. He looked so relaxed and boyish as he stood on the carousel behind the black stallion that Sam rode. Sadie stood next to him, after asking a young girl to take their photo. It was a rare moment when they had been a *real* family.

Sam had brought them all together. Once upon a time.

She sighed. "What happened to us?"

The last page in the album held photos taken a few months ago. On Valentine's Day, at the parade downtown. People were lined up on both sides of the street. Sam's class had gone there on a field trip, and Sadie had volunteered to meet them there and help. The moment he had spotted her in the crowd, Sam had beamed a smile and blown her a kiss. That's the second she snapped the picture.

Sadie blew a kiss back. "You'll always be my Valentine, Sam."

Her smile froze. She squinted at the photo. There was a man in the crowd. It would be difficult to miss him. He was dressed in a clown suit. He didn't look exactly like Clancy, but there was something about him that set off alarms. Perhaps because while everyone was watching the parade, he seemed to be watching Sam.

Since the photo was too small to make out any details, she rushed to her laptop and opened up the file where she had saved all the family photographs. Chewing her bottom lip, she scrolled down until she found the one of Sam at the parade. She enlarged it until it filled the screen.

She let out a muffled gasp.

Although his face was half hidden by shadows, the man was definitely staring in Sam's direction. Unsmiling. Intense. Familiar.

And holding six red balloons.

"Gotcha, you *bastard*."

∞ ∞ ∞

Seated at the kitchen table with an oil lamp and the fireplace for light, Sadie tried to eat her supper, but she barely tasted the chef salad she made. She picked at it, unable to get The Fog out of her head. He'd been watching Sam for weeks, maybe months, plotting his abduction, and she hadn't had a clue.

She had to get the photo to Jay, and there was only one way she could do that without having to drive all the way back to Edmonton.

Digging through her purse, she found Jay's card. Under his office phone number was an email address.

"Tomorrow," she murmured.

She glanced at the bin on the chair across from her. LaToya's letter lay on top, mocking her. She reached for it, then hesitated, resisting the temptation to read it again.

Her purse rang.

Without thinking, she retrieved her cell phone and flipped it open. "Yeah?"

"Are you okay, Sadie?" Leah's voice was tentative, distant.

"I'm fine."

"I was…worried about you, my friend. You left so suddenly."

Sadie didn't know what to say, and she didn't feel like explaining herself. Not even to Leah. Or anyone, for that matter.

"So…" Leah said. "How's the book coming along?"

"I'm almost done. Maybe another week."

"Want me to come keep you company, wherever you are?"

She was hinting, trying to get information from her, but the last thing Sadie wanted was company. She was already a bit pissed at herself for getting friendly with the locals. Irma, Ed, Martha…they were all nice people.

Too nice to be exposed to what I'm planning.

"Sadie?"

"I'm not ready for company. I have stuff to take care of."

"Why are you pushing me away?" Leah's voice trembled. "I'm your friend, or supposed to be. But ever since Sam—"

"Look, I can't talk about this right now. I'm sorry that things are the way they are." *But they just are.*

Leah tried again. "Friends are supposed to stick together in bad times. You know I'm here for you. Any time, day or night. If you need to talk, just call me." Quiet desperation echoed in her voice.

"I have to go now, Leah. Don't worry about me. I'll be fine."

Sadie hung up and turned off her phone. To preserve the battery, she told herself. In actuality, she didn't want any more interruptions.

Annoyed by Leah's call, she washed the dishes and wiped down the counters. When she was done, she picked up the rum bottle, intending to mix a stiff drink. It held less than half an ounce.

"No point in wasting it."

She drained the rum and wiped her mouth with the back of one hand. Then she tucked the empty bottle in the cupboard, out of sight.

Philip's Cabernet teased her, calling out to her.

"No way. I'm saving *you* for last."

Resolved to a night without the comfort of an alcohol-induced sleep, she slumped down on the sofa, stared into the fire and tried to look at the positive side.

"At least you won't see ghost girls if you're sober."

An hour later, she was bored. With nothing better to do, she sat at the kitchen table and caved in to the seductive pull of LaToya's letter. She read it again, wondering why it felt so wrong. Afterward, she sorted through the folders and placed them in neat piles, her gaze skimming over them. They were legal documents, nothing exciting.

Until she found a letter that Philip had written two years ago, but never mailed.

Dear L.,

I can't stop thinking about you. I know you wanted it just as much as I did, so don't bother threatening that you'll tell Sadie. I'll tell her you led me on, seduced me. After all, you kissed me first. Sadie will never look at you the same way again. Especially if I tell her about Sam. I'm looking forward to your next birthday party, and I'm sure I can arrange to drive you home again.

Philip.

Sadie reread the last line. "What the hell?"

The truth hit her, hard and fast.

She swept aside the piles of paper until she found the first letter, the one she'd thought LaToya had sent to Philip. Then she snatched up her purse, rooting around for a sympathy card she'd received at Sam's funeral. She set the card and letter side-by-side, her eyes widening in horrified realization.

She let out a pained gasp. "What?"

There it was. All the proof she needed. Philip's name, in capital letters. Exactly the same as the card. That's what had teased at the corners of her mind, something subliminal daring her to recognize Leah's writing.

A cry ripped from her throat. "No! Not them!"

Sordid thoughts raced through her mind, taunting her, each competing for her attention. Philip had driven Leah home and they had sex. Her husband and her best friend. Betrayal cut her like a knife, resisting at first and then slicing clean through her heart.

Philip and Leah.

She bolted from the chair and paced the cabin. Clenching her hands, she pounded on the counter. "Damn you, Philip, you fucking asshole!" She gritted her teeth. "And damn you, Leah. You were supposed to be my best friend."

Leaving the oil lamp burning on the table, she walked in a haze toward the bathroom. The bottle of sleeping pills waited on the counter. She shook two out and swallowed them dry. Then she made her way to the bedroom. In the dark, she climbed into bed and curled up into a ball.

It wasn't long before her despondent sobs filled the room.

23

Sadie didn't wake up until almost lunchtime. After a mug of instant coffee, she grabbed her purse and laptop, then made her way down the path. When she reached the Mercedes, she climbed in and turned the key in the ignition. The car let out a gravelly sputter. Then it died.

"Not now, damn it!"

It took two more attempts before the engine finally caught.

The drive to Hinton was uneventful, and Sadie kept her mind off Leah and Philip by thinking of the photograph of the clown and Sam.

"Nothing will bring you back, Sam," she said to the empty back seat. "And they'll probably never find The Fog. But I can't just ignore it. I have to tell someone. Then it's out of my hands."

"Time to charge up already?" Ed asked when she entered the pub.

"Actually, I need to ask you something."

Ed smiled. "Ask away, dear."

"Is there wireless Internet somewhere in Hinton?"

He gave her a startled look. "Yeah, Cuppa Joe's. It's a coffee shop by the liquor store. There's a big sign right out front. Can't miss it."

"Thanks."

Ignoring the concerned looks he threw her way, Sadie said goodbye and sped off down the road. Just as Ed said, a sign advertising free wireless Internet with the day's special brew sat on the ground in front of Cuppa Joe, a tiny cafe with four tables. The boy behind the counter gave her a vacant stare when she asked about Internet.

"You gotta order coffee though," he said. "Vanilla okay?"

"Whatever you've got," she replied, handing him a five dollar bill.

A minute later, she had her laptop open on a table and the photograph of Sam and the clown was sent via the Internet fairy to Jay's computer. The Styrofoam cup of coffee was still on the table, untouched, when she left.

Before heading home, she took a detour to the liquor store and bought another bottle of rum—the largest she could find—and a case of cola. A cashier wearing a University of Alberta t-shirt eyed her suspiciously and seemed shocked when Sadie brought out a VISA card.

"I'll have to see some I.D.," the girl said, chomping on a mouthful of pink bubblegum. "We've had lots of fake credit cards lately."

Sadie slid her driver's license across the counter.

Gum Girl scrunched her face. "Doesn't look like you. Your hair's a lot shorter now and you—"

"And I'm having a bad hair day. I know."

The irony was Sadie hadn't even bothered to brush her hair that morning. Or her teeth. She hadn't bathed or put on any makeup either. In the past month, she'd lost at least fifteen pounds, maybe closer to twenty, and her clothes hung loosely on her thin frame.

Gum Girl moved with the uninspired zombie-like speed of a young person who had nowhere to go and nothing better to do than breathe. Even that seemed to take some effort.

Finally, she handed back the cards. One at a time.

"Do you want that in a paper bag?" the girl asked, pointing to the rum.

"No."

Sadie snatched the rum and cola, then strode toward the exit. She was almost out the door when a gunfire pop sounded behind her. Startled, she jumped, nearly dropping the bottle. When she turned, she saw the girl peeling sticky pink gum off her mouth.

"Sorry," Gum Girl said with a giggle. "Jeesh. You look like someone shot you or something."

Sadie opened her mouth to reply, then clamped it shut.

In the car, she flipped down the visor and gazed into the mirror. "Okay, the verdict is in, folks. Sadie O'Connell, New York Times bestselling author, looks awful. No, she looks like *shit*."

This swearing business was a breeze.

When she got back to the cabin, she called Jay.

"I got the photo," he said, sounding so far away.

"It's him, Jay. The Fog."

"We're checking into it, Sadie. There are some surveillance cameras in the area. We're hoping maybe one of them caught his license plate or the make of his vehicle. Something. We might get him yet."

"Great," she said, her voice hollow. "Better late than never, I guess."

"Sadie, we're doing everything—"

"I know." Her dull eyes wandered around the cabin and settled on Sam's photo on the wall. "But it's too late. No matter what you do, it won't bring Sam back. Will it, Jay?"

She heard him sigh.

"I'll call you as soon as we know anything," he said.

∞ ∞ ∞

Jay called late the next day with bad news.

"There's nothing on camera. We're going to canvas the streets, see if anyone remembers him. It might take a few days."

"Do what you have to, Jay."

Sadie pushed aside thoughts of The Fog. Finding him meant very little to her. She didn't want to think of a long drawn-out court case, of the media frenzy it would create, and she just couldn't comprehend sitting across from the man who had murdered her son. Or testifying before a jury that she had watched him leave with Sam.

And let him.

Sometimes her thoughts drifted to Matthew Bornyk. When they did, she would shake her head. If The Fog had so brutally butchered and murdered Sam, then Cortnie surely was dead as well. Matthew was lucky, she told herself. He didn't have to watch his child die before his very eyes.

For the next two days, she threw herself into finishing the illustrations for Going Batty. Every time she glimpsed the title, she'd laugh aloud. Truthfully, it was more of a hoarse cackle.

"Yes, you're going batty," she told herself.

At night, she ignored the relentless squawking of the crow and slid into a rum-induced haze before retiring to bed. In the morning, she opened the sliding door to the veranda, wondering what strange gift would be waiting for her. After the chocolate bar and envelope, she'd found a piece of licorice. The day after that, nothing. This morning, she'd found a pen, which she dropped into a jar near her art supplies.

During the day, she wrestled with images of Leah and Philip.

With quiet resolve, she re-read Leah's letter. She sensed deep-rooted remorse in each word. But that didn't make up for betraying a best friend.

Doesn't she know that secrets only destroy things?

"For three years you pretended to be my friend, while all along you kept this horrible secret. You and Philip. You could've told me, Leah. Maybe I would've understood. Maybe I could have forgiven you. But keeping this from me? I don't understand that."

She thought of the day Leah had shown up in Philip's office, the day she was looking for a lost book.

Another piece of the puzzle slid into place.

"Ah, I bet you were looking for *this*."

She folded Leah's letter and placed it on the coffee table.

Despondent, she picked up the photo of Leah. "How could you sleep with my husband? How *could* you?" Fury gripped her and without hesitation she threw Leah's photo in the garbage can.

The walls felt like they were closing in on her.

"I need to get out of here."

So she escaped to Hinton to charge her laptop and phone.

She sat in Ed's Pub, nursing a rum and cola and doodling on a napkin while planning the last few paintings for Sam's book. It was practically finished. With a weary sigh, she leaned back in the chair and closed her eyes. The sweet sound of Sara Westbrook filtered through the room. Innocent, pure…and hopeful.

But there's no hope for me.

"You want another?" Ed asked softly.

She opened her eyes, shook her head. "You sure have an eclectic selection of songs on that thing." She nudged her head toward the jukebox.

Ed smiled. "I like to support Canadian talent."

As she stood to leave, she began to crumple the napkin, but something she had drawn unconsciously made her hand shake. The napkin was covered with infinity symbols, and one word was written in the middle.

SAM.

"My little man," she whispered.

"You okay, Sadie?" Ed asked from behind the bar.

"No, but I will be."

He gave her a sad look. "Drink's on me."

With a quick nod, she packed up the laptop and cell phone charger. Out of curiosity—and not because she intended to call anyone—she checked her messages. Two from her parents, one from Leah and four from Philip.

"Must be wondering where his *documents* are."

The phone disappeared into her jeans pocket.

Furious at not seeing what had been going on right under her nose, she sped back to the cabin. By the time she reached it, she had convinced herself that Leah and Philip had been messing around for years, that her entire marriage and her friendship with Leah was a sham.

She dropped the laptop case near the door and stormed into the kitchen. She yanked one of the bottles of Cabernet from the cupboard and poured a tall glass. To hell with Philip. She'd celebrate her freedom from him by drinking the bastard's precious wine.

Sadie smiled sardonically. "To truth and freedom."

She stopped counting after the fourth glass. What was the point? She knew what she was.

Weak.

She welcomed the giddy infusion of alcohol in her blood. It almost made her forget about her philandering husband and her traitorous best friend. It almost blocked her visions of them having wild sex. It almost made her forget about Sam.

Almost.

That night, she wished she were already dead.

∞ ∞ ∞

Terrifying images assaulted her. The bloody finger. Sam's little toe. The gruesome carnage in the tree nursery. Faces fluttered before her, mingling with snatches of angry conversation that crept through the stupor of her mind. Philip, blaming her for Sam's death. Leah, doubting her decision to remain silent about seeing The Fog. Her parents, embarrassed by her drinking. They all pointed a finger in Sadie's direction, accusing her.

"It's all your fault," they shouted.

Then she saw *him.*

The Fog.

He skulked in a shadowed corner of the cabin bedroom, his eyes gleaming in the dim light cast by the oil lamp simmering beside the bed. When he stepped into the light, his face was painted like Clancy's.

She whimpered and backed up against the headboard.

"Shh," he whispered, as if comforting a child.

"Stay away from me!"

He paid no attention and moved soundlessly toward the bed. He held up a hand brandishing a gleaming butcher knife, and in the other hand, two small blue and white marbles rolled in his palm.

But they weren't marbles. They were eyes—Sam's eyes.

Sadie stared at them, horrified. "Sam?"

"Your son is dead." The Fog's mouth moved closer, rotting breath spilling from him like raw sewage. "Now I'm going to carve you into pieces. Little bloody pieces."

As the knife swiftly arced downward, she squeezed her eyes shut and screamed. "No!"

A breeze wafted over her. But that was it. No searing pain, no agonizing death. Just silence.

When she opened her eyes, he was gone. Confusion swept through her. Where was he? Hiding in the shadows?

She reached out and touched the oil lamp.

It was cool.

The Fog had been nothing more than a hideous dream.

"But it seemed so real."

A sob caught in the back of her throat and she shivered uncontrollably. Then she frowned. *Why is it so cold in here?*

With a grunt, she sat up, her eyes fastening on the one thing that was out of place.

The open window.

She thought of the night Sam had been taken, the night that had been filled with signs—if she had only seen them. His window had been open too, just like hers was now.

But the Fog isn't here. So who's playing tricks on me?

She felt like a participant in a demented game of cat and mouse, and she had no illusions—she was the mouse. And she was sick and tired of playing.

"What do you want from me?" she moaned.

Every inch of her body tightened. Her hands clamped into fists and she wanted to pound something. Someone. Philip. Leah.

Him.

"No more!" she screamed. "No fucking more!"

With a deep breath, she leapt from the bed. Then she reached up and slammed the window shut. Outside, the moon shone above the trees, its crescent shape radiating a hazy light. A glistening fog floated above the ground. She stared at it, wondering if that was what had inspired her nightmare.

She leaned her forehead against the cool glass.

Nothing stirred outside.

But someone opened my window.

"Well, there's no way in hell you're going back to sleep now."

She fumbled for her robe. Blinded by the dark, she made her way through the gloomy living room and approached the fireplace, where glowing embers pulsed ever so faintly. She felt for the kindling in the basket on her left. When she tossed a few pieces in, sparks licked the undersides of the wood. She placed two logs on top, but they merely smoldered and crackled, laughing at her. Knowing they'd catch sooner or later, she squinted at the two windows, the sliding doors and the back door.

"By the time I'm done, this cabin'll be locked down like Fort Knox," she muttered. "But first, I need a flashlight."

She trailed her fingers along the coffee table, searching for the flashlight she had bought in town. All she met was empty space.

"I'm sure I left it here." *It must have fallen.*

Her hands swept the floor.

Nothing.

"What the heck did you do with it?"

A glaring light blinded her.

With a shriek, she jumped back, her heart racing.

"Looking for thith?"

24

A boy of about six with closely shaved hair sat cross-legged on the sofa. Covered by a blanket, he watched her with a curious expression in his fathomless eyes.

He held something in his hands. "You want it?"

It was the blue flashlight. The one Irma had given her. The one Sadie had lost in the woods.

She shook her head, confused.

It was happening again. The hallucinations. The boy was a figment of her insane imagination. Or a mirage, compliments of Philip's blasted wine. But she hadn't had that much to drink. Had she?

"What's your name?" the boy lisped cheerfully, as though it were perfectly normal for him to be sitting in her cabin in the middle of the night.

She swallowed hard. Figments of imaginations weren't supposed to talk, or be heard.

The boy huffed. "Lady, dontcha talk?" He waved the flashlight and the light bounced off the walls.

"There are no children here," she said.

The boy grinned. "Yeth there are. Me."

She crept forward. With an outstretched hand, she reached for the phantom boy, positive that she would touch his cheek and—*poof*—he'd vanish into thin air.

But he didn't vanish. Her hand met soft skin.

She snatched her hand back. "Who are you? And what are you doing here?"

The boy didn't answer. Instead, he slid off the blanket, revealing a pair of navy-blue and light gray striped flannel pajamas.

She frowned. "You should be home in bed. It's late."

"My thithter made me come," he said.

She stared at the boy, her mind reeling. What kind of sister would make her little brother wander around the woods at night?

"She wanted me to give you something," he continued with a soft lisp. "She was gonna come herself, but Father sent her to the dungeon because she got out the other night."

Jumping to his feet, he shoved a hand deep into his pants pocket and pulled out something round.

"Your sister sent you out in the middle of the night to give a complete stranger an *onion*?" She gaped at him. "Do your parents know you're here?"

"Father's sleeping. We're not supposed to go outside unless he's with us."

"Then he'll be very worried if he finds you gone. Let's get you home." She moved toward him.

"But I don't want to go."

The fear in his eyes made her breath stop. It reminded her of how Sam reacted when Philip got angry with him.

The boy started sobbing. "Don't make me go back. *Pleathe!*"

Alarmed, she scooped him up in her arms and hugged him close. His warm body felt good, like he belonged.

Like Sam.

She mentally slapped herself.

This boy is alive and safe. And he's not Sam.

As the boy's sobs subsided, she sank down onto the sofa.

"It's okay. We can stay here. Just for a bit. Okay?"

The boy sniffed. "'Kay."

She stroked his shaved head. "My name is Sadie."

"A-Adam."

"Where do you live, Adam?"

The boy flicked a look at the sliding door.

"Ah, across the river," she guessed.

He nodded, his wet eyes staring up at her. About to say something, he opened his mouth, like a hatchling waiting to be fed. Abruptly, he changed his mind and clamped it shut.

"How about some hot chocolate," she said, sliding him onto the sofa.

"Got any *marthmallowth*?"

She grinned. "Jumbo ones."

After she lit the lamp, she prepared the hot chocolate on the Coleman stove. From the corner of her eye, she studied the boy sitting in the shadows. Adam was small and thin—and deathly pale. No wonder she had thought he was a ghost.

"Is it ready yet?" he asked, bouncing on the sofa.

"Almost."

Minutes later, they were sitting side-by-side, sipping hot chocolate and staring into the fire. Neither of them said a word.

Sadie knew she'd have to take him home eventually.

But not yet.

"This is *so* good," he said, plopping a melting marshmallow in his mouth. "Ashley's gonna be jealous. Hey, wanna hear a poem she taught me?"

"Sure."

Adam grinned. "One fine day in the middle of the night, two dead boys got up to fight. Back-to-back, they faced each other, drew their swords and shot each other. A deaf policeman heard the noise, got up and shot the two dead boys. If you don't believe this story's true, ask my blind uncle. He saw it too."

"Well, that was....interesting," she said. "But maybe next time Ashley could teach you something nicer."

Even in the faint light, she could see that he was a handsome boy. Somewhere out there was a lucky mother.

"Won't your mom be worried about you?" she blurted.

A shadow crossed Adam's eyes. "She's dead."

"I'm so sorry, honey."

Unfazed, he held out his mug. "Can I have some more?"

When she returned with a full mug, Adam was asleep on the sofa. Curious, she watched him, taking in the chocolate mustache smear above his contented smile and the gentle rise and fall of his chest.

There was no denying it. She had a real live boy in her cabin.

"Great," she mumbled. "Now what am I supposed to do?"

The grandfather clock showed four in the morning.

She looked at Adam. Maybe it would be okay to let him sleep, take him back in a few hours. Hopefully, she could get him back before his dad woke up. But she'd sure like to have a few words with his sister, whom she suspected was the girl she'd seen in the woods.

Sitting beside Adam, she recalled something that he had said earlier, something that hadn't registered because he had distracted her with the onion.

"Father sent her to the dungeon."

Surely, the dungeon wasn't referring to the basement.

She couldn't fault a father for not wanting his kids to talk to strangers or go out at night. But why were they seeking her out in the first place? Why were they giving her gifts? And who had tackled her in the woods—their dad?

Her eyes wandered to the sleeping boy.

What will happen when his dad discovers he snuck out?

She tugged the blanket over Adam's shoulders. When he inched forward in sleep and placed his head in her lap, she held her breath, startled by the close contact. A yearning deep in her heart made her eyes water. She closed them, conscious of Adam's small, warm hand sliding into hers before she too fell asleep.

When she awoke a few hours later, he was gone—along with the gray blanket. She would have thought she had dreamt it all, if it weren't for the blue flashlight on the coffee table and five items lined up on the kitchen counter. The chocolate bar, envelope, licorice, pen and...an onion.

"You and your sister are very weird, Adam."

Without hesitation, she slid the wrapper from the bar, crumpled it and tossed it in the garbage can.

"Hot chocolate and a chocolate bar for breakfast. Lord, Sadie, you're gonna get fat."

She devoured the bar in seconds.

After she dressed, she headed outside.

"Time to have a little chat with my landlady."

∞ ∞ ∞

The interior of Irma's cabin was decorated in a wild hodgepodge of country and cowboy. Antiquated horseshoes were nailed to the rough log walls, and photographs of rodeo performers framed the doorway, remnants of her husband's career as a bull rider.

Irma tapped a photo. "This here's old Diablo."

Sadie peered at the mangy looking bull. The angry glint in the animal's eyes was fearsome and raw. Why would anyone get into a ring with an animal like that—a killer?

"Clifford loved the thrill of beating 'em," Irma murmured, as if reading her mind. "He'd dig in his heels and hold on for the ride. Until that last time. Diablo tossed him in the air like spit." She stared wistfully at the photo.

"I wanted to talk to you about something," Sadie said.

"'Bout what?"

"The children across the river."

Irma walked to the kitchen table, poured some tea and set a porcelain cup in front of Sadie.

"Have a seat," she said. "I'm a bit worried about you."

"Why?"

"I saw the liquor you've been buying. And I know the signs."

"Signs?"

Irma's mouth thinned. "Of an alcoholic. I know what it can do to you, to your mind. It destroyed my Clifford. That's why Diablo tossed him. That beast could smell booze a mile away. And Clifford's eyesight was so poor he couldn't get away. Diablo trampled him to death."

"Look, I'm sorry, but I didn't come here to talk about your husband. Or my occasional drinking. I came because of the boy and girl across the river."

"What boy and girl? I told you there aren't no kids here."

"Of course there are," Sadie argued.

Irma gave her a sad look and shook her head. "I knew the moment I first saw you, Sadie, that something awful haunted you."

"I saw them."

"Okay...then tell me their names."

"Ashley and Adam."

The cup in Irma's hand trembled. "Is this a joke?"

"Of course not. I *saw* them, talked to them. I ran into Ashley in the woods the other night. And last night Adam came to visit me."

The woman's eyes watered. "That's not true, dear."

"Why is it so difficult for you to believe me?"

Irma hastily set her cup on the saucer and tea sloshed over the side. "Sadie, you couldn't possibly have seen Adam and Ashley."

Sadie let out a frustrated sigh. "Why not?"

"Because, dear...they're both dead."

25

Irma's revelation sent ripples of disbelief through her body.

"But I saw them, Irma. I spoke to them."

"You couldn't have," the woman insisted. "Adam and Ashley died in the fire with Carrie."

Sadie gasped. "Sarge's kids?"

"Died five years ago."

Sadie slumped forward, cradling her head in her hands. One of them had completely lost their mind. She knew it wasn't Irma.

"I *am* seeing dead people," she moaned. "What's happening to me?"

"Maybe it has to do with why you're out here, Sadie. By yourself. Sam, perhaps?"

Sadie raised her head, her eyes swollen with unshed tears.

"My son. He was kidnapped…murdered. But I still see him. I dream of him all the time." Her face twisted in pain. "And now I'm seeing other dead children."

"It sounds as if you haven't let your son go."

Sadie swallowed. "How can I do that? He was my baby."

"Yes, he was. And always will be. But he's gone, Sadie."

There was a stifling pause.

"I'm so tired, Irma," Sadie whispered.

Irma patted her hand. "I know, dear. But life goes on. It has to. And your son needs you to live it—fully—with all its ups and downs, no matter what life throws at you. There's no peace in giving up."

Sadie twitched. Did Irma know about the gun?

"I-I have to get back," she said, rising swiftly to her feet. "I'm sorry, Irma."

"For what, dear?"

"For bringing my troubles to your home."

"Now don't you be fretting over that. It ain't been all roses in my life either. Us gals gotta stick together."

Sadie smiled tremulously. "Your daughter is very lucky."

"Now don't you be getting me started on Brenda," Irma grumbled. "You need anything, dear?"

"Just some uninterrupted sleep."

Irma followed her outside and lit up a cigar. "You know," she said, "even after the worst storm, the sun always comes out and shines again."

"It stopped shining for me the day Sam died," Sadie replied.

Irma grunted, then went back inside.

The path back to Infinity Cabin seemed to take longer than normal and Sadie reflected on the old woman's words. Irma was wrong. There would be no sunshine. Ever. There was nothing to live for. Sam was dead, Philip was in jail, and Leah…well, she meant nothing anymore.

She estimated she had two or three days left before Going Batty would be finished. She plotted out her remaining time, listing the things she needed to take care of. No loose ends.

Whirr…

Her pocket was vibrating.

She withdrew the cell phone and scowled at the display.

Philip.

"Shit." She flipped the phone open. "What do you want?"

"Are you okay?" He sounded worried.

"Yeah. Why are you calling, Philip?"

"Leah's worried about you. I thought you were going to stay with her." Pause. "Where the hell are you?"

"That's none of your business," she said, seething at the mention of Leah's name. "You lost the right to question me when you started sleeping around." *With my best friend.* "Is that the only reason you called me?"

"No…I, uh, was hoping you'd come visit me."

"Why would I do that, Philip?"

She heard him sigh.

"Look," he said. "I know I messed up. And I know I don't deserve your forgiveness, but I need to talk to you."

"I'm done talking. We have nothing more to discuss."

"Sadie, I know you have it," he said in a tight whisper. "I know you have the gun."

Her breath lurched to a stop. "Why do you think I have it?"

"Because it wasn't in my office when you packed up."

"How would you—?" She broke off, fuming. "Leah."

Her friend hadn't been after the bloody bottles of Screaming Eagle Cabernet. Or the letters. She wanted the gun.

"I asked her to find it," Philip said. "To get rid of it."

"Unbelievable. Asking my *friend* to do your dirty work. Now why would she do anything for you?"

He didn't answer.

"Maybe I should ask *her*," she said sourly.

"Where's the gun?"

"I got rid of it," she said, gritting her teeth. "Along with your letter and hers."

There was dead silence on the other end.

"What have you got to say about that, Philip?"

"Sadie...I...we—"

"Save it, Philip! I don't want to hear how my husband was screwing my best friend behind my back."

"It was one time," he said, like *that* made it any better. "Three years ago."

"Yeah. The night of her birthday party."

"She was loaded," he insisted. "And all over me."

"Oh, right. So it's all Leah's fault, is it?"

"No, it's mine. I knew she was drunk and I took advantage of her. I should've walked away."

"But you didn't, Philip. You slept with my best friend. And neither of you had the guts to tell me."

Everything started to fall into place. Leah and Philip's blatant animosity, their vicious bantering back and forth, their inability to be in the same room.

"That's why you've tried so hard to get me to dump her," she said, disgusted. "You were afraid she'd confess your mutual sins."

"She would never tell you. She didn't want you to get hurt. Yes, she feels guilty. Me too. So we agreed to forget about it."

"Well, obviously *you* didn't. Her letter makes it sound as though you've been pursuing her ever since. What were you doing, Philip? Blackmailing her into having sex with you because you couldn't get it from me?"

More silence.

What could he say? She'd caught him—and Leah—just as if she had walked in on them. It pierced her to the core. Philip sleeping with Bridget, LaToya or some other co-worker was one thing. But Leah? It was the harshest of infidelities.

She thought of Leah, recalling their last stilted conversation. She had known something was off. Now she knew what. Leah was afraid that in all the chaos of Sam's disappearance, his murder and the sale of the house, the truth would come out.

Philip cleared his throat. "We never slept together after that one time. I swear it on our son's grave."

"Don't you dare bring Sam into this!" she shouted. "How—?"

"He saw us, Sadie."

She almost dropped the phone. "What the hell are you talking about?"

"Sam walked in on us."

"How could he have walked in on you if you were at her—?"

The air was sucked from the room.

"I assumed it happened when you drove her home," she said, dazed. "But that's not true. Is it, Philip?"

"No."

She covered her mouth, horrified, sick to her stomach. "You both disappeared during the party for almost half an hour. Leah told me she'd gone to lie down."

"She did, but—"

"And you said you were in your office."

"I went upstairs to get my glasses," he mumbled.

"So you had sex with my best friend. In our bed."

There was a brief pause. Then he said, "One time, Sadie."

"Once is more than enough," she replied. "We're done, Philip. Don't call me again."

"Sadie, wait! What about the—"

She calmly flipped the phone shut and stuffed it into the laptop case. Taking a slow, deep breath, she released it. "No loose ends."

Determined to complete Sam's book, she shrugged off her gloomy mood and set to work on the illustrations. Before long, she had finished a painting of Batty flying backwards into a tree. Next, she started on one of him cheerfully soaring toward the cave. By nightfall, it was finished.

She looked up at Sam's photo. "Soon."

Exhausted, she grabbed the wine bottle. There was no way she was taking any chances. She was not going to see dead children. Not that night.

Not ever again.

Later, she fell into bed and slept soundly...dreamlessly.

Until a shrill scream sent her staggering to her feet.

26

In the dark, Sadie's pulse quickened.

"What the hell was that?" she mumbled, still intoxicated.

After a long moment of silence, she let out a disparaging chuckle. It was the raging storm outside that had woken her. Or at least that's what she tried to convince herself. Rain pounded overhead, while the wind whipped against the cabin and rattled the windows. The drape caught her eye. It fluttered as if someone was blowing on it from behind.

"Just look outside, you coward."

She crossed the room in two swift—though unsteady—strides, and yanked back the drape.

Small black eyes blinked at her.

"Good grief! Don't you ever sleep?"

In response, the crow flew off into the night.

She was about to turn away when two apparitions emerged from the storm. They moved around the side of the cabin, until they were out of sight.

She pinched herself. It hurt.

"Okay, you're not dreaming. But you're definitely seeing things. No one would be outside in this—"

Knock, knock!

"Who's there?" She giggled drunkenly. *I am insane.*

Holding the lamp, she cracked open the back door.

Two shivering children stared up at her as they huddled together beneath a drenched blanket.

"Can we come in?" they asked in unison.

Apparently, even the dead needed to get in out of the rain.

Sadie opened the door wider, expecting the children to vanish. When they didn't, she nudged her head and they stepped inside. As she helped the smaller child slide the blanket from his shoulders, she recognized his shaved head immediately.

"Adam."

He gave her a brief smile.

The girl had to be his sister. Ashley. The girl from the woods.

Then she remembered what Irma had told her. Adam and Ashley were dead.

So who are they?

She watched while they made themselves comfortable on the sofa. They were a peculiar pair. Ashley's damp blond hair was cut dreadfully short—far too short for a girl—and it hadn't been brushed in a while, much less washed. She was dressed in a pink cotton nightgown this time. Adam's blue-striped pajamas had been replaced by solid gray ones and he wore boots that matched his sister's. He looked thinner and paler than the other night. Then again, trekking through the woods in a storm wasn't altogether healthy.

Their presence made no sense.

Unless I'm delusional.

"I'm cold," Adam whined.

She hurried into the bathroom, returning a minute later with some bath towels, all the while telling herself that the children didn't exist. They'd be gone when she returned to the living room.

But they were still there.

Sadie passed a towel to Adam. "Make sure you dry off good or you'll catch a cold." She handed the other towel to the girl. "Ashley, right? Adam's sister?"

"Yes," Ashley said in a subdued voice.

"I'm Sadie."

"We know," Adam said. He grinned and she saw that a front tooth was missing.

"I hope the tooth fairy came last night," she said.

His smile faded. "There *is* no tooth fairy."

"Of course there—"

"Father doesn't like us talking about make belief things," Ashley cut in. "We're too old for that stuff."

"You sound ancient," Sadie said with a chuckle. "Don't be in such a hurry to grow up."

"I'm almost nine," the girl said, straightening.

"I'm six," Adam piped up.

Ashley handed her the wet towel. "Thanks."

"Why don't I brush your hair?" Sadie offered. "It's a mess."

"It doesn't matter. It's always a mess."

"I promise I'll be gentle."

The girl trudged into the bathroom behind her, and when Sadie reached for her, she half expected her hand to move through insubstantial waves, but her hand touched wet hair.

How could these children be real?

I'm drunk, that's how.

She carefully separated strands of Ashley's neglected hair, while Adam perched on the toilet seat, watching them.

"Can I have hot chocolate?" he asked.

"Sure. With extra marshmallows."

He made a face. "Yuck! I hate marshmallows."

"Well, you ate them last time," Sadie said, surprised.

"No, I didn't."

"Adam doesn't know what he likes," Ashley interjected. She smiled at the mirror. "Hey, my hair looks…pretty."

And it did. The soft glow of the lamp brought out golden lights in the girl's naturally blond hair, and because it was so short, it was almost dry.

"You should let it grow a bit," Sadie suggested.

Ashley's smile disappeared. "I can't. Father—"

"Won't let us," Adam finished.

There was an awkward silence.

"Go sit by the fire," Sadie said. "I'll make the hot chocolate."

She went out to the veranda to get the milk jug from the cooler. An arctic wind whipped at her hair, but the overhang protected her from the drizzly rain. In the kitchen, illuminated by the lamp, she unsteadily scooped hot chocolate powder into a pot, filled it with milk and set it on the Coleman stove. It took her three tries to light the damned thing, but she finally got it working.

Her gaze drifted toward the children. Big sister Ashley had grabbed Sadie's blanket, the one she'd left on the chair. They sat side-by-side, covered with it, anxiously waiting for her return. Occasionally, their heads would move close and they'd whisper to each other, their expressions serious.

Sadie rubbed her eyes.

The children were still there when she opened them.

When the hot chocolate was ready, she handed them each a mug and offered Ashley a bowl of marshmallows. The girl picked out two and dropped them in her mug. When she took the first sip, the smile with which Sadie was rewarded was one of complete bliss.

"This *is* the best hot chocolate," Ashley said in awe. "Adam was right."

"Yeah, Adam was right," her brother mumbled between sips.

Sadie frowned. Not many kids referred to themselves in third person. It was more than a little weird.

Ashley and Adam.

Why would they lie about their names?

The wine she had polished off earlier still made her brain fuzzy and she took a deep breath. "Listen, this prank has gone on far enough. I know your names aren't really Ashley and Adam."

Ashley jumped to her feet, a terrified look on her face.

"That's a lie! My name is *Ashley*."

"Ashley and Adam are dead," Sadie said gently. "Who are you really?"

Adam, his mouth trembling, tugged on Ashley's arm. "We gotta go." He pulled her toward the back door, yanked it open and stepped outside.

In the doorway, Ashley whipped around. "He told us you'd come for him. For us. We thought you were the one. I don't know how we could've been so wrong."

Sadie lurched toward them. "Wait! Who—"

But she was too late.

The children darted across the grass. At the edge of the woods, Adam skidded to a stop and spun around. *"Saa-deeeee!"* His voice sounded desperate and clear—no lisp.

In fact, now that she thought about it, he hadn't lisped during the entire visit. Not once.

"What the hell is going on?" she murmured.

She moved down the steps, thinking to call them back, but then the strangest thing happened. Before her eyes, Adam and Ashley multiplied into four small shapes. Then six. Like human cells duplicating and separating.

Sadie blinked, but they remained, cloaked in shadows, indistinguishable. Six ghost children.

"Jesus…"

Voices began to chant. *"One fine day, in the middle of the night, two dead boys got up to fight…"*

"Stop it!" she screamed.

The chanting died instantly.

In the distance, they studied her, and it made her skin crawl.

"Leave me alone!" she yelled.

At first, none of them moved. Then, one by one, the children withdrew, merging into the colorless void of night.

Sadie stepped back into the cabin, slammed the door and leaned against the wall. Her breath came in quick pants and she dug her fingernails into her palms.

What did these illusions, these children, want from her?

Giving into temptation, she grabbed the second to last bottle of Cabernet and staggered back to bed. By the time she had nearly finished the wine, she had convinced herself that Ashley and Adam's visit had been nothing more than another alcohol-induced hallucination. That's why she'd seen six of them. She had conjured them up because of her own loss and culpability.

"You saw them because you want to, because you're nothing but an alcoholic, Sadie. And a useless drunk. There's no other explanation."

But there was.

27

Six objects on the kitchen counter were the first things she saw when she managed to make it past the bathroom the next morning. She stood motionless, two feet from the sink, and eyed the wrinkled chocolate bar wrapper, envelope, licorice, pen, onion and a new addition—a handful of Smarties. Something about their careful alignment bothered her.

Were they mere apparitions?

She reached out hesitantly and swept the Smarties in her hot hand. They began to melt.

"Well, you're real at least."

She ate them, happy to camouflage the sour taste of vomit.

Before her trip to the bathroom where she had thrown up until she was left with dry heaves, she had woken to thoughts of the strange children. There was only one explanation that made any sense. Since Irma swore that there were no children around and that Ashley and Adam were dead, Sadie—in a perpetual drunken stupor—had conjured up the entire thing.

She scowled.

That meant *she* was responsible for the items on the counter.

She swept them into the garbage can, then proceeded to make a pot of coffee. Recalling Ed's advice, she added an extra half scoop of dark roast coffee. Not wanting to fight with the temperamental stove, she slid the grate over the fire and plopped the percolator down on it.

Then she set up her art supplies.

∞ ∞ ∞

As the sun departed to make room for the moon, Sadie drained the rum, drinking from the bottle, welcoming the giddiness it brought. She had been gripped by a blur of activity and intoxication the entire day. Illuminated by two oil lamps and a blazing fire, she had worked in frenzy, painting the final illustrations for Sam's book and fighting the panicky feeling that rumbled in the pit of her stomach.

Now, she tried to ignore the desperate voices in her head.

But she couldn't.

"We needed you."

"The one person who ever needed me is dead," she wept.

She caught sight of the calendar near the sink.

It was already two weeks into May.

She squinted at the clock. *9:50.*

"A few hours and it'll be Mother's Day," she slurred. "Well, if ever there was a sign, this is it." She circled the date with a black marker. "D-Day. Dying Day."

She let out a drunken laugh, then lurched into the bedroom, careful not to look at Sam's photograph. She set a flashlight on the nightstand and directed the beam at the bottom of the bed.

"Oh, it's dying time again, I'm gonna leave you," she sang off-key as she sank to her knees. *"I can see that faraway look...in your eyes."*

She floundered under the bed and pulled the gun box closer. Once it was clear of the bed, she picked it up and tucked it under her arm. Then she stood up. Too quickly. The sudden shift in equilibrium made her head spin and she fell against the nightstand. The box tumbled to the floor, the lid toppled off and the gun slid under the bed.

"Shit!"

On her knees again, she lifted the edge of the bedspread and peered into the shadows underneath the bed. The gun was lodged against one of the headboard legs. She inched her head sideways and stretched out her arm, but still couldn't reach it. She wriggled closer, her body blocking all the light. The floor was cool and rough, and she found a handful of dust bunnies. But no gun.

An unexpected light beamed from the opposite side of the bed, as though someone had entered the room behind her and shifted the flashlight. Then, bit by bit, the bedspread began to lift.

What Sadie saw next practically stopped her heart.

A familiar face and two solemn sapphire eyes.

Sam's eyes!

"Sam?"

The bedspread dropped back into place.

Scrabbling from under the bed, she lurched to her feet and threw a scared glance at the flashlight. It was right where she had left it, pointing exactly where she had aimed it.

"What's going on here?" she whispered.

She steadied herself with one hand against the dresser, her eyes drawn to the far end of the bed.

"Sam, come on out."

Nothing moved.

She forced herself to walk around the bed. The space on the other side was empty—no sign that anyone had been there, except for a faint layer of dust that had been disturbed. A trail of clean floor disappeared under the bed.

She crouched low and peeked underneath.

There was only one thing there.

The gun.

It glinted in the dim light, menacing in its deadly promise.

She waited, expecting Sam's eyes to peek at her from the other side. When nothing happened, she warily reached for the gun and withdrew it, its cool metal reassuring. She was about to stand when a disturbance in the air made her chest tighten. Holding her breath, she straightened slowly, the gun in hand.

Someone or something had moved the flashlight. It was now pointing to the open bedroom door.

She frowned and shuffled toward it, but saw nothing out of place. Then, as a last thought, she pushed the door closed.

"Oh, Jesus!"

Behind the door, someone had carved an infinity symbol.

She slumped against the dresser. "Stop it!"

A sob ripped from her throat, followed by another. She wanted to pound her head against the wall.

She glared at Sam's photo and fury rose from the very depths of her soul. "Why are you haunting me?" She rubbed her face, smearing hot tears over her cheeks. "Why, Sam?"

There was no answer. But then, she didn't really expect one.

Staggering into the living room, she shone the flashlight on every surface. As the beam grazed the kitchen counter, her hand trembled. Everything she had tossed in the garbage was once again arranged in a line on the counter.

In an uncomprehending daze, she stepped closer.

On the envelope someone had drawn an infinity symbol. The licorice was twisted in the same shape.

That's when her mind shattered, completely.

In the small room, her pained howl echoed, raw and savage.

"No more! I can't do this anymore. God!" She shook her head, weeping and laughing hysterically. "Wait, what am I saying? There is no God. Because if there is, he's taken everyone I've ever loved away from me." Sobs wracked her body and she caved in to her misery. "No...*I* let a monster take my baby. I let him torture Sam—*kill* Sam. It's *my* fault. I admit it. But I'm done with this! Do you hear me? It's over!"

She had no idea if she was talking to Sam, the ghost children or God. It didn't matter anyway. No one heard her. No one cared. She was alone, dead inside.

"Just do it!" she screamed, gritting her teeth. "Kill me now or let me die. I...don't...care!"

∞ ∞ ∞

An hour later, Sadie sat at the kitchen table.

She was ready. Ready to die.

She had downed two handfuls of assorted pills and most of the Screaming Eagle Cabernet. Her mind swirled with random thoughts, while the gun with its single bullet waited on the table.

On the mantle above the fireplace, an envelope addressed to Leah mocked her, an account of the madness that had gripped her like a noose crushing the air from her lungs. Next to the portfolio with Sam's completed book was a letter for Philip. It was a will of sorts, although she wasn't sure a judge wouldn't contest her sanity. She had left Going Batty to Philip, to do with whatever he pleased—get it published or burn it. It was out of her hands.

"I loved you, Philip," she said numbly. "But you're right. I loved Sam more. He was a part of me that you never understood. The *best* part of me. He kept me whole. Sober. Sane."

The grandfather clock emitted another garbled gong.

Almost time.

She turned half-glazed eyes toward the newspaper on the table. She cringed at the sight of the man on the front page. His face had haunted her nightmares and ravaged her sanity. This fiend had crept into her house, abducted her son, then viciously butchered him and burned him alive.

"Monster!"

She ripped off the front page and shredded The Fog's face, tearing at the newspaper until her hands were black. In a fury, her arm swept across the table, sending the paper bits into the air. As the freak snowstorm of dead gray flakes floated to the floor, she gave voice to her rage.

"I hope you rot in hell!"

Tears slid down her cheeks as she gazed at the sparsely furnished cabin. What she saw instead was Sam's empty bed, the gaping window in his room and the police officer holding the clown's shoe. She closed her eyes and when she opened them, she saw Sam in the car, bound and gagged. The entire explosion played itself out like a horror film that had been incorrectly fed into the projector, jerking and skipping until it froze on a shot of the scorched baseball cap.

Sadie picked up the gun. It was as if a stranger held it.

"I'm sorry I couldn't save you, Sam," she wept.

Through the kitchen window, she saw them. Six small bodies.

"One fine day, in the middle of the night..."

Outside, a pale hand reached for the window.

"You're not real," she cried, even as her hand pressed against the icy glass. "You don't exist."

She looked down at the gun in her hand and caressed it.

"No!" the ghost children screamed.

A final gong echoed in the small room. Midnight had arrived.

"Happy Mother's Day."

She took a steadying breath, pressed the gun to her head and flicked back the safety, shuddering at the soft click.

"Mommy's coming, Sam."

Against her will, her eyes settled on the gifts on the counter.

Why are they always arranged in the same order?

In the nanosecond before she pulled the trigger, the answer became crystal clear.

28

Sadie's death didn't go according to plan.

She expected to hear a deafening roar, maybe feel a twinge of heat and then sink into a black abyss. However, there was only silence. No booming blast, no pain, no blood spatter. Just a faint click.

She jerked the trigger again, this time with more force.

Nothing.

She batted away a stray tear. "You can't do anything right, Sadie. Not even kill yourself with a fucking loaded gun."

If it weren't so tragic, she would have laughed.

With a trembling hand, she dropped the gun on the table, hoping it would go off and finish the job she hadn't been able to. She glared at it, wondering why she felt sober all of a sudden. The overdose of drugs and alcohol should have knocked her out at the very least.

Maybe I'm unconscious. Or in a coma.

But she knew she wasn't.

"Maybe I *am* dead," she rasped, hopeful.

The sound of her voice assured her this wasn't true either.

Sensing that she was being watched, she turned toward the window. Outside, the children had ceased their chanting. With the shifting veil of fog behind them, they stood motionless, watching her…waiting.

She flicked a look at the counter, at the message—for that's what it was. She could see it so clearly now.

Hershey, envelope, licorice, pen, onion.

"*H…E…L…P.*" Seeing the onion, she frowned. "One of you needs to learn how to spell. Un-yun. *U.* And I ate the Smarties. *S.*"

HELP US.

In a shocked trance, she walked to the back door. When she opened it, three nearly identical boys and three almost identical girls silently stepped inside. None spoke a word, but moved as one, almost gliding toward the warmth of the fire. She surveyed each child, noting the close shaved dark hair of the boys and the butchered blond of the girls. The boys wore two-piece pajama sets in gray, yellow and navy blue, while the girls wore matching nightgowns in mauve, aqua and pink.

"Who *are* you?" she croaked.

The girl wearing mauve stepped forward. "I'm Ashley."

"No, you aren't." Sadie pointed to the girl in pink. "She is."

The girl in aqua smiled. "We're all Ashley."

"And we're all Adam," said the boy in gray.

"Adam and Ashley are dead," Sadie said in a dull tone.

"We know, Thadie," Gray Adam said.

The boy who likes marshmallows!

She groaned in confusion. "Why would your parents name you after dead children? And why would they give you all the same names?"

"Father named us," Pink Ashley said tightly.

"I don't under—"

"Come with uth!" Blue Adam pleaded. "But you have to hurry."

Without hesitation, she snatched up a flashlight and followed them out into the tempest. The winds raged and the clouds released a torrential downpour, but the canopy of evergreens sheltered them somewhat from the storm. The single beam from her flashlight lit the ground as they picked their way through the woods and down to the river's edge.

Sadie noticed the rock bridge. Before she knew what they were planning, two of the girls began to file across the slippery surface, arms outstretched for balance. They were followed by two of the boys.

"Wait!" she yelled.

"What's wrong?" Blue Adam asked, reaching for her hand.

"It's too dangerous. Someone might fall in."

"We won't."

"We should stay on this side," she argued. "The river's going to flood."

She shone her flashlight on the boulder on the far shore. The water level had almost risen to the orange line.

"Trust me," he said, tugging her hand.

She sucked in a breath and followed him onto the first rock. It was dry and ridged, making for easy footing. The next slab was damp and covered with a thin slime of algae. She made her way across, praying that she wouldn't drop the flashlight or plunge into the turbulent river. Minutes later, she was on the other side, racing along the shore, winded and trying to keep up. She was nearly sober—nearly sane—for the first time in weeks.

Maybe months.

"This way," Gray Adam called, waving her on.

She moaned. "Can't you slow down a bit?"

Pink Ashley took pity on her and waited. "We don't have a lotta time. C'mon."

Sadie shot her a brief smile. "I'm not as young as you. And I'm a bit out of shape."

"No, you're not," the girl said. "It's the booze and drugs."

Sadie stumbled. *How'd she know?*

"I just do," Pink Ashley said.

"So you're a mind reader now, are you?" Sadie said, slightly amused. "What am I thinking now?"

Pink Ashley took a few steps away, then hesitated. "You're thinking that you should've bought more bullets."

As the girl disappeared into the heavy brush, Sadie plodded behind, pondering her words. Ashley was right about the bullets.

Soon, the babbling of the river faded. When the trees parted, an icy field stretched out before them. A few yards to the left stood a rusted utility shed with metal sides and a corrugated tin roof. As the rain clanged down, a strange humming sound emanated from within the shed.

Sadie started toward it, but something drew her attention.

At the far end of the field, the blackened hull of what was once a two-story house created a sharp contrast to the opalescent ice around it. The house resembled a false front in a ghost town, its empty window frames scorched by a previous fire that had trailed its way up to the roof. A collapsed doorway revealed a deteriorated stairway that climbed to a non-existent second floor. The back wall had buckled and was mostly gone.

Sadie shuddered. "Sarge's house."

Mauve Ashley nodded. "Yeah."

"So Sarge is your neighbor?"

"Not quite," Pink Ashley replied softly. "Follow me."

Sadie followed her back into the bushes, away from the field. The others trailed close behind. Once they had climbed over an uprooted tree trunk and up a steep incline, Ashley stopped in a heavily wooded area. The children crowded around her, watching her expectantly while she wrestled with a tree stump. It would have been comical, except that it was the middle of the night and the rain was chilling everyone to the bone.

Sadie stared at her, baffled. "What are you—?"

Pink Ashley grunted and tugged on the stump. "Help me!"

The desperation in the girl's voice made Sadie react fast. She handed her flashlight to the nearest Adam, then joined Ashley.

"Pull on it!" the girl ordered.

Sadie yanked on the stump with all her might. To her surprise, it flipped over, taking a perfect rectangle of sod with it—along with a hinged metal door.

She gasped, stunned. "An underground bunker."

Retrieving her flashlight, she moved forward and shone the light into the hole. A wooden stairway led down into the musty depths and ended at a dirt floor several yards below.

God only knows where that leads.

"It's our back door," Aqua Ashley said.

Sadie's jaw dropped. "You can't be serious. You don't really expect me to believe that you live down *there*. That's ridiculous."

"But we do," Yellow Adam insisted.

Bewildered and dismayed, she looked at the children.

Nothing was making any sense. Nothing except the fact that she had gone around the bend and was standing outside in the middle of the night, staring into a pit that led underground.

I can't go down there.

"You have to follow us," Pink Ashley begged. "If you do, you'll understand everything."

Sadie let out a frazzled groan. "Why can't you just tell me what this is all about?"

"We tried," Blue Adam said. "But we made a promise and we can't break it."

"Then what good is it if I go down there?" she asked him.

He tugged on her hand. "We can *show* you."

"Trust us," Pink Ashley said before disappearing into the pit.

Sadie hesitated near the edge, confronted by a sudden image of Sam's casket being lowered into the earth. Gathering her courage, she swung the flashlight toward the hole and moved forward, cautious and alert to the texture of the ground beneath her feet. Her boots hit a clump of moist dirt and she watched it tumble into the void. She didn't hear it land.

Prodding the top step with her foot, she eased onto it, fearful that it would collapse beneath her weight and send her plummeting to her death. When the step held, she said a silent prayer and began the descent.

Blue Adam followed. "You don't got claustrophobia, do you?"

"Not until now." She tried to laugh, but it came out a moan.

Suck it up, princess. If they can do this, so can I.

For balance, she held onto the railing that someone had anchored to the smooth wood walls. As the sides closed in around her, she tried not to think of how far underground they were going, concentrating instead on the pungent scent of moist earth and plywood that hung in the air, trapped by the stillness and dark. By about the tenth step, she lost count and was beginning to relax—until a sudden bout of vertigo made her miss a step.

Blue Adam grabbed her arm. "Careful."

She glanced over her shoulder, up past the children, and saw the faintest glimmer of moonlight. For a second, she panicked.

Oh God, what am I getting into?

"I can't do this."

"It's okay," Blue Adam lisped. "As long as Father doesn't find you here, you're safe."

"Great," she muttered. "That makes me feel so much better."

"Just a few more steps," he promised.

When she finally connected with solid ground, she released a pent-up breath. The children gathered around her, while she took a final look at the light at the top of the stairs.

"Well, that wasn't too bad," she said. "Now what?"

"That," Blue Adam said, pointing.

A metal door barred their way.

"It's locked," she said, indicating the card-swipe security system above the handle.

"No, it's not," Pink Ashley said. "Father had no reason to."

"Well, here goes nothing then."

Sadie opened the door and sudden light blinded her.

29

"Oh...my...God."

However, it had been human hands—not divine ones—that had built the underground bunker. Someone had spent a lot of time, energy and money to fashion it with all the necessities of life, including electricity, running water and pumped-in air. Why someone would want to live underground, away from sunlight and fresh air, was beyond Sadie's comprehension.

With a sinking heart, she took a step forward, leaned against a cubicle divider and surveyed the strange sight. Wood paneling covered every wall of the bunker, and soft lighting gave the room a warm, cozy feeling that clashed with the scarcity of furniture and lack of any color other than brown or gray tones. At the opposite end of the room, another metal door glinted. Near it, a card table and three padded chairs sat in an open kitchen area. In the middle of the room, a camel brown leather recliner with pieces of duct tape across the armrests faced a television and microwave. They sat side-by-side on a picnic table bench.

She frowned. "What shall we watch? TV or microwave?"

Moving further inside, she noticed a desk, chair, computer and other electronic devices behind the cubicle divider. An open doorway beside it led to a small washroom with a shower stall.

"All the comforts of home," she said in disbelief.

Except something was missing.

There was not one single toy, not one picture book, nothing to indicate the existence of the children.

Guardedly, she approached the door at the end of the room. She stopped and sniffed, wrinkling her nose at the acrid scent of smoke.

"That's our front door," Pink Ashley said.

Sadie spotted another door, a narrow one that blended into the wall by the kitchen. Beside it was an alphabetical keypad.

Awful lot of security for a home.

"What's in there?" she asked.

"The *dungeon,*" Blue Adam said. "Where we thleep. You—"

"That's father's bedroom," Pink Ashley interrupted, pointing to another door half-hidden between two shelves.

Sadie turned in a slow circle, taking in the eccentricities of the bunker. It was far more intricate and spacious than she had first thought.

"I don't get it," she said. "Why are you living down here?"

Mauve Ashley stepped forward. "It's our home."

"But you can't live here. It's unhealthy. You have to leave."

"We can't leave," Yellow Adam said. "He won't let us."

"Who, your dad?"

Yellow Adam pulled her toward the desk. He pointed to a drawing tacked on the wall beside the computer. When her eyes fastened on it, her world tipped and spun out of control.

Her drawing.

The Fog.

The murkiness of her mind lifted—like the sun burning off a morning mist—and she was left with a horrific revelation.

She had found The Fog. *And* the children he had abducted.

She set the flashlight on the desk and stared at the newspaper clippings that surrounded her drawing. Faded photos of the children stared back at her, each circled in red marker. Their names were all there, in the headlines, next to the anguished faces of their parents.

"Oh, Jesus," she moaned. "We have to get out of here."

As she turned away, her eyes latched onto another familiar face. Sam's. His photo, next to an article covering his death, had also been circled.

"My beautiful boy."

It was too late for Sam. But not for the others.

She faced Pink Ashley. "Your name is Marina Fisher."

She turned to the Ashleys wearing aqua and mauve. "And you're Brittany Atherton and Kimber Levine."

The girls gave her a blank stare.

"Holland Dawes, Jordan Jaremko and Scotty McIntyre," Sadie added, indicating the boys in navy blue, yellow and gray. She shook her head, stunned. "Why didn't you just tell me?"

Pink Ashley—*Marina*—stepped forward. "We couldn't. Father made us swear. He said he'd kill us if we ever said our real names out loud."

"Or if we ever tried to leave him," Holland added. "He said he'd hunt us down and cut us up like the other boy."

Scowling, Kimber folded her arms across her chest. "Father

wouldn't hurt us. He loves us."

At first, the defensive remark seemed strange, especially coming from a girl who had been kept hostage for three years, until Sadie recalled that it wasn't uncommon for a hostage to bond with his or her captor. There was a name for it. Stockholm syndrome. Like Patty Hearst and Elizabeth Smart.

More pieces of the puzzle slid into place and she kicked herself for not putting it together sooner. The real Adam and Ashley had died in a fire, one that had left their father grotesquely *scarred*—not pockmarked.

"This man," she said, tapping the drawing, "took you from your homes. From your parents." Her eyes were drawn back to the newspaper clippings.

Eight-year-old Kimber and six-year-old Jordan were the first two children abducted by The Fog, back in April 2003. Brittany and Scotty were taken the following April. Last year, Marina and Holland. And this year, Sam and…

"Wait!" she said, grabbing Marina's arm. "Where's Cortnie?"

"We don't know," the girl said. "She snuck out."

"When?"

"A couple nights ago. She took Adam with her."

Sadie shook her head. "What?"

"The other Adam," Brittany said. "She took him and ran."

Sadie was completely confused. "What other Adam?"

Holland tapped a photo on the wall. "Him."

Sadie fainted.

∞ ∞ ∞

The shadows around her shifted, becoming more distinct. She groaned. When her vision cleared, six worried faces stared down at her.

"What happened?" she asked in a groggy voice.

"You passed out," Kimber said. "When you saw the picture."

Sadie grabbed Holland's hand. "What did you say? Before I fainted." She moved to the photo of Sam. "You said he was—"

"Cortnie took him away," Marina cut in.

"The boy in this picture," Sadie said carefully.

"Yes, *that* boy. The one who doesn't talk."

Sadie's heart skipped a beat. "And that was a few days ago?"

"Yeah."

Sam's dead, her mind argued. She had seen the car explode.

But you never truly believed he was gone.

"Where's Sarge now, Marina?"

"He's gone looking for them again."

Sadie released Holland's hand. "We have to go back to my cabin and call the police."

And I have to find Sam.

"Before *he* does," Jordan whispered.

Without warning, heavy footsteps echoed down unseen stairs behind the far door. The sound grew more menacing with each step.

"He's coming!" Holland lisped.

"Come on then," she urged. "Back up the stairs."

"We're right behind you," Marina said.

Sadie took the steps two at a time, ignoring the drizzle that dripped in from the open trap door.

"Careful!" she warned. "The steps are slippery."

Halfway up, she realized that she'd forgotten the flashlight. She almost turned back, but the children's safety edged her onward, toward the fading light.

"We're almost there."

Climbing onto the slippery grass, she rolled over, arms outstretched for the first child. "Hurry up!"

The pit was still, silent.

"Marina! Holland! Where are you guys?"

No reply.

She began to shake.

Had The Fog—*Sarge*—caught them trying to escape? Had she left them behind with a killer?

Her stomach coiled and rumbled. "Think, Sadie!"

If he had them, there was no way she could force him to let them go. She had to leave them behind, get to her cabin and call the police.

"Who's up there?"

At the sound of a man's booming voice, Sadie ran for her life. She scurried through the woods, feeling her way, trying to remember the path she had taken with the children. But it all looked the same in the dark.

"You gotta get to the river," she panted.

She darted around trees and bushes, pausing to listen for the sound of running water. But she couldn't hear anything over her ragged breath and thumping heart.

"Help me," she cried softly. "I have to save them."

A gleam of light drew her out of the trees. When she broke from the woods and skidded onto the rain-drenched rocks of the riverside, she heaved a sigh of relief, then threw a nervous glance over her shoulder, half-expecting Sarge to jump out from the trees. Facing the river, she found on the rock bridge a few yards to her right. But there was one major problem. Kimree River was rising fast. Many of the slabs were submerged and the water that rushed between them moved swiftly.

"Oh, God," she moaned.

Knowing she had no choice, she climbed onto the slick surface of the first slab. With one foot, she prodded the water for the next and cried out when her ankle high winter boot filled with icy water. She found the rock and stepped forward. Feeling for the third slab, she wobbled precariously. "Steady, Sadie." She hopped to the next slab, arms stretched out for balance.

Four more...somewhere.

She surveyed the water's surface. "Where are you?"

Her boot hit something solid and she eased forward, the water now up to her calves.

"Two more."

But she didn't make it. She miscalculated and her foot slid between two slabs. She plunged into the frigid water. Swept downstream, she flailed her arms to keep her head above the surface. The river pulled at her from all directions and tossed her about, as if she were nothing but a piece of deadwood

Then her head went under.

Panicking, she swallowed a mouthful of grit. She clawed at the water, coughing and spitting, until she finally surfaced and sucked in a lungful of air. Her hair stuck to her face and she swatted it away. Then she began to inch diagonally toward the shore, while allowing the current to take her downriver.

Up ahead, something glistened in the moonlight.

The roof of Infinity Cabin.

30

As the river swept her around the bend, Sadie was drawn toward the shore. She snatched at tufts of dry brush that overhung the bank. Fumbling, she cursed, then tried again. She gripped a wiry root and pulled her aching body onto dry ground.

She lay in the grass, panting. When her breathing slowed, she dragged herself to her feet and a shooting pain flared through her left ankle. She examined it in the faint light. It was bruised and swollen, maybe broken and definitely sprained. Gritting her teeth, she moved away from the shore and studied the churning water.

In some areas, the river had already flooded its banks.

"The bridge!"

Recalling Irma's warning, she knew she had to hurry. She suddenly had a horrible vision of Sarge herding the children into his pickup and whisking them away. And what about Sam and Cortnie?

She took a reinforcing breath, then jogged toward the cabin, ignoring the jolting pang in her ankle. She ran inside, slammed the door and lit the lamp with shaking hands.

"Okay, call the police."

Her purse was lying on the coffee table. She checked it, but no cell phone. She opened kitchen drawers and rummaged through them. "Okay, where'd you put your cell?"

Fear crept into her mind, but she pushed it away. "Focus!"

When had she used it last? A few days ago, a week? She couldn't remember.

In her panic, she tripped over the laptop case.

"A-ha! There you are."

She flung it on the kitchen table and unzipped it. Relief rushed through her. The cell phone was right where she had put it earlier, in the inside pocket. She flipped the phone open and let out a groan. No power, no signal…nothing.

"Come on!" She stabbed at the power button. It flashed, then died. "You left it on, you idiot!"

She dropped the useless phone on the table, knowing she would have to drive into town and bring the police back. Spurred into motion, she changed jackets. At least the heavy winter one was warm and dry. She tugged her purse strap over one shoulder, then fumbled in the jacket pockets and pulled out a set of keys.

"Thank God something's going right."

Ducking her head against the howling wind and another deluge of rain, she stepped outside, the small flashlight in one hand, car keys in the other. She limped down the path and within minutes, she was at Irma's cabin. She almost pounded on the door before she recalled that Ed had taken his sister to Edmonton.

Philip's Mercedes sat dejectedly off to the side of the road. Fat raindrops battered it, then rolled off the hood. She unlocked the door, tossed the flashlight and her purse on the passenger seat and climbed in. Muttering a quick prayer, she shoved the key into the ignition and turned it. A faint raspy sound greeted her. Then, like the cell phone, it too was out of commission.

"For crying out loud!" she cried. "Give me a fucking break!"

Furious, she tried again.

This time the engine was dead silent.

For a moment, she just sat there. Then she slumped over the steering wheel and tears poured from her, unbidden and unrestrained. A crack of thunder made her body jerk. She bolted upright, terrified, and gripped the wheel until her knuckles turned white. The windows were starting to fog over and she wiped the side one with her sleeve. When lightning streaked across the sky, she saw a black hulk off to her left. Another jagged flash lit up the surrounding area, spotlighting a sedan of indistinguishable color. It was parked next to the other cabin, the one near the road.

She shoved the door open, gathered her belongings and bolted from the car. Fighting the storm, she ran toward the cabin. She practically jumped out of her skin when a rectangle of light appeared.

A bulky shadow moved in the open doorway. "Someone out there?"

"Hey!" She waved the flashlight in the air. "Over here!"

By the time she reached the cabin, she was out of breath and fighting back tears. "Help me…please…we have to help them."

She looked up at the sign over the door. *Hope.*

Sadie was ushered inside by a burly, red-bearded man in a dingy, stained t-shirt and faded jeans, the latter held up by a leather belt that was half-hidden by his drooping belly. He had maybe a decade on her and had kind, pale green eyes.

"What's wrong with you, lass?" he asked in a thick Scottish accent. "You look like you seen a ghost."

"I need to use your phone," she panted.

She tried not to look at the deer and moose heads that were mounted on the walls of the log cabin or the empty beer cans that littered the floor.

"That'll be a problem, then. Don't got one."

"But we have to call the police!"

The man frowned. "Now why would we do that?"

She took a deep breath. "Sarge kidnapped some children. He's holding them in an underground bunker."

"Sarge has a bunker? In the ground, you say?"

Sadie groaned with frustration. "He's The Fog!"

"'Tis a wee bit foggy out there," the man said, distracted. "Why don't you rest up a bit, lass? Your ankle's swelling. You should raise it, put it up on the other chair. I'll be right back."

He disappeared outside, returning a minute later with a bag of ice. He led her to a chair. "Put the ice on your ankle."

She sat down and watched him move toward the kitchen.

"We have to do some—" Her breath caught in her throat.

Bulging eyes stared back at her. Eight fish in various stages of cleaning were belly up on the counter. Some were still alive, their mouths opening and closing, gasping for breath. Eventually, they gave up trying.

The man picked up a fishing knife, its curved blade glinting dangerously. When he saw her watching him, he smiled. "Once I finish this, I'll make us some warm apple cider. Unless you'd prefer ale."

Sadie was mesmerized by the knife. "I don't want anything."

"Cider'll warm you up. Name's Fergus, by the way."

"Sadie."

"Aye, I know all about you." Fergus sliced through the belly of a small fish and scraped the guts onto a blackened metal cookie tray that rested across the top of the sink. "Irma said you had man trouble and was hiding out here."

"I'm not hiding."

"What do you call it then?"

She opened her mouth, floundering for words. But like the half-dead fish, she quickly gave up.

After a minute, she said, "We have to help the children."

"Sarge's wee ones are dead. Don't know why you'd think otherwise."

"I don't mean them. I'm talking about my son and the others that he took. They came to me for help. I have to do something."

"Best wait 'til the morning, lass. 'Til this squall is over."

"I can't wait. My son is out there somewhere. We need the police *now*."

A gust of wind rattled the door. Sadie jumped.

Fergus frowned. "You planning to take that Mercedes into town in this weather?"

"The battery's dead. I need to borrow your car."

The man rinsed off the knife and wiped his hands on a dishtowel. "Perhaps 'tis the booze talking."

"I am *not* drunk. I'm perfectly sober."

He cocked his head. "Aye, you don't look drunk."

"Please. Help me, Fergus."

"Tell you what…I'll take my car into town and call the cops for you."

She gave him a thankful smile.

Fergus reached for a jacket hanging beside the door. "You rest here and keep that ice on your ankle."

He was out the door before she could blink.

A car engine rumbled to life and headlights swept past the window at the back of the house. Then all was still.

She shot out of the chair. "There's no way in hell I'm going to sit around and do nothing."

Especially when she had a weapon. *The gun.* Before leaving the house earlier, she'd stashed it back in the box and hidden it under the bed.

She headed for the door, but paused when her eyes landed on the fishing knife. She slipped it into her jacket pocket.

"Better to be safe than sorry."

31

Infinity Cabin was in danger of being swept away. At least the veranda was. The river had climbed almost four feet up the supports. Another six inches and the water would be over the bank, turning the grass into a swamp.

Once inside, Sadie locked the back door, tossed her purse and flashlight on the table, aiming the latter into the center of the room. The cabin was freezing and dark, lit only by flashes of lightning from outside. The hearth had long turned to ash, but there was no time to build a fire, even though she was soaked to the bone.

She was about to go into the bedroom when a sound made her glance over her shoulder. A tall shadow shifted past the draped kitchen window. A shadow wearing a cowboy hat.

Sarge.

Pulling the knife from her pocket, she pressed herself against the wall and held her breath.

The doorknob rattled. A muffled curse was followed by something solid slamming up against the door.

Her eyes flared with fear. *Please don't let him get in.*

Then the footsteps plodded away.

Sadie released a slow breath, until she heard Sarge moving alongside the cabin. Horrified, she gazed across the room to the sliding door. The door she had left *un*locked. There was no time to secure it now, not without being heard. She had to hide. But where?

Desperate eyes latched onto the rug in the middle of the floor.

The root cellar!

She flicked the flashlight off, praying he hadn't seen the light. Then, crossing the room, she bent over and flipped the corner of the rug. Someone had used double-sided carpet tape to keep it in place. With a trembling hand, she tugged on the metal ring and let out a soft sob of gratefulness when the trapdoor opened. She moved down a few stairs, grabbed the door and pulled it over her head.

She was thrown into a dark abyss.

Oh, God....

The cellar was worse than the bunker. For one thing, it was pitch black and smelled musty, and she felt cramped even though she couldn't see the size of it. She felt as though she had just been buried alive, which couldn't possibly be that much different from being trapped in an ice-cold cellar with a murderous kidnapper above hunting for her.

Footsteps clumped overhead.

Closer...

Her pulse quickened and the knife shook in her hand.

Above her, something clattered to the floor. An angry grunt followed. Then there was a soft thud near the trapdoor.

Terrified, she covered her mouth with one hand.

Silence.

He was listening.

Sadie's heartbeat pounded in her ears. Could he hear it?

Footsteps gradually receded and a door slammed.

She shivered uncontrollably. *Is he still here?*

The waiting was excruciating, the silence endless—until the gong of the grandfather clock interrupted it. To be safe, she waited few more minutes. Once her breathing had calmed, she tiptoed up the cellar stairs and pressed her ear to the trapdoor.

She heard nothing. Not a sound.

I have to get help.

Inching the trapdoor open, she peeked out. She couldn't see anything or anyone. The cabin was too dark, and she'd left the flashlight on the table.

Serendipitously, a bolt of lightning streaked across the sky, illuminating the room. No one was hiding in the shadows. But then again, she could only see three sides of the cabin. What if he was standing behind the trapdoor?

He's gone. I can't stay down here forever. The children need me.

She eased back the trapdoor and crawled out, waving the knife in the air. When no one attacked her, she strode to the sliding door, locked it and pulled the heavy drape across. Her hands were numb with cold. She knew she had to get warm or risk hypothermia. If that happened, she wouldn't be good to anyone.

"Dry clothes first," she said, tucking the knife back into her pocket. "Then the gun."

After lighting a lamp and turning it as low as possible, she carried it into the bedroom where she removed her jacket and tossed it over the back of the chair. She stripped off her wet clothes, leaving them in a heap on the floor, and vigorously dried off with a bath towel she had left on the bed earlier. Once dressed in warm jeans and a sweater, she sat down on the chair and pulled on two pairs of socks, wincing at the sight of her bruised and swollen ankle.

"Looks like you had a little accident," a voice sneered.

Her head jerked up as a shadow slithered into view. With his hat in one hand, a man leaned cockily against the doorjamb. His shaved head gleamed in the lamplight and his beady eyes carefully scrutinized the room. Then his gaze rested on her and his disfigured face twisted into a sinister smirk.

"We meet again, Sadie O'Connell."

She gaped at him and swallowed hard. "The Fog."

At first glance, Sarge only vaguely resembled the sadistic monster that had beaten her, abducted Sam and brutalized him. In a way, he looked like an ordinary man, someone she'd see at the Calgary Stampede or a local bar and never think twice about. Until she looked into his eyes. A madman resided there.

"H-how did you get in?" she asked in a weak voice.

He held up a key. "Irma keeps a spare under the welcome mat. Not very original, is she?"

Her heart plunged when he took a step forward.

"What do you want?" she demanded.

"I'm returning something that belongs to you." He dropped a flashlight—the blue one she'd left in the bunker—on the dresser. "Says *Infinity Cabin* right on it, so I took that as an invitation. Su casa es mi casa. Remember?" He frowned. "I'm surprised it's you though, and not some nosy old greaser."

She inched back in the chair. "The police are on their way."

"You called 'em, did you?"

She nodded.

"Kinda hard to do, since this ain't working." He flung her cell phone at her feet.

"It was working when I called," she lied.

She moved slightly. Something shifted under her thigh. She glanced down and saw a glimmer of metal. The knife. She was sitting on part of the blade.

"There's no service out here when it storms," Sarge said.

"Maybe," she replied, her hand creeping toward the knife. "But someone's gone to get the police. They'll be here any time."

"You mean ole Fergus? He's stuck on the road a few miles back. Looks like it's just me and you." He started across the room.

"Don't come any closer!" she shrieked, jumping to her feet.

Sarge sniggered. "You gonna whip me with that towel?"

"No, but I have this." Boldly, she flourished the fishing knife.

"Better be prepared to use that...*bitch*."

It happened so fast that she had no time to react. One minute she was pointing the blade at the bastard—the next, the knife was knocked from her hand.

An arm snaked around her throat. "One more sound outta you," he hissed in her ear, "and I'll snap your neck."

Light bounced off something slim and razor-sharp.

"A little something to calm you down," he murmured.

A hypodermic needle jabbed her arm, right through her sweater. She tried to fight him, tried to scream, but all that came out was a faint sob. Then her vision blurred, and the room morphed into fuzzy shadows. Within seconds, her legs buckled. If it weren't for Sarge holding her up, she would have fallen to the floor.

Hot breath teased her ear. "How the fuck did you find me?"

She moaned. "The children..."

With a mewling whimper, she gave up fighting.

32

An earsplitting shriek woke her.

She groaned.

The shriek came again, this time louder.

She tried to cover her ears, but her hands wouldn't move. She forced her eyes open and blinked, wondering why her vision was so hazy. Had she gotten drunk? Passed out?

And why was she so cold?

The ceiling above the bed swam into view, just out of focus. It was morning. She knew that much. An early dawn crept in through the parted drapes and the air in the room was icy, as though she had walked into a deep freeze.

I have to put a log on the fire.

Disoriented, she turned her head.

Sam stared back at her—from the photo beside her bed.

Then she remembered.

The children. I have to help them. And Sam! He's alive!

She tried to call his name, but the sound was muffled. A second later, she realized why.

A sock was stuffed in her mouth.

Fear infused her to the core as she inhaled through her nose and strained to regain complete consciousness. She struggled to sit up, but that resulted in a sharp pain in her ankles and wrists. Her eyes drifted over her inert body. She shuddered in terror at what she saw. She was lying on top of the blankets and tied spread-eagle to the bedposts.

With nothing on but her bra and panties.

She screamed, but the gag restrained the sound. She screamed again. And again, until her throat burned and her cries subsided into whimpers of uncontrolled terror.

Something fluttered outside the window.

The crow peered through the glass, watching her.

Sadie stared at it with pure dread. Crows were the harbingers of death. The bird was here for one reason. To claim her soul. She knew that now.

I am not going to die! Not here. Not like this.

Adrenaline surged through her veins. Behind the gag, she let out an angry yowl and tugged on the coarse ropes above her head. Squeezing her hands, she tried to make them small enough to slip through the ropes. She twisted and pulled, but the ropes cut deeper into her flesh until her wrists were on fire and her arms ached from being stretched into such an unnatural position.

A trickle of blood dripped down one arm. For a moment, she watched it, captivated by the bright red against her pale skin. Then she lifted her head and fixed wild eyes on the open doorway. *Is he gone? Will he be back?*

Her near nakedness made her feel defiled.

Did he—? No, don't think of that!

The wintry air made her shiver uncontrollably.

A door slammed. Footsteps drew near and a shape moved into the doorway.

"Good, you're awake. And looking a might...perky."

Sarge stepped into the room and set a gas can on the dresser.

Sadie's heart kicked into overdrive. *No, please...*

With a shudder, she squeezed her eyes shut, desperately wishing she could close her legs too. She felt him watching her, taking in every inch of her body.

Something skittered across the floor.

Her eyes flashed open in alarm.

Sarge had dragged a chair next to the bed. With one hand, he flipped it around. Then he straddled it and folded his arms across the back—like he had all the time in the world.

When his hand moved toward her, a wave of repulsion made her stomach heave. She gave a muffled cry and yanked her head away. But that only made her dizzy. Whatever he had injected her with was still in her system.

"Such perfect skin," he whispered. "Same as your kid."

She shuddered as his calloused fingers trailed up her arm to her neck, caressing it, circling it. For a moment, she thought he was going to strangle her. Then his sandpaper hand skimmed over her right breast, cupping it roughly.

"You know, it don't gotta be like this," he said. "If you're nice to me, I could be nice to you. Maybe tell you where your kid is."

She whipped her head around and grunted persistently.

Take off the gag, you bastard.

Sarge's eyes narrowed in suspicion. "I'll take the sock outta your mouth, but if you scream, no one'll hear you and I'll just shove it back in. Understand?" He drew his hand away from her breast and removed the sock.

Swallowing repeatedly, she cleared her raw throat. Cotton fibers clung to her tongue, the inside of her cheeks and the roof of her mouth.

"I saw Sam die," she said in a hoarse voice. "You killed him."

"You *thought* you saw him."

Sadie recalled the boy in the car. He had been bound in such a way that very little of his face was exposed. And since The Fog had told her it was Sam, she had...

Assumed.

"I took that boy last year," Sarge admitted. "But his time was up. So I dressed him in your kid's stuff, tied him in the car and called you."

"You killed him right in front of me."

He let out a huff. "Nah, he was already dead. I put him to sleep a week before I took your kid."

His admission horrified her. "Why would you do that?"

"He'd served his usefulness."

"But why make me think he was Sam?"

"You're not very smart, are ya?" he said, shaking his head. "To kill two birds. You gave the cops my picture and I had to show you I was serious, so you wouldn't say nothing else. I wanted the police to back off. Plus, I figured they'd go slower if they knew I'd kill 'em."

In the living room, the grandfather clock let out an ominous gong. Time was running out, and Sadie knew she had to keep Sarge talking. She had one chance to survive. And that rested with a red-bearded Scot.

Please, God...let Fergus get the cops!

"What about the blood? The police said it was—"

"Your kid's," he said with a shrug. "I was a medic in the Forces. Until they discharged me. Collecting a little blood and leaving it on some bushes was nothing." He rubbed his chin. "Cutting off his toe and finger took a bit of work though. Your kid's a fighter."

Sadie's blood turned to ice. "What kind of monster are you?"

"That's the price of warfare. You should never have fucked with me. I warned ya."

"Where is my son?"

"Not so fucking fast!" he snarled. "I want something first."

"What?"

His tongue swept over cracked lips. "Something I ain't had in five years."

When he smiled, acid boiled up into her throat.

Change the subject! Get him thinking about something else!

"I know about Carissa," she rasped. "And your kids, Ashley and Adam."

"What the hell do you know?"

"I know they died in a fire. That's how your face got burned. You tried to save them."

"Yeah, except that's not what happened. Not really."

A sound erupted from him and his entire body twitched.

It took a moment before Sadie realized he was laughing.

"Tell me then. What happened?"

Sarge gripped the back of the chair. "Carrie was gonna take them away from me. Said I was different after I came back from Iraq." There was a baffled look in his eyes. "Do you know what she told me? That my kids were afraid of me. I tried to tell her that wasn't true, that I was a good dad. Sure, I had nightmares. Awful ones. So did most of the guys when we got back home."

"Maybe she was right," she mumbled.

"Bullshit! She wanted me to go see some shrink, like I'm insane or something. She was gonna use that against me to keep them kids. I found her all ready to leave. So I had to stop her."

"What did you do?"

"I backhanded the bitch. She blacked out, so I set her on fire."

Sadie's sickened gaze moved to the gas can. "You didn't have to kill her. You could have worked something out."

"I wasn't gonna let her take them from me."

"Maybe you could have shared cust—"

Sarge leapt to his feet. "They were *my* kids! Mine!"

Sweat poured down her brow. "But you...k-killed them."

"That was an accident," he said, pacing the floor. "They were supposed to stay in the bunker where I left 'em. Carrie was on the floor in the living room when I set the fire. I didn't know Ashley and Adam had gone back into the house through the basement." He stood by the bed, reliving a memory she couldn't see. "They were in the window, staring at me, crying. Soon as I opened the front door, the goddamn house went up like a pack of matches."

"Then you're right. It was an accident."

Sarge stared off into space. "She wanted to take them away. They always wanna leave me. That's why I have to kill them."

"No, you don't," she argued, straining against the ropes.

After a long pause, he let out a sigh. "Maybe you're right. Maybe they'll stay now that I found them a mama." He noticed her shocked expression. "You said you'd do anything for your boy."

"You expect me to live here?"

"We'll be one big happy family."

"The children won't be happy. Why won't you let them go?"

The look he gave her was deadly. "Because they're mine!"

He stomped to the dresser, grabbed the gas can. "And I won't let you or anyone try and take 'em away from me, Carrie. If I can't have them, no one will. Ever!" He twisted off the cap and the scent of gas quickly permeated the air.

Sadie knew her time had just run out. He was going to burn her alive if she didn't agree to be a mother to the children he had abducted. But he'd have to let her go to do that, she reasoned, which meant maybe she could escape. *With* the children.

"Okay!" she cried out. "I'll do whatever you want."

"And what might that be exactly?"

"I-I'll take care of them. I'll be their…m-mother."

A satisfied look crossed his face. "You'll be more than that."

Sarge recapped the gas can and placed it back on the dresser. Without a word, he removed the heavy winter jacket and kicked off his boots. Then he peeled off his clothes and approached the bed.

"Let's seal the deal then."

33

Sarge stood before her, his body covered in dense black hair, interrupted by old battle scars and faded tattoos. Between his legs dangled a half-erect, pale worm.

Terror suffocated her when she saw his growing arousal. She wanted to look away. But she couldn't.

"No! I said I'd stay, look after them—"

"Me *and* them." He gripped her chin. "You'll look after all of us."

"Please," she whispered.

He stroked his arousal eagerly, his heavy-lidded eyes drifting shut for a moment. "Sure, I'll please ya. You'll be begging for more by the time I'm done. Then I'll tell you where he is. Your kid."

"Tell me where Sam is first."

"Not until you gimme what I want."

Horror engulfed her when he reached out with his free hand and fondled her breasts beneath the bra. She shivered uncontrollably, realizing she had no choice. He was going to rape her. And she had to let him. It was the only way to get the gun.

It's only sex. It doesn't mean a thing.

He tugged aside the bra, his mouth latching onto her nipple.

Sadie wanted to curl up and die. She wanted to throw up, scream with rage. She longed to beat him with her hands, claw out his eyes, kick him in the balls—anything to keep him away from her.

Instead, she forced herself to remain still, unresponsive.

Tap, tap.

Her eyes locked on the crow. It was still in the window.

"What the hell do you want?" she shrieked.

"I wanna fuck you," Sarge replied, biting her breast.

She cried out in agony.

With a grunt, he stretched out on top of her. The coarse hair on his chest scratched her delicate skin and his weight crushed her.

This isn't happening, she told herself. *This is a nightmare. You drank too much, passed out.*

Sarge lowered his face close to hers and she could smell the foulness of his rancid breath. Everything about him smelled like disease—putrid...evil. He groped between her legs and she whimpered and automatically clenched her thighs, desperate to close everything off from him.

Gain his trust, Sadie. Get him to untie you. Then get the gun.

"If you remove the—"

A fist connected with her face. "Shut the fuck up! I know how to do this."

Stunned, she went limp. This was no drunken dream.

Again, he fumbled.

She drew in an agonized breath. "I can help you."

His eyes narrowed into suspicious slits, but he said nothing.

"I need to put my legs up," she said, biting her lip until she tasted blood. "I'll make it good for you."

"Why would you do that?"

"So you won't hurt Sam. Or the others."

"Just for them?"

"No! For you too." She tried to smile. "And me. I haven't had good s-sex...in a long time."

He contemplated the lie. "If you try anything, I'll make you suffer. Then I'll kill him." He flicked the photo of Sam that sat on the nightstand and it toppled over. "You got that?"

"Yes," she said. "But there's one problem."

He eyed her warily. "What?"

"The bed is too soft. I need everything...hard."

There was a salacious gleam in his eyes. "The floor, then."

He climbed off her and untied the ropes. Once she was free, she stretched cautiously and covered her breasts, until she saw his angry expression.

"It's cold in here," she murmured.

"I'll heat you up."

She bit back a reply. Easing herself to a sitting position, she flexed her limbs. "My hands and feet are numb. Give me a minute to get my circulation back and get warm."

He snickered and thrust his hips toward her. "You could warm *this* up."

If she hesitated any longer, Sarge would have her doing something revolting. Not that the alternative was any more pleasant, but at least she'd have a chance to get the gun.

It was her only chance.

You can do this, Sadie. For Sam. For the others.

"I'm going to put the bedspread on the floor," she mumbled, conscious of his fiery gaze on every part of her body.

He licked his lips, then nodded. "Hurry up."

She grabbed the bedspread and watched it settle on the floor.

"Let me straighten it," she said, praying she could get to the gun in time.

She knelt on the blanket.

That was the wrong thing to do.

Sarge dropped to the floor behind her, pressed up against her and shoved her forward until her face hit the blanket. She blinked, stunned and gasping for air.

Then she saw it.

The gun box.

It was tucked under the bed, inches away from her left hand.

"Now that's a sight to see," Sarge said. "You'll make a good mama."

When he stroked her raised buttocks, she bit her tongue hard to keep from screaming. She reached out—fingers flexed—and slid her hand under the bed.

"Don't move 'less I tell ya to!" he snarled, cuffing the back of her head. "Now, be a good little doggy."

"Wait!" she cried. "Let me turn over."

Her hand bumped against the gun box. She curled her fingers over it and slid the top open. Once she touched cool metal, her heart soared. She clenched the gun in her hand, then carefully withdrew it and cradled it under her chest.

"Give me what I want!" Sarge commanded.

She fingered the gun. "You owe me something first."

"What?"

"Tell me where Sam and Cortnie are."

"Dunno."

"Yes, you do. And you're going to tell me."

He smirked. "Now why would I do a stupid thing like that?"

With lightning speed, she rolled away and jumped to her feet.

Sarge sat up, his eyes flashing in anger. "What the fuck do you think you're doing?" He probably would have lunged at her, but he noticed the glint of metal in her hand. "Oh, my," he said with a snort. "Mama's got a gun."

She aimed the weapon at his chest. "And Mama's prepared to use it, you fucking bastard."

He stood slowly, the worm between his legs now miniscule.

"Don't move!" she shrieked.

The web of scars on Sarge's face twitched. "If you shoot me, you'll never know where they are."

He was right. And they both knew it.

"Put down the gun and I'll take you to them," he said.

"If I do that, you'll kill me...*and* them."

He took a step forward. "You're right."

She leveled the gun. The gun with one bullet. The gun that wouldn't fire. "Where are they, Sarge?"

"You won't do it," he sneered. "You *can't* do it."

As he stalked toward her, she prayed to God, to Buddha, to the universe, to every higher power that he was wrong. She prayed that this time when she pulled the trigger, the gun would go off.

It did.

34

The shot reverberated in the small cabin, and Sadie stumbled backward from the recoil just as a silver object whizzed past her arm. The fishing knife clattered to the floor behind her. She kicked it past the doorway, then turned to face her tormentor.

Sarge sagged against the wall, clutching his stomach with both hands while a crimson tide rippled between his fingers.

"Don't move!" she ordered.

He gave her a surprised, almost hurt, look. "You shot me."

With lightning speed, she grabbed the robe from the closet and shrugged it on to cover her nakedness. A blossom of blood stained the sleeve. She turned to the man by the wall and raised the gun again, even though there were no bullets in it. "Tell me where Sam and Cortnie are."

Sarge began to quiver and she wondered if he was going into shock. But then she heard his mocking laughter.

"You told me you knew where they were," she yelled.

"I lied." He slid down the wall, leaving a trail of blood. "They took off on me. It's Ashley's fault."

"Cortnie!" she snapped. "They have names. Their *own*."

"She's too smart for her own good. We'll have to punish her."

"Of course," she said with a fake smile. "But first I'll have to get them, bring them back. Where are they, Sarge?"

On the floor, he blinked vacantly.

"Tell me," she insisted.

"I dunno."

"I'm going to find them," she said. "And then we're all going home. Back to Edmonton."

"But they wanna stay with me," he whined. "With us. We could be happy, Carrie. We could be a family again. How could you take our children from me? They're mine."

Sadie gaped at him. Sarge had completely cracked.

She shook her head. "They'll *never* be yours."

Instantly, Sarge was back with her. "You belong to me too," he said with a weak smirk. "You'll never forget me. You'll think of me every time you fuck someone."

"You're a disgusting pig," she seethed. "I won't waste a second of my life thinking about you. I hope you rot in prison. When all the children get back to their parents, they'll make sure you do. None of them want to stay with you. Not Marina or Holland. None of them."

"What the fuck you talking about?"

"I'm taking them all out of here."

Sarge laughed. The sound gurgled up from his chest, liquid and abrasive. A bubble of saliva spewed out of the corner of his mouth, followed by bright red blood. He didn't notice.

"You won't ever find 'em," he rasped. "Not before they blow up into itty bitty pieces." He raised a shaky hand and stared at his watch. "In one hour."

Sadie's pulse quickened. "A bomb?"

"And you don't know the code," he sneered. "Aw, too bad."

"What code?"

He stared at her, mute and defiant.

"You're dying," she said. "Do something right for a change. Tell me the code."

"Go to hell."

"I've been there. And back. It's your turn now. The code!"

He mimicked a zipper sliding across his lips.

"Help me save them," she pleaded.

"I've saved enough lives. In the Forces. Look where that got me." He coughed up more blood. "Discharged on medical with a measly pension that a dog couldn't live on. I watched my buddies get blown into bits. They wanted me to stitch 'em back, and when I couldn't, I had to amputate their legs, their arms. But I saved them. And they hated me for it."

As Sadie watched him, a bout of intense dizziness gripped her. She held back a moan, then surreptitiously examined her injured arm. The knife had sliced into her skin, maybe half an inch deep. She needed to tie something around it, stop the bleeding.

But she couldn't leave Sarge. Not until he gave her the code.

"You'd be a hero," she said, grasping at anything.

"I'm already a hero. I fought overseas for my country. I was in the Gulf War. Iraq. For what—peacekeeping? What a fucking joke!" Another grating cough. "I get home, my wife is ready to leave me and take my kids. She was gonna leave me with nothing. Just bills and this ugly face." He spit a dark clot of blood on the floor. "That's a hero's payment."

"Come on. What's the code, Sarge?"

He snickered. "Mi casa...es...su casa."

The familiar words made her sick to her stomach.

"Give me the code!"

"You can't get into mi casa," he taunted.

His head dropped to his chest, a long wheeze of air erupting from his mouth.

"Sarge?" She crept forward and touched his neck.

He had a pulse. A faint one.

She shook him. "Sarge!"

When he lifted his gaze, thick lips beamed a malevolent smile. But he said nothing. He just stared at her, his mouth stretched into a sick grin.

"What's the fucking code?" she screamed.

She slapped him and his head lolled lifelessly to one side.

Sarge was dead.

A sound behind her made her jump.

The crow waited on the window ledge, its beak pressed against the glass. The bird was so motionless that if she didn't know any better, she would have thought it was nothing more than a plastic lawn ornament.

"What the fuck do you want?" she yelled, fists clenched.

She crossed the room, but the bird's gaze remained fixed.

On Sarge's body.

She hesitated, finally realizing the bird's mission.

The crow bobbed its head. Then it flew off with a loud squawk. It had gotten what it had come for.

Grabbing a pair of clean, dry jeans, a sweater and socks, Sadie headed for the bathroom. Before dressing, she scrubbed away every trace of Sarge. No one had to know the disgusting things he had done to her. He had kidnapped her son, then come after her, drugged her and tied her up. Surely that was enough.

She took the belt from her robe, and using her teeth, she secured it around two facecloths padding her arm. She'd lost a lot of blood from the knife wound. But she couldn't stop now.

"You have to save the children," she said to her reflection.

Before the bunker explodes.

When she stepped out of the bathroom, she kept her eyes on the main part of the cabin. She was conscious of Sarge's body in the bedroom, but she didn't want to think about it. Not now. It would probably take years before she could accept that she had killed a man. And even longer to admit that she had wanted to.

Pulling on her jacket, she winced at the pain that shot through her arm. She should have fashioned a makeshift sling, but she needed both hands to wrestle the tree stump. With her good arm, she opened the back door. The sudden bright light seared her eyes and she staggered outside. Straight into a solid, breathing body.

Jay Lucas' grizzled face swam into view. "Sadie?"

"Jay! Wha—how did you get here so fast?"

The detective lifted his eyes skyward. "Helicopter."

"But you're afraid to fly!"

"I had no choice. This man insisted."

Sadie saw Fergus standing behind Jay. She opened her mouth to thank him, but her knees gave in. "Oh, crap."

Jay's eyes wrinkled in concern. "Are you hurt?"

"It's just a scratch." She gave Fergus a wry look. "Your fishing knife paid me back for stealing it."

"Let me see," Jay demanded, moving closer.

"No, we don't have time. We have to find the bunker. Sarge has it rigged to explode in less than an hour."

Jay tugged a radio from his pocket. He muttered something into it. Then he looked at her. "Can you show us the entrance?"

"Yes. I think so."

"Where's Sarge?" Fergus asked, eyeing the woods nervously.

She nudged her head toward the cabin. "In there. He's dead."

"Dead?" both men said in unison.

"He drugged me and tied me up," she murmured, looking away. "When he untied me, I shot him."

Jay disappeared inside. A moment later, he returned, a grim look on his face. "Where'd the gun come from?"

Sadie opened her mouth to answer, but Fergus beat her to it.

"I suspect 'tis Sarge's. He had a collection. Some legal, some not." He gave her a hard stare, as if to say, "Don't argue with me, lass!"

"Someone should stay here," Jay said to Fergus. "With the body. Are you up for that?"

The Scot nodded. "Aye, you can count on me, Detective Lucas."

"And the children are counting on me," Sadie said.

Jay's eyes drifted to the trees. "I can't believe they're alive."

Fergus sighed. "And I canna believe Sarge took 'em. Don't know what he was thinking, that man."

"He wasn't," Jay replied gruffly. He turned to Sadie. "So they're all in the bunker?"

"Except Sam and Cortnie. They ran away." Her eyes watered. "We have to find them. It's too cold, especially at night."

"Do you have any idea where they would have gone?"

"No, but maybe the other children do."

35

Two police helicopters waited in the middle of the field, their blades whirring. A dozen uniformed police officers wearing Kevlar vests combed the area surrounding what was left of Sarge's house. Some had search dogs, but the dogs seemed more interested in sniffing the cinders of the house than finding a trail through the woods. On Jay's command, two female officers had moved to the exterior of the house, guns drawn.

No one knew what to expect, but as Jay told Sadie, it was better to be prepared for anything.

Yesterday's storm was over, the river already receding. The raging wind had died to a calm, intermittent draft, leaving everything in its wake fresh again.

"Anything yet," Jay barked into his radio.

Sadie heard a muffled, *"No,"* and her heart sank.

They'd been searching for half an hour and they were running out of time. Already, a team had investigated the shed, confirming the existence of a generator, hot water tank, water filter and air purifier, but all the pipes and cables were buried far underground. It would take hours, maybe days, to excavate them and follow them to the hidden bunker.

They didn't have hours.

She stood with Jay, mere yards from the house.

"This is impossible," she moaned. "We've been all over these woods and nothing seems familiar. How do we find one tree stump in a forest filled with them?"

"Hey, it was dark and raining out. No one blames you."

"*I* do."

She blamed herself for not paying attention. She had followed the children through the woods and helped Marina dislodge the stump. Yet every stump Jay had tried only uprooted dirt and mud.

Frustrated, she pounded a fist against her thigh. "I know I'm forgetting something. Something important."

It gnawed at her, this thought that she knew how to find them. Was it something the children had said? Something Sarge had said?

"Shit!" she muttered. "It was something about the doors."

"Doors? As in plural?"

"That's it!" She slapped her forehead, feeling stupid. "Jesus! There were *two* entrances. The stump and another door."

"Where did it lead?"

Her heart sank. "I don't know. I never opened it. Sarge came in that way. We heard him thumping down the stairs." She grabbed Jay's arm. "Wait! When I was by that door, I smelled smoke. And Sarge said Ashley and Adam went back into the house from the bunker the night of the fire. Via the basement."

"They're in the basement!" Jay shouted into the radio.

From the woods, a swarm of men emerged. Like bees converging on a hive, they raced toward the house.

A detective wearing a yellow vest waved to Jay. "We're ready," he yelled. "But we gotta be careful. We don't know how it's been rigged."

"Stay here, Sadie," Jay ordered, pressing his radio into her hand. "Don't forget to take your finger off the button when you're done speaking." He disappeared into the wreckage.

Sadie leaned against a tree and watched the house.

The radio crackled. *"Sadie? Can you hear me?"*

She pressed the button. "Did you find anything?"

"There's a hole leading to a basement. We're going down—"

A sharp crack of static interrupted him.

"Jay?"

Silence.

Then the radio sputtered. *"Sa...at the...you know..."*

"What?" she yelled. "I missed what you said. Repeat, please."

"We're in the bunker...no kids in the main room or Sarge's bedroom. There's one other door we haven't opened yet."

"That's the children's room!"

"Sadie...we need a code for that door."

The code. *Shit!* She had forgotten about it.

"Oh, God. I tried to get Sarge to tell me."

There was more hissing static.

Then Jay's voice came across, clear and gentle. *"Sadie, we get one chance at this. Do you understand? He's got it wired so the whole place will go up if we punch in the wrong code."*

She clawed at her throat, unable to breathe.

"Sadie!"

She began to weep. "I don't know it, Jay. Oh, Jesus...I don't know the code. We can't save them."

There was another crackle.

"Don't give up. The keypad is alphabetical. The code is six letters."

She wracked her brain for a code.

Sarge would make it something easy to remember, yet important, like a name. Adam...Ashley—no, he wouldn't pick one child over the other. Carissa...

"Carrie!" She was so excited she forgot to turn on the radio. She jabbed it again. "I think it's Carrie—his wife's name."

"Carrie. Are you sure?"

"Not really, but it's six letters."

"Okay, good job. Codes usually mean something to a perp."

"It has to be Carrie."

Even as she said it, she began to doubt whether Sarge would have used the name of the one person who wanted to take everything away from him, including his children. In the end, he hated her. Enough to set her on fire, kill her.

"Wait!" she yelled into the radio. "I think I'm wrong."

No reply.

"Jay! It's not Carrie!"

The radio hissed, then Jay's voice cut in. *"We have to hurry, Sadie. We have less than ten minutes."*

"No!" she sobbed. "That's not enough time to figure this out."

"If you don't have another suggestion, we'll have to try Carrie."

A sudden motion caught her eye.

Men streamed out of the ruins, moving a safe distance away. Everyone was out of the house—except the bomb squad detective in the yellow vest...and Jay.

"Maybe you should get out of there," she urged him.

"Six letters, Sadie. Maybe he told you and you just didn't know it."

She recalled Sarge's final words. *"You can't get into mi casa."*

"You can't get into my house."

Jesus! It had been right there in front of her. *The bastard!*

"MI CASA!" she shrieked. "M...I...C...A...S...A."

"You sure?"

"I'm sure, Jay. The bastard was laughing at me when he said it. He never thought I'd figure it out. Mi casa. My house."

The line went dead silent.

Her pulse quickened. Was she wrong?

"Please, God...watch over Jay and the children. Keep them safe." She lifted her head to the sky. "And please help us find Sam and Cortnie."

She waited, holding her breath. Surely the time was up.

"Jay?" she said into the radio.

Static.

She stared at the house. No smoke, no explosion.

Five minutes passed. Still nothing.

The radio crackled.

"The code worked, Sadie," Jay said, his voice sounding tired.

"And you found them?"

Pause. "Yes. We found them."

Sadie released a long, ragged breath. Elated, she clicked off the radio, shoved it into her jacket pocket and strode toward the house. She was a jumble of emotions. She wanted to dance in the field. In that moment, she made a promise. To God, herself...and Sam. She would never drink again. It was a promise she would keep.

"Thank you, God," she said. "I'm clean."

She paced in the grass, excited to see the children again. One of them must have an idea where Sam and Cortnie had gone. Maybe Cortnie had said something before they left, given them a clue.

The officer in the yellow vest appeared first. He looked her way, then veered toward a group of men near the shed. He said something to one of them and they set off for the house.

When Jay finally materialized, he headed straight for her. His face was smudged with soot and he looked drained.

She ran to him, smiling. "We did it, Jay!"

He didn't answer.

She tugged his arm. "Come on, the least you can do is smile."

"Sadie..."

She peered over his shoulder. "Where are they? How come they aren't out yet?"

Jay gave her a helpless look. "Sadie, they're..."

She couldn't breathe. "What's wrong? Why are you looking at me that way?"

"They're dead, Sadie."

"What?"

"They're dead. All of them."

"But that's impossible. They were all fine when I left them here. You're wrong. Go check them. They're alive."

Jay's wrinkled eyes clouded. "There are seven bodies down there. All in different stages of decomp, which means some of them have been dead awhile. And we know he blew up one boy in the car. That makes eight kids. That's how many The Fog took."

"Eight," she said, numb.

"Including Cortnie...and Sam. I'm sorry, Sadie."

"But I—" She shook her head. "You have to be wrong."

She closed her eyes, trying to rationalize it all. She had brushed

Marina's hair, watched Holland drink hot chocolate with marshmallows and they had left gifts on her doorstep. She had even followed them through the woods to the bunker. How else would she have known where it was?

She pictured six sweet, trusting faces.

Marina, Holland, Brittany, Scotty, Kimber, Jordan…

"Marina said Sam and Cortnie ran away," she insisted. "Sarge said the same thing."

"He must have found them," Jay said gently. "Before he came after you. He was messing with your head, Sadie."

There was only one way to see if Jay was telling the truth.

She sprinted toward the house.

"Wait!" Jay yelled. "Come back! You don't want to go in there. Trust me."

But she was beyond trusting anyone. This was something she had to see for herself.

Tripping over chunks of blackened wood, she made her way through the damp cinders, kicking up sticky soot that had found refuge under slabs of wood and melted metal. In one corner, she saw a broad-shouldered detective standing near a hole in the floor. He looked up as she approached.

"I need to get down there," she said.

The officer peeked over her shoulder.

"It's okay," Jay huffed behind her. "Help her down."

The two men secured a rope around her waist, then lowered her into the hole in the floor. The air thickened as ash wafted down around her, loosened by the motions of the men above. The pungent tang of smoke was everywhere—in her mouth, clinging to her skin and hair, but at least she could see. The basement was lit by strategically placed heavy-duty flashlights, and she was thankful that she wasn't descending into darkness. She'd had enough of that lately.

When she reached the ground, a young rookie unfastened the rope. "This way," he said, his face etched with green pallor.

As he led her through the rubble, she was surprised to see that the fire had not reached the basement. Most of the damage had been done by rain and soot seeping in through the floor and the gaping hole. Everything was covered with a layer of grime, and black rain dripped around her, looking as eerie as it sounded.

She spotted a crib in one corner and a toy box overflowing with games, Disney movies, dolls and Star Wars figures in the other. Beside the toy box, an air hockey table held about two inches of murky water.

"It's behind here," the rookie said, distracting her.

He pulled aside a metal shelf that was attached to a sheet of moldy drywall. Behind it, stairs led downward to another level.

Within minutes, Sadie was back inside the bunker.

"At least I didn't imagine this," she said, her eyes skimming over the room.

"What?" the rookie asked.

"Nothing."

The young man led her to the door with the keypad.

"Mi casa," she said, as he keyed in the code.

The door unlocked with an audible click.

The rookie stepped aside and gave her a worried look. "You sure you want to go in there, ma'am?"

Sadie opened the door.

36

The children were laid out on blanketed crib mattresses on the concrete floor—girls on one side of the room, boys on the other. A blue light above them shed little light in the room, casting the bodies in a ghostly pallor. They were dressed in their pajamas, their hands folded sweetly in their laps.

Sadie's gaze grazed the lifeless bodies. It was too dark to see them clearly and it was obvious from the ripe smell that some were, as Jay had put it, in *decomp*.

Tears welled in her eyes. "They look like they're sleeping."

She counted them and stifled a sob. "Seven."

Jay's right. All the kids are here. Even Sam.

She let out tight, unsteady gasps.

"Are you okay, ma'am?" the rookie said behind her.

"No." She turned away. "I have to get out of here."

She was raised up again, into the light and breathable air, and Jay escorted her away from the opening and far from the house.

"I couldn't look at their faces," she moaned. "I didn't want to see Sam. Not like that." She raised her eyes. "Does that make me a terrible mother?"

"No," Jay said, his voice cracking. "It makes you human. You can look at Sam when you're ready."

"I'll never be ready," she wailed. "I *saw* them, Jay! I spoke to them, fed them. I just don't understand. Marina said Cortnie and Sam had escaped. I believed her. For the first time in weeks, I had hope." She held her hands out. "And for what?"

"Sadie, we never would've found them. Not without you. They would've been down there forever. Maybe that's why you saw them, so you and the other parents can get closure, so the children can have a proper burial."

Jay's words made her angry.

"I already buried my son once. I can't do it again." Her sobs came in angry gasps. "I refuse to!"

"You did a good thing here, Sadie. Don't forget that."

But she wanted to forget. Forget the bodies, forget everything.

She fled across the field. When she reached the shed, she slumped with her back against it and sank to the damp ground.

"You imagined it all. There were no kids...no Sam. It's all a lie!" She smacked her head against the shed. "Stupid, stupid drunk!" Tears streamed down her face, momentarily blinding her, and she cradled her head and wept for the children, for Sam and for herself.

"Ssssadie..."

Hearing her name, she lifted a tear-streaked face and saw a gray fog rolling toward her. The sight of it paralyzed her as it churned and separated. Then seven ghostly forms stepped forward.

The children. The *dead* children.

"What do you want from me?" Sadie cried.

Marina moved toward her. "We want to thank you."

"Thank me for what?"

"You came back for us."

"But it's too late."

"It's never too late." Marina reached out with both hands, framing Sadie's face. "You did *exactly* what we asked you to."

"What do you mean? I didn't do anything."

"Remember the things we left you?"

"Your message, 'help us'?"

Marina nodded. "Well, you did. Help us, I mean."

Sadie moaned. "No, I didn't."

"Yes, you did," the girl insisted. "You saved us from being with *him*. You've given us peace. And our freedom."

Sadie struggled to her feet. "Freedom? You're all dead!"

"And you brought us all *home*." Marina hugged her. "Thank you, Sadie O'Connell."

Before Sadie could say a word, the girl tore herself away and ran across the field. As she reached the edge where the dead grass met the swirling fog, the other children joined her. They stood in a row, holding hands, facing Sadie...smiling. Then, one by one, the children began to merge with the fog, until only Marina was left.

"Wait!" Sadie pleaded. "Don't go!"

"We have to. But we're leaving you three last gifts."

Marina turned away, then peered over her shoulder, a glowing smile shaping her lips. "There's a light beyond the fog, Sadie. The most beautiful light. It's warm and peaceful, and filled with so much love it takes your breath away. Make sure you tell my parents that. Tell them I love them and that I'll always be a part of this world. I'll be in every sunrise and every sunset. We *all* will. It's our destiny."

A finger of pulsating ethereal light reached out and caressed Marina, gently pulling her into its core. Then laughter, soft and sweet, mingled with the breeze, and the fog dissipated, as if it had never existed.

"Goodbye," Sadie wept.

A startling squawk shattered the calm, and her bleary eyes snapped skyward. Beyond the trees, a crow circled the peak of a rocky hill. Even from the distance, she could make out a dark recessed area near the top. A cave.

"We're leaving you three last gifts," Marina had said.

Sadie's heart skipped a beat. "Wait! I saw *seven* children, but no Sam."

She stared at the crow.

And then she knew.

Sam was alive, and there was just one place Sam would feel completely safe.

Cadomin Cave!

Clamping a hand over her wounded arm, she raced through the woods until she reached the base of the hill. Then she began to climb. The trail—if one could call it that—was about a foot wide and barely detectable in some places. It had most likely been carved by a meandering stream trickling down the hillside.

Half an hour later, the radio in her pocket crackled.

"Sadie?"

"Yeah," she panted.

"Where the heck are you? I thought you went back to your cabin."

"I'm on my way to Cadomin Cave."

"What? What the hell are you—?"

"Sam is in the cave."

Pause.

"Listen, Sadie, you're hurt and you've lost a lot of blood. You're not thinking—aw, hell. Never mind. I'm on my way. Wait for me."

But there was no way in hell she was waiting.

The higher she climbed, the more the landscape changed. The dense forest at the base of the steep slope thinned, and evergreens and low shrubbery with early spring buds gave way to loose, chalky gray rock and ridges with sheered edges.

Somewhere on the other side was the common path, the one the tourists took to Cadomin Cave. And somewhere behind her, she guessed, Jay was trying to navigate the same path she was taking. But he wouldn't be catching up any time too soon.

She wiped a grimy hand across her brow and squinted up at the peak. Martha said it would take an hour and a half from base to cave. For Sadie, it was a grueling two hours. As she finally glimpsed the cave entrance, she let out a sigh of relief.

"Cawww!" the crow cried above her.

"There's nothing for you here," she yelled.

Distracted, she didn't see the sinkhole until her foot—the same one she had twisted earlier—sank into it and disappeared up to the knee. She plunged forward and went down, hard and fast, her injured arm slamming into the ground. She howled in pain, not knowing which to clutch first, her arm or her foot. As she lay on the ground, she prayed she hadn't broken anything.

After a few minutes, she took a deep breath and withdrew her leg from the hole. With a disdainful chuckle, she said, "You're going to end up in a body cast at this rate."

She took a quick inventory. Her jeans were torn and her leg had a patch of angry scrapes and welts, but no broken bones.

Her gaze wandered toward the cave. Doubt set in. Maybe she was wrong. Maybe she had climbed up this godforsaken hill, risking limbs and life for nothing.

The cave beckoned her.

She limped toward it, ignoring the numbness in her arm and the shooting pain that flared up her leg.

Beside the entrance, a plaque was mounted on a metal stand.

"Welcome to Cadomin Cave," she read.

The greeting was followed by a number of safety rules, including one on carrying sufficient lighting.

Sadie cursed under her breath.

Resigned to another dark journey, she moved toward the mouth of the cave. The ledge above it was low and she ducked her head.

"Sam?"

Her voice echoed back, teasing her mercilessly.

"Sam, are you in there?"

Then the mouth of the cave swallowed her.

37

The cave was bone cold. Even dressed in a winter jacket, Sadie felt an extreme drop in temperature. She groped at the damp wall, feeling her way as the light faded. The ground was slick with mud, so each step was measured and cautious. A few yards in, a foul odor slapped her in the face.

"Jesus!"

She kept moving.

Finally, the narrow corridor opened up to a cavern about thirty feet wide by fifteen feet high. She moved on autopilot, walking until the light behind her was almost gone and she could hardly make out the path or the rock formations ahead.

An imperceptible shift in the air made her pause.

"Sam?"

"Sam...Sam...Sam..." the cave mocked.

Something stirred in the shadows.

"Sam? It's Mommy!"

The ground began to vibrate and a frigid current of air made her shiver. Before she knew what was happening, a black mass swarmed toward her. She screamed and ran towards the light.

Bats—hundreds of them—whirred past her, scratching her face, desperate to escape the cave. One flew into her hair. She swatted at it, shrieking and crying at the same time. Covering her head, she sank into the mud and pressed her body against the wall. When the bats were gone, she stood shakily and was about to continue on her way when she heard a soft murmur.

Voices. And they were coming closer.

Two shapes emerged from the depths of the cave.

"Hello?" she said softly.

With a whimper, a small body flung itself at her.

She touched a cool shaved head. *Could it be?* "Sam?"

There was a shudder, then quiet sobs. Recognizable sobs.

It *was* Sam.

"Oh, my God," she cried, stroking his head. "You're alive."

Sobbing with relief, she rocked him in her arms. "I found you, Sam. Mommy found you."

She leaned back and studied him. His skin was clammy, caked in mud. She stroked his dirty face. He raised his eyes and the terror she saw there made her heart stop beating.

"You're safe, honey. Mommy's here."

"Are you taking us home?" a girl said from the shadows.

Shocked, Sadie held out a hand. "Cortnie?"

"Ashley," the girl said, shuffling closer. "Father said no one can call me by my old name."

Sadie's eyes swam with tears. "He's wrong. Your name is Cortnie Bornyk. And your real dad is waiting for you."

Cortnie let out a sob. "I want my daddy, not that other man."

Sadie grabbed the girl, hugged her close. "It's okay, Cortnie. That man can't hurt you anymore."

"Father wanted us to go to sleep with the others."

Sadie cringed at the girl's words and stood up quickly. A little too quickly. *I have to get them out of here. Before I pass out.*

"Come on," she said.

Cortnie took Sam's hand, but neither of them moved.

"Sam, Cortnie," Sadie said softly. "Let's go home."

She was relieved when they moved toward her, and she led them to the mouth of the cave. A few feet from daylight, her head started pounding. She leaned against the wall.

Just for a moment, until I catch my breath.

In the muted light, she caught sight of Sam's muddy pajamas and his bloody, bandaged hand. He held it close to his chest and she didn't want to think of what lay beneath the strips of cloth.

Then she saw the yellow happy face on Cortnie's nightgown.

"You're the girl I saw in the woods."

Cortnie looked at the ground. "I was trying to get away. I'm sorry Father hurt you."

"I know."

Sadie's vision blurred and she closed her eyes.

"Mommy, can we go now?"

"Yes, honey," she said, fighting another dizzy spell.

A few steps from daylight, she lurched to a stop, turned and gaped at Sam. "D-Did you say something?"

His sapphire eyes blinked. Then he signed *I love you, Mom.*

She tried to smile, but her face hurt. She was imagining things again. She knew she was in rough shape. Too much blood loss, combined with being battered and bruised. *And raped.*

She shook her head. *Don't think about that now.*

She was running out of time…and energy. She could have kicked herself for being so stubborn. For coming to the cave alone.

"Follow me," she said as she stepped out into the light.

The sun's rays bouncing off gray rock blinded her. Then she saw something wonderful. Jay was standing off to one side of the entrance, a flashlight in his hand.

She moved away from the mouth of the cave. "Jay!"

"I was just coming in after you," he said, visibly relieved.

"How…?" Her eyes trailed upward. "Ah, the helicopter."

"That's twice," he said, puffing out his chest. "In one day."

"There may be hope for you yet." She swayed and let out a moan.

"Sadie, are you all—" Jay noticed the children standing in the cave entrance. "Jesus Christ, Sadie! You were right all along."

"A mother knows," was all she could manage.

After that, everything happened in such a flurry of activity that she had to hold onto Jay for support. The droning black blot in the sky above them lowered a harness and she watched as the children were lifted to safety. Then she was hauled up into the air.

Once aboard the helicopter, a paramedic unfastened the harness and she collapsed in the seat beside Sam, emotionally and physically drained. She closed her eyes and heaved a sigh as small hands lovingly stroked her face. She was losing consciousness, until she heard the *click* of her seatbelt.

"Thanks, honey," she said, fighting to open her eyes.

Sam smiled—thumbs up—and said, "Snug as a bug."

Sadie's jaw dropped in shock. "You *can* talk."

She recalled Marina's words—*three gifts*—and looked at Sam and Cortnie. "One, two…and now this."

She reached for her son's hand. "I love you, Sam."

"I love you too, Mommy," he said.

Then a winged black bird swept them away.

∞ ∞ ∞

Sadie was feeling better by the time Jay wheeled her into the University of Alberta Hospital. The first person she saw was Matthew. He was pacing in the waiting room, and the second he saw her, his eyes brightened.

"Sadie! Are you okay?"

"I'm great."

"You, uh, don't look great."

She made a face. "Gee, thanks."

"The police told me to come to the hospital, but I didn't know why. I thought maybe…well…you know."

She smiled tearfully. "We brought you a gift."

Matthew's puzzled gaze flickered toward Jay. Sadie knew the exact second that he noticed his daughter standing behind the detective.

"Cortnie," he said, his voice raw with emotion.

The girl stared up at him, her lower lip quivering. "Daddy?"

Sadie watched Matthew swing Cortnie up into his arms and hold her so tightly that she was sure he'd never let her go. Blinking back tears, she smiled when Sam slipped his warm hand in hers.

She'd never let go either.

epilogue

Sadie paced anxiously on the front porch of the townhouse. It had been ten days since she had shot and killed The Fog, and brought Sam and Cortnie home. Life was slowly returning to normal, although she knew it would never be quite the same.

Leah had rushed to the hospital as soon as she'd heard. It had been difficult and awkward at first, but Sadie realized that the past had its place. In the *past*. Right now, she desperately needed a friend, and Leah was her best friend, her soul sister, a piece of her heart.

Leah didn't recall much about the night she had slept with Philip. She'd been too drunk. However, she did remember that Sam had walked in on them. Philip had grabbed Sam by the arm and threatened that Sadie would leave if he ever said a word. That was why Sam had refused to speak. In a way, he had been held hostage by his own father—a more subtle version of Stockholm syndrome. Sadie was still working on forgiving Philip, but that would take time.

A horn blasted and she jumped.

Philip's Mercedes pulled up to the house, and the sight of an old woman driving it made her laugh. Ed was sitting beside Irma, a grim look on his face. In the back seat, Martha and Fergus looked serious and pale. Car doors slammed as everyone rushed from the vehicle.

Sadie waved. "You made it."

"Barely," Ed grumbled.

"'Course we made it," Irma said. "You think I woulda missed driving *that*?" She nudged her head in the direction of the car.

Ed scowled. "My sister beat me to the driver's seat and refused to budge. We white-knuckled it the whole way."

Irma swatted his arm. "I wasn't driving *that* fast."

"As long as you made it safely," Sadie said, grinning.

She opened the front door and ushered them through to the backyard, where the others were waiting for Sam's belated birthday party to begin. Captured by the sight and sounds of sheer joy, she hovered in the doorway, watching her friends and family.

She glanced at the photo of Sam on the wall behind her.

It was difficult not to feel guilty. Her son had survived while the others had not. She slept restlessly, haunted by nightmares and the urge to check on Sam. She must have gotten up at least eight times last night. Each time, she hesitated at his door, fighting the fear that when she opened it, he'd be gone.

He wasn't gone…but he *was* different.

Sam was adapting to his missing finger and toe, and was mourning the loss of Joey, his imaginary friend. But he had other friends now, or so he told her. He often talked about them. Marina, Holland, and the others. He seemed oblivious to the fact that they were dead—had been dead all along. He told her that Cortnie couldn't see them. She thought Sam was making them up so she'd feel better, but she *had* seen the bodies. Sarge had made them sleep in the same room.

It was Sam who had watched Sarge enter the numerical code on the keypad that led to the stairs, to freedom. He had memorized the four digits. The night he and Cortnie had escaped, Sarge had fallen asleep in his chair after supper. They crept past him and headed into the woods with no particular destination in mind, until Sam remembered seeing the signs for Cadomin Cave.

The rest was history. Or as Sadie believed, fate.

The trauma Sam had endured left him severely depressed. During the first few days, he was almost a stranger to her, cringing when she touched or hugged him, jumping at every loud sound, and fearful of any man who came near. Victim Services had told her that his behavior was common for abduction survivors. They said it would take time, that she had to be patient.

Then there were the nightmares that would leave him writhing, screaming and sweating so badly that she had to move him into her bed. Even worse were the triggers. She'd taken him to McDonald's the other day and a teenager dressed as Ronald was there in full clown gear visiting the children. The instant Sam saw the clown he let out the most god-awful scream and started beating on Sadie with his fists until she took him out.

The doorbell rang, interrupting her thoughts.

"Nice house," Jay mumbled when she let him inside.

"It's a rental. For now." She hugged him, catching him off guard. "Thank you, Jay."

"Yeah, well…you're welcome."

She took a deep breath. "What's going to happen to me?"

"You'll be fine."

"But I killed—"

"It was self-defense, Sadie. No jury in their right mind would convict you."

There was an uneasy silence.

"I wanted to kill him," she whispered.

"I know."

She sighed. "What about the two extra…bodies?"

Jay looked as if he had swallowed something slimy. "His own kids. Ashley and Adam." At her shocked expression, he added, "The bastard dug them up. He couldn't let go of them."

Sadie's eyes fluttered shut. "And the boy in the car, the one I thought was Sam?"

"Holland Dawes. The boy Sarge took last year."

Blue Adam. The boy who spoke with a lisp and loved marshmallows.

Her eyes watered. "Poor Holland."

"He was dead long before the explosion, Sadie."

She nodded. "I know. He was drugged, right?"

"An overdose of sedatives. Like the others. They fell asleep and never woke up."

Sadie's heart ached for the children. For their parents.

"You know," Jay said uneasily. "I always wanted to ask you how you knew."

"Knew what?"

"That the man who took your son was in Cadomin."

She looked him in the eye. "Honestly? I didn't have a clue. I've always been a big believer in fate. I asked Sam to tell me where to stop, show me a sign."

"And what did he show you?"

"A crow, a sign about bat caves…I know that sounds hokey, but as soon as I saw them I just *knew* that's where I was supposed to go. It was fate."

"Fate." Jay tested the word on his tongue.

She glanced at Sam's photograph. "I've got to believe in something, otherwise none of this makes sense. I know what I saw, what I heard and felt. They were there. The children. I think their spirits were collectively strong enough to bring me there, show me signs, help me find them. And Sam."

"You gave them peace."

"So…what do we do now?" she asked.

Jay smiled. "That's easy. You go out there and spend time with your friends and family. And your son."

She crooked her head toward the door. "Why don't you join everyone outside? I'll be out in a minute."

"I, uh, wasn't planning on staying, Sadie. This is for family."

"That's just what you are," she said, taking his arm.

Smiling, she led the old detective out into the sun.

∞ ∞ ∞

After everyone except Matthew and Cortnie had left, Sadie stood on the deck and peered around the side of the house to the street in front. For a second, she could have sworn she saw a man dressed in black watching her.

She shook her head and he dissolved into thin air.

One day you won't haunt me anymore.

It was a momentous task fighting the daily bouts of sadness, shame, fear and extreme rage that sometimes hit her at the most inopportune moments. She still dreamt of a scarred monster, of his hands touching her. She hadn't told a soul about that part—not even Leah.

It didn't take much to remind her of everything that had happened, and even the smallest thing, like seeing Sam's book, had an adverse affect on her mood. She decided to put Going Batty away, for now at least. One day, maybe, she'd get it published.

Sam waved at her. "Mom! Watch this!"

He rode his new bike, the one she had bought for his birthday a lifetime ago. Cortnie had set up two small pieces of wood, creating a jump, and he rode up one side, lifted a few inches into the air and landed with a soft thud.

Her gaze was captured by a slow-drifting mist that glided across the manmade lake beyond the back fence. Her smile faded ever so slightly as she recalled the bizarre fog that had haunted the woods near Infinity Cabin.

The fog…and the children.

There was no logical explanation for it. For *any* of it. Over the past days she had come to accept all that had happened as an act of God. Or Fate. There was no doubt in her mind that Sam had been a conduit for the spirits of the dead children, that he had helped them reach out to her. And he had reached out on his own too. That's why she'd *seen* him everywhere. He had sent the crow to her, knowing she would think of bats and the cave…eventually.

Jay was right. The children had been bound to this world by unfinished business, by bodies that needed to be buried and loved ones who needed closure. And maybe by vengeance and the need to see Sarge brought to justice. They couldn't tell her who they were because they were sworn to secrecy, and even in death, they were held captive by their promise to a madman.

Sam tugged on her sleeve. "Mom, are you listening to me?"

Sadie patted his hair. It was growing so quickly. "I'll always hear you, little man."

"Aw, Mom," he said, scowling. "Don't call me that."

She hugged him close. When he pulled back, he traced the first half of an infinity symbol over her heart. "S is for Sam."

She added the reflecting half. "S is for—"

"Sadie," he interrupted. "Sadie and Sam for all eternity."

With a loud whoop, he jumped on his bike and sped away.

As she watched him, she wiped away a stray tear.

"You all right?" Matthew asked, joining her on the deck.

She smiled. "I am now."

Unexpectedly, he slipped his warm hand in hers. "Thank you," he whispered.

Lost in overwhelming emotions, they watched Sam and Cortnie for a long time, thanking the universe that fate had intervened and their children had been brought back to them, alive. They were the lucky ones.

The fate of the other children weighed heavily on her heart. They had not been as lucky and neither were their parents. Except now they had closure. That had to count for something.

"Mom!" Sam shouted.

She shook away the gloomy clouds. "What, honey?"

"Listen to what Marina taught me. One fine day in the middle of the night…"

"Two dead boys got up to fight," Cortnie joined in, grinning.

In unison, they chanted, "Back-to-back, they faced each other, drew their swords and shot each other. A deaf policeman heard the noise, got up and shot the two dead boys. If you don't believe this story's true—"

Sadie smiled. "Ask my blind uncle. He saw it too."

Sweet innocent laughter wafted in the air, and in that single moment of fate, all was infinitely perfect in the world.

If you enjoyed this book, please consider writing a short review and posting it on Amazon, Goodreads and/or Barnes and Noble. Reviews are very helpful to other readers and are greatly appreciated by authors, especially me. When you post a review, drop me an email and let me know and I may feature part of it on my blog/site. Thank you. ~ Cheryl

cherylktardif@shaw.ca

"One fine day in the middle of the night" (Journal Versions)
One fine day in the middle of the night,
Two dead boys* got up to fight, [*or men]
Back-to-back they faced each other,
Drew their swords and shot each other,
One was blind and the other couldn't see
So they chose a dummy for a referee.
A blind man went to see fair play,
A dumb man went to shout "hooray!"
A paralyzed donkey passing by,
Kicked the blind man in the eye,
Knocked him through a nine inch wall,
Into a dry ditch and drowned them all,
A deaf policeman heard the noise,
And came to arrest the two dead boys,
If you don't believe this story's true,
Ask the blind man he saw it too!
~ Anonymous

Source: http://www.folklore.bc.ca/Onefineday.htm#Onefine

Note from Cheryl: The following version was taught to me by my childhood friend, Cathy Magill, may she rest in peace.

One fine day in the middle of the night,
Two dead boys got up to fight,
Back-to-back they faced each other,
Drew their swords and shot each other.

A deaf policeman heard the noise,
Got up and shot the two dead boys,
If you don't believe this story's true,
Ask my blind uncle, he saw it too!
~ Anonymous

**And now here's an excerpt from Cheryl's international bestselling
thriller, SUBMERGED...**

Prologue

Near Cadomin, AB – Saturday, June 15, 2013 – 12:36 AM

You never grow accustomed to the stench of death. Marcus Taylor
knew that smell intimately. He had inhaled burnt flesh, decayed
flesh...diseased flesh. It lingered on him long after he was separated
from the body.

The image of his wife and son's gray faces and blue lips assaulted
him.

Jane...Ryan.

Mercifully, there were no bodies tonight. The only scent he
recognized now was wet prairie and the dank residue left over from a
rainstorm and the river.

"So what happened, Marcus?"

The question came from Detective John Zur, a cop Marcus knew from the old days. Back before he traded in his steady income and respected career for something that had poisoned him physically and mentally.

"Come on," Zur prodded. "Start talking. And tell me the truth."

Marcus was an expert at hiding things. Always had been. But there was no way in hell he could hide why he was soaked to the skin and standing at the edge of a river in the middle of nowhere.

He squinted at the river, trying to discern where the car had sunk. He only saw faint ripples on the surface. "You can see what happened, John."

"You left your desk. Not a very rational decision to make, considering your past."

Marcus shook his head, the taste of river water still in his throat. "Just because I do something unexpected doesn't mean I'm back to old habits."

Zur studied him but said nothing.

"I had to do something, John. I had to try to save them."

"That's what EMS is for. You're not a paramedic anymore."

Marcus let his gaze drift to the river. "I know. But you guys were all over the place and *someone* had to look for them. They were running out of time."

Overhead, lightning forked and thunder reverberated.

"Dammit, Marcus, you went rogue!" Zur said. "You know how dangerous that is. We could've had four bodies."

Marcus scowled. "Instead of merely three, you mean?"

"You know how this works. We work in teams for a reason. We all need backup. Even you."

"All the rescue teams were otherwise engaged. I didn't have a choice."

Zur sighed. "We go back a long way. I know you did what you thought was right. But it could've cost them all their lives. And it'll probably cost you your job. Why would you risk that for a complete stranger?"

"She wasn't a stranger."

As soon as the words were out of his mouth, Marcus realized how true that statement seemed. He knew more about Rebecca Kingston than he did about any other woman. Besides Jane.

"You know her?" Zur asked, frowning.

"She told me things and I told her things. So, yeah, I know her."

"I still do not get why you didn't stay at the center and let us do our job."

"She called *me*." Marcus looked into his friend's eyes. "*Me*. Not you."

"I understand, but that's your job. To listen and relay information."

"You don't understand a thing. Rebecca was terrified. For herself *and* her children. No one knew where they were for sure, and she was running out of time. If I didn't at least try, what kind of person would I be, John?" He gritted his teeth. "I couldn't live with that. Not again."

Zur exhaled. "Sometimes we're simply too late. It happens."

"Well, I didn't want it to happen this time." Marcus thought of the vision he'd seen of Jane standing in the middle of the road. "I had a...hunch I was close. Then when Rebecca mentioned Colton had seen flying pigs, I remembered this place. Jane and I used to buy ribs and chops from the owner, before it closed down about seven years ago."

"And that led you here to the farm." Zur's voice softened. "Good thing your hunch paid off. *This* time. Next time, you might not be so lucky."

"There won't be a next time, John."

A smirk tugged at the corner of Zur's mouth. "Uh-huh."

"There won't."

Zur shrugged and headed for the ambulance.

Under a chaotic sky, Marcus stood at the edge of the river as tears cascaded from his eyes. The night's events hit him hard, like a sucker punch to the gut. He was submerged in a wave of memories. The first call, Rebecca's frantic voice, Colton crying in the background. He knew that kind of fear. He'd felt it before. But last time, it was a different road, different woman, different child.

He shook his head. He couldn't think of Jane right now. Or Ryan. He couldn't reflect on all he'd lost. He needed to focus on what he'd found, what he'd discovered in a faceless voice that had comforted him and expressed that it was okay to let go.

He glanced at his watch. It was after midnight. 12:39, to be exact. He couldn't believe how his life had changed in not much more than two days.

"Marcus!"

He turned...

Chapter One

Edson, AB – Thursday, June 13, 2013 – 10:55 AM

Sitting on the threadbare carpet in front of the living room fireplace, Marcus Taylor stroked a military issue Browning 9mm pistol against his leg, the thirteen-round magazine in his other hand. For an instant, he contemplated loading the gun—and then using it.

"But then who'd feed you?" he asked his companion.

Arizona, a five-year-old red Irish setter, gave him an inquisitive look, then curled up and went back to sleep on the couch. She was a rescue hound he'd picked up about a year after Ryan and Jane had died. The house had been too damned quiet. Lifeless.

"Great to know you have an opinion."

Setting the gun and magazine down on the floor, Marcus propped a photo album against his legs and took a deep breath. *The photo album of death.* The album only saw daylight three times a year. The other three hundred and sixty-two days it was hidden in a steel foot locker that doubled as his coffee table.

Today was Paul's forty-sixth birthday. Or it would have been, except Paul was dead.

Taking another measured breath, Marcus felt for the chain that marked a page and opened the album. "Hey, Bro."

In the photo, Corporal Paul Taylor stood on the shoulder of a deserted street on the outskirts of a nondescript town in Afghanistan, a sniper rifle braced across his chest and the Browning in his hand. He'd been killed that same day, his limbs ripped apart by a roadside bomb. The IED had been buried in six inches of dust and dirt when Paul, distracted by a crying kid, had unwittingly stepped on it.

One stupid mistake could end in death, separating son from parents and brother from brother. Resentment could separate siblings too.

"I wish I could tell you how sorry I am," Marcus said, blinking back a tear. "We wasted so much time being pissed at each other."

As a young kid, he'd hidden his older brother's toy soldiers so he could play with them when Paul was at school. In high school, Marcus had hidden how smart he was, always downplaying his intelligence in favor of being the cool, younger brother of senior hockey legend Paul Taylor. Marcus had learned to hide his jealousy too.

Until his brother was killed.

He stared at the warped dog tag at the end of the chain. It was all that was left of his brother. There was nothing to be jealous of now.

He glanced at the gun. Okay, he had that too. He'd inherited the Browning from Paul. One of his brother's war buddies had personally delivered it. "Your brother said you can play with his toys now," the guy had said.

Paul always had a warped sense of humor.

"Happy birthday, Paul."

He knew his parents, who were currently cruising in the Mediterranean, would be raising a toast in Paul's honor, so he did the same. "I miss you, bro."

Then he dropped the tag and flipped to the next set of photos in the album. A brunette with short, choppy hair and luminous green eyes smiled back at him.

Jane.

"Hello, Elf."

He traced her face, recalling the way her mouth tilted upward on the left and how she'd watch a chick flick tearjerker, while tears steamed unnoticed down her face.

Marcus turned to the next set of photos and sucked in a breath. A handsome boy beamed a brilliant smile and waved back at him.

"Hey, little buddy."

He recalled the day the photo had been taken. His son, Ryan, a rookie goalie on his junior high hockey team, had shut out his opponents, giving his team a three-goal lead. Jane had snapped the picture at the exact second when Ryan had found his father in the crowd.

"I love you." Marcus's voice cracked. "And I miss you so much."

He couldn't hide that. Not ever.

There was one other thing he couldn't hide.

He had killed Jane. *And* Ryan.

For the past six years, whenever Marcus slept, his dead wife and son came to visit, taunting him with their spectral images, teasing him with familiar phrases, twisting his mind and gut into a guilt-infested cesspool.

The only way to escape their accusing glares and spiteful smiles was to wake up. Or not go to sleep. Sleep was the enemy. He did his best to avoid it.

Marcus glanced at the antique clock on the mantle. 11:06.

Another twenty-four minutes and he'd have to head to the Yellowhead County Emergency Center, where he worked as a 911 dispatcher. He'd been working there for almost six months. He was halfway through five twelve-hour shifts that ran from noon to midnight. He worked them with his best friend, Leo, who would undoubtedly be in a good mood again. Leo liked sleeping in and starting his day at noon, while Marcus preferred the midnight-to-noon shift, the one everyone else hated. It gave him something to do at night, since sleeping didn't come easily.

He closed the photo album, stood slowly and stretched his cramped muscles. As he placed the album and the gun and magazine back in the foot locker, a small cedar box with a medical insignia embossed on the top caught his eye, though he did his best to ignore it.

Even Arizona knew that box was trouble. She froze at the sight of it, her hackles raised.

"I know," Marcus said. "I can resist temptation."

That box had gotten him into trouble on more than one occasion. It represented a past he'd give anything to erase. But he couldn't toss it in the trash. It had too firm a grip on him. Even now it called to him.

"Marcus..."

"No!"

He slammed the foot locker lid with his fist. The sound reverberated across the room, clanging like a jail cell door, trapping him in his own private prison.

Behind him, Arizona whimpered.

"Sorry, girl."

One day he'd get rid of the box with the insignia and be done with it once and for all.

But not yet.

Shaking off a bout of guilt, he took the stairs two at a time to the second floor and entered the master bedroom of the two-bedroom rented duplex. It was devoid of all things feminine, stripped down to the barest essentials. A bed, nightstand and tall dresser. Metal blinds, no flowered curtains like the ones in the house in Edmonton that he'd bought with Jane. The bedspread was a mishmash of brown tones, and it had been hauled up over the single pillow. There were none of the decorative pillows that Jane had loved so much. No silk flowers on the dresser. No citrus Febreeze lingering in the air. No sign of Jane.

He'd hidden her too.

Stepping into the en suite bathroom, Marcus stared into the mirror. He took in the untrimmed moustache and beard that was threatening to engulf his face. Leaning closer, he examined his eyes, which were more gray than blue. He turned his face to catch the light. "I am *not* tired."

The dark circles under his eyes betrayed him.

Ignoring Arizona's watchful gaze, he opened the medicine cabinet and grabbed the tube of Preparation H, a trick he'd learned from his wife Jane. Before he'd killed her. A little dab under the eyes, no smiling or frowning, and within seconds the crevices in his skin softened. Some of Jane's "White Out"—as she used to call the tube of cosmetic concealer—and the shadows would disappear.

"Camouflage on," he said to his reflection.

A memory of Jane surfaced.

It was the night of the BioWare awards banquet, nineteen years ago. Jane, dressed in a pink housecoat, sat at the bathroom vanity curling her hair, while Marcus struggled with his tie.

He'd let out a curse. "I can never get this right."

"Here, let me." Pushing the chair behind him, Jane climbed up before he could protest. She caught his gaze in the mirror over the sink and reached around his shoulders, her gaze wandering to the twisted lump he'd made of the full Windsor. "You shouldn't be so impatient."

"*You* shouldn't be climbing up on chairs."

"I'm fine, Marcus."

"You're pregnant, that's what you are."

"You calling me fat, buster?"

Five months pregnant with Ryan, Jane had never looked so beautiful.

"I'd never do that," he replied.

She cocked her head and arched one brow. "Never? How about in four months when I can't walk up the stairs to the bedroom?"

"I'll carry you."

"What about when I can't see my toes and can't paint my toenails?"

"I'll paint them for you."

"What about when—"

He turned his head and kissed her. That shut her up.

With a laugh, she pushed him away, gave the tie a smooth tug and slid the knot expertly into place.

He groaned. "Now why can't I do that?"

"Because you have me. Now quit distracting me. I still have to put on my dress and makeup."

Marcus sat on the edge of the bed and waited. Jane always made it worth the wait, and that night she didn't disappoint him. When she emerged from the bathroom, she was a vision of sultry goddess in a designer dress from a shop in West Edmonton Mall. The baby bump in front was barely noticeable.

"How do I look?" she asked, nervously fingering the fresh gold highlights in her hair.

"Sexy as hell."

She spun in a slow circle to show off the sleek black dress with its plunging back. Peering over one glitter-powdered shoulder, she said, "So you like my new dress?"

"I'd like it better," he said in a soft voice, "if it was on the floor."

Minutes later, they were entwined in the sheets, out of breath and laughing like teenagers. Sex with Jane was always like that. Exciting. Youthful. Fun.

After dressing, Jane retreated to the bathroom to fix her hair and makeup. "Camouflage on," she said when she returned. "Now let's get going."

"Yes, ma'am."

He heard her whispering, "Six plus eight plus two…"

"Are you doing that numerology thing again?" he asked with a grin.

Jane had gone to a psychic fair when she'd found out she was pregnant, and a numerologist had given her a lesson in adding dates. Ever since then, whenever something important came up, she'd work out the numbers to determine if it was going to be a good day or not. She even made Marcus buy lotto tickets on "three days," which she said meant money coming in. They hadn't won a lottery yet, but he played along anyway.

"What is it today?"

She smiled. "A seven."

"Ah, lucky seven." He arched a brow at her. "So I'm going to get lucky?"

"I think you already did, mister."

They'd been late for the awards banquet, which didn't go over too well since Jane was the guest of honor, the recipient of a Best Programmer award for her latest video game creation at BioWare. When Jane had stepped up on the stage to receive her award, Marcus didn't think he could ever be prouder. Until the night Ryan was born.

Ryan…the son I killed.

Marcus gave his head a jerk, forcing the memories back into the shadows—where they belonged. He picked up the can of shaving cream. His eyes rested, unfocused, on the label.

To shave or not to shave. That was the question.

"Nah, not today," he muttered.

He hadn't shaved in weeks. He was also overdue for a haircut. Thankfully, they weren't too strict about appearances at work, though his supervisor would probably harp on it again.

The alarm on his watch beeped.

He had twenty minutes to get to the center. Then he'd get back to hiding behind the anonymity of being a faceless voice on the phone.

Yellowhead County Emergency Services in Edson, Alberta, housed a small but competent 911 call center situated on the second floor of a spacious building on 1st Avenue. Four rooms on the floor were rented out to emergency groups, like First Aid, CPR and EMS, for training facilities. The 911 center had a full-time staff of four emergency operators and two supervisors—one for the day shift, one for the night. They also had a handful of highly trained but underpaid casual staff and three regular volunteers.

When Marcus entered the building, Leonardo Lombardo was waiting for him by the elevator. And Leo didn't look too thrilled to see him.

"You look like your dog just died," Marcus said.

"Don't got a dog."

"So what's with the warm and cheerful welcome? Did the mob put a hit out on me?"

Leo, a man of average height in his late forties, carried about thirty extra pounds around his middle, and his swarthy Italian looks gave him an air of mystery and danger. Around town, rumormongers had spread stories that Leo was an American expatriate with mob ties. But Marcus knew exactly who had started those rumors. Leo had a depraved sense of humor.

But his friend wasn't smiling now.

"You really gotta get some sleep."

Stepping into the elevator, Marcus shrugged. "Sleep's overrated."

"You look like hell."

"Thanks."

"You're welcome." Leo pushed the second floor button and took a hesitant breath. "Listen, man…"

Whenever Leo started a sentence with those two words, Marcus knew it wouldn't be good.

"You're not on your game," Leo said. "You're starting to slip up."

"What do you mean? I do my job."

"You filed that multiple-car accident report from last night in the wrong place. Shipley's spent half the morning looking for it. I tried covering for you, but he's pretty pissed."

"Shipley's always pissed."

Pete Shipley made it a ritual to make Marcus's life hell whenever possible, which was more often than not. As the day shift supervisor,

Shipley ruled the emergency operators with an iron fist and enough arrogance to get on anyone's nerves.

The elevator door opened and Marcus stepped out first.

"I'll find the report, Leo."

"How many hours you get, Marcus?"

Sleep?

"Four." It was a lie and both of them knew it.

Marcus started toward the cubicle with the screen that divided his desk from Leo's. Behind them was the station for the other full-timers. He waved to Parminder and Wyatt as they left for home. They worked the night shift, so he only saw them in passing. Their stations were now manned by casual day workers. Backup.

"Get some sleep," Leo muttered.

"Sleep is a funny thing, Leo. Not funny *ha-ha*, but funny *strange*. Once a body's gone awhile without it or with an occasional light nap, sleep doesn't seem that important. I'm fine."

"Bullshit."

They were interrupted by a door slamming down the hall.

Pete Shipley appeared, overpowering the hallway with angry energy and his massive frame. The guy towered over everyone, including Marcus, who was an easy six feet tall. Shipley, a former army captain, was built like the *Titanic*, which had become his office nickname. Unbeknown to him.

"Taylor!" Shipley shouted. "In my office now!"

Leo grabbed Marcus's arm. "Tell him you slept six hours."

"You're suggesting I lie to the boss?"

"Just cover your ass. And for God's sake, don't egg him on."

Marcus smiled. "Now why would I do that?"

Leo gaped at him. "Because you thrive on chaos."

"Even in chaos there is order."

Letting out a snort, Leo said, "You been reading too many self-help books. Don't say I didn't warn you." He turned on one heel and headed for his desk.

Marcus stared after him. *Don't worry, Leo. I can handle Pete Shipley.*

Pausing in front of Shipley's door, he took a breath, knocked once and entered. His supervisor was seated behind a metal desk, his thick-lensed glasses perched on the tip of a bulbous nose as he scrutinized a mound of paperwork. Even though the man had ordered the meeting, Shipley did nothing to indicate he acknowledged Marcus's existence.

That was fine with Marcus. It gave him time to study the office, with its cramped windowless space and dank recycled air. It wasn't an office to envy, that's for sure. No one wanted it, or the position and responsibility that came with it. Not even Shipley. Word had it he was positioning himself for emergency coordinator, in hopes of moving up to one of the corner offices with the floor-to-ceiling windows. Marcus doubted it would ever happen. Shipley wasn't solid management material.

Marcus stood with his hands resting lightly on the back of the armless faux-leather chair Shipley reserved for the lucky few he deemed important enough to sit in his presence. Marcus wasn't one of the lucky ones.

Bracing for an ugly reprimand, his thoughts drifted to last night's shift. A drunk driver had T-boned a car at a busy intersection in Hinton, resulting in a four-car pileup. One vehicle, a mini-van with an older couple and two young boys, had been sandwiched between two vehicles from the impact of the crash. The pileup had spawned numerous frantic calls to the emergency center. Emergency Medical Services (EMS), including fire and ambulance, arrived on scene within six minutes. The Jaws of Life had been used to wrench apart the contorted metal of two of the vehicles. Only three people extracted had made it out alive. One reached the hospital DOA. Then rescue workers discovered a sedan with three teenagers inside—all dead.

They'll have nightmares for weeks.

Marcus knew how that felt. He'd once been a first responder. In another life.

He straightened. He was ready to take on Shipley's wrath. At least this time it would be done privately. Plus, if he was honest, he had messed up. Misfiling the report was one of a handful of stupid mistakes he'd made in the last week. Most he'd caught on his own and rectified.

"Before you say anything," Marcus began, "I know I—"

"What?" Shipley snapped. "You know you're an idiot?"

"No. That's news to me."

Pete Shipley rose slowly—all two hundred and eighty pounds, six feet eleven inches of him. Bracing beefy fists against the desk, he leaned forward. "I spent three hours searching for that accident report, Taylor. Three hours! And guess where I found it?" A nanosecond pause. "Filed with the missing persons call logs. Whatcha think of that?"

"I think it's ironic that I filed a missing report in the *missing* persons section."

"Shut it!" Shipley glared, his thick brows furrowed into a uni-brow. "Lombardo says you've been sleeping better, but I don't believe him. Whatcha got to say about that?"

"Leo's right. I slept like a baby last night."

Shipley elevated a brow. "For a baby, you look like shit. You need a haircut. And a shave." He wrinkled his nose. "Have you even showered this week?"

"I shower every day. Not that it's any of your business. As for the length of my hair and beard, sounds like you're crossing discrimination boundaries."

"I'm not discriminating against you. I simply do not like you. You're a goddamn drug addict, Taylor."

Everyone in the center knew about Marcus's past.

"Thanks for clarifying that, *Peter*."

Shipley cringed. "All it'll take is one more mistake. Everyone's watching you. You mess up again and you're out on your ass." His shoulders relaxed and he folded back into the chair. "If it were up to me, I would've fired you months ago."

"Good thing it isn't up to you then."

Marcus knew he was pushing the man's buttons, but that wasn't hard to do. Shipley was an idiot. A brown-noser who didn't know his ass from his dick, according to Leo.

"This is your final warning," Shipley said between his teeth. "We hold life and death in our hands. We can't afford errors."

"It was a misfiled report. The call was dispatched correctly and efficiently."

"Yeah, at least you didn't send the ambulance in the wrong direction." A smug smile crossed Shipley's face. "That was the stunt that got you knocked off your *high* horse as a paramedic. Got you fired from EMS."

Marcus thought of a million ways to answer him. None of them were polite. He moved toward the door. "I think our little meeting is done."

"I'm not finished," Shipley bellowed.

"Yes you are, Pete."

With that, Marcus strode from the office. He left Shipley's door ajar, something he knew would tick off his supervisor even more than his insubordination.

He tried not to dwell on Shipley's words, but the man had hit a nerve. Six years ago, Marcus had been publicly humiliated when the truth had come out about his addiction problem, and his future as a paramedic was sliced clean off the minute he drove that ambulance to the wrong side of town because he was too high to comprehend where he was going.

That's when he'd taken some time off. From work…from Jane…from everyone. He'd headed to Cadomin to clear his mind and do some fishing. At least that's what he'd told Jane. Meanwhile, he'd secretly packed his drug stash in the wooden box. Six days later, while in a morphine haze filled with strange images of ghostly children, he answered his cell phone. In a subdued voice, Detective John Zur revealed that Jane and Ryan had been in a car accident, not far from where Marcus was holing up.

That had been the beginning of the end for Marcus.

Now he was doing what he could to get by. It wasn't that he couldn't handle the career change from superstar paramedic to invisible 911 dispatcher. That wasn't the problem. Shipley was. The guy had been gunning for him ever since Leo had brought Marcus in to fill a vacant spot left behind by a dispatcher who'd quit after a nervous breakdown.

"What did Titanic have to say?" Leo asked when Marcus veered around the cubicle.

"He doesn't want to go down with the ship."

"He thinks you're the iceberg?"

Marcus gave a single nod.

"I got your back."

Leo had connections at work. He knew the center coordinator, Nate Downey, very well. He was married to Nate's daughter, Valerie.

"I know, Leo."

As he settled into his desk and slipped on the headset, Marcus took a deep breath and released it evenly. The mind tricks between him and Shipley had become too frequent. They wreaked havoc on his brain and drained him.

Because Shipley never lets me forget.

The clock on the computer read: 12:20. It was going to be a very long day.

In the sleepy town of Edson, it was rare to see much excitement. The center catered to outside towns as well. Some days the phones only rang a half-dozen times. Those were the good days.

He flipped through the folders on his desk and found the protocol chart. Never hurt to do a quick refresher before his shift. It kept his mind fresh and focused.

But his thoughts meandered to the misfiled report.

Was he slipping? Was he putting people's lives in danger? That was something he'd promised himself, and Leo, he'd never do again.

Remember Jane and Ryan.

How could he ever forget them? They'd been his life.

The phone rang and he jumped.

"911. Do you need Fire, Police or Ambulance?"

Marcus spent the next ten minutes explaining to eighty-nine-year-old Mrs. Mortimer, a frequent caller, that no one was available to rescue her cat from the neighbor's tree.

Then he waited for a real emergency.

Chapter Two

Edmonton, AB – Thursday, June 13, 2013 – 4:37 PM

Rebecca Kingston folded her arms across her down-filled jacket and tried not to shiver. Though May had ended with a heat wave, the temperatures had dropped the first week of June. It had rained for the first five days, and an arctic chill had swept through the city. The weatherman blamed the erratic change in weather on global warming and a cold front sweeping down from Alaska, while locals held one source responsible. Their lifelong rival—Calgary.

"Can we get an ice cream, Mommy?" four-year-old Ella said with a faint lips, the result of her recent contribution to the tooth fairy's necklace collection.

Rebecca laughed. "It feels like winter again and you want ice cream?"

"Yes, please."

"I guess we have time."

They hurried across the street to the corner store.

"Strawberry this time," Ella said, her blue eyes pleading.

Rebecca sighed. "Eat it slowly. Did you remember Puff?"

Her daughter nodded. "In my pocket."

"Good girl." Rebecca glanced at her watch. "It's almost five. Let's go."

Her cell phone rang. It was Carter Billingsley, her lawyer.

"Mr. Billingsley," she said. "I'm glad you got my message."

"So you've decided to get away," he said. "That's a very good idea."

"I need a break." She glanced at Ella. "Things are going to get ugly, aren't they?"

"Unfortunately, yes. Divorce is never pretty. But you'll get through it."

"Thanks, Mr. Billingsley."

"Take care, Rebecca."

Carter had once been her grandfather's lawyer and Grandpa Bob had highly recommended him—if Rebecca ever needed someone to handle her divorce. In his late sixties, Carter filled that father-figure left void after her father's passing.

Her thoughts raced to her twelve-year-old son. Colton's team was up against one of the toughest junior high hockey teams from Regina. With Colton as the Edmonton team's goalie, most of the pressure was on him. He was a brave boy.

She bit her bottom lip, wishing she were as brave.

You're a coward, Becca.

"You're too codependent," her mother always said.

Rebecca figured that wasn't actually her fault. She'd been fortunate to have strong male role models in her life. Men who ran companies with iron fists and made decisions after careful consideration. Or at least worked hard to provide for their families. Men like Grandpa Bob and her father. Men who could be trusted to make the right decisions.

Not like Wesley.

Even her grandfather hadn't liked him. When Grandpa Bob passed away two years ago, he'd sent a clear message to everyone that Wesley couldn't be trusted. Grandpa Bob had lived a miser's lifestyle. No one knew how much money he'd saved for that "rainy day"—until he was gone and Colton and Ella became beneficiaries of over eight hundred thousand dollars from the sale of Grandpa Bob's house and business.

Grandpa Bob, in his infinite wisdom, had added two major conditions to the inheritance. Money could only be withdrawn from the account if it was spent on Ella or Colton. And Rebecca was the sole person with signing power.

Wesley moped around the house for days when he heard the conditions. Any time she bought the kids new clothes, he'd sneer at her and say, "Hope you used your grandfather's money for those."

Once when he'd gambled most of his paycheck, he begged her for a "loan," and when she'd voiced that she didn't have the money, he slapped her. "Lying bitch! You've got almost a million dollars at your fingertips. All I'm asking for is thirty-five hundred. I'll pay it back."

She'd refused and paid the price, physically.

Rebecca wanted him out of her life. Once and for all. But for the sake of the children, she had to find a way to forgive Wesley and deal with the fact that he was her children's father. He'd always be in their lives.

Every time she looked at Colton, she was reminded of Wesley. Unlike Ella's blonde hair and blue eyes that closely resembled her own, both father and son had dark brown hair, hazel eyes, a light spray of freckles across their noses and matching chin dimples.

She'd met Wesley at a company Christmas party shortly after she started working as a customer service representative at Alberta Cable. The son of upper-class parents, Wesley had created his independence by not joining the family law firm, as was expected. Instead, he went to work at Alberta Cable as a cable installer. At the party, he'd been assigned to the same table as Rebecca. As soon as Wesley realized she was single, he poured on the charm. He was a master at that.

The next morning she'd found Wesley in her bed.

After nearly four years of dating, he finally popped the question. Via a text message, of all things. She was at work when her cell phone sprang to life, vibrating against her desk. When she glanced down, she saw seven words.

"Rebecca Kingston, will U marry me?"

She'd immediately let out a startled shriek. "Wesley just proposed."

This sent the entire room into a chaotic buzz of applause and congratulatory wishes. The rest of Rebecca's shift was a blur.

"Is Daddy gonna be at the game?" Ella said, interrupting her memories.

"No, honey. He's at work."

At least that's where Rebecca hoped he was.

Wesley had left Alberta Cable six months ago, escorted from the building after being fired for screaming at a customer in her own home and shoving the woman into a wall. It hadn't been the first complaint lodged against him. He'd been employed off and on since then, but no one wanted an employee with anger management issues.

When Rebecca had asked what had happened, he mumbled something about an accident, arguing that it wasn't his fault. "No matter what that ass of a supervisor says," he said.

She'd given him a look that said she didn't believe him. She paid for that look. The black eye he gave her kept her in the house for nearly a week. That's when she filed for separation.

Since leaving Alberta, Wesley had wandered from one dead-end job to another. For the past two months he'd hardly worked at all. She hoped to God he wasn't sitting at his apartment, surfing the porn highway.

Last time she saw him, Wesley had blamed his unemployment situation on the recession, which had, in all fairness, wreaked havoc with many people's lives and crushed some of the toughest companies. But the economy, or lack of a strong one, wasn't Wesley's problem. The problem was his lack of motivation and the inability to handle his jealousy and rage.

Perhaps Wesley was experiencing a midlife crisis.

Maybe she was too.

It was getting more and more difficult to keep it together. But she did it for her children. Besides, she'd endured worse than uncertainty when she lived with Wesley. Much worse.

Rebecca glanced down at her daughter. Ella was a petite child who'd been born two months premature. Wesley had seen to that.

She shook her head. *No. What happened back then was as much my fault as his. I stayed when I should've left.*

"Hurry, Mommy!" Ella said, tugging on her hand.

The hockey arena was a five-minute walk from where she'd parked the car, but with the ice cream pit stop, Rebecca was glad they'd left early.

"Ella, do you think Colton's team will win today?"

Her daughter rolled her eyes. "Of course. Colton is awesome!"

"Awesome," Rebecca agreed.

Tamarack Hockey Arena came into view, along with the crowds of hockey fans who gathered outside the doors to the indoor rink.

Rebecca took Ella's hand and drew her in close.

In Edmonton, hockey fans bordered on hockey fanatics. It wouldn't be the first time that a fight broke out between fathers of opposing teams. Last year, a toddler had been trampled in a north Edmonton arena. Thankfully, he'd survived.

"Stay close, Ella."

"Do you see Colton?"

"Not yet."

"Becca!"

Turning in the direction of the voice, she scoured the bleachers. Then she spotted Wesley near the home team's side. He wasn't supposed to be there. The terms of their separation were that he could see the kids during scheduled visitations. Once the divorce was final, those visits would be restricted to visits accompanied by a social worker—if Carter Billingsley, her lawyer, came through for her. She hadn't given Wesley this news yet.

"I saved you some seats," Wesley hollered. The look he gave her suggested she shouldn't make a public scene. Or else.

Rebecca released a reluctant sigh. *Great. Just great.*

"Are we gonna sit with Daddy?" Ella asked.

"Yes, honey. Unless you want to sit somewhere else." *Anywhere else.*

Despite Rebecca's silent plea, Ella headed in Wesley's direction, pushing past the knees that blocked the aisle. Rebecca sat beside Ella and tried to tamp down the guilt she felt at placing their daughter between them.

"There's a seat beside me," Wesley said.

Her gaze flew to the empty seat on his right and she winced. "I'm good here. Thanks for saving the seats."

Looking as handsome as the day she'd married him, Wesley smiled. "You look lovely. New hairstyle?"

She touched her shoulder-length hair. "I need a trim."

"Looks good. But then you always do."

She stared at him. He was laying on the charm a bit thick. That usually meant he wanted something.

Wesley chucked Ella under the chin. "So, Ella-Bella, how's kindergarten?"

"We went on a field trip to the zoo yesterday."

"See any monkeys?" he asked, his arm resting over the back of Ella's chair.

"Yeah. They were so cute."

"But not as cute as you, right?" He caught Rebecca's eye and winked. "You're the cutest girl here. Even though you have no teeth."

"Do too!" Ella opened her mouth to show him.

After a few minutes of listening to their teasing banter, Rebecca tuned out their laughter. Sadness washed over her, followed by regret. If things had gone differently, they'd still be a family, and the kids would have their father in their lives. But Rebecca couldn't stay in an abusive relationship. Her mind and body couldn't endure any more trauma. And she was terrified he'd start lashing out physically at the kids.

So she'd made a decision, and one sunny Friday afternoon, she'd summoned up the courage to confront Wesley at his current *job de jour*.

"We need to talk," she'd told him.

"This isn't a good time."

"It's *never* a good time." She took a deep breath. "I want you to move out of the house, Wesley."

He laughed. "Good joke. What's the punch line?"

"I'm not joking."

His smile disappeared. "You're serious?"

"Dead serious. It's not like you couldn't see this coming. I want a separation. You know I've been…unhappy in our marriage."

"I'll try to make more time for you."

"It's not more time that I want, Wesley. Neither of us can live like this. Your anger is out of control. You're out of control."

"So this is all my fault?" Wesley sneered.

"You nearly put me in the hospital last week."

"Maybe that's where you belong."

She clenched her teeth. "Your threats won't work this time. I've made up my mind. I'm leaving tonight, and I'm taking the kids with me."

There was an uncomfortable pause.

"Seems to me you're only thinking about yourself, what *you* want. Have you even thought about what this'll do to the kids?"

"Of course I have," she snapped. "They're all I think about. Can you say the same?"

"You're going to turn them against me. Like your mother did to you and your father." His voice dripped with disgust.

"Don't bring my parents into this. This has nothing to do with them and everything to do with the fact that you have an anger problem and you refuse to get help."

"What'll you tell the kids?"

She shrugged. "Ella won't understand. She's too young. Colton's getting too old for me to keep making excuses for you. He's almost a teenager."

Wesley didn't answer.

"You know what he said to me last night, Wesley? He said you love being angry more than you love being with us. He's right, isn't he?"

She stormed out of his office without waiting for a reply. She already knew the answer.

That evening, Wesley packed two suitcases.

"I'll be staying at The Fairmont McDonald. I still love you, Becca."

His actions had stunned her. She'd been prepared to take the kids to Kelly's. She was even ready for Wesley to try to hurt her. What she hadn't expected was his easy submission. Or that for once he'd take the high road.

"You're leaving?" she said, shocked.

"That's what you wanted," he said with a shrug. "So that's what you get."

For a second, she wanted to tell him she'd made a mistake. That she didn't want a separation. That she'd be a better wife, learn to be more patient, learn to deal with his rages.

Then she remembered the bruises and sprains. "Good-bye, Wesley."

"For now."

She'd watched him climb into his car and waited until the taillights winked, then disappeared. Then she let out a long, uneasy breath and headed down the hallway. She wandered through their bedroom and into the en suite bathroom, all the while trying to think of the good times. There weren't many.

She stared at her reflection in the mirror, one finger tracing the small scar along her chin. Wesley had given her that present on Valentine's Day two years earlier. He'd accused her of flirting with the

UPS delivery guy.

"You deserve better," she said to her reflection. "So do the kids."

Now, sitting two seats away from Wesley at the arena, Rebecca realized that her husband was still doing everything in his power to control her.

"Penny for your thoughts," he said.

"You're wasting your money."

"What money? You get most of it."

"That's for the kids, Wesley, and you know it."

She dug her fingernails into her palms. *Don't fight with him. Not here. Not in front of Ella.*

She caught his eye. "Next time Colton has a game, I'd appreciate it if you didn't bother showing up."

"Wouldn't miss it for the world." He gave her an icy smile. "That's *my* son down there."

"What part of 'scheduled visits' don't you—"

Cheers erupted from the stands as both hockey teams skated out onto the ice and joined their goalies. Everyone stood for the national anthem, then a horn blasted.

Rebecca released a heart-heavy sigh.

The game was on.

After the game, the arena parking lot was a potpourri of car exhaust and refinery emissions, and a breeding ground for irritation. Everyone wanted to be first out. Especially the losing team.

Rebecca was glad she'd parked her Hyundai Accent down the street.

"Mommy, are we going home now?" Ella asked.

"Yes, honey. It's almost supper time."

"Is Daddy coming home too?"

"No, honey. Daddy's going to his own house."

As they made their way through the parking lot, Rebecca was sure Wesley would veer off toward his van, but he stayed at her side. Doing her best to ignore him, she reached for Ella's hand as they crossed the street. Behind them, Colton lugged his hockey bag and stick.

When they reached the sedan, Rebecca unlocked the doors, sank into the driver's seat and started the engine, while the kids said good-bye to their dad. Stepping out, she moved to the back door and wrenched on it, gritting her teeth as it squealed. Colton climbed in back. Ella looked up at her with a hopeful expression.

"Back seat," Rebecca said.

Ella obediently climbed in beside her brother, and Colton helped her with the seat belt for her booster seat.

Rebecca shut the door using her hip. Catching Wesley's eye she said, "You always said we should use the sticky door, that if we did it might not stick so much. Hasn't worked."

Wesley studied the exterior of the car. "Can't believe you haven't bought a new car."

The Hyundai *had* seen better days—and today wasn't one of them. They'd bought the used car back in 2003, when they'd gone from a two-door Supra—Wesley's toy—to a four-door vehicle that wasn't so "squishy," as the kids had called the Supra. The red paint was now worn in places, the hinges of the trunk groaned when lifted and the back door on the passenger side stuck all the time, making it impossible for either of the kids to open. The latter was a result of an accident. Wesley had been sideswiped by a reckless teen texting on her cell phone. Or at least that's the story he'd given her.

"This works fine," she said. "I don't need a new one." *And I can't afford one.*

Colton cracked the door open and poked his head out. "Dad said he's getting me a cell phone for my birthday next month. One that does text messaging."

Rebecca shut the car door and turned icy eyes in Wesley's direction. "You what?"

"Before you say anything, hear me out. Colton's old enough to be responsible for a phone. Besides, I'm taking care of it, bills and all. When he's old enough to get a job, he'll take over paying for it."

"I told you a while ago that I do not agree with kids walking around glued to a cell phone. It's ridiculous." She walked around to the driver's side.

"What if there's an emergency and Colton needs to call one of us?" he asked, following her.

"Then he uses a phone nearby or has an adult call us. It's not like he's driving any—"

"Rebecca, this is *my* decision. As his father."

"Well, I'm his mother, and I say no cell phone."

She scowled at him, mentally cursing herself for falling into old habits—childish habits. Truth was, she'd been thinking of the whole cell phone argument ever since Wesley had first brought it up. But her pride wouldn't let her back down. Not now.

"I think you're being a little unfair," Wesley said.

"Unfair? You really want to go there?"

She turned when she heard the whir of the power window.

"Did you tell her, Dad?" Colton asked.

"Hey, buddy, give me a second—"

Rebecca frowned. "Did you already tell him he's getting a cell phone?"

"Let's table the phone idea for another time."

"Fine."

Wesley shuffled his feet. "Becca, I have a favor to ask."

She held her breath. *Here it is.*

"I want Colton to stay with me in July."

From inside the car, Colton nodded. "Say yes, Mom."

She was livid. Motioning for Colton to roll up the window, she turned to Wesley. "What are you doing? This is something you should've discussed with me first."

"I *am* discussing it with you."

"You should've called me, not mentioned this right in front of him." She tried to ignore Colton, who had his grinning face pressed up against the window. "Why didn't you call me so we could discuss this?"

"I tried calling. I left you two messages last week."

Rebecca blinked. She checked the answering machine every day, and there'd been no calls from Wesley.

Wesley's mouth curled. "I'm not lying."

"Maybe I accidentally erased them."

"Probably. You always had problems with technical things. And managing money."

"For the last time," she snapped, "our financial mess isn't my fault. We both overspent."

"But you've got your secret stash, don't you?"

"You know that money is for the kids' college funds," she said.

When Wesley had found out about the money that had been set aside for the kids, it had enraged him to the point that he deliberately drove his van into the side of the bridge on the way home from dinner at a restaurant.

Rebecca hadn't come away unscathed. She suffered a multitude of scrapes and bruises, easily explained by the crash. The doctor had no idea Wesley had beaten her after pulling her from the wreck. She barely recalled that incident. But she remembered the others that followed in the days after the crash. The broken wrist. The bruises on her back and hips.

Every day afterward, Wesley had said he loved her. But love wasn't supposed to hurt physically. Was it?

She eyed him now, thankful he had never touched the kids. At least she'd done that right, gotten out before he was tempted to unleash his fury on Colton or Ella.

"Becca, why are you staring at me like that?"

"I'm reminding myself of why you'll soon be my *ex*-husband."

Wesley flinched, and she knew her words had hurt him.

Good. He deserves it.

"Do you think it's possible to be civil to each other?" he said.

She glanced over her shoulder at Ella and Colton. "If you're willing, I am."

"For the kids' sake, right?"

She caught his eye. "For all of us."

Silence.

"Look, Becca," he said in a contrite tone, "I've been seeing a psychologist, and I've taken an anger management class. I'm doing everything I can to show you I can be trusted with the kids. I would never hurt them."

"Like you'd never hurt *me*?"

He looked away. "I've apologized for my past. I'm not like that anymore."

She mulled over his words, her heart conflicted with such a heavy decision. If she was wrong and something happened to Colton, she'd never forgive herself.

But what if he's telling the truth? I can't keep him away from the kids. They need him.

She peered over her shoulder at Colton. He had a smile on his face and his hands clasped in front, pleading. How could she resist that?

Finally, she said, "How long do you expect Colton to stay with you?"

"One week. In the middle of July."

She bit her bottom lip. "I'm not sure…"

"I know it's not what we agreed on, but I'm taking that week off and I was hoping to spend it with my son."

"Just you and Colton?"

He rolled his eyes. "And Tracey."

Tracey Whitaker used to be a receptionist at his father's law firm. Wesley and Tracey had started seeing each other a few months before Rebecca had asked him to leave. She'd found out about the "other woman" when she'd called her father-in-law one day. Walter revealed to her he hadn't seen Wesley in weeks. Then he asked if she'd called Tracey's place. Everyone at the law firm, including her father-in-law, knew about Tracey and Wesley. Her husband hadn't bothered to keep his affair secret.

Except from Rebecca.

Wesley's father had been supportive enough to fire the woman after Rebecca stormed into his office, accusing him of trying to break up his son's marriage. She'd heard Tracey had resumed an earlier career as a caregiver in a senior's complex.

"So you're still with Tracey," she said.

"I'll dump her in an instant if you let me come home. We can rip up that separation agreement and make our own agreement." He arched his brows suggestively.

"How come she didn't come to the game?"

Wesley shrugged. "Tracey has a cold. Picked it up from the old folks. She didn't come because she didn't want to pass it on to Colton."

"How considerate of her," Rebecca sneered.

"Becca…"

She ignored the warning in his voice. "You two planning to tie the knot?"

As soon as the words were out of her mouth, she wished she could take them back. Why had she asked him *that*, of all things? It made her sound like she was jealous.

Am I?

Wesley smiled, as if reading her mind. "I'll be sure to send you an invite when we do."

She reached for the car door handle. "Don't bother."

"You haven't answered my question, Becca."

With a heavy sigh, she faced him. "Fine. You can have Colton for the week. But not a day more." A grin spread across his face and she scowled. "And please don't go getting any ideas about changing the custody agreement after that, Wesley. The kids need stability."

"Thanks," he said.

"You can thank me by making sure you look after him." She hesitated. "I guess I should tell you I'm going away for a couple of days. The kids will be staying with my sister."

"When are you leaving?"

"Tomorrow evening. After supper. I'll be back Monday afternoon."

"That's kind of last minute, don't you think?"

Her eyes narrowed. "I decided to do it today. And I do not owe you any advanced notice. I'm telling you now."

He held up his hands in surrender. "Okay, okay. So where you going?"

"Cadomin. You know I always wanted to see the bat cave."

"I was going to take you."

She shrugged and climbed into the car. "But you didn't."

"I could." He regarded her with suspicion as he held onto the door. "Why aren't you taking the kids?"

"They have school on Monday."

"Who are you going with?"

"Me, myself and I." She scowled. "I'm going alone, Wesley. I need a break, so I'm taking a few days off."

"I'd babysit the kids, but I'll be busy this weekend."

She resisted the urge to tell him it wasn't *babysitting* when the kids were his own. "It's already arranged, Wesley. Kelly's expecting them."

"Doesn't she already have her hands full?"

Wesley was right. Her sister did have her hands full. Kelly was happily married with four kids—eight-year-old Evan and five-year-old triplets, Aynsley, Megan and Jacob.

"Kelly can handle it. She's a great mother."

Rebecca wouldn't admit it, but she envied her sister. Kelly was married to the perfect man, an electrical engineer who doted on her and their kids. Steve was highly respected, financially stable and he would never lay an angry hand on anyone. Except maybe Wesley. More than once, Steve had offered to help Rebecca *"toss that bastard out on his ass"*—or words to that effect.

"Well, I'll have Colton's visit to look forward to this summer," Wesley said.

She was starting to have second thoughts about that.

Grasping the door handle to close it, she eyed him. "We have to go."

"Have fun in Cadomin." He didn't sound too sincere.

She aimed a tight smile at him. "I will."

As she pulled the car away from the curb, Rebecca peered into the rearview mirror. Wesley stood on the sidewalk, watching her drive away.

"Did you say yes, Mom?" Colton asked.

"Yes."

In the back seat, her son did a seated jig and jabbed Ella in the side.

"Mommy, Colton's poking me."

"Don't worry, Ella," Colton said, "I'll be outta your hair for a whole week."

Rebecca peered into the mirror. "How did you know it was for a week?"

"Dad told me last weekend he was gonna ask you."

Her lips curled. "You should've said something to me."

"Nah, Dad said he'd ask you himself. And I didn't wanna jinx things."

Colton stuffed two ear buds into his ears, then sat back with a grin. She watched for a minute as he bobbed his head to whatever tune he was listening to on the iPod his father had bought him for his birthday last year.

It was going to kill her to be away from her son for an entire week.

You'll still have Ella.

As if on cue, her beautiful daughter giggled in the backseat.

Come July, Rebecca would keep busy with Ella and enjoy some real mommy-daughter time. But that wouldn't stop her from missing Colton. A week was a long time.

Too long.

Depressed, Rebecca pulled onto Whitemud Drive and headed for home, all the time wondering if she should cancel the summer plans with Wesley.

"You can do this," she whispered. "It's only a week."

It would be the longest week of her life. After it was over, she'd convince Wesley to go back to their original summer plan. Alternating weekends during the summer holidays. There was no way on earth she was ever going to be separated from either of her children for longer than that.

Colton and Ella are my life and soul.

"Can we get pizza to celebrate?" Colton asked.

"Sure. Pepperoni and mushroom?"

"Yeah."

"With double cheese?" Ella piped up.

"With double cheese."

Somehow, pizza made the world seem right again, and Rebecca smiled. She was in the proverbial driver's seat, in control of her life again.

She should have realized that life is never predictable.

Chapter Three

Edson, AB – Thursday, June 13, 2013 – 4:55 PM

The afternoon had crawled past at worm speed. Using the Kindle application on his iPhone, Marcus downloaded an eBook on sleep disorders and spent the time between calls reading about somniphobia—the fear of sleeping—something Leo was adamant Marcus had.

He yawned and stretched his legs beneath the cramped desk. Three calls had come in during the first three hours of his shift, and neither had warranted emergency vehicles.

"Pussy Willow's back home," Mrs. Mortimer said when she called in the second time. "One of my neighbors was kind enough to coax her down from the maple tree. They bribed her with—"

"Thanks for calling back," Marcus cut in, "but 911 is for emergencies, Mrs. Mortimer."

"This *is* an emergency. I didn't want you to trouble yourself by sending out a fire truck."

Marcus gritted his teeth. "Thank you, Mrs. Mortimer."

"You're welcome, dear. You have a nice day now."

He couldn't help but grin.

The third call had been a false alarm. Some kid had pulled the fire alarm at the elementary school. School staff had conducted a thorough check of the school and found nothing. No smoke, no fire. That was one of the good calls.

"Supper time," Leo said behind him.

"You read my mind."

Leo and Marcus preferred to take the five-o'clock slot, while the casuals—Carol and Rudy—took the six-o'clock supper break. That way there were always two people on the phones. They alternated the two fifteen-minute breaks the same way. Of course, if there was a major emergency during that time, Leo and Marcus would rush back to the phones.

Marcus followed Leo into the cramped break room with its bare walls and mismatched chairs. He grabbed a plastic container from the bar fridge, popped the lid and placed it in the microwave.

"Got anything good today?" Leo asked, eyeing him hungrily.

"Leftover lasagna."

"That's three days in a row, Marcus."

"I thought Italians were supposed to love pasta."

Leo scowled. "Not three-day-old lasagna. Besides, I was hoping you made one of your fancy dinners."

It was no secret that Marcus enjoyed cooking. He spent hours flipping through the cable channels on the prowl for the next great recipe. He watched Gordon Ramsey, Jamie Oliver and a few others, then concocted his own recipes using fresh herbs and lots of vegetables. He'd cook, day or night, depending on his shift. There was something almost magical about cooking up something delicious in the early hours of the morning, when the sun hadn't even made an appearance yet and his neighbors were all sleeping soundly in their beds.

With the container of hot lasagna in hand, he sat down at the single table in the break room, a warped slab of melamine with deformed metal legs, one of them propped up by a bent piece of cardboard. As Leo sat down in the chair across from him, Marcus rocked his chair back and forth, waiting for the legs to settle into the grooves in the old linoleum.

He took a bite of lasagna. "What about you, Leo? What's on the menu?"

"KFC." Leo held up a crispy drumstick.

Marcus laughed. "Again? Haven't you had *that* the past three days?"

"It's KFC."

Fried chicken was Leo's weakness. Marcus was concerned that one day all the grease would catch up to Leo and his arteries. The man was already overweight. And *exercise* wasn't in Leo's vocabulary, unless it was picking up the phone to order take-out on the way home.

But Leo did love Marcus's cooking.

At least someone does, Marcus thought.

"You and Val should come over for dinner Monday. Before work."

"Maybe. We might be busy that night."

"What, you got a hot date planned?"

"Naw, man."

"Why's your face so red? What's going on?"

"Val wants to try again."

"Try what?"

Leo leaned close. "She wants a kid."

"Ah, and Monday is D-Night."

"Yeah. De night for love."

Marcus chuckled. "Then how come you don't look too happy about it?"

"It's so…I don't know…planned. You know. Feels like the damn doctor is standing over us, telling us where to put what and for how long."

"You mean you haven't figured that out yet?"

Leo took an angry bite of a drumstick. "Hey, stop laughing. This ain't funny. Trying to have a kid puts a lot of pressure on a guy."

"At least you're getting laid."

A rumble of laugher came from deep within Leo's burly chest. "Yeah, there's that."

Marcus scraped the last bite of lasagna from the container. "You're a lucky man, Leo."

"And don't I know it."

Marcus studied his friend. Leo would make a great dad. The kind that would always be there, always be cheering his kid on.

And God forbid anyone dumb enough to bully his kid.

"Why you staring at me like that?"

"I'm trying to imagine you with a teenage son."

Leo beamed. "A son? That what you think I'll have?"

"Yeah, a big, burly kid who looks just like you. Talks like you too. We'll call him Smartass Junior. What do you think?"

"You talkin' to me?" Leo said in his best De Niro.

Marcus laughed. "Yeah, I'm talkin' to you." Unfurling his long legs, he walked over to the sink and washed the empty container.

"You coming to the meeting tonight?" Leo asked, licking greasy fingers.

"I'm not sure."

"Marcus…"

There was a piece of onion stuck to the bottom of the plastic container, and Marcus spent a minute trying to scrape it off with his fingernail. It kept him from having to see the disapproval he knew was in his friend's eyes.

Leo grunted. "This'll be the second week you've missed. That's not good."

"So who's counting? Except you, Leo."

"*You* should be."

Marcus placed the container on a dish towel to air dry, then glanced at Leo. "Hey, don't look so pissed. I'm still good."

"Are you? Like I said before, you don't look too hot."

Marcus let out an exaggerated sigh. "Fine, I'll go. Happy now?"

"Yeah, happy as a snitch in concrete blocks."

"Careful, Leo. Your inner mobster is showing."

"And don't you forget it." Leo threw the empty KFC carton in the garbage can and let out a loud belch. "I'll drive tonight."

"Great," Marcus drawled. "I'll call ahead to the traffic cops. I'm sure they can use the extra ticket money." He turned abruptly as footsteps approached.

Carol Burnett entered the break room. Though allegedly named after the witty television comedian from the '80s, that's where the resemblance ended. Carol was a scrawny-looking gray woman—gray in hair color, pallor, attire and personality. There wasn't much evidence of a sense of humor either.

"It's 6:05," she said, unsmiling.

Leo gave Marcus a look of mock horror. "Good God! We're late."

"We've got a date…with *destiny*," Marcus said in an overdramatic tone.

Carol glared at them, then shook her head and wandered over to the fridge.

"One day we'll make her laugh," Marcus said to Leo.

His friend responded by taking a low bow, which showed off his butt crack in Carol's direction.

"Funny, Leonardo," she muttered. "Very funny."

Leo winked at her. "Someone around here has gotta be."

"You're the class clown of 911," Marcus said as they made their way back to their desks. "The guy who always gets a laugh."

Leo pouted. "From everyone except Carol. She's ruining my mojo."

"Hey, even Shipley thinks you're funny, which is pretty damned amazing considering he rarely cracks a smile for anyone."

"Taylor!"

Marcus grimaced. "Shit. Speak of the Devil."

Shipley stood in the doorway to his office. He raised a hand, and at first Marcus wondered if he was going to wave. But he didn't. Instead, Shipley pointed two fingers at his own eyes, then pointed at Marcus.

Marcus nodded. *Got it. You're watching me.*

He strode to his desk while his supervisor's stare followed him. He knew exactly what the man was thinking. Shipley was praying he'd mess up again. But he'd already messed up enough.

Marcus's addiction had led to countless lies, theft of drugs and forging doctors' prescriptions. And though he didn't feel he deserved their support, his EMT-P platoon had gone to bat for him, defending him to the higher-ups. The powers that be agreed to rehabilitation and counseling, as long as Marcus promised to abide by the rules. It was a fair deal. He would serve no prison time for the theft of the drugs and had to abide by other conditions, and in exchange he'd work at the center as part of his rehab.

He recalled the day he started at the center five years ago. The first time he'd stepped into Shipley's office he knew he'd have problems with the man.

"So you're a druggie," Shipley said, referring to a folder in his hands.

"A recovering addict."

Shipley's eyes narrowed. "A druggie. I have no use for people who refuse to value life. Our job here is to save lives." He stared at Marcus. With a sigh, he slapped the folder on the desk. "But my hands are tied, and you've been assigned the job. Don't screw it up."

"I won't."

The man's mouth lifted in a sneer. "We'll see. Won't we? Personally, I doubt you'll make it a month here."

Marcus had smiled then. He knew an alpha male when he saw one. He also recognized a challenge. "I don't give a shit what you think, Mr. Shipley. I'll do my job."

"Don't forget the mandatory drug testing every week."

"I know the drill."

Yeah, he knew the drill well. He adhered to the rules, pissed in a plastic bottle on demand and stayed away from his old dealer haunts. It was the price he had to pay. Whenever the cravings teased him—and some nights they hit with a vengeance—he pictured Jane and Ryan. He recalled the look of despair and disappointment in her eyes when she'd first learned of his addiction.

Everything had started out so innocently. As a paramedic he was surrounded by drugs. He'd administered them to victims when needed. He stocked them, counted them and restocked them. After three grueling multiple car accidents and an apartment fire, both claiming dozens of lives and injuring dozens more, he'd suffered from burnout and back and shoulder pain.

The first time he used, he convinced himself it was only going to be that one time. He popped a couple of misappropriated Vicodin, and the rest of his day was a productive fog of pain-free activity. In the beginning, it was easy to "accidentally misplace" the drug when he needed more. On one occasion, he faked dropping a bottle so the pills spilled out on the ambulance floor. As he and Ashton Campbell, his partner, cleaned up the mess, Marcus furtively pocketed every other handful. Not one of his proudest moments.

When Ashton began to notice the missing Vicodin, Marcus resorted to Tylenol 3s, an easy prescription to get. He broke them down in cold water and separated the codeine, an opiate used for pain relief. The concentrated codeine numbed the pain and had the added effect of making him high. Unfortunately he liked the feeling a bit too much. He tricked himself into believing he was more efficient as a paramedic when he was high. It made him feel more confident, alert, in control.

Who the hell was he kidding?

Over time, his addiction became more demanding. Codeine stopped working, and he returned to Vicodin and Percocet. Occasionally, he'd inject himself with morphine, when the pain became unbearable. Soon his dilated pupils gave him away.

Jane broached the subject one evening, but he walked out of the house, pissed that she'd accused him—a paramedic, for God's sake—of being an addict. Then Ashton told Marcus he knew about the pilfered drugs.

Within days, Marcus's deep, dark secret was out. He was exposed, humiliated and ashamed. He was given a choice—rehab or jail.

Wasn't much of a choice.

Jane had stood by him. She was wonderful that way, always forgiving. She even supported his decision to take off to Cadomin for a week, without her or Ryan. Fishing, he told her.

In actuality, he'd gone there to contemplate his life and the terrible choices he'd made. The box with the insignia had gone with him. It would be his last time using, he promised himself. Then he'd bury the box and be done with it all. He swore he go to meetings, get clean, whatever it took, as soon as he returned home. But he spent most of the time in the cabin high on morphine and sleeping. That was back in the days when he *could* sleep.

He remembered sitting in the candlelit cabin, a hypodermic needle in his arm. He was dozing, embracing the flow of lightness, when his cell phone rang.

"Marcus, it's John Zur." The detective went on to tell him Jane and Ryan had been involved in a serious car accident.

Marcus ripped the needle from his arm and jumped to his feet. "Where?"

"Not far from Cadomin."

"I'm on my way."

"Marcus, you should—"

Marcus shifted into autopilot. He hung up the phone before Zur could finish what he was saying, grabbed his coat and ran from the cabin to his car. It was raining, freezing rain, but he barely noticed. All he could think of was his wife and son, hurt and dazed. They needed him.

He sped down the highway until he saw the police cars and fire truck. He pulled up behind an ambulance, parked, then leapt from his car.

Zur strode toward him. "Marcus, I don't think you should—"

Ignoring the detective, Marcus skidded down the muddy embankment toward the water-filled ditch.

Then he saw it. Jane's car. It had flipped over and was half submerged in deep, murky water.

"Jaaaane!" he screamed. "Ryan!"

Two rescuers using the Jaws of Life ripped open the side door, the metal grinding and squealing in rebellion, water pouring to the ground. In the driver's seat a body hung upside-down, water up to the waist.

Marcus recognized Jane's jacket immediately. *"Nooo!"*

The remainder of that night was a blur of flashing lights and sirens. And death.

He had a lot to make up for. Penance was his middle name.

The phone rang, tearing him from his dark thoughts. Over the next few hours he filed paperwork, forwarded a suspicious arson call to Fire and Police and sent an ambulance to a possible home invasion, while doing his best not to think of the meeting he'd promised Leo he'd attend.

There was a brief second when he stared at the computer monitor and thought of why he went to the meetings in the first place. To make amends. To help assuage the guilt.

To be forgiven?

Was that even possible?

**SUBMERGED is available at
Amazon, B&N and more.**

In the tradition of Stephen King, The Twilight Zone and The Hitchhiker, comes a terrifying collection of short stories in…

Skeletons in the Closet & Other Creepy Stories

Thirteen stories take you from one hold-your-breath chapter to the next.

Enter the closet…

A Grave Error
The Death of an Old Cow
Maid of Dishonor
Atrophy
Picture Perfect
Sweet Dreams
Separation Anxiety
The Car
Deadly Reunion
Remote Control
Ouija
Caller Unknown
Skeletons in the Closet

ISBN: 978-0-9866310-2-3 (ebook)
ISBN: 978-1-926997-05-6 (trade paperback)

Available at various retailers, including Amazon, Chapters and KoboBooks

Check out Cheryl Kaye Tardif's terrifying thriller...

The River

How far do we go until we've gone too far?

The South Nahanni River has a history of mysterious deaths, disappearances and headless corpses, but it may also hold the key to humanity's survival—or its destruction.

Seven years ago, Del Hawthorne's father and three of his friends disappeared near the Nahanni River and were presumed dead. When one of the missing men stumbles onto the University grounds, alive but barely recognizable and aging before her eyes, Del is shocked. Especially when the man tells her something inconceivable. Her father is still alive!

Gathering a group of volunteers, Del travels to the Nahanni River to rescue her father. There, she finds a secret underground river that plunges her into a technologically advanced world of nanobots and painful serums. Del uncovers a conspiracy of unimaginable horror, a plot that threatens to destroy us all. Will humanity be sacrificed for the taste of eternal life?

And at what point have we become...God?

"Tardif specializes in mile-a-minute potboiler mysteries." —*Edmonton Sun*

ISBN: 9781412062299 (trade paperback)
ISBN: 978-0-9865382-3-0 (ebook)

Available at various retailers, including Amazon, Chapters and KoboBooks

Book 1 in the Divine series by Cheryl Kaye Tardif...

Divine Intervention

CFBI agent Jasmine McLellan is assigned a hot case—one that requires the psychic abilities of the PSI Division, a secret government agency located in the secluded town of Divine, BC.

Jasi leads a psychically gifted team in the hunt for a serial arsonist—a murderer who has already taken the lives of three innocent people. Unleashing her gift as a *Pyro-Psychic*, Jasi is compelled toward smoldering ashes and enters the killer's mind. A mind bent on destruction and revenge.

Jasi's team, consisting of *Psychometric Empath* and profiler, Ben Roberts, and *Victim Empath*, Natassia Prushenko, is led down a twisting path of dark, painful secrets. Brandon Walsh, the handsome, smooth-talking *Chief of Arson Investigations,* joins them in a manhunt that takes them across British Columbia—from Vancouver to Kelowna, Penticton and Victoria.

While impatiently sifting through the clues that were left behind, Jasi and her team realize that there is more to the third victim than meets the eye. Perhaps not all of the victims were *that* innocent. The hunt intensifies when they learn that someone they know is next on the arsonist's list.

The case heats to the boiling point as Jasi steps out of the flames...and into the fire. And in the heat of early summer, Agent Jasi McLellan discovers that a murderer lies in wait...*much closer than she imagined.*

ISBN: 9781412035910 (trade paperback)
ISBN: 978-0-9865382-2-3 (ebook)

Available at various retailers, including Amazon, Chapters and KoboBooks

Book 2 in the Divine series by Cheryl Kaye Tardif...

Divine Justice

CFBI agent and Pyro-Psychic Jasi McLellan battles a serious infection that threatens to claim her life. Slipping in and out of consciousness, she remembers the Parliament Murders...

One by one, members of Ontario's Parliament are disappearing, only to be found days later, disoriented and drugged. Or worse dead. Police are stumped and the CFBI brings in a covert PSI team, agents with special psychic abilities.

Accompanied by Psychometric Empath Ben Roberts and new team member Victim Empath Natassia Prushenko, Jasi heads for Ottawa and uncovers a plot so devious that Canada's national security is at risk. If that isn't enough to deal with, Jasi bumps into old flame, Zane Underhill, who wants to rekindle their relationship that ended three years earlier.

But the investigation takes precedent and Jasi is forced to place her feelings for Zane on hold in order to find a killer who has more than justice in mind for his victims, and in the end she makes a gut-wrenching decision—one that will cost the life of someone close to her.

ISBN: 978-1-926997-00-1 (trade paperback)
ISBN: 978-1-926997-06-3 (ebook)

Available at various retailers, including Amazon, Chapters and KoboBooks

Check out this novelette by Cherish D'Angelo...

Remote Control

In this dark, suspenseful and somewhat comical look at one man's desires, Remote Control by bestselling author Cheryl Kaye Tardif delivers a strong message: Be careful what you wish for!

Meet Harold Fielding—plumber by part of the day, slacker/tv addict the rest of the day and night. Harry believes that fame and fortune will come to him if he wishes hard enough. God forbid if he should actually work for it.

Beatrice Fielding is Harry's hardworking wife. She holds down multiple jobs so her husband can laze about on his recliner, eating popcorn and drinking cola while watching his favorite shows. She has many wishes-- some aren't so nice.

ISBN: 978-0-9866310-0-9 (Kindle ebook
ISBN: 978-0-9866310-1-6 (Smashwords ebook)

Check out this romantic suspense by Cherish D'Angelo...

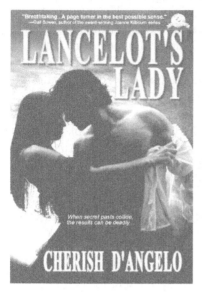

Lancelot's Lady

A Bahamas holiday from dying billionaire JT Lance, a man with a dark secret, leads palliative nurse Rhianna McLeod to Jonathan, a man with his own troubled past, and Rhianna finds herself drawn to the handsome recluse, while unbeknownst to her, someone with a horrific plan is hunting her down.

When palliative care nurse Rhianna McLeod is given a gift of a dream holiday to the Bahamas from her dying patient, billionaire JT Lance, Rhianna has no idea that her 'holiday' will include being stranded on a private island with Jonathan, an irritating but irresistibly handsome recluse. Or that she'll fall head over heels for the man.

Jonathan isn't happy to discover a drop-dead gorgeous redhead has invaded his island. But his anger soon turns to attraction. After one failed marriage, he has guarded his heart, but Rhianna's sudden appearance makes him yearn to throw caution to the wind.

To live fully in the present, Rhianna must resolve her own murky past, unravel the secret that haunts JT, foil the plans of a sleazy, blackmailing private investigator and help Jonathan find his muse. Only then can Rhianna find the love she's been searching for, and finally become...Lancelot's Lady.

ISBN: 978-0-9865382-8-5 (ebook)
ISBN: 978-1-926997-04-9 (Trade paperback)

Available at various retailers, including Amazon's Kindle Store, KoboBooks.com and Smashwords.

Cheryl Kaye Tardif is an award-winning, bestselling Canadian suspense author. Her novels include Children of the Fog, The River, Divine Intervention, and Whale Song, which New York Times bestselling author Luanne Rice calls "a compelling story of love and family and the mysteries of the human heart...a beautiful, haunting novel."

Her next thriller, Divine Justice (book 2 in the Divine series), will be published in spring 2011, in ebook and trade paperback editions.

Cheryl also enjoys writing short stories inspired mainly by her author idol Stephen King, and this has resulted in Skeletons in the Closet & Other Creepy Stories (ebook) and Remote Control (novelette ebook).

In 2010 Cheryl detoured into the romance genre with her contemporary romantic suspense debut, Lancelot's Lady, written under the pen name of Cherish D'Angelo.

Booklist raves, "Tardif, already a big hit in Canada…a name to reckon with south of the border."

Cheryl's website: http://www.cherylktardif.com
Official blog: http://www.cherylktardif.blogspot.com
Twitter: http://www.twitter.com/cherylktardif

You can also find Cheryl Kaye Tardif on MySpace, Facebook, Goodreads, Shelfari and LibraryThing, plus other social networks.

IMAJIN BOOKS

Quality fiction beyond your wildest dreams

For your next eBook or paperback purchase, please visit:

www.imajinbooks.com

www.twitter.com/imajinbooks

www.facebook.com/imajinbooks

CPSIA information can be obtained at www.ICGtesting.com
Printed in the USA
LVOW04s1721290515

440464LV00010B/217/P

9 780986 631061